A SIREN'S SUMMER FOR LOVE
THE LAVENDER FALLS SERIES

ISABEL BARREIRO

Published by Isabel Barreiro

Copyright © 2025 Isabel Barreiro

All Right Reserved

Paperback ISBN: 979-8-9902878-2-2

No part of this book may be reproduced in any form or by any electronic or mechanical means, including information storage and retrieval systems, without written permission from the author, except in the case of a reviewer, who may quote brief passages embodied in critical articles or in a review.

This is a work of fiction. Names, characters, businesses, places, events and incidents are either the products of the author's imagination or used in a fictitious manner. Any resemblance to actual persons, living or dead, or actual events is purely coincidental.

A Siren's Summer for Love

Genre: Small town paranormal romance

Cover Design: Jennette Perdomo

Editor: Michelle Prado

❦ Created with Vellum

But a mermaid has no tears, and therefore she suffers so much more.
-Hans Christensen

And what about a merman?

For the ones who are everyone else's sunlight.
For the ones who carry everyone else's burdens.
For the ones who are tired of being everything for someone else.
You are deserving of joy, of rest, of love, laughter and
most importantly a space to drop your mask.
While this book is the ending of a chapter I never thought would come,
It is also the beginning of so much.

THINGS TO KNOW

This is the fourth book in the Lavender Falls series. While I tried my best to make sure you won't be lost I do recommend reading the other books first!

This an **open door romance** book so there are **adult scenes.**

TW: Grief over loss of parent, depression, anxiety

Spicy Chapters:
   21, 23, 24, 28, 29, 30, 31

Playlist:

PROLOGUE

Crystal

Clammy hands. Erratic heartbeat. Light nausea.

This is how I've always felt right before a meeting, and even though my meeting was already over I still felt anxious. The anxiety was like a monster clawing at me just beneath my skin, wanting and waiting to be released. On the outside I was the picture of calm and cool, just how my father had taught me to be, but on the inside, I felt like a cracked egg on a sidewalk, burning up under the summer sun.

Sharp blue eyes captured me. I swallowed.

"I think this could be the start of a good partnership," Mr. Calder said, his voice rough. He was taller than me, with slicked back blonde hair. Compared to our last face to face meeting in the fall, he had a new glow about him. He must be spending some time outside now that it's almost summer.

I gave him a practiced smile as I readjusted the strap of my laptop bag.

"I think so! We are looking forward to helping Coralia Coast rebuild its structures. I hear it's a beautiful seaside town," I said, earnestly. Ever since I was little, I was fascinated by the ocean. While my pixie magic was made for the Earth, there was always something that drew me to the water. Maybe it was the way it was unapologetic with its emotions. It has always brought me solace. Mr. Calder's hand slipped beneath the strap on my shoulder as we made our way to The Drunken Fairy Tale Tavern.

"Let me," he offered. My eyes widened slightly in shock. I nodded silently; afraid my voice would squeak. It's not that I was attracted to him. At least, I didn't think so, although my experience is lacking so it might be hard for me to tell. I'd spent so much time working for my father's company Hale's Lumber Industry that I'd had little time to interact with my peers'. Plus, I was an introvert who is always a little lost when it comes to interacting with other beings.

As we continued to walk in silence I remembered how during the winter I got to reconnect with my older sister, Eleanor. Eleanor was vibrant, warm, and talkative. She loved being surrounded by beings and thrived with attention.

When she'd left for college and had a falling out with my father I'd felt like I'd lost a piece of myself. Ever since we were reunited, I've been introduced to her friends, and I've slowly felt myself breaking out of my shell. But now here I am, walking with my business partner and at a loss for words.

"Well, you'll be spending time in Coralia Coast soon," Mr. Calder said. I glanced up at him. Mr. Calder wasn't exactly cold, but I've learned that he's fairly reserved and calculated. We both agreed that I would help oversee the construction of the town's buildings and therefore I was going to be spending the summer in town. Honestly, I was excited to start an adventure somewhere new, a place untouched by my family. It's not that I didn't love being in Lavender Falls. Here I was always 'Eleanor's little sister', or 'Mr. Hale's baby girl'. In Coralia Coast, I'll *just* be Crystal Hale Silva.

"My friends have visited before. Lilianna with her partner Celestino and my sister Eleanor with her boyfriend Caleb," I commented. Mr. Calder sighed.

"I heard and I do apologize for my town's...cold behavior," he said. I bit my bottom lip. That's what I'd heard. They had told me there was something off about Coralia Coast, the beings there seemed to be wary but also lonely. We turned the corner, and I could see the door to the tavern was propped open. I had been curious about the town ever since Eleanor visited.

"I hope I'm not prying but is there a reason why?" I asked curiously. Mr. Calder's eyes flickered to mine a swirl of emotions in them. They reminded me of the turbulent sea. Just like Sailor anytime someone brought up Coralia Coast. *I wonder if Mr. Calder knows who Sailor is.*

According to Eleanor, Sailor didn't like talking about his hometown, and when they had visited to get some magical ingredients to heal the Hollow Tree and break Caleb's curse, he'd stayed hidden. My cheeks warmed at the thought of Sailor. He was like the sun on a warm beach day. He was that friend who made me nervous.

I don't think friends are supposed to make you nervous, but I think in a way I liked that he did. He had the same warmth as my sister, which is why I liked being around him. In a flash Mr. Calder's demeanor softened.

"It's okay Ms. Hale. I understand my town gives off a much different feeling to Lavender Falls. We lost someone important to us. Or shall I say they ran away from their responsibility," he said. I raised an eyebrow in confusion. He gave a slight chuckle that sounded rough, as if he wasn't used to expressing that emotion. "This person had a responsibility to the town, to his people. Because of his absence the ocean has been upset," he said cryptically. *The ocean?*

"Is this person like the heart of the town or something?" I asked. My cheeks heated and I bit the inside of my cheek in embarrassment. I probably sounded like a child. Mr. Calder gave a weak smile.

"He was the heart of the town *and* our family so yes," he said. I nodded as we stepped into the tavern. I noticed my friends in the back corner.

"Would you like to meet my sister and our friends?" I asked him. When I looked up at Mr. Calder, his eyes were elsewhere. He was staring at someone with a glare.

"Yes, please introduce me to your friends Crystal."

Caspian

"But it's so hot!" Eleanor exclaimed. I leaned against the booth, laughing with my friends. Caleb dropped off our drinks as Eleanor begged him to do a renaissance themed weekend where Caleb would be dressed as a knight. Caleb glared lovingly at his girlfriend.

"I agree. I would love to see Flynn in some tights," Lola said grinning at Flynn, who was standing behind the booth, hands on his girlfriend's shoulders. I glanced at Lily who was staring at Celestino with a faint blush. I didn't need to read her energy to know what she was thinking.

"I honestly think it's a good idea," I said. Everyone looked at me.

"See!" Eleanor exclaimed. I chuckled.

"There used to be a renaissance festival that came through Coralia Coast every year and it was a lot of fun," I said as a pain radiated through my heart. The winter season was the first time I had been back home in a year. When I had left, I'd packed up my things and walked away from my family and my town. I stared at the empty finger of my right pinky. I had left everything behind to come to Lavender Falls.

Here I was just Sailor. I was a bartender and a carpenter. I didn't need to hear about everyone's problems. I didn't need to be in ridiculous meetings making decisions. Here I could just be me. Just Sailor.

"Sailor," Lily called. My eyes widened.

"Sorry, spaced out," I said, sheepishly. While everyone rolled their eyes and laughed, Lily's eyes were filled with worry. Although she couldn't read energies the way I could, she was good at reading beings. I looked around the group of friends I had found for myself. People who liked me for me and not my last name. They all knew I was hiding a secret, and I *wanted* to tell them, but I was afraid they would look at me differently.

"I think you should do it. I know *I* look good in tights," I said, hoping to lighten the mood. I smiled as my friends joined in laughter.

"*This* is where you've been?" a familiar cold voice said from behind. I froze. Everyone's eyes stared behind me. *No.* This couldn't be happening. He wasn't really here. "Turn around," he ordered. I closed my eyes briefly. Turning around I saw a pair of hazel eyes first. My heart thumped. *Fuck, what was Crystal doing here next to him?*

"Sailor?" Crystal hesitated. I finally looked at him. He was still tall with broad shoulders., his blonde hair was a bit longer since the last time I saw him and pulled back. I see he finally decided to let himself grow a beard. His eyes were stormy, eyes that matched mine. Eyes that screamed brother.

"Sailor? That's what you call yourself? Really? Couldn't have been more creative?" he grumbled. Crystal placed a hand on my brother's arm, stepping forward. I looked between them. *Why was she touching him so openly? What is their relationship?* I noticed her patchwork laptop bag was around his shoulder. I grinded my teeth.

"What's happening?" Eleanor said from behind them. My eyes were still glued to the hand on my brother's arm. *Why was she touching him?*

"Sailor?" Crystal said again, much softer. I swallowed. Her voice was like the whisper of a sea breeze, pulling me in, and I was unable to resist it. My brother crossed his arms.

"I hope you know this means you're coming home," he said. I clenched my fists.

"No," I said sternly. My brother's eyebrows shot up in surprise.

"Yes, you will. You need to," he said, his voice laced with authority. I looked at the floor, away from his compelling eyes.

"Don't even try. It won't work on me," I said. I had spent years building up a tolerance to a siren's voice. I refused to let our own people's magic be used against me.

"You need to come home," my brother's voice softened for half a second. I glanced at Crystal quickly.

"Why are you two even together?" I asked, ignoring what he said. I couldn't have masked my tone of jealousy even if I'd wanted to. My brother must have sensed it because his lips twitched.

"Ms. Hale and I have an agreement," he said, placing a hand on her shoulder, a little too close to her neck. Crystal didn't flinch. She didn't shrink away from his touch, not like she usually did around beings. My stomach churned. *What fucking agreement was he referring to?*

"She'll be coming to Coralia Coast with me for some time," he said, nonchalantly. My blood boiled.

"Oh! Wait, you're Mr. Calder!" Eleanor said. My brother nodded and gave a practiced smile.

"Yes, I am. I'm Ronan Coralia Calder, Mayor of Coralia Coast," he said, facing my friends before turning back to me. "Now, Cas. You need to return home," he said, refocusing the conversation.

Return home.

Return to the life I never wanted. Return to the life of having the responsibility of my people on my shoulders. Not *just* my people, the ocean and every living creature there. I ignored him and instead took Crystal's bag from his shoulder and placed it on my own.

"You know what this year is," my brother said. I sighed. I knew what this year was, which is why I'd wanted a year to myself, to live how I wanted to. This year marked something important, and every Calder had to be there to perform the ceremony. I needed to do my duty no matter how much I hated it.

"Cas?" Crystal asked, confused.

"Are you going to tell them or shall I?" my brother asked. I felt another twist in my stomach and a pang rang through my heart. I breathe deeply and stepped away from the booth. I faced each of my friends. I didn't want the truth to come out, and even if I had, I didn't want it to be this way. There were so many opportunities for me to tell them the truth.

But I'd shied away. A small part of me had hoped I'd never have to, although deep down I knew it would come to light eventually. I finally glanced at Crystal who'd taken a step towards me. I gave her a weak smile. *Would she still think of me as her friend after this?* I hope they all will.

"My name isn't Sailor. It's Prince Caspian Coralia Calder. Second Prince of Coralia Coast, and of the Atlantic Ocean."

CHAPTER 1
BITTERSWEET FEELINGS

Crystal

"I-I'm sorry about all of this," I said to Mr. Calder over the phone. He let out a warm chuckle. I sit on the bed that used to belong to my older sister, Eleanor. Looking out the window I can make out the warm friendly community of Lavender Falls. This small town was the place I grew up in, yet it's been so long since it's felt like home. I'm not even sure if it has ever felt like home.

We used to be a happy family. I remember following my mom in the kitchen as she cooked. Eleanor would make me play dress up and my dad...laughed. Then mom passed away in a car accident when I was 10 and my family shattered on the floor of a cold hospital floor.

I remember my mom but then sometimes her memories felt like sand slipping between my fingers. Where she fell away, Eleanor filled in the gaps. Dad threw himself into his work and building his company.

Eleanor went from helping take care of me to wanting her freedom. She did what I couldn't. She lived, went out, and partied. When she was in high school dad tried his hardest to mold her into a version of himself. That's when she began hanging out with her friends more, leaving me behind.

They fought all the time. They fueled each other's fire with their stubbornness. College came around and she seized the opportunity to leave. She left and our strenuous relationship collapsed.

In the beginning I was unhappy. I felt abandoned by both her and dad. I understood she wanted to live her life, to be her own person.

"*If you walk out* that door you'll never be welcomed back," my dad yelled. My heart sank. I clutched my pillow tightly against my chest as if to shield myself from their yelling. Despite the years of fighting between the two of them, it still felt like a knife to my heart, mainly because I ended up being the one that picked up their broken pieces.

"Well, that's fine by me!" Eleanor yelled, slamming the door in her wake. I swallowed, turning to stare at the ceiling. Dad took in a breath, banging a fist to the front door before padding his way to the office, which used to be our playroom. It was my favorite room because it looked out towards the Gasping Greenwood Forest. But when mom died, Eleanor and I stopped playing with toys.

I sighed, giving my dad a few minutes of silence before going to check on him. Their fights were constant in my life, but I knew this time it was different. Eleanor was off to college. She would finally be away from him like she'd always wanted, and I was going to be the one to take care of him. Like always.

I wiped my tears and take a breath, calming myself before going into dad's office. Outside his door I could hear him tapping away on his computer. He was either responding to emails or adjusting a spreadsheet.

My dad owned Hale's Lumber Industry, one of the top companies in the northeast to provide high-quality and affordable lumber. I snorted. I was already saying 'we'. I was about to be a sophomore in high school, and I already knew what my place in life was going to be. The dutiful daughter that takes over Hale's.

"Dad?" I called out, lightly knocking.

"Come in," he said tensely. The door creaked open with a gentle push. He was at his giant, oak desk, shoulders hunched. He had the same tan skin as Eleanor, which deepened during the summer. Their auburn hair was also the same, but he had a few white hairs around his temples.

I walked over to him and placed a hand on the back of his chair. He tensed. I bit the inside of my cheek. He turned his dark eyes to me.

"What's for dinner?" he asked before I could say something about Eleanor. Whenever he was upset about her, he always changed the subject and I allowed it, not wanting to rock the boat. Bringing her up or asking about his feelings would only cause him to shut down further. I already had to deal with the ghost of my father. What could be worse than a ghost?

"I'm making chili," I said. He nodded. That was the end of our conversation, and the last time that Eleanor had come home.

My dad has always kept a watchful eye on me, especially after Eleanor left. He was worried that I would leave him like she did. But I couldn't. Everyone in my house was broken and it felt like I needed to be their glue.

So, I'd spent months dropping hints about missing Lavender Falls, missing mom, and our family. I talked about the festivals, and my dad had taken the bait. I mentioned how the town needed more sponsors and reminded him that the winter festival had been mom's favorite.

At first, he was against it, but I'd assured him I could lead the sponsorship. I would be in charge and show him that I could be responsible for leading a big project. I told him if he wanted me to prove I could take over the company one day, then this was my chance. He begrudgingly agreed.

Once I had started working on the winter festival and I'd started updating my dad on everything (including Eleanor), something had shifted in him. One day I brought up bumping into Lilianna's mom and I could see the emotion on his face. Lilianna's mom had been my mom's best friend. The three of them always hung out.

Since then, he's been going to therapy, and he's changed a bit. The winter festival was a step towards reconnecting to the town we were once a part of. I've been able to have a civil lunch with him and Eleanor every few weeks. I could see how he was changing. He'd even trusted me to land a major partnership with another supernatural town, Coralia Coast.

My eyes drift to the pink blanket that was draped across my bed. It was my sister's. She left here when she decided to move in with her boyfriend, Caleb. Another reminder that this wasn't mine. The apartment was my sister's. My job was because of my dad. Everything about me was made up of pieces of someone else. I close my eyes as a familiar ache washes over me.

Eleanor was loud and therefore I was quiet. When mom had passed away, I'd retreated further into my shell, not wanting to add any stress. Between Eleanor and my dad constantly fighting, I didn't want to fuel the fire that threatened to burn down our family. Yet even in my attempt to keep the peace I always ended up being the one to get burned.

I had taken on the role of a perfect child and dutiful daughter. I molded myself to be what my father had needed, my teachers had wanted, and society had expected of me. My mask had shifted so many times throughout my life that when I looked in the mirror, I didn't know who I was.

Now I have a new adventure waiting for me. My fingers trembled and my chest felt heavy as tears threaten to pour out. I had just begun settling into Lavender Falls and was now leaving. I glance around at the boxes around the apartment. I'd barely unpacked since moving in and that served me well. My phone buzzed on my nightstand, and I shove the sadness into its familiar box.

> ELEANOR
> ladies night at your place?

I cringe. I didn't want to see anyone today. It was an overwhelming day with mixed emotions. But the ladies wanted to discuss Sailor– I mean, *Caspian*. My stomach twists. I hadn't even had time to process *that*. I sigh.

> ME
> sure. Im packing so please bring food and drinks

There was a knock at my door and when I pull it open the ladies were there, dressed in sweats. My sister gave me a wide smile from where she stood, holding a bag filled with food.

"I knew you would say yes!" she said, stepping inside. I force my lips upward. I wonder what would have happened if I'd said no. But even if I had, Eleanor would have begged me until I caved.

"Hey Crys!" Lola said, pulling me into a tight hug. I squirm. Lola Luna was the local vampire vet who gave incredibly tight hugs. Her braids were placed on either side of her head in two space buns. I noticed a sunflower necklace around her neck. She'd finally gone official with Flynn Kiernan. He worked for his family's whiskey distillery and was the occasional bartender at The Drunken Fairy Tale Tavern which his brother, Caleb, Eleanor's boyfriend co-owned.

Lily placed a hand on my shoulder, offering me a small smile. I relax a bit. I have always liked Lily since I was little. She was more reserved like me and had wavy brown hair. She was dating Celestino, the warlock who was her childhood best friend. He was an amazing carpenter, and I enjoyed working with him during the spring festival and collaborating with his new carpentry shop.

The ladies made their way to the couch and began passing around food. Today they'd brought over Jamaican food, and my stomach growled. *Did I eat today?* It had been so crazy between my meetings with Mr. Calder and packing up to move for the summer. Eleanor made me a plate of rice and peas with curry lentils. I smiled.

Lola came back with a tray of mojitos. "Alright ladies. It is time for Sip n' Spill!" she said brightly. Once we all settled around the coffee table with our food, Eleanor took the first sip.

"Well, my father texted me to ask how I was doing, which was fucking weird but nice, I guess," she said, rolling her eyes. My stomach tighten. Eleanor and I had very different relationships with our dad.

"Did you respond?" Lola asked.

"I said 'Fine'," she said nonchalantly. I bite my tongue, feeling Lily's eyes on me. Eleanor had no idea how hard everything was for dad. I already knew that this simple text had probably taken him hours to write. That he'd gone back and forth on whether to do so.

Granted, he had a lot to apologize for, but this was him extending an olive branch and all she did was send him one word. I took a bite of food, reminding myself that I didn't need to fix their relationship. It's easy to say but hard to believe. Lola took a sip next.

"Flynn and I are officially together, and my mother is already planning the wedding," she said giggling. Lilianna's eyes widened.

"You've barely been together a month!" Lily exclaimed. I nodded in support. Lola rolled her eyes.

"Like your mom and Celestino's haven't been doing the same thing since you guys were in diapers," Lola pointed out. Eleanor laughed.

"We haven't even said I love you," she pointed out. My eyes ping pong between all three ladies.

"We're still up for our plan this month, right?" Eleanor asked. Lily wanted to go all out for her big 'I love you' confession. She nodded, a blush staining her cheeks.

"I can't wait," Lola said, eyes sparkling. I reach for my drink, hoping it can help me get through this night.

"She finally sips and now she must spill," my sister said, smirking. I fight the urge to groan. I knew there was a hidden agenda with showing up to my place. Eleanor was always sneaky, manipulating conversations. Not in a bad way. My sister loves helping people. She just hasn't realized that my problems weren't hers anymore and they haven't been for a long time.

"What am I spilling?" I ask. My sister rolled her hazel eyes at me, one of the few things we had in common.

"Um the fact that you just moved here and are now moving away? That your *friend* Sailor is not Sailor but Caspian? He's a freaking prince!" she said animatedly. My sister and her friends—*our* friends loved bringing Sailor–*Caspian* up all the time. He and I are just friends. I take another sip, feeling parch.

"One: it is true that I just moved back but this project in Coralia Coast is a big opportunity for me to prove to dad that I can lead a project of this caliber," I said. My sister's eyebrow twitched.

"You don't have to take over the company," she said, crossing her arms. I reach under the table to grip my knee. I had a feeling this would happen at some point. She thought that just because she walked away I could too. But I couldn't. Eleanor always had lofty dreams while I was chained down by the duty she'd passed down to me.

"I want to," I said, fighting to keep my tone at bay. "I like what I do," I said, honestly. Even if I'd started working for my dad out of obligation I *did* like my job. I helped plan workshops so that Hale's could partner with local communities. We helped those in need during disasters. I liked overseeing projects where we turned broken, overlooked places into something new and filled with welcome warmth. "And two: as for Sailor, I don't see the big deal," I said.

The ladies leaned forward, staring at me as if I'd grown a second hydra head. I shrugged my shoulders. "He's a prince!" Lola said.

"He's still Sailor–*Caspian*," I correct myself.

"He has a crown! And he kept that from us," Eleanor said, leaning in. Lilianna pushed Eleanor's hair back to avoid getting it in her food.

"You saw how he reacted to his brother. Also remember how he was behaving when you had to Coralia Coast in the winter," Lily said, looking at Eleanor.

"I mean...yeah. I knew he was keeping a secret. I just figured it was more like his family owned the town, not the town and the entire freaking Atlantic Ocean!" Eleanor said. I sip on my drink quietly. That *was* a surprise.

Sirens tend to be secretive. None of us knew much about them, we just knew that the seven seas are ruled by seven different royal siren families.

"We all knew that he wanted to tell us something. And now we know he was running from whatever responsibility he has within his family," Lily said.

"You should be able to understand," I said, quietly. Eleanor's eyes snapped towards me. Fuck. I wasn't supposed to say that out loud.

"Excuse me?" my sister said, her voice pitching up. My hands dig into my knee again. Kraken's crap, she was upset and now all three of them were staring at me.

"I'm just saying, you didn't want to take over the company, right? You felt trapped, bound by something you never wanted. He probably felt the same way," I said, hoping to ease the storm brewing.

"Remember how alone you felt in college? He probably felt the same way until he met us," Lily said, trying to soften Eleanor up.

"It was hard," Eleanor said, staring at her hands. My eyes prick with tears and my heart hammers in my chest. I want to scream, *"What about me? What about the fact I was left alone with dad. I was alone at the house. I didn't have time to make friends. All I'd had was me, dad, and the company."*

But if I said that, Eleanor would feel guilty and this whole night would be ruined because of me.

"Exactly. He probably needs us more than ever," Lola said, wrapping an arm around Eleanor. Lily placed a hand on her shoulder.

I watch them console my sister as uneasiness grows inside me. I was an outsider in their friend group; someone they once knew. It didn't matter that I'd spent months reintegrating into the town that was once mine. It didn't matter that we laughed, shared drinks, and shared ladies' nights in. I had spent so many years away that all I am is Eleanor's little sister and Mr. Hale's perfect daughter. They didn't see me, or my pain.

I settle into my practiced smile. "Maybe we should all hang out before we leave," I suggest, the mask falling snug into its place. My sister beamed, her pain forgotten.

"That's a great idea, Crys!" she said. Her smile turned into a smirk. My sister is now back to her devious, bubbly self. "So, are you guys' carpooling?"

CHAPTER 2
I'LL ALWAYS BE SAILOR

Caspian

This wasn't how it was supposed to happen.
My friends' faces were perfectly painted in my memory, the look of surprise and hurt across their faces. They knew I'd been hiding something, and I'd assured them that one day I would tell them what that was. I just didn't think today would be that day, let alone that my brother would be involved.

I glance over at him as he caught up with Carrie. It's been a year since we were in the same room. He cracked a small smile at my boss, Carrie, the only other siren in town and the owner of The Siren's Saloon, where we now sat.

Carrie grew up in Coralia Coast. She was Ronan's high school sweetheart. Last year, after the anniversary of my dad's death and the reminder of my duty for this year's ceremony, I ran. I *ran* to Lavender Falls, to Carrie, who kept my identity a secret from everyone.

I just wanted a fucking break from everything and everyone. And I had that here. Here, I didn't need to be some prince or protector of the Atlantic Ocean. I glance back at my brother. But I must now. He found me, so it's time to go back.

"So, I guess I can call you Caspian again," Carrie said, pulling her long red hair into a braid. My brother frowned.

"You couldn't have thought of a better fucking name?" he said, his voice deep. My hands clench at my side.

"What does it matter now?" I spoke. His blue eyes narrowed.

"Caspian," he warned. I roll my eyes.

"Don't like my tone, *your highness?*" I sneer. My brother's nostrils flared, and Carrie slapped the back of my head. "What the fuck was that for?" I ask.

"He's your brother before he is your king," she said. I click my tongue.

"He's your ex, too," I grumble. She placed a hand on his shoulder.

"And before that he is my friend," she said, her tone softening. I squirm in my seat. I'm not used to soft Carrie. She is badass, strong-willed, and took shit from no one. She'd left Coralia Coast to take over her family's bar and she'd made it into something on her own. My brother sighed, my focus redirected towards him.

"I'm sorry for the way the truth came out to your friends. That wasn't easy. But Caspian, I'm serious about needing you home. Things...things aren't the same there," he said. My stomach sinks. I knew what he was talking about. During the winter I had secretly gone to Coralia Coast with Eleanor and Caleb to help them break a curse.

The town felt cold...isolated. I know one of the reasons the town was in shambles was because of the pain I had caused in leaving, and that broke me. I grimace.

"I...heard," I said, not wanting to admit I was there. He crossed his arms, giving me a look I knew well. Of course he knew. He is King of The Atlantic Ocean. The second I had dove into the water for Eleanor and Caleb; I knew that news would spread.

"The royal families will be gathering in the coming weeks for the ceremony," he said. I groan into my hands, leaning against the bar. Every king or queen of the ocean had a protector, their second in command. Since I was the second and only other sibling, the responsibility fell to me, something I'd always known and actively avoided.

When I'd left, I'd had one year before the ceremony that solidify my place and title. So, I ran. But now there was no more running.

"I promise to come back," I mumble.

"Are you riding with Crystal?" he asked. His tone shifted up at the mention of Crystal's name. My head snaps towards him. I knew that Crystal was working on a project in Coralia Coast. I just didn't know it involved my brother or that they were so close. I bit the inside of my cheek remembering the way he'd placed a hand on her shoulder.

"Why?" I ask, searching his eyes for something that would indicate what kind of relationship they had. He shrugged his shoulders nonchalantly.

"I'm only asking. She will be staying in town for the summer as we rebuild some of our structures," he said, his voice shifting from brotherly to kingly.

"Please tell me you're bringing back the meadery," Carrie said, wiping the bar. My brother let out a small smile.

"It is on the list," he assured her. Carrie smiled, her blue eyes sparkling.

"Remember when the renaissance festival would come into town? All the events the meadery would have?" she said, lost in the memories of when our town was warm and vibrant. My brother swallowed, his shoulders tightening.

"I'm hoping to bring the town back to life, back to how we were before..." he trailed off. I inhale sharply.

"You mean before dad died," I said, finishing his sentence. My brother paused for a moment.

"Yes. Before he died," he said.

"Well, good luck with that," I said, pushing out of my seat.

"You know you will be helping," he practically demanded. I lean towards him; my hands balled into fists.

"Why?" I ask.

"It's your *duty* as my second. We must work together to heal the town and the ocean," he said. I freeze. I raise an eyebrow.

"What do you mean the ocean?" I ask, my heart sinking.

The last time I dove into the spring in Coralia Coast the water had felt off. It felt sick. All the rocks, corals, and creatures looked dull. I had assured myself it was just because they were dealing with a harsh winter. Now looking into my brother's solemn eyes, I knew I had been wrong.

"A lot of things have changed Cas," he said and my stomach twists at the old nickname. Carrie poured us a beer. I reluctantly sit down. "The ocean is sick, and I have no idea what I can do," he said, sounding defeated.

"The ocean gets sick sometimes. We have to deal with humans plaguing our waters all the time," I said. Granted, there were plenty of humans doing all they could to help the ocean. *I'm grateful for those humans*. My brother shook his head, taking a sip of beer.

"I know that, but something is just off. I'm hoping with you back... you could...," he trailed off and downed more of his beer. It had been a while since I tapped into my powers. I stare at my hand, trepidation growing.

"Ronan...I haven't used my magic in a long time. I-I don't know if I'll be of much help," I admit. There was a tick in his jaw. But instead of yelling at me like he used to, he just nodded.

"Do you think you could give it a try?" he asked. I glance at him and Carrie. The man standing before me was not the same brother I'd left a year ago. Sure, he looked slightly older and grumpy, but my brother was a confident siren. He was someone who *always* knew what to do, held a demanding presence. Yet the being sitting before me looked broken and lonely. The taste of guilt soured my beer.

"I'll do what I can."

○ ○ 🐚 🐚 🐚 ○ ○ ○

THE MOMENT I've dreaded has finally arrived. My friends and I gathered at The Drunken Fairy Tale Tavern for a long-awaited chat. After talking to my brother last night, I'd barely slept and Celestino had graciously given me the day off to pack.

But now we were sitting, looking like knights at the round table with drinks all around. Eleanor sat in Caleb's lap while Flynn sat across and was toying with one of Lola's braids. Celestino sat on my left and was holding Lily's hand. I could tell from the way her energy was buzzing she was ready to diffuse whatever emotions were going to pour out.

My knee bounces up and down as I glance at Crystal, who was on my right. I had grown close to her for the past few months. She is quite the beauty with long dark hair and warm hazel eyes. My magic pushes for me to wrap my arms around her.

I bite the inside of my cheek. I knew in my heart that Crystal was my destiny. The siren in me begs to sing melodies in her name, to hold her, touch her. But I'm painfully aware that Crystal occasionally feels nervous around me. She isn't someone that likes attention.

Sirens have many different abilities, one of mine is to read the energy of others and associate those energies with feelings. Crystal's energy always comes off as anxious, and the last thing I want to do is stress her out.

While I know in my heart that our fate is intertwined, she has no idea, and I can make myself okay with keeping it that way.

"So, you have money," Eleanor blurted out, breaking the tension. I chuckle.

"I mean, I guess I'm well off," I said. She snorted and everyone chuckled.

"That's something rich people say," Eleanor said, crossing her arms.

"Do we call you Caspian or Sailor?" Lily asked. Everyone stared at me. I had lied to everyone at this table and town about my identity for a year. I'd grown accustomed to the name Sailor and in some way, it was now a part of me the way that Caspian was.

"Either is fine," I said earnestly. "You guys, I'm sorry," I rush out.

"Why?" Lola asked, leaning her arms against the table. I stare at each of them. Crystal was avoiding my gaze and a pain travelled through me. I didn't like that she was hiding her eyes from me. I sigh, running my hands through my hair.

"I have a responsibility as the second son, and I needed a break. I needed a break from my duties, from my family. So, I ran. When I ran, I came here because I knew Carrie and I made her promise to hide who I really was," I began. "I wanted a chance to live as just a siren from a supernatural town," I said. My heart is in my throat as my feelings begin bubbling up again.

"I understand that," Eleanor said. Crystal flinched next to me and when I glance over, her eyes held a blank expression. "I ran away from home too, although I didn't hide who I was," she said, reaching for her water.

"You just erased your last name," Crystal muttered. I look at her again and her eyes were still downcast. No one heard what she said. Something in Crystal's expression was pulling me toward her.

"But you know we don't care about that shit. We care about *you*," Eleanor continued.

"We knew you were hiding something, Sailor, and we were giving you the space to tell us," Celestino said. I nod.

"I know that. Trust me. I was going to tell you soon. But I wanted you to find out through *me*, not my brother," I said. There was a quiet pause.

"Your brother is hot," Eleanor said, breaking the tension. Caleb slapped her thigh, and she giggled. "I still think you're the hottest," she said. Caleb grunted, leaning to whisper something in her ear. I look away, not wanting to see the kind of energy they are emitting (*although honestly, they are hot for each nearly 24/7*).

"Is there anything you need from us?" Flynn asked. I hold a ghost of a smile.

"Your friendship?" I ask. Everyone laughed but I was serious. I spent my whole life with beings who knew my title and used me half of the time for it. But here in Lavender Falls, beings liked me for me.

"You're still our friend," Lily assured me. I sit back in my chair feeling grateful for their kindness. They all looked at each other and once again, Crystal twitches in her seat. I need to talk to her alone. Something is up with her.

"Accepted," Eleanor said. I sigh. When I moved to Lavender Falls, I only had Carrie. I didn't know anyone else.

For the first time I had been alone. For the first time no one had known my family or my royal status. I got to be silly and loud. I didn't need to watch what I said, how I sat or how I held a damn spoon. It was freeing.

In Coralia Coast I felt like a fish trapped in a tank, limited to fulfilling my duty and playing my role in the community. Lavender Falls was like the deep part of the ocean where I was free from the chains of royal duty. And now I'm returning to my tank.

Eleanor looked over at her sister, a gentle smirk on her lips. "So, are you guys' carpooling?" she asked. Crystal groaned and something told me she had already been asked this question. I smile at everyone, feeling slightly more myself.

"Well, that's for Crystal to decide," I said.

CHAPTER 3
LAST GUY'S NIGHT

Caspian

Tonight is guys night at Caleb's apartment, which was above his bar. If I'm honest I have a feeling this isn't going to be our normal game night, where we ate food, drank beer or cocktails. We have our own version of "Sip n' Spill" but it is more like "Bros n' Brews". With my identity now out in the open, they probably have a lot of questions.

Flynn was mixing some cocktails with his new whiskey while Caleb brought over some pizza that Greg, his older brother had made. Occasionally Greg would join us, but tonight he is working late to prep for Alex's birthday.

Celestino was currently helping Flynn, and for the first time I feel left out amongst my friends. I anxiously sit on the couch waiting for someone to say something. I swallow, standing up to help Caleb set the plates. He eyed me and silently nodded, handing me a stack. I go back to the living room, getting the coffee table situated.

"I heard Nessie and Lucky are leaving Boogeyman's Swamp this weekend," I said, hoping to break the uncomfortable feeling that is slowly consuming my body. Flynn sighed.

"As much as I'm going to miss them, I swear I still smell dead fish every time I walk by," Flynn joked. During the spring he had assisted Lola in helping Nessie, The Loch Ness monster, give birth. We all let out a chuckle.

"The spring season was crazy," Celestino commented. I nod, remembering the number of floats we had to prepare for the Parade and the amount of times I nearly sawed off my fingers. Caleb grunted.

"And the winter festival?" Caleb said with a raised eyebrow.

"You broke your curse," I point out. He crossed his arms, glaring at me.

"And the Hollow Tree was dying, and we know how that affected the spring festival," Flynn said. He handed Celestino and Caleb their drinks.

During the winter festival the Hollow Tree (which provides the pixies with their magic) had started to die. It was pretty touch and go for a second. Flynn handed me my glass, and we all sat around the table. I sit on the floor giving the Kiernan brothers the couch. I take a sip, enjoying the sweet burn of whiskey mixed with citrus juices.

"So, what you're saying is that past year has been crazy," Celestino pointed out. Caleb sighed.

"I wonder what the summer will bring," Flynn said. Caleb's lips twitched and my face grows warm.

"I have a feeling *our* summer will be okay but..." he trailed off, staring at me. I swallow. *Fuck.* "You took a sip. You know what that means," Caleb said. I sigh as I feel the weight of their stares. I knew this moment was coming but it didn't make it any easier.

"What else do you want to know?" I ask. Sirens were secretive. We grew up having to be, with the way we were always treated and hunted by humans.

"Well how are you feeling?" Flynn asked. He watched me and I took another sip of whiskey, hoping to gain some courage. Flynn was like Caleb in a lot of ways– he hung back, was observant, and assessed situations to step in and help.

"I...feel sad and anxious. Sad because I love you guys and I hate the thought of leaving what I created here," I said. When I'd moved to

Lavender Falls, I stayed with Carrie, working at her bar until I could have my own place. Then I started working with Celestino, building props for the Haunted House in the fall. It felt good to do things that were for me. I was selfish.

"Now I'm returning home and...I won't be Sailor anymore," I said. Celestino handed me a plate of pizza.

"What exactly are your duties?" he asked. I tilt my head, remembering what I'd learned in my lessons on how to be a proper prince.

"Protect the ocean, essentially serve as a liaison between the land and sea, fill in on meetings when the king cannot," I said, remembering my father's words. My heart sank.

"CASPIAN, YOU MUST PAY ATTENTION," my father ordered. I was 13 and sitting in his office which overlooked the ocean. The sun was high up, making the water glitter. I felt the pull, the urge to dive in, swim, and be free.

"I am paying attention," I said, lying. My older brother Ronan snorted as he continued working on some essay about how the increase of pollution was detrimental to coral health. I glared at him as my father cleared his throat.

My father was a tall man with sunburnt skin, blonde hair blue eyes so light they passed for grey. I gripped my hands beneath my desk.

"Yes, father," I said. He tapped his own shoulder, and I immediately sat up straight. A prince must always sit up straight, shoulders back, to command a room. At least that's what he always said. Honestly, having perfect posture was exhausting. Ronan stood straight all the time, and it just made him blend in with the house plants.

"What did I say?" my father asked, and I grimaced. He knew I wasn't truly paying attention. I never did. I found our lessons boring. I hated reading about our history of the ocean. Why read about it when I

could dive right into the real thing? My father sighed for the tenth time today and I cringed inwardly.

"Caspian, you are the Second Prince of Coralia Coast and of the Atlantic Ocean. I know right now that might not mean much to you but one day you will help your brother rule. You will be second in command, the one that our ocean's creatures turn to in their time of need. You will be the connection between your brother, the ocean and all of the beings," he said. My heart began pounding. Every time my father spoke like this it sent a wave of panic through me, as if he was saying goodbye. I nodded solemnly.

"Yes father," I said, quietly. My father, the king, got down on his knee and placed a hand on my shoulder. His lips stretched into the warm smile I was familiar with.

"You have so many gifts," he said. I rolled my eyes.

"Yes, talking to fish and seeing energies is a gift not many have," I said in a bored tone, reciting the sentences everyone around me has told me. My father let out a deep chuckle.

"Those are abilities that you were born with. Your true gift is the way you connect with those around you, the way you make all of us laugh and smile. Even Ronan here," my father said. Ronan shook his head but couldn't fight back a smile. I nodded and my father squeezed my shoulder. "Your heart is your gift. Never lose that."

· · · 🐚 🐚 🐚 · · ·

"THAT'S A LOT," Flynn said, pulling me out of a bittersweet memory. I nod. "You grew up under a lot of pressure," he continued. I sip my whiskey, closing my eyes briefly. I knew Flynn understood where I was coming from. He was the middle child and his siblings were outspoken, confident, and always knew what they wanted. He too felt pressured to be something amongst his successful siblings.

"You know we're only two hours away if you need us," Caleb said, his tone firm. I move to hand them the rest of the pizza.

"I know, and I seriously would like for all of you to come to the ceremony," I said.

"You mean the ceremony you want to avoid but clearly can't?" Celestino asked. I let out a hollow chuckle.

"Maybe I can find a loophole," I said nonchalantly.

"I think we can agree that this isn't something you can run away from again," Celestino stated. I lay my head back on the backrest of the couch between Caleb and Flynn.

"No, I can't," I said quietly, staring at the ceiling.

"You'll have Crystal," Caleb pointed out. A flush crawls up my face. He was right. I was going to have Crystal with me…in my hometown…for the entire summer. My mind flashes back to Ronan and how close he was to her. My hand tightens around my glass. I hum in agreement. Caleb and Flynn both looked at each other.

"What was that look?" I point out. Flynn chuckled and Caleb shook his head. Celestino tossed a napkin at me, and I threw it back, annoyed.

"You know damn well why," Celestino said. I down the rest of my glass, shaking my head.

"We're friends," I said. Caleb snorted.

"You and Crystal are *"just friends"* the same way Celestino and Lilianna were just friends," Caleb pointed out. I shove his knee.

"We are *just* friends," I said through gritted teeth, my heart pounding. I was lying and they knew I was lying. Crystal was sensitive and wary of everyone. Sure, I felt like there was something between us. No, I *knew* there was, but she was dealing with too much. Between the weird tension with Eleanor and her dad and now discovering that I was lying she was overwhelmed. I groan.

"She's probably upset I've kept this from her," I said. I was hoping to have an easy summer after the craziness of the past few months but maybe I was asking too much from the Fates.

"Only one way to find out," Celestino said.

I'VE BEEN STANDING OUTSIDE of Crystal's apartment for the past ten minutes, trying to find the courage to knock. The image of her face while I encountered my brother has been replaying in my head. Her eyes were filled with confusion, but I could also sense hurt, and it gutted me to know that I had hurt her feelings.

I still remember meeting her for the first time when she came to Lavender Falls. She was sitting with the rest of the group. I had walked up to the table during ladies' night at the tavern. She was fidgeting with her drink. When our eyes connected, I felt it. My magic awoke, beckoning me to sing a siren's song.

A siren's song is a powerful thing. We can influence those around us, though no one can understand the words we say. Not even sirens can make out each other's words. When a siren discovers their soulmate, they are the only ones who can understand the words we are singing. The day I met Crystal, an ache to sing our song nearly took me over.

I could tell she was shy. She held back amongst the crew. Unlike Flynn who acted like a wallflower Crystal was a true introvert. Watching others reactions, careful of her words and oh, so fucking sweet.

I knew I needed to take my time with her. I wanted to be her friend, even if nothing came out of it. She was kind to everyone around her, funny when given the opportunity to be, and stubborn.

After the winter festival she moved back to Lavender Falls, and we slowly began hanging out. She tapped away on her laptop while I came up with designs for the floats that were used in the spring festival.

· · · 🐚 🐚 🐚 · · ·

"HEY, what do you think of this design?" I asked Crystal during one of our many hangouts at Coffin's Coffeeshop. I was busy drawing a float for the bar, The Plastered Pixies. She stopped typing on her laptop, her

hazel eyes meeting mine. She had dark eyelashes that curled up, drew me in.

Her eyes drifted down as I handed her my sketch. Her nose wrinkled once as her eyes moved all over the paper. Crystal was quiet but like her sister she was a visionary. She brought her fingers to her lips, lightly tapping them, and I looked away. I needed to remind myself that we were just friends. I reached for my glass of water.

"You need more glitter, and to add a few different shades of pink around here. Maybe include an area where they can pour some drinks and hand them off here, it could work as a bar after all the float's park," she suggested. My mouth broke into a grin. Fuck, that was brilliant.

"You're a genius!" I said. She turned the prettiest shade of pink, reaching to play with her hair.

"I mean, it was just an idea," she mumbled, shrugging her shoulders. I shook my head.

"It was brilliant and exactly what I needed," I said, holding her gaze. Her lips twitched as they stretched into a tentative smile.

"Thank you," she said, her smile growing more confident.

I SIGH for the thousandth time as I stare at her door. I had a bag of fried rice and sweet and sour chicken ready for her. I was being griffin shit about this but before I could knock, the door opened. My eyes widen.

Crystal was in grey leggings with an off-the-shoulder, oversized sweatshirt. Her hair was tossed into a messy bun and her fingers twitched at her side.

"You've been out there for 15 minutes," she said, matter-of-factly. I flush under her gaze. I guess she had been watching me struggle the entire time.

"Yes," I admitted. Her head tilted to the side.

"Why?" she asked, stepping away to let me in. Her apartment used to be Eleanor's, and she's barely moved in by the state of all the boxes. But I guess it didn't matter anymore considering she was temporarily moving to Coralia Coast. I set the bag on the kitchen island trying to not let the thought of the ceremony ruin what I had planned to discuss with Crystal.

As I begin laying out the food I catch a whiff of Crystal's signature citrus scent. She opened the fridge, pulling out two Portuguese beers. She offered me one.

"I'm going to need one," I mumble, taking it from her. Our fingers brush and my eyes close briefly, enjoying the rush of electricity that always happened when our skin met. Her cheeks flushed.

"You didn't have to bring me food," she said, nestling on top of one of the bar stools. I pull one next to her. She managed to fit both her feet on the stool, reminding me of an anime character. I don't know how she managed to fit on the chair considering her height.

"I know but…if I'm honest the food is more of an apology," I said, sheepishly. Confusion was written all over her face. My brows furrow. "I lied about who I was," I said, quietly. Her eyes skirted away, focusing on the food.

"It's okay," she said, voice softening. My eyes widen. *Okay?*

"Crystal, no it's not," I said, firmly. She bit down on her bottom lip. Her hands began fidgeting with the beer bottle.

"Yes, it is," she said, a bit assertive. I snort. It didn't matter that I'd chatted with her and the rest of our friends, I know my secret has caused pain and uneasiness. Which is understandable. I spent a year with everyone thinking they knew all of me when they only knew a fraction of who I was.

"Why?" I ask, waiting for her to meet my gaze. Once again, her hazel eyes wandered back to the food. I knew she hated confrontation. She is more comfortable in her shell.

"You were probably running away from your duty, needing a break to be Sailor and not C-Caspian. It happens," she said. My heart hammers at my true name on her lips. Fuck, did she make my name sound so sweet.

"You've met other royal sirens?" I ask, raising an eyebrow. She rolled her eyes and finally looked at me. Her cheeks were still stained pink.

"No, it just makes sense," she said. "It's okay that you kept this secret. You had your reasons," she said, setting the beer on the counter. I take a breath and a chance, reaching for her hand.

"And you were hurt that I kept this from you," I said, gently. She sniffed and her fingers tightened around mine. I hid a secret from her, but I knew that she hid a lot of herself and what she feels from all of us. She swallowed before looking up.

"Friends don't always tell each other everything," she said.

"True but I kept a pretty big piece of myself from you," I said, squeezing her hand. "Crystal, I'm sorry I kept this from you. I didn't want you to treat me differently." She nodded.

"So, you're a prince," she said, trying to be casual. I chuckle and her shoulders eased.

"I'm not the crown wearing type," I said, cracking a smile. Crystal pulled her hand away and I immediately missed her warmth. She grabbed a plastic fork and began munching on her fried rice. The corners of her mouth tilted up. I join her and we eat quietly together.

I slowly relax, enjoying Crystal's company. I grew accustomed to always being the life of the party– outgoing, cracking jokes. But with Crystal I could simply be me and enjoy the beauty of silence. Her fingers drummed against the counter, and I raise an eyebrow.

"What is it?" I ask. She turned to me in surprise. I point to her hand which was still tapping. She immediately froze and gave me an awkward smile. I cover my mouth to keep from laughing. She bit her bottom lip before tugging on her hair.

"Well, I'm going to Coralia Coast for the summer," she began. I nod, motioning for her to spill whatever was occupying her pretty brain. She took a breath. "Okay as you can see, I'm packing up which honestly isn't much work considering I never really unpacked. But everyone keeps asking if we're going to carpool," she continued. "*If you are indeed going back*," she rushed out. I bite the inside of my cheek to keep from laughing at her adorable ramble.

"Everyone keeps bugging you about it huh?" I ask. Her face scrunched and she crossed her arms.

"Yes, it's frankly annoying but then I remind myself that they're just asking because they care," she said, eyes glancing away. I didn't know much about Eleanor's and Crystal's past. From what I gathered they lost their mom at a young age and then when Eleanor went to college, they stopped speaking. It was just her and her dad.

My stomach twists. A box of memories in the corner of my mind threaten to open again. But now was not the time, there might never be a time.

"I have to return," I said, begrudgingly as I reach for my beer. Crystal took a bite of her food, watching me.

"Some ceremony?" she asked. I nodded. "Do you want to talk about it?" she asked.

In a few days I'll be home. I'll be taking the mantle of second in command, protecting Coralia Coast and the Atlantic Ocean. It's a lot of responsibility. My whole life will be centered around this job. No longer would I belong to myself, not that I ever did. I won't *just* be Caspian and I'll never be Sailor again.

My whole life was going to change, and I'd spent the last 29 years running from it. I'm selfish.

"Soon," I said.

"That's understandable," she said, clinking her beer against mine. Her hazel sparkled with mischief causing my heart to race. I craved these tiny moments when Crystal let her guard down. "So, how much trunk space do you have?"

Chapter 4
On the Road Again

Caspian

My jeep was packed with a small trailer attached. I was moving back to Coralia Coast and said goodbye to the apartment I'd made into a home. I was parked outside of Crystal's apartment when I placed the last box of hers inside. Everyone had gathered around to help us load and say goodbye.

"You'll always be our Sailor," Lola said, crushing me in a hug. I laugh as Flynn pulled her away.

"If you need anything, you let us know," Caleb said with a rough nod. I smile, looking at the group of friends I'd found for myself. The ladies were huddled together around Crystal. She gave them a smile but the closer I watch her the more I notice how her eyes moved back and forth between them all. Her hands were clasped behind her back, fidgeting with the end of her graphic t-shirt.

"Remember you can always call us for anything," Eleanor said, her eyes misty. Crystal's nose twitched and I felt my own stomach tighten. There had been something off between their interactions lately. I couldn't place what it was, and Eleanor seemed completely oblivious to it.

"I know but I'll be fine, seriously," she said. Lily placed a hand on Crystal's arm, probably trying to soothe her anxiety with her magic.

"Seriously, if you need anything, let us know," Celestino said, patting my back. I smile. Celestino and I had grown close since he'd moved back to town. "I'm going to miss having my carpenter buddy," he said teasingly.

"You mean you're going to miss telling me what to do," I said with a snort. He let out a laugh that caught Lily's attention. Both their energies were warm and calm. They were each other's perfect match.

"Well yeah, but I'm also being serious," he declared. I swallow.

"I promise to text you when we get there, *mom*," I tease. He rolled his eyes and patted my back again. I turn to see Eleanor who was pouting,

"I guess no more tequila shots under the moonlight," she said, sighing dramatically. I wrap my arms around her.

"Please, like you need me to take tequila shots," I joke. Eleanor and I were the party goers in our group. She smiled wide.

"True, but who else helps me get this crew of beings to let loose?" she said. I ruffle her hair, and she pulled away, straightening her appearance.

"I'll always be down for a party," I said, crossing my arms. She raised an eyebrow.

"Really your highness?" she teased. It might have been a joke, but it left a sour taste in my mouth. I hadn't thought about that. I was going to be confirming my position to the royal sirens. That meant maintaining a certain image.

Does that mean no more dance parties?

No more magical beer pong or celestial charades that led to running around town in feather boas. The second I cross into Coralia Coast I would be leaving all of that behind. I force myself to smile, the smile I had perfected over the years.

"I will always be the life of the party, with or without a crown," I said. There was a tug on my shirt and Crystal motioned towards the car. I nod. Eleanor jabbed a finger into my chest.

"Take care of her," she demanded. I swallow, my cheeks flaming.

A SIREN'S SUMMER FOR LOVE

CRYSTAL and I spend the two-hour drive listening to music. As badly as I want to talk to her, I could tell from our little goodbye party that the last thing she wanted to do was talk. Instead, she sat in the car, tapping to the beat of music while reading a romance book.

"Why don't we stop to eat before I drop you off," I suggest.

"That would be nice," she said, eyes still focused on her book. My grip on the steering wheel tightened as the "Welcome to Coralia Coast" sign came into view.

Fuck.

I'm really back. This time to stay. The last time I'd briefly came it was during the winter season to help Caleb and Eleanor get the ingredients they needed to break Caleb's curse and save the town. I had stayed hidden, but my aunt had figured it out. She came to my cottage, but I'd stayed tucked away. My cousin had even written me a note that Eleanor received when she picked up lunch.

I want to puke. I'm not ready for this. There was no way I could face everyone after running away. The closer we got, the more nauseous I was becoming. A yellow gummy came into my view. I glance at Crystal.

"Ginger gummy. It helps with nausea," she said. I lean my head down, careful not to touch her fingers. When I look at her again her cheeks were pink. The corner of my lips tilt up. I begin chewing slowly.

"How did you know I was nauseous?" I ask. She looked up from her book to the road.

"Your hands have been fidgeting against the wheel ever since we passed the welcome sign. You're probably anxious, and when I'm anxious I get nauseous. Hence the ginger," she said. I sigh. Crystal was insanely preceptive, which I partially worried about. What caused her to be so hyper aware?

"I am nervous. It's been a year," I said. She closed her book, tucking her legs under her as she lowered the music. I guess now she was in a talking mood.

"Have you really not contacted anyone from Coralia since you left?" she said. I shake my head. She let out a quiet "Oh" and my heart sank.

Is she disappointed in me? I thought back to when I got into my jeep and took off. I had left a note for my mom and brother, telling them I needed space. I wanted to cut myself off from everyone. I also assumed Carrie had told them where I was but given my brother's surprise, I guess I was wrong about that.

"Why?" she asked. I take a deep breath as my quiet seaside town came into view. The usual morning fog had disappeared now that it was early afternoon.

The main street was littered with eclectic-colored buildings. Some of them still had life in them with their bright colors and open signs, while some were faded brick and wood buildings with spiderwebs lingering in the corner of their windows. I gaze at the town that I'd grown up in.

Once upon a time it was a vibrant, bustling seaside town that tourists came to every year, especially in the summer. But now it looked deserted, hanging by a thread. I see why my brother was desperate to work with Hale's Lumber Industry. Our town needed a major facelift.

"I ran, and when I ran, I didn't want anyone to have the chance to bring me back. I wanted to have the opportunity to live, and I knew if my mother or brother knew where I was, they would drag me back before I'd had a chance to explore who I am," I said quietly as I pull into the parking lot of Calder's Diner.

The outside was made of white, weathered wood with big windows and a blue steel roof. It hasn't changed a bit since I've been gone. There were a few cars in the lot, and I was already mentally prepared to run into someone I knew. My cousin Mira would probably be the first, considering she worked here.

"Did you?" Crystal asked. I put the car in park and turned to meet her gaze. "Did you figure out who you are?" she asked quietly, reaching for her bag. I think back to my time in Lavender Falls. I'd made friends, lasting memories, and had felt more like myself than I ever had. I lick my lips, my mouth dry.

"I did, and now that I'm back I'm afraid I won't be that person ever again."

"Ow!" I said, as Mira kept hitting my shoulder. I forgot how strong she was. Since my secret visit in the winter Mira had dyed her hair dark purple. Her brown eyes shimmered with annoyance. "Is that how you greet your favorite cousin?" I asked. She rolled her eyes.

"Please. A text would have been nice, or did you change your number too, *Sailor*?" she said. I wince. I'd changed my number when I left. Mira crossed her arms, glaring at me.

"I am sorry for the way I left, and I promise I'll do anything for you to forgive me," I said, placing my hands on her arms. She raised an eyebrow.

"Anything?" she asked, and I swallow. Mira was three years younger than me, but she and I hung out all the time since our mothers are sisters.

We used to always get in trouble together, running off to look for treasure around Calder's Beach. I shared everything with her. I'd told her when I'd had my first kiss, we shared our first alcoholic beverages together, and she took care of me when I got hungover for the first time. I know I hurt her when I'd run, but I also knew she understood why. I nod slowly.

"Great. When the time comes, remember this moment," she said, her frown turning into a smile. That was the Mira I knew. She was always mischievous. She finally turned to Crystal who was quietly standing behind me during this whole exchange.

"Um Mira, meet Crystal. She's Eleanor's younger sister. The pixie-"

"From Lavender Falls. Yes, we all know about Eleanor and Caleb," she said, her eyes sparkling. I forgot how gossip travels in small towns. If Mira remembered Eleanor and Caleb, then the whole town must have known I visited.

"She'll be-"

"Helping rebuild our town. Your brother made us all aware of the upgrades that will be happening over the next few months," she said, smiling at Crystal. "We're very happy to have you," she said. Despite her blushing, Crystal reached out her hand.

"It's a pleasure to meet Sai-Caspian's cousin and I hope my company can provide what you all need and do your town justice," she said. My own cheeks blush at hearing my real name.

I stare at her. It was as if the shy pixie I knew wasn't standing next to me anymore. In her place was a confident businesswoman. Mira nodded and motioned for us to follow. We sat in my favorite spot– the last booth against the window that overlooked the ocean.

The sun hung high in the air and the ocean was calm. My magic flowed beneath my skin, pushing me to transform and swim.

In the year I had been gone I had only transformed once, and it was painful. Typically, I would go for a swim almost every day or every other day. I know going so long without stretching my tail meant that the next time would be painful.

"The usual Cas?" Mira asked. I nod. "Get her chili cheese fries and a lime soda," I said. Crystal blushed and Mira smirked. I bite the inside of my cheek. I knew I wasn't going to hear the end of this. When Mira walked away to place our order, I sigh.

"She seems cool," Crystal said, glancing back. I nod.

"She is. Her and I were always thick as thieves," I said, my tone somber.

"Until you left," she pointed out. I nod again. "Looks like you have a lot of apologies to make," she said. A hollow laugh escapes me.

"You have no idea. The worst is going to be my-" The door to the diner dinged and the words die on my tongue. Crystal turned around to see who had caught my attention. My heart rattles against my chest.

She'd gotten visibly older in the year I had been away. She had new wrinkles across her face and her once golden hair was turning pale with age. She was skinnier too. She wore a loose sundress with a warm yellow colored cardigan. Her blue eyes, which matched mine, filled with tears. She walked towards me robotically and I stood up. Once she was a foot away, my years of royal training kicked in. I place a hand over my heart and bowed my head.

"Your highness," I said, my voice cracking. I keep my eyes on the floor, worried about what kind of look I was going to face. She was probably angry with me, which she had every right to be. I left her. I never called. I'd mistakenly assumed that Carrie had told her where I was. A shaky hand covered in aging beauty spots came into view.

"Raise your head," she said, her voice as calm as the ocean before a high tide. My eyes slowly meet hers and the tears I desperately held back trickled down my face, mirroring hers.

"I'm your mom before I am a royal," she said with a shaky breath. I nod quietly. "Are you too old for a hug?" she asked, cracking a smile at our inside joke.

Once I became a teenager, I would get embarrassed by my mom's warm affection even though she loved reminding me that one day she wouldn't be around. And now seeing how much time I'd lost with her I understood what she meant more than ever.

"I'm not," I said, pulling her into my arms. Instead of feeling small in my mother's embrace, she was the one who felt tiny and fragile. "I'm sorry," I whisper, holding her close.

"I know," she said gently. She pulled away, wiping her tears and returning to her regal composure. She turned to Crystal with a warm smile and offered her hand. "Ronan has told me much about you and I'm very excited to see the progress you'll bring," she said. Crystal's eyes were bright with tears as she shook my mom's hand.

"I'm very grateful for the opportunity," she said, her tone sounding corporate. My lips twitch watching the two women interact. It made me smile. It felt right watching their gentle natures interact.

"If you don't mind, could I pull my son away for a moment?" my mom asked, and nerves coursed through me again. Crystal nodded and my mom motioned for me to follow her to the opposite side of the room.

Was this the moment where she was going to yell at me? Disown me? I shake my head. She couldn't disown me. I'm the only siren who could take up second in command. We both slide into a booth. I stare at my mom, waiting for her to lead the conversation.

"I knew where you were," she started. My eyes widen and she motioned for me to wait. "Carrie kept me up to date on your life in Lavender Falls. And I didn't tell your brother because I knew you needed time for you. You were always against your royal duties, and I wanted you to have a life outside of it," she said. Guilt weighs on my heart. She knew the entire time. She never dragged me back, instead giving me a chance to live.

"I'm sorry mom," I said. She nodded, wiping a tear away.

"But you know you must stay now. You can't run away again," she said, her voice hardening. I swallow. The queen in her is showing. She straightened her spine. "The ceremony is at the end of the summer, and you need to prepare and hone in your powers," she began. I bite the inside of my cheek. I'm like a child again, listening to my parents recite what was required of me. I'm given no choice. I nod.

"You're almost thirty, you know. It's time you think about settling down," she said. My eyes widened.

"Mom," I whine. She tsked.

"Don't. It's time for you to be serious. You're the Second Prince. You have duties to yourself, the beings of this town, and the Atlantic Ocean," she said. I groan. Honestly, it's like I never left. "There will be a few princesses coming and I was hoping-"

"No," I said, firmly cutting her off. There was no way in a kraken's lair that I'm going to be walking around entertaining a bunch of spoiled princesses. My mother sighed dramatically.

"You are worse than your brother," she said. I rub my eyes.

"Shouldn't you be getting on Ronan's case about finding a queen?" I ask, hoping to put the pressure off of me and onto him. *It's what little brothers are for, right?*

"Your brother is very busy with the summer tourism, rebuilding the town, maintaining order in the ocean, and preparing for your ceremony," she rattled off, her lips twisting into a frown. My stomach tightens. My brother had mentioned that something was wrong with the ocean and even though I hadn't been here for long I felt the pull towards it.

There was no way I can manage dealing with whatever is happening with the ocean, my powers, the ceremony, *and* entertaining princesses.

"Well, I can't meet with any princesses," I said. My mom raised an eyebrow. *Dragon's piss.* I need an excuse for my mom to not set me up. Faintly I heard Crystal thank Mira for the food. "I already have a girlfriend," I said, a tentative smile stretching across my face.

AFTER A PAINFUL REUNION with my mom, Crystal and I ate our food and left. If I was anxious about entering the Coralia Coast, I'm bouncing with nerves on the way to my cottage.

I glance at Crystal who was focused on taking in the scenery. She hadn't asked about my conversation with my mom, and I was grateful for the quietness because I needed to come up with something *fast*.

Making a turn near the edges of our woods a small, cream-colored cottage with a blue wooden door came into view. The windows held potted plants that were blooming. *I wonder if my aunt has kept up with it.* Crystal's eyes widened and her face broke out in a smile.

"It's beautiful," she said, her eyes sparkling. My body heated. She liked my place. It filled me with pride and made me want to sing.

I step out and quickly run to open her door. Her eyes bounced everywhere. From the white fence to the flowers and lemon trees tucked in the back. She tilted her head out the side before turning to me. "This is your house?" she asked. I nod.

"It was my grandmother's," I said, looking at the old thing. "When she passed away my father had it fixed up a bit. I spent more time here than at my own house, and because of that my grandmother left it to me," I said, smiling at the memories of running around the backyard. Crystal placed a hand on my arm, and it eased the nerves that were swimming around my stomach.

"It really is beautiful," she assured me. Her brows furrowed for a second. "But I thought you were dropping me off at the bed and breakfast," she said. I take a deep breath and scratch the back of my head. Crystal pulled away, crossing her arms. The look she was giving me reminded me of Eleanor's.

"Tell me," she demanded. I bite the inside of my cheek hard. I didn't need dirty thoughts of her telling me what to do behind closed doors filling my head.

"Well, you can't stay there," I said. She shook her head.

"But I booked it. It's the other B&B that needs to be remodeled," she said. I swallow.

"Very true."

"Sailor," she demanded in that same sinful tone. She was going to kick me in the balls for this. I know it. She arched an eyebrow, her patience waning.

"It wouldn't look right," I state, buying myself useless time. I struggle under her gaze.

"Why wouldn't it look right…Caspian," she asked. I inhale sharply and close my eyes briefly. *Fuck*. She truly can make me do anything by just saying my name. I glance between her and my cottage.

"It wouldn't look right if my girlfriend wasn't staying with me."

CHAPTER 5
SINGLE PRINGLE

Crystal

I had decided to get lunch at the Siren Saloon. It was one of the many pubs in Lavender Falls. I don't remember much of this one. Each pub in town had its own aesthetic and crowds. Growing up, my mom favored the Plastered Pixie where one of my cousins worked.

But I didn't want to be around my family. Family always meant questions, and I've been disconnected from mine for a long time. Their questions would include me having to explain the rift between Eleanor and my dad, and I wasn't ready for that.

The family was aware of the separation, but if they asked it was probably because they wanted to be nosey. They didn't really seem to care for us, anyway. They never really tried to contact us. They just liked hearing dramas to make themselves feel better about their own lives.

"Ms. Crystal Silva Hale," a smooth voice said from behind me. I turned to see the siren I'd met a few days ago.

Sailor.

My stomach twisted. Sailor was beautiful like most sirens. Enchanting, alluring. Just like in all legends humans have written. There was something about Sailor that grabbed my attention. When his eyes were on me, I felt like we were in our own bubble.

I wasn't used to being someone's complete focus. Something about the calming blueness of his eyes kept me tethered, easing my constant anxiety. He wore a white shirt that made his golden skin glow. His blonde hair was tousled back.

"You remembered," I murmured. I sounded stupid or like I was a sad pixie who felt isolated, which I was. I was a being that blended into the background. I always had, and I was comfortable with that.

Instead of having his usual one liners, Sailor simply smiled and slid into the seat next to me. My eyes widened slightly in surprise.

"The COO of Hale's Lumber Industry. The one helping us with our workshops to make our community stronger," he said. He almost sounded like he was in awe of me, and that made my cheeks pink. "Of course, I remember who you are."

I bit the inside of my cheek. He didn't say I was Eleanor's little sister or Mr. Hale's daughter. No. I was my own being with my own work and accomplishments.

When I was younger, I didn't mind being Eleanor's little sister. She was the constant sun in our family, outgoing and warm. My proximity to her made me feel welcomed by all. Being Mr. Hale's daughter also came with its benefits of respect and money.

At some point being attached to them made it difficult to breakaway, for people to see me for me. And yet none of that seemed to matter to Sailor. For the first time someone saw me, for me.

I grinned. "You guys are doing great with your workshops," I said. Sailor helped Celestino run his carpentry shop and was often the leader of their Saturday morning workshops. I only knew this because I would occasionally peek in to take photos for marketing. Work reasons, you know. It's not like I would show up just to catch a flash of blue eyes and soft blonde hair.

Sailor waved his hand, being bashful. "Tis' nothing when you have a great boss," he said, still grinning.

I glanced around. The Siren Saloon wasn't busy. A few beings *loitered in the background. Carrie, the owner, was somewhere in the back. I couldn't help but wonder why he was sitting here talking to me. It couldn't be because of the workshops.*

My hands fidgeted with the keys of my laptop. I swallowed, unsure of how to continue the conversation. But I didn't need to because Sailor was very talkative.

"Are you working or having a lunch break?" he asked, glancing at the laptop. I tapped a key.

"Um, both?" I said, my voice wavering. Sailor's chuckle almost had a musical quality to it. It made me wonder what a full laugh would sound like.

He shook his head. "No ma'am. You need to stop working and eat. Take a break for a bit. Let that brain of yours relax," he said. I tried not to grimace. I had a mountain of things on my to-do list. I hadn't even stopped to think about lunch. My stomach growled. Sailor raised an eyebrow, and I blushed again.

"I just need to finish this email," I said, my eyes flicking back to the screen. He placed his hand on my laptop pushing the screen down. I gasped.

"You are so lucky I have autosave," I sassed. His eyes widened and he removed his hand as if it was on fire.

"I am so sorry," he rushed out.

"I'll accept the apology if you give me a milkshake." His blue eyes brightened.

"You got it but also if you're having lunch then that means you're having a break," he reminded me. He moved to stand up, hands on his hips.

I folded my hands in my lap, chewing the inside of my cheek. I knew he was right. It's what most working-class beings did. Take a lunch break. Pause work to breathe.

I spent so many hours running myself ragged for my father and the company. A thirty-minute break wouldn't hurt, right?

"So, what do you wanna eat?" he asked, a slight curve to his lips. I stared in confusion.

"Why are you asking me that?" I questioned. Sailor kept his slight

smile, his blue eyes softening.

"Because I also work here," he said. My surprise lasted for a second. "So, tell me. What do you wanna eat, M'Lady?" he asked. My hands twitched while my heart skipped under his unwavering kind gaze.

"Chili cheese fries."

· · · 🐚 🐚 🐚 · · ·

HIS CRYSTAL-CLEAR blue eyes are wide with worry. I know my mouth is hanging open, my face redder than a ripe strawberry. My mouth opens and closes as I try to process the words that came out of his mouth. Did Sailor really say what I think he just said? *Girlfriend?* I bite the inside of my cheek. I'm still getting used to calling him Caspian.

"Can you repeat that? I don't think I heard you properly," I said. He lets out an awkward chuckle and scratches the back of his head nervously, which I find adorable.

"It wouldn't look right if my girlfriend wasn't staying with me," he said softly, cheeks pink which makes his sun kissed skin glow. I swallow.

"And by girlfriend you mean a friend that is a girl—woman, technically. A woman friend," I clarify. The corner of his lips tilted up into a lazy smile.

"No, I mean girlfriend as in a girl I'm dating," he said. A laugh bubbles out of me. There is no way. First, I find out he is a prince and that I've been working on a deal with his brother for half a year. Then I've had to deal with being the middleman between my dad and my sister, and now *this?*

"Sailor, what do you mean?" I ask, trying to dig into my memory and find when I possibly became his girlfriend. Was it after crossing town lines? When he brought food over to the apartment? His mouth turned down.

"Remember how we ran into my mom?" he asked. I nod. His mom is beautiful, and they look so much alike. I could tell she was heartbroken but happy to have her son back. I understood her pain. Eleanor left for college, and I had no idea what she was doing without the occasional social media hunt.

I could have reached out to her plenty of times, but I knew it would hurt my dad, and she'd seemed content with living her life. I didn't want to ruin what she had.

"And you know how there's a ceremony I have to do? To solidify my position?" he said, sounding annoyed. I nod again, trying to figure out how this connects. "Well, my mom was insisting I meet with some princesses, in a "settle down" kind of way," he said, face still flushed. "I already feel pressure by being back and this whole ceremony, I didn't want to deal with my mom setting me up too. So, I said we were dating," he rushed out at the end. They were gone for like 15 minutes, and in 15 minutes I became a girlfriend. I stare at him in shock. There is no way this can work.

"No," I said, softly. His eyes widened.

"You don't have to be my real girlfriend. Just think of it as fake dating. Like the books you read!" he said. I swallow. While in theory I enjoy fake dating there is no way I can do this. How the fuck am I going to convince people we are in a relationship when–

"No, I can't," I said, my heart hammering. I can see the panic in his eyes. He really is against his mom setting him up. *But why?* Soon the town will be filled with princesses, and he's a prince. It only makes sense. A prince dates a princess. Royal life 101.

"Crys–"

"Sailor, I can't be your girlfriend because I don't know how to be," I blurt out. I've never been a girlfriend, hellhound, I've never been on a damn date. How can I fake a relationship when I don't know what having a real one is like? He stared at me, his expression matching my earlier one.

"But how?" he asked. I sigh, covering my face in embarrassment. I wasn't expecting this conversation to ever happen, especially not with him.

"I spent most of my time working at the company, taking care of my dad. I didn't exactly have time to go out with anyone. My life was always busy," I said. I glance back at the beautiful cottage. I didn't often dream of what I wanted in life. My thoughts were consumed with making sure my dad was okay.

"Have you ever…kissed? Went on a date?" he asked. His gaze shifted from my eyes and to the ground. I've never seen Sailor squirm so much. Typically, he was oozing with confidence.

"First kiss was at a frat party, and it was horrible. He had fish breath," I said. He nodded. "As for a date…never."

Sailor took a deep breath. "Forget everything I said, okay? I'll talk to my mom. Don't worry about it," he said with a smile. But I recognize that smile.

It's fake. He is saying all of this to not stress me out and instead of agreeing to help him out with this fake plan I nod. How can I fool everyone in town? Fool all those royal princesses when I'm just me? My phone beeped and I glance at it.

"I have a meeting with your brother. Could you drop me off and I'll get my bags later?" I ask. Sailor's shoulders relaxed and he nodded. For some reason, my heart sinks slightly. I hate not being able to help him. I want to. But I have too many things to worry about.

I ASSURE Sailor I'll be fine at the diner. I'm early to my meeting with Ronan but it's because I want to have time alone. I need time to process all that had just occurred. My thoughts drift to Eleanor and a pain rings through me. I know in my heart she was being a nice older sister just offering her help, but it hurt.

I spent so many years taking care of myself. When I needed her, she wasn't there and now that she was back in my life it was hard to accept. I know her and our dad don't get along. They had fought since she'd started high school, but he was really trying to reconnect with her now and she just kept brushing it off with an eye roll.

I glance over at the ocean and felt its pull. My feet sink into the sand as I walk closer, feeling compelled by its song. I stare into the turbulent ocean feeling the wind cut through the heat of the sun shining against my skin.

There was a melancholic air around me. If I were like my sister, I would find a way to banish these feelings and fill my mind with rainbows instead of dark clouds. But I wasn't my sister. Unlike her, I welcome this feeling. I find solace in being and feeling alone.

I used to think something was wrong with me. I never truly felt grounded. I didn't have a group of people that I could call true friends. I never had anyone to rely on. Whenever I thought I did, they would leave. My mom passed away leaving a giant rift in my family. Eventually Eleanor left and as for my dad, well, he was never the same without mom.

In Lavender Falls I felt like a ghost. I was someone trying to be someone else. I wasn't outgoing or bubbly like my sister and her friends. Putting forth such effort left me exhausted and guilty for disrupting their established relationship.

And now I'm in Coralia Coast: a small coastal town that is draped in a blanket of solemn beauty. The waves crash against the shore, singing a bleak melody. I wonder if the ocean feels my pain and longing, and that's why it's comforting. My phone rings, pulling me back to reality.

"Hey dad," I said, doing my best to sound cheery.

"Hello, Crystal. How was the drive?" he asked. I bite my cheek. Was he really interested in knowing? Our bond never felt like father and daughter, more like boss and employee.

"Smooth sailing," I said, mentally laughing at my own pun.

"You'll be meeting with Mr. Calder soon, correct?" he asked. My heart sinks.

"Yes. I'm waiting for him as we speak. I'll report back later on how the meeting went," I begin. "The town has a lot of charm, and I can see some areas that need help," I said, knowing what he wanted to hear. He grunted, his version of saying good.

"How was your sister when you left?" he asked. Tears prick my eyes as jealousy washes over me. I hate the pain his words gave me. Obviously, he would be concerned for Eleanor, he was trying to mend their relationship. But couldn't he see that our relationship needed fixing as well?

"She was sad to see me go, but overall happy. She's happy in Lavender Falls," I said. I close my eyes, willing the tears to go away. "She's not used to you wanting to talk to her, but I can tell she'll open up soon if you just show her that you want to reconnect in an honest, accepting and warm way," I said, hating every word coming out of my mouth. It was like I was digging a knife into my own heart.

"I have a lot to apologize for," he admitted. He means he has a lot to apologize *to her for.*

"Little by little," I said, echoing my mom's words. She was always a believer that you couldn't rush things. Little by little you could mend anything. My dad let out a chuckle.

"Little by little," he repeated. For a second I felt the ghost of my mom's hug but as quickly as I felt it, it vanished in the ocean breeze. "Well, I'll let you go to your meeting. I'll be waiting for the updates," he said firmly.

"Yes," I said, hanging up. I slide my phone into my bag, wiping my face. I take one deep breath, relishing the ocean's embrace. All that was left for today was to meet with Ronan and then check into my room.

Ronan shows me around town and introduces me to the places that Hale's Lumber Industry will be rebuilding. We had two cottages, a meadery, a bookstore, the other bed and breakfast, and the outdoor stage on the north shore of the beach. There are a lot of projects but thankfully they aren't in too bad of a condition and we of course have the help of magic.

"The outdoor stage really needs a new main deck," Ronan said, tapping on the floor with his hands. I type away my notes on my tablet.

"I know which spell to use on the wood since it's so close to the ocean," I said. Ronan cracked a smile. The sun is beginning to set, and, in this lighting, I can see glimpses of Sailor in Ronan. "We can start with that stage first since you'll need it by the end of the summer for your ceremony," I said. He nodded, his eyes darting between the stage and the ocean. Something is troubling him.

"Everything okay?" I ask. He sighed and I have a feeling this was going to be about Sailor. Which I understand. Eleanor is my oldest sister who ran away, and Sailor was the younger brother who ran away. "It must have been a hard year," I said. His eyes were clouded with grief.

"If only it was just a year," he responded. "I wasn't surprised when he ran. I always expected it," he added. I swallow, a familiar pain coursing through me. I always knew Eleanor would leave too. With every fight between her and my dad, I waited for her to walk out. And even though I was expecting her to walk out, it still hurt when she did.

I follow Ronan as we walk across the shoreline towards the diner. It is peaceful. There weren't many beings out which is sad to see. In Lavender Falls beings were always outside, popping into shops and bars just enjoying themselves. But here in Coralia Coast, it almost felt like a ghost town.

"It still hurt, didn't it?" I ask, tentatively. Ronan's eyes flickered back to the ocean.

"It did," he affirmed. I understand what Ronan is feeling, and I want to know if he feels the same resentment that I do. But if I ask that, it will mean admitting how much jealousy and anger I harbor towards Eleanor. It wasn't right because I understood why she left. His blue eyes meet mine again and I feel an understanding pass between us. Maybe I don't need to ask.

"And of course he would run away to Lavender Falls," he said, cracking the smallest hint of smile. I cock my head to the side. Where Sailor is warm and vibrant, Ronan is reserved and a little grumpy–cold, even. But I can feel his warmth when he speaks of his town. It's why I agreed to this project.

"What do you mean?" I ask, the diner coming into view. He scratched the back of his head and once again I'm reminded of Sailor.

"Carrie," he said. A light bulb flickered. *That's right. He knew Carrie.* From what I'd heard Carrie had come to Lavender Falls in her early 20s to take over The Siren's Saloon which was left to her. "They were always close," he said with a wistful smile. My stomach tightens.

Of course. Naturally, both of them had very vibrant and warm personalities. Ronan let out a rough chuckle.

"Not like that. They didn't have that kind of relationship," he said, smirking. I bite the inside of my cheek. "I did." My eyes widen in disbelief. While Ronan and Carrie are both pretty as most sirens are, Carrie is like fire and Ronan is like ice.

"You two?" I ask. He nods, dipping his hand into the water. He seems more at ease the second it washes over his hand.

"We dated all through high school, but then my father passed during my senior year. I had to begin preparing to take over as king once I graduated. I had a lot more responsibilities," he said. A shadow passed over his eyes. I place my hand on his arm. I offer a smile, knowing we shared the same weight. "I missed taking her to prom. I was stressed with all the royal duties. Showed up an hour before it ended. Everyone in town–*small* town, saw that I'd forgotten about her. She yelled at me in front of the whole senior class and faculty," he said, pointing to his eyebrow where there was a jagged scar. "I ran out after her and tripped into some rocks," he said with a sigh.

"One, some people find scars to be distinguished," I said. He chuckled again, the warmth coming back to his eyes.

"On a king no less." His eyes flickered behind me. "And two, Ms. Hale?" he asked.

"Well, how are you two now? I assume you saw each other back ho–in Lavender Falls," I stuttered, cursing inwardly for correcting myself. Lavender Falls is my home even if I didn't always feel a part of it.

"Mhmm. Well, she didn't kick me out of her bar, so I'd say all is forgiven," he said, tilting his head.

"Then that means two, it has all worked out," I said. A phone beeps and Ronan checks his message with a frown.

"Everything okay Mr. Calder?" I ask, worry gnawing at me. He rubbed his forehead before looking up.

"Unfortunately, there was a water leak at the other bed and breakfast," he said. I swallow. *Oh no.* "Guess we have another thing on the to do list," he said, placing his phone in his pocket. "Good thing you're staying with Caspian," he said with a slight smirk.

Griffin's shit. How fast did that news travel?

CHAPTER 6
MY TAIL AND ME

Caspian

The sun is setting by the time I make it to my favorite spring. The water is tumbling over rocks twenty-five feet high. It has a beautiful pool at the bottom. While there is a rocky area to lay or sit in behind the waterfall, it's what is beneath that rock that I'm looking forward to.

I missed my tail. In the water I felt free, but the closer we get to my dreaded ceremony the less I feel at home in the ocean.

I typically have this waterfall to myself since it was a part of my property. I quickly shed my clothes and enter the water, sighing deeply. It feels cool against my heated skin as I walk further in. Once under I feel the water pull at my feet and slowly they merge together. I hiss at the sensation of my feet joining, bones fusing and stretching to form a tail. I breathe heavily, knowing the pain will eventually pass.

"Fuck," I whisper. When I open my eyes, the water is blue, and the sunlight reflecting in it makes my tail sparkle. Fish swim around me and I chuckle at their excitement. With a flick of my tail, I head towards the waterfall. Diving under the rocks, I make out a small hole. My heart races. I haven't been back to my secret place in so long.

Through the hole, a small underwater cave opens up. It was my hideaway growing up. A small cave was carved on the other side of the waterfall. There are also two entrances, one from the waterfall and another that led to the ocean. I used to spend a lot of time here.

I hop up onto the sandy shore, enjoying the feel of my tail swishing in the water. I lay against the sand, stretching. My eyes wander up to the opening and I notice that the sun has already passed its highest peak. I glance around the cave. It hasn't changed much in all the years I've been coming here. It has the same dark rocks with jagged carvings. This place was one of the few things that has remained constant in my life.

A pang races through me, and I shut my eyes, trying to push the memories back. The only reason I knew of this cave's existence was because of my dad. He brought me here when I was 10.

"I THOUGHT *you said I needed to focus on my studies,"* I whined as I followed my dad. He shook his head with a small smile.

"We still have a lesson. We are just changing locations," he assured me. I rolled my eyes. I had finally finished my homework for the weekend and had planned to take a swim with Mira before the other royal kids showed up. I always hated them when they did. They were snotty and made fun of her.

"Aren't the other royals arriving?" I asked. The royal family of the Pacific Ocean were staying for the weekend. Apparently, my father had a meeting with their King. My dad let out a sigh.

"Yes, and I expect you to treat their kids with some kindness," he said, looking back at me. I shrugged my shoulders as the familiar spring came into view.

"How I treat them depends on them," I said. For instance, if what's his face decided to call Mira a shrimp again, I would simply dump

water on him. "You said to treat people with respect if they treat you with respect," I pointed out. My dad let out a laugh.

"Aye, that I did my boy," he said.

Once transformed and in the water, I swam behind him. He led me under the rocks towards a hidden opening that led to an underwater cave. I stared in amazement. I had no idea this place existed. We rose toward the shore. Before my dad could pull up onto the rocky sand, I swiped away some of the big rocks. He smiled thanks. I stayed in the water, enjoying its warmth.

"This place is awesome!" I said. My dad glanced around.

"It is, isn't it?" he said. His blue eyes were bright, and his tail was almost identical to mine, a blue ombre with reflections of iridescence. "This place always brought me peace," he said. I swam towards him.

"Does Ronan know about it?" I asked quietly. He shook his head and I grinned. If Ronan didn't know about this place that would mean it was our little secret. "So...this place is just ours?" I asked. He nodded.

"It'll be our secret place," he said. I swam in a circle. It was pretty big. Looking down, I could make out another opening. My dad must have noticed.

"That one leads to the ocean," he said. My eyes widened in excitement. He let out a laugh, noticing my expression. "This was always my little hideaway," he said. I stared in disbelief.

"You? Hide from what?" I asked. My dad let out a sigh. Looking at him now, I noticed the dark circles under his eyes. I swallowed.

"Being a prince was hard and being a king is even harder," he began. His tail swished back and forth in the water. "It's a lot of responsibility Caspian," he said. I looked away, already knowing where this was going. "Sometimes we need a place, a person that helps to ease the weight off of our shoulders. Sometimes we need to be reminded of why we do what we do, but also that we can't do everything," he said. I pulled myself up to sit next to him.

"Is that why you have mom and Uncle Seward?" I asked. Uncle Seward was Mira's dad and second in command. He smiled at me.

"Aye. Your mother brings me peace, the same peace I feel here. Uncle Seward helps me with my duties as a king. They remind me of my duty to our people, the ocean, and the duty I have to myself," he said, softly. My brows furrowed.

"To yourself?" I asked.

"You cannot take care of others if you don't take care of yourself. Remember that," he said.

AND MAYBE THAT'S why I ran. There is no way in a kraken's lair I can possibly take up my role as General of The Atlantic Ocean. I would be the king's second in command and a failure to my dad, to our name.

I fit in better as the royal jester than as the prince.

There is a giant splash in front of me, and I sit up. A young seal swims before me. It's a harbor seal with sleek blue-grey fur and dark speckles. It has big dark eyes and a face that reminds me of a puppy. While it isn't uncommon for seals to appear on Coralia's shoreline, I'm surprised one has managed to discover my secret place.

I dip back into the water and the seal swims to the opposite side of the cave, watching me. Nerves crawl up my body as we continue to stare at each other. My heart races as my magic begins resurfacing.

In Lavender Falls I normally kept my magic to a minimum. Reading energies was like breathing to me but there were other aspects of my magic that I tucked into a corner of my mind, hidden, much like my tail.

The seal tilts its head, and I take a breath, letting my magic heat my body. I roll my shoulders, feeling all of my muscles relax. It's as if I have spent a year in a fish tank and now am finally free. I smile.

"Wow, that feels great," I said. The seal snorted. "How did you know how to get in here?" I ask.

"*Me?* Why are *you* in my secret place?" it asked. With my magic flowing freely I can understand what it is saying. Its voice is sweet and curious. The seal is only four feet tall and still young from the looks of it. I let out a laugh.

"Yours? I think you mean mine," I said. Its eyes filled with annoyance, and it swam back and forth in a no gesture. "I'm sorry to break it to you, but I've been coming here since I was ten," I said, mimicking its motion.

"Wait, how old are you?" it asked. The seal swims closer, sizing me up.

"29," I said, confidently. It lets out a noise that I believe is a laugh.

"Wow, you're old," it said. My jaw drops.

"I assure you in siren years I'm young," I said. The seal lays on its back, staring up.

"Since you're so old I guess this place *was* yours first," it said. Its voice sounded sad.

"We can always share this place," I said, offering a peace deal. The seal sighs again and something inside me said there is something else. The seal's head pops up as I swim across.

"Wait! I know that symbol," it squealed with delight, catching a look at my tattoo. "You're with King Ronan!" it said excitedly. My stomach tightens. It seems so happy at the mention of my brother.

"He is my brother," I said. Its eyes widen and it swims so close its flippers rub against my side.

"Are you Prince Caspian?" it asked. I nod solemnly. "We've been waiting for you!" it said. I raise an eyebrow.

"What could you possibly need me for?" I ask. Its eyes cast down, staring into the depths of the cave's pool.

"It's best if I show you, your highness," it said.

I DO my best to follow behind the seal as we swim out into the ocean and bit back a sigh. It has been way too long since I stretched out my tail. All around us were seaweed, fish, sea urchins, starfish and more. I smile as a stingray swim by.

There is a weird sensation flowing through me the further down we swim. The water is a bit murky as the sun begins to set. The coral's vibrant shades of bright yellow, orange, green and red have begun to fade. They look dull and lifeless.

"What is this?" I ask. We come upon an open area where I can sit comfortably against the ocean sand. Surrounding me are dying coral. If I look up, I can see the way the mackerel keeps swimming away from this area. It is like this is a dead zone. I swallow. Something is wrong. I can feel it. The seal swims up to me.

"King Ronan has been trying to find a way to slow down the decay," it said. I shake my head.

"But how could this be happening? I've only been gone a year," I said. There is no way my leaving is tied into this, right? I glance around. Is it magical? A mundane reason? "Wait, why would you be waiting for me?" I ask, already dreading the answer.

"You are the bridge between us and them. You can help!" it said. I shake my head again. What can I possibly do? I can read energies, compel others with my siren songs, and talk to sea creatures– that's where my magic ends. I don't have healing abilities. There is no way I can help with this. The seal shakes its head, clearly not believing me.

"Talk to King Ronan. I know you can both figure this out," it said, looking up as a school of fish swims by. "You need to, before it's too late."

※

ACCORDING TO MY MOM, my brother lived at the lighthouse. He had moved there last year and felt like he could keep a better eye on the ocean that way. I walk inside, not bothering to knock. I know he leaves it open. It's a habit of his.

"Ronan!" I shout once inside. I slip out of my shoes and made my way to my dad's–*his* office. I swallow the pain I always feel when I walk inside.

The door is ajar, and my brother is at his desk, surrounded by books, a computer, and papers. He has his glasses off, sitting back in his chair. I look around. This place is a mess. Behind him was an entire wall filled with books about every ocean creature imaginable, especially the magical.

"Nice of you to show up," he said with a roll of his eyes. My nostrils flare. "I take it you saw the coral," he said. I glare at him.

"Yes. I met a lovely seal who seemed convinced that I could somehow fix this mess?" I said, placing my hands on the desk. My brother's eyes harden.

"And you think the seal is wrong?" he said. I huff out a hollow laugh.

"What could I possibly do to save the coral?" I ask. "Can't you ask Aunt Meryl for a magical recipe?" I ask, remembering how she'd helped save the Hollow Tree in Lavender Falls. Ronan's mouth twist in a frown.

"No shit shrimp brain. We've been trying everything. Why do you think in the year *you've* been *gone* it hasn't gotten worse," he snapped.

"I can't believe you let this happen," I said, instantly regretting my words. My brother slams a book close.

"You think I *let* this happen? You've been gone an entire fucking year Cas. A year. While I've been left to take care of all of this by myself," he said. I swallow at my brother's righteous intensity.

"You've been taking care of it by yourself since you were 18," I point out. Ronan glares at me.

"Maybe I was doing it all by myself but at least you were still around. I thought I could rely on you when things got tough. Did you always plan to leave? Were the years of talking about you taking up the general's position just talk? Making me believe that my brother had my back?" he asked, voice booming.

"I could never take Uncle Seward's place," I said quietly.

"You always knew you would," he said harshly. I swallow the guilt.

Since graduating high school I've been biding my time. I did everything that I was told. I studied the books and attended all the meetings. But the closer I got to the ceremony the more I felt Uncle Seward's ghost swimming around me. He was an amazing general, a great father and brother. How could I compete with that?

I sit in a chair, the familiar weight resting on my shoulders again. "Ronan, there is nothing I can do," I said. He shakes his head.

"Do you truly believe that or are you trying to run away from your responsibility again?" he asked. I keep my mouth shut, knowing that a small part of his statement is right.

"I just don't know what I could do," I said. My brother leans his head against the chair, staring at the ceiling.

"I'm hoping that Prince Kai of the Pacific might have some ideas. He's in charge of his own ocean, a responsibility you share. Maybe he knows something," he said. His fingers gingerly trace his forearm. Hidden beneath his long sleeve was the same tattoo I wore on my chest. Our family insignia, what bonded us and represented our royal status. "I've been looking into the Trident of King Atlas," he said quietly. I freeze.

"Ronan the trident is a legend," I said. He raises a dark blonde eyebrow.

"Sirens are a legend too, Caspian," he said, crossing his arms. I take a deep breath. I know my brother and I recognize that look in his eyes. He has something planned for me.

"What do you want from me?" I ask with gritted teeth.

"I want you to work with Kai and find what you can about the Trident of Atlas," he said, checking his watch. "Aunt Meryl just got some new books courtesy of Professor Luna. I heard she is a friend of yours from Lavender Falls," he said, standing. I bite the inside of my cheek, recalling when Mrs. Luna, Lola's mom, handed her a book about sirens. I had to translate some of the texts. My brother pauses at the door.

"One more thing Caspian," he said, turning to face me. His eyes glow mischievously.

Fuck, now what?

"Tomorrow's dinner is to welcome Kai and a few other royals. You will be in attendance, and I assume I should have an extra plate set for your girlfriend Crystal, yes?"

CHAPTER 7
FIRST DAY FRUSTRATIONS

Crystal

The sun hasn't risen and I'm already out of Sailor's cottage. When Ronan told me about the second bed and breakfast flooding, I knew that meant I would be staying at Sailor's. My options were limited. So, I shot him a quick text that I would stay with him and locked myself in one of the bedrooms. His response? He would be home late, which was fine by me.

I spent all night tossing and turning. My meeting with Ronan to discuss a plan of action went smoothly and I wrote a neat report for my dad. It wasn't the minor issues I'd run into at work that kept me up. It was Sailor's pained face when I declined to be in a fake relationship with him and the fact that when Ronan said it was a good thing I was staying with his brother, I didn't clarify that we were friends.

Just friends.

Sailor is a nice friend. A terribly handsome friend who makes me feel comfortable. I should have clarified that, and yet I stood there with my throat so tight I could hardly let out a squeak. And now I'm avoiding Sailor.

The sound of the ocean crashing against the shore pulls me

forward. Mira had mentioned they served breakfast starting at 5am when Sailor left me to talk to his mom.

I swallow. His mom is beautiful. I could see the pain in her face when she faced her son. It was the same expression my dad wore when he saw Eleanor. At least, that's what I saw. It was a look that screamed, *'I know you're hurt. I know I carry the blame, but I don't know how to fix it.'*

My chest tightens. I was acutely aware of everyone's perception of my dad, which I understood. I grew up with him. I saw what they saw.

But they didn't see him skipping meals every time he fought with Eleanor, or the countless hours of sleep he lost just waiting for her to come home. It was so fucking painful to watch and the only thing I could do was be the good daughter. He was stressed enough between the company and Eleanor that I couldn't be another burden to him. Or to anyone else for that matter.

I sigh. I don't have to meet Ronan until 10, so I wander towards the ocean. When I get to the sandy beach there are a group of beings already there. They are swimming, laughing and enjoying themselves. My stomach twists. They all seem to be having a wonderful time. I bite my bottom lip. *Maybe I should just go to the diner.*

THE DOOR CHIMES over my head and Mira looks up, a smile breaking across her face. Her purple hair looks a bit lighter today. Her eyes move to look behind me, probably thinking Sailor is with me. I give her a small smile.

"Just me," I said, quietly. She nods and motions for me to follow her. Across from me are a group of beings around my age. There are three young women and a man, all very beautiful. They have deep tan skin, dark arched eyebrows, wide noses, dark eyes, and amazing cheekbones. They are gorgeous. I quickly look away, not wanting to get caught gawking. I hear a snicker.

"Mira where is our coffee?" one of them said. Mira looks at me and rolls her eyes.

"The coffee is brewing," she said with fake sweetness. I quietly watch their interaction. One of the women snorts and Mira takes a deep breath. She clearly doesn't like these beings.

"First we had to stay in one of those ugly cottages because this town is so old their b&b is run down, and *now* we have to deal with such rude service," she said, sounding snotty. My nose twitches. I can immediately tell their type. Spoil out of towners. I'm an out of towner too, but–

"Do you have to have an attitude at 7AM?" the man said, glaring at the women. He makes eye contact with me and winks. My nose wrinkles and I look back at Mira. She sighs, leaning towards me.

"Sorry about that. Royals can be a pain in the fin," she whispers. My eyes widen. That's right. Ronan had mentioned royals would be arriving in the coming weeks for the ceremony. "What can I get you?" she asked. I quickly flip through the menu.

"Bacon, hash browns, and scrambled eggs," I said. She nods, not bothering to write it down. "And a coffee but when it's ready," I said, slightly raising my voice. The women glance over at me, and I keep my face neutral. Just because I'm quiet, it doesn't mean I can't be passive aggressive. Mira grins.

"I knew I liked you," she said, turning around with a pep in her step. I lean my back against the booth, a small smile tugging at the corner of my lips.

There is a dull ache forming in the back of my head that I hope the coffee will soothe it. I pull out my tablet to go over my to-do list.

Ronan had acquired a team of workers to begin on the stage. They need to pull some wood out so my team can come in and replace it around noon. Then, we will take the old wood to our lumber yard to have it magically restored for future use.

My nose twitches happily as a steaming cup of coffee interrupts my view. Mira smiles and I nod, taking it from her. There is a scoff.

"Didn't we order first?" one of the ladies said.

"Yes, but *you* were rude," the man commented. I smile. At least someone is putting them in their place. Mira walks her tray over and quietly hands them their coffee. "Looking beautiful as ever Mira," he said, laying on the charm. Mira rolls her eyes. This piques my interest.

"Kai, that smile will never work on me," she said, her voice sounding bored. My eyes dart between them. He shrugs his shoulders.

"One day you'll fall for my charms," he said. The women with him gag. "Excuse my cousins. Their parents got tired of their snotty attitude and decided to stick them with me," he said. The ladies gasp and I place a hand over my mouth to stifle a laugh. Mira simply sighs and walks back towards the kitchen.

I smile to myself, enjoying my coffee quietly. This morning was proving to be slightly entertaining.

I SIGH in relief as I leave the diner and the royals that keep complaining about everything. Thankfully Kai kept putting them in check but if I was exhausted just listening to them, I couldn't imagine how tired he was having to deal with them. Mira had given me a burrito that I could take for lunch. Knowing me I would probably forget otherwise, so I had accepted and thanked her profusely.

I make my way down the beach, towards the stage where I can already see Ronan and his crew. They are ten minutes early. My shoulders drop. I like punctuality, I crave it. I have less anxiety when things occur at the times previously agreed upon. Ronan turns around, sensing my approach.

"Good morning Ms. Hale," he said. Today he is in jeans and an old slightly cropped shirt that read, Coralia's High School Swim Team. I'm faintly surprised by it, my cheeks heating. I didn't expect the King of Coralia Coast to dress so casually.

"Good morning Mr. Calder," I pause. "Wait, should I say, "Your Majesty" or something?" ask. I bite the inside of my cheek. I'm not used to dealing with royalty. I don't know how I'm supposed to properly address him. He lets out a dry chuckle.

"Mr. Calder works, or dare I say *Ronan* is fine too," he said with a slight tilt to his lips. I nod. He hands me a coffee, and I gladly take it.

This is definitely going to be a day that requires multiple cups. I glance around at the beings he has gathered.

"Everyone, attention please!" Ronan said. Everyone huddles closer and the grip on my drink tightens. "This is Ms. Hale. She is helping lead the project to restore Coralia Coast. Hale's Lumber Industry is providing the lumber we need as well as restoring what we are removing. We shall be working together to remind people what makes Coralia Coast so great," he said, warmth pouring out of him. I stare at him. I can see why he is king. Sure, he can be a bit grumpy and cold, but when it comes to Coralia Coast, he is a light.

Looking at the crew I can't help but smile. They look at Ronan with complete trust. He has told me most of the crew are from Coralia Coast and that he trusts them to get the job done. He turns to me, and I step forward.

Typically, I'm the quiet one who stands idly by. But in moments like these where I'm in work mode, I take charge. I know how to lead a project.

"Good morning, everyone. Hale's is very excited to start this new partnership with Coralia Coast. If all goes well, we have many projects lined up to get Coralia Coast back on the map," I said with a genuine smile. "My crew will be hauling in the new lumber that will be replacing the stage at around noon. All I ask is that you be mindful when pulling up the wood. If you can remove whole planks that would be best, though we'll make it work either way," I continue. I point to the stage.

I'm hoping that this wood can be salvaged and used on the b&b's new flooring. Whenever I take on these projects, I like to make sure that I don't let anything go to waste. Whatever leftover wood I have I use as supplies for workshops.

You would be surprised at how many people enjoy woodworking; Celestino offers Saturday workshops with the wood we supply. Early mornings are free workshops for the kids, while the afternoon is for the older crowd. It's a great way to bring the community together. Ronan's crew nod in understanding.

"Alright, let's get started folks!" Ronan said and everyone quickly disperses to do their jobs. There is a light tap on my shoulder, and I turn to face Ronan. "I'll let you know when your crew has arrived and keep you updated. I know you probably have other work to do," he said. I raise an eyebrow.

"Wait, are you going to help them?" I ask, staring at him in shock. For the first time he offers me a wide grin. His smile reminded me of Sailor's, wide and open-mouthed, his blue eyes shining brightly. They really were brothers.

"It is my royal duty to help my people," he said, casually. I let out a giggle, shaking my head in disbelief.

"You are not the king I thought you were," I said honestly. He shrugs his shoulders before walking away, leaving me standing in the sand.

CORALIA COAST HAS one coffee shop, The Seaside Bistro. It is cozy with a rustic, ocean charm. From outside the window, I can see the ocean and that brings me comfort. It wasn't until I moved to Lavender Falls that I realized how much nature soothed me, and now being in Coralia Coast reaffirmed this.

Granted, I'm a pixie who literally specializes in nature, but I hardly ever tap into that part of myself. I believe magic should be used when needed, not just because. Also, most of my job revolves around me being on my computer and running meetings.

I had spent the better part of two hours filtering through emails and updating shipments for different clients across the east coast when my phone pings. It's from my sister. I take a breath. I'm still not used to us talking again. I could have reached out plenty of times, but I'd become comfortable with the hand life had dealt me. I had gone so many years with her silence that I'd become comfortable with it.

But now? Now I was constantly confused by the emotions that would rack through me from a simple text.

> ELEANOR
> just checking in.

A SIREN'S SUMMER FOR LOVE

> **ME**
> Im good

> **ELEANOR**
> What do you think of the town?

I glance back out the window. What *did* I think of Coralia Coast? It has a bleak melancholic air about it, but that's been comforting. I enjoy its quietness. The buildings have a rustic charm and have clearly been here for longer than I've been alive.

The ocean is a soothing melody that puts my soul at ease. I haven't seen much of the other beings. They tend to keep to themselves at the moment. Ronan has mentioned there was a shift when his dad passed away, and then again when Sailor left. The people grew reclusive.

> **ME**
> I like it

> **ELEANOR**
> I knew you would
>
> But

> **ME**
> But??

There is a tick in my jaw and a surprising flash of defensiveness courses through me. Coralia Coast isn't my town. I technically belonged to Lavender Falls, and yet something about Eleanor's but bothers me.

> **ELEANOR**
> Don't think it has a sad vibe?

> **ME**
> Just because it's quiet doesn't make it sad. It's clear these beings are missing someone or something.

> **ELEANOR**
> How's Sailor?

I frown. She is ignoring what I said. I glance back out the window quickly. I haven't seen much of Sailor. We'd only arrived yesterday, and I had ditched him as fast as I could, even hiding from him this morning. We haven't talked since the fake dating conversation. My cheeks heat.

> ME
> It's only been a day
>
> ELEANOR
> right. Well let me know if you need anything.
>
> ME
> Okay.

I take a breath trying to simmer down the anger her last text. In my heart I know she is coming from a good, caring place. I'm her younger sister and we're back in each other's lives. Of course she would offer help.

But at the same time, it's been eight fucking years, *years* of just dad and I. Years of me figuring out shit by myself. I don't need her. I haven't needed her in a long time.

I rub my temples and decide I needed more coffee. I need something to get me through the rest of this day. My crew will arrive soon, and then I had an afternoon meeting and a follow up with my dad. My phone beeps again with a text from Ronan.

"THE STAGE IS ALMOST DONE," Ronan said, wiping the sweat off his face with his shirt. I quickly glance away.

"Let your crew break for lunch while mine finishes the demo. We can start building this afternoon," I suggested. Ronan nods and walks back to tell everyone the plan. I glance at my workers.

The stage stood about four feet high and was around 24x32 feet, a good size to accommodate a seven-to-ten-piece band. Ronan says there was a magical ward around the stage to keep any humans from seeing the crew use their magic.

I smile. Magic came in handy during times like this and I'm grateful for it. I walk over to my crew and smile. I've been working with them since I was 20, so around four years.

"Hey everyone," I said, brightly.

"Ms. Hale!" they greeted. They have palettes of fresh wood behind them.

"How was the drive?" I ask, checking to see if any of them look tired despite the drive only being two hours long. Some of them roll their eyes.

"We're fine. Ms. Hale," Connor said. Connor is close to my age and around my height.

"We're just excited to be at the beach," Mr. Whitman, the supervisor, said. I nod.

"I told Mr. Calder that his crew could break for lunch while you finish taking apart the stage. Afterwards I think if we combine our magic and muscles, we should have the stage done by tomorrow," I said, making sure to look at each of them. "I sent you an email with the hotel you'll be staying at. I'm sorry that the bed and breakfasts aren't ready," I said, regrettably. They wave their hands off. While my dad was a bit cold, he always hired the warmest, hardworking beings.

"Just put us to work Ms. Hale," Connor said. I smile, feeling relaxed. With them here I have a piece of my normal life with me.

I SMILE from my seat upon a rock, taking pictures of the progress, our teams have made. By the time we were ready to clock out the stage was almost done, which meant we would be able to shift our timeline up.

"We work well together," Ronan affirmed, walking towards me. Ronan rarely took a break the whole day. He demonstrated his leadership amongst his beings, and it was admirable. I can't remember the last time I saw my dad working hand in hand with his crew. Granted, he has a lot on his plate with taking care of company, but I know deep down that he misses working with his hands. I nod.

"It was a great first day. I have a good feeling about this," I said confidently. Ronan took a seat next to me, sighing.

"It felt good to be doing something that doesn't involve shaking hands or signing papers," he said, staring out into the water.

"For the moment the wood for the stage is dark, but it'll lighten to a really pretty pale gold with the exposure to the sea salt and sunshine over time," I note, pointing to the stage and he nods.

"I trust your judgment," he said. I can't fight back a smile. It is a relief for someone to trust me. I always second guess myself because my dad is always double-checking everything, I do to the point of feeling suffocated.

The sun is setting, making the ocean glitter. "I have to get ready for tonight," Ronan said, standing up. He offers me a hand.

"Tonight?" I ask, letting him pull me up. The side of his mouth twitches and his eyes sparkle with amusement. My stomach sinks.

"Don't tell me Cas forgot to tell you about the welcome dinner?" he teased.

Shit, dinner?!

"You'd think my brother would be a better boyfriend," he said. I blush but before I can correct him, he continues. "We're having a welcome dinner for Cas and some of the royals from the Pacific Ocean," he said. My eyes widen.

A dinner…with royalty and my apparent fake boyfriend.

Just lovely.

CHAPTER 8
ONCE UPON A TIME

Caspian

A *flash of dark hair caught my eye. I saw her walking from afar and without a thought my body compelled me to move towards her. Crystal was like a lighthouse, every time I saw her, her presence made me follow in her wake.*

Lalalala lala lalalala

A melody played every time I thought of her, saw her. It was soft, sweet, and demure; a tune that rocked my body gently like a soft wave.

I didn't know why, but it was always there in the back of my mind. There have been a few times when I almost began singing around her.

She made a left and my lips twitched. Where was this pixie heading today?

*I had the day off, and usually on my days off I take a dip in Boogeyman's Swamp. Without changing, of course. It didn't feel right shifting in a lake when my heart belonged to the Atlantic Ocean. **I** belonged to the Atlantic Ocean.*

Carrie has done it, of course. She's been living here for ten years.

I quickened my steps, wanting to open the door for Crystal. Her hand reached for the handle, and I stepped right behind her, aligning our bodies. I breathe deeply. She smelled like citrus.

My hand gripped the door handle before hers. Surprisingly she didn't flinch. Instead, she turned around and gave me a smile that made my heart race.

"Sailor," she said grinning. I smiled down at her. She was a beauty, with her hazel eyes that either looked like warm honey or melted jade. Her long dark hair was twisted in a messy bun, and she wore an oversized hoodie, and this time only had a satchel with her. No laptop.

I raised an eyebrow. "No laptop?" I asked. She shook her head.

"Giving myself a break," she said quietly. My grin widened. Crystal was always working. It was admirable. I could tell she was like Eleanor and worked herself too hard.

Or maybe I just wasn't working enough. I was trying to live an easy life, away from responsibility. But I felt it. The call to the ocean came from deep within bones.

"Would you like to hang out today?" I asked, hopefully. Her cheeks turned the prettiest shade of pink. Fuck, I liked making her blush.

I inhaled her scent once more before reminding myself we were just friends. She nodded. I pulled open the door and we stepped inside Coffin's Coffee Shop.

"What's the plan?" I asked as I followed her to the front. She tilted her head back and forth.

"I wanted to have breakfast here, then maybe go to Boogeyman's Swamp to do some reading by the water," she said. I nodded.

"I don't have a book. Care to share?" I asked. She blushed again and I inwardly cheered. Every time I made her blush it felt like a win.

"It's a romance book," she said, eyeing me as we stood in line. I shrugged my shoulders.

"If it's something you like, that's all that matters."

CRYSTAL WAS GONE in the morning. I had planned on making breakfast for us, something to ease the awkwardness of yesterday's conversation, but she had vanished by the time I woke up.

It was fucking stupid of me to tell my mom that I was dating Crystal. Of course she would say no to me. I was her friend, *just* her friend.

My hands clench. How the fuck had she never had a boyfriend? Even asked out on a fucking date. She is gorgeous and so sweet.

"Book," Aunt Meryl said, slapping a worn weathered book in front of my face. I'm with my aunt in her apothecary shop. I spent most of my childhood in and out of this place, fascinated by the potions and sea crystals she would gather. I crack a smile. I wasn't sure how Aunt Meryl was going to react to seeing me.

When I visited during the winter I'd stayed hidden, but she knew I was there. She didn't push, wanting to keep my whereabouts a secret, and I was grateful for that.

"Thanks," I said, eyeing her. Aunt Meryl's vibrant red hair was streaked with grey, and her green eyes sharpen in my direction. I swallow. She is totally pissed at me. "I'm sorry," I blurt out. She stares at me for a second before sighing.

"I understand why you ran Caspian," she said, her voice tired. Aunt Meryl is–*was* married to Uncle Seward, my dad's brother. Her husband had held the duty that I was next in line for.

The thought of taking the last thing that belonged to him made me sick to my stomach. Uncle Seward's name was still written in the royal book of the Atlantic Ocean as the Second Prince/General. But by performing the ceremony, his name would be washed away and replaced by mine.

Aunt Meryl looks at me again, her eyes filled with sadness. "But you didn't have to keep it from us," she said, quietly. I swallow. I'd told no one I was leaving except Mira, who I'd sworn to secrecy.

"I know I just…I didn't want people to try and stop me, convince me to stay. I needed to…" I trail off trying to find the right words.

"Be you?" she suggested. I nod solemnly. She sighs greatly. I'd hurt a lot of beings when I left, and I wasn't sure how I was going to fix it.

"I am sorry," I said, earnestly. She taps my chin once; her eyes trained on me. With a whisper of smile, she pulls away.

"Well, you are back now and taking on your brother's research from the looks of it," she said, pointing to the book.

"How long has this been going on?" I ask. I should have pressed my brother for more details, but I'd been so annoyed with him last night I couldn't think. Aunt Meryl shook her head back and forth.

"Honestly hard to say. No one noticed the coral dying until maybe two months after you'd left?" she said. My eyes widen.

"And there is no hypothesis on how or why it started?" I ask. She shrugs her shoulders.

"Who's to say this isn't the natural order of things, Caspian," she said. I frown. "You see the way humans treat the world. This could just be the direct result of their overconsumption," she said, sounding bleak. I shake my head.

"Even so, there are some who are on our side, fighting for the world and the ocean. And we're magical beings. None of your potions have worked?" I ask, thinking back to how we managed to save the Hollow Tree in Lavender Falls. She glances around, taking in her shop.

"So far nothing has purified the coral. We've slowed it down, yes, but we haven't found an actual solution," she remarked. I glance at the book Mrs. Luna let us borrow. It was old. The worn leather was a deep blue, the color of the ocean, with the title carved in. Its pages were jagged, used. I brush my fingers across them, feeling its magical history.

"That's why we're looking into the legend of the trident?" I ask. Aunt Meryl's lips twitch.

"Legends are born from truth, Caspian," she pointed out, sensing my distrust. Her words reflect my brother's. I nod, opening the book and doing what my brother wanted. While it annoys me to listen to his royal authority, I want to save the ocean too. Because even when I was running from my duty, I'd felt the ocean's call.

King Atlantis was a mighty and fair king. He ruled the Atlantic Ocean for 800 years with an open mind, righteous fist, and heart of mercy. But he felt immense pressure because of his duty as a king to all beings and the ocean. His younger brother, Atlas, proposed a solution that was then implemented throughout all oceans for years to come.

King Atlantis would govern the sirens and the ocean, but his younger brother Atlas would act as the link between the oceans' creatures and other beings. As second in command Atlas' duties revolved around making sure the ocean was safe and healthy. Given Atlas' special inclination to speak with sea creatures, a rare ability, the kingdom of The Atlantic Ocean was able to thrive for hundreds of years.

However, as the human population grew and evolved, their actions made our oceans become sick. And thus, the trident of Atlas came to be.

It is a magical item crafted from coral from the depths of the Atlantic Ocean, imbued with Atlas' royal blood. As a mystical tool, the trident became a conduit for Atlas' many magical abilities.

One stormy night Atlas and King Atlantis got into a fight. King Atlantis wanted to keep the sirens hidden from the humans, while Atlas wanted to seek a home for himself on the shore as he had fallen in love with a human woman.

The kingdom was divided for some time. When King Atlantis passed away, Atlas ascended the throne and the kingdom reunited and established Coralia Coast, a shoreside town that became a sanctuary for the sirens of the Atlantic Ocean.

King Atlas and the kingdom thrived until his own passing. With the kingdom in peace, his son decided to hide the trident. Its powers no longer needed for the time being. When needed again, the trident will awaken, and its rightful owner will hear its siren call.

I sit back in my chair, taking a breath. My fingers tremble slightly as I stare at the pages. I grew up hearing about Atlas, the Second Prince, then king, and all the good he had done with his magical trident. As a kid it was just a story, a story my dad told my brother and I to help us get along. But as an adult, I couldn't deny the connection my brother and I had to Atlantis and Atlas.

"Well, did you learn anything?" Aunt Meryl asked. I close the book carefully and tuck it into my bag. I look at my aunt.

It's been a year since I saw her and, like my mom, I now notice the slight wrinkles by her eyes and the new beauty spots on her arms. She still looks beautiful. Most supernatural beings aged very slowly, but that didn't mean I couldn't see the differences as the years go on.

"Like most magical adventures Aunt Meryl, we have a lot of "wait for something magical to happen"," I said, and my aunt laughs at my annoyance.

I'M DRESSED in the kitchen for tonight's welcome dinner. The dinner is for me as well as Prince Kai and his family. I haven't seen the siren in almost five years. He is one of my closest royal friends. He is kind, loves getting under Mira's scales, and shares my sense of adventure.

When I turn around, Crystal stands at the edge of the kitchen in khaki slacks that hid her slender curves and long legs. She's wearing a linen blouse, no doubt because of the sun.

Her cheeks are slightly pink, but I can't tell if she is blushing or it's from being kissed by the outdoor heat. I heard from the townsfolk that they were working on the stage. Her long dark hair is wrapped in a tight bun.

Fuck, she is beautiful.

"Hey," I said, trying not to sound awkward. She nods and walks in as I pour her a glass of water. She offers me a small smile. "How was your day?" I ask, casually. Because I *am* casual. *Totally* casual about the fact that Crystal is staying in my home, with me, just me. Her and I. Sharing space as two friends who did not have an awkward moment like a day ago.

Fuck. I need to get a grip.

"Long but productive," she offered. I hum and point to the fridge.

"I have some pasta in the fridge if you want to heat it up for dinner," I said as I turn to dry the dishes I'd used. She chokes on her water.

"You made me dinner?" she asked, in shock. I don't turn around. I can't face her quite yet. I still haven't told my mom or my brother the truth about our relationship. But I plan to tonight. They are expecting Crystal, and I plan on showing up alone and setting everyone straight.

"I figured you'd had a long day and would be too tired to cook," I said. She walks over and the smell of summer and citrus wrap around me. I glance slightly down at her. Her brows are furrowed in confusion.

"But we have that welcome dinner," she said softly. I swallow, nervous.

"You were mainly invited because they think you're my girlfriend. I'll tell them the truth at dinner. You don't have to go. It's been a long day for you," I said. Her lips twist in a frown.

"I would appreciate you telling them the truth, but Ronan expects me to go," she said. Crystal crosses her arms, the blouse tightens around her breasts, and I look away. My gaze focuses on our reflection in the window. "I already made up my mind and I'm going," she said, firmly.

My lips twitch. I have a habit of forgetting how assertive Crystal can be. At times I forget her quiet and gentle nature is just one aspect of her and not who she is all the time.

"Okay, well then you can go get ready and I promise to tell my mom and Ronan the truth," I said, turning back to her. She nods, her eyes skirting away from mine though I notice her cheeks becoming more rosey.

ISABEL BARREIRO

"We are pleased to welcome you all to Coralia Coast. I know for some of you it is your first time here and I would like to apologize for the construction that will occur during your stay as we work to revitalize our small coastal town," my brother said, a champagne glass in hand. I glance at the crowd.

Some lower-level royal families from the Pacific coast have gathered. My mom stands behind my brother in a beautiful blue dress, admiring him. I can't blame her. So far, he hasn't fucked up his speech.

"I would also like to welcome my little brother Caspian back, who has spent a year connecting with other small towns in the hopes of strengthening Coralia's partnerships," he continued. I smirk. Oh, my brother is fucking good.

Look at him up there covering up the fact that I ran away from home. Someone presses into my side, and I glance to see it is Crystal. She offers me a reassuring smile and for a second, I feel at peace.

"You okay?" she whispers, her hand brushing mine. What I would give to slide my fingers between hers. The warmth of her side is enough to ease the tension in my body created by the guilt of my brother's lie. I tune out the rest of my brother's speech. My sole focus was on the vision that stood next to me.

There is no fucking way in a kraken's lair that I will be able to focus on this damn dinner with Crystal looking gorgeous. She wore a fitted pantsuit in a shade of red that made me want to fall on my knees. With her heels, she reaches my height and fuck, it's hot. I just need to survive this dinner and tell my family the truth.

"I am since I'm here with you," I whisper, handing her my glass. She takes it, taking a tentative sip with a roll of her eyes.

"He makes a good speech," she said, leaning towards me. I glance at my brother, droning on about how we hope to flourish as a town, and we strengthen our connections. His speech fills everyone else with hope, but it only makes me feel guilty.

. . .

AFTER DINNER it is time for the part I hate: mingling and dancing. I excuse myself to the restroom and when I return, Crystal is laughing at something my brother has said. Weird, since my brother isn't funny.

"Caspian!" a shrill voice called. I inwardly groan. The main thing I hate about these welcome dinners is all the two-faced personalities trying to kiss fins. I turn to see Tati, Kai's younger cousin.

She is a beautiful young siren, but if I remember correctly, she is a spoiled princess. A literal spoiled princess.

"Princess Tati," I said, with a slight bow. She loops her arm through mine, and I bite the inside of my cheek. She presses her chest into mine, as if that will seduce me.

"You should ask me to dance," she said, batting her eyes. I do my best to not gag. We are in my kingdom and surrounded by royals. If I make any sort of disgusted face or utter rude words, I won't hear the end of it from everyone, Coralia or out of town.

"To dance?" I hesitate, my eyes drifting back to my brother. Crystal has disappeared somewhere in the crowd.

"I thought you'd never asked!" she said, dragging me to the center of the room where a few couples are swaying to the music. I take a deep breath. I was hoping my first dance would be with Crystal. I *wanted* it to be with her.

I place my hand on the middle of Tati's back and take her other hand as we waltz. Every time she steps towards me and presses her body against mine, I take a step back. I can see what she wants with me, and I'm not interested.

"It's been a while Caspian. How have you grown more handsome?" she said. I bite back a laugh.

"Why thank you. You look beautiful this evening," I said, politely. She smiles, stepping close to me again.

"So, your brother says you hope to improve this town," she said. My jaw ticks at her statement. Something about how she said it leaves a sour taste in my mouth.

"Yes," I said, maintaining a neutral tone. She nods.

"I would start with that diner," she said, eyes looking around. I smirk. She is probably looking for Mira. My dearest cousin loves putting the other royals in their place.

"I believe the diner is fine, just needs a few minor upgrades," I said, gauging her reaction.

"Probably a new hire," she mutters.

"I see you met my cousin Mira," I said. Her eyes snap to me. "You do remember she is my cousin. My *favorite* cousin," I emphasize. Her face flushes in embarrassment.

"That's right. Her attitude was probably due to the fact that it was early," she said. I hum knowing damn well, she avoided taking responsibility over her attitude towards Mira.

"Anyway, I'm tired of beating around the coral," she said. I raise an eyebrow, spinning her. When we come together, she leans her face towards me but a hand on my arm cuts her off. Her gaze turns dark at the intrusion.

I look to see who my savior is. My heart thumps. Crystal offers her a grin. My cheeks heat. *Look who decided to be my knight in shining armor.*

"Excuse me, may I cut in?" Crystal asked politely.

"We were—"

"I *will* cut in," Crystal demanded, pulling my hand away from Tati's. She glared at Crystal.

"Do you know who I *am*?" she asked, sounding exactly like a snotty princess. Crystal ignores her tone, glancing at me shyly. I stare at their interaction, questions racing through my mind. Crystal straightens her shoulders.

"Yes, I do but you're dancing with *my* boyfriend," she said. My heart rattles in my chest. *Fucking barnacles.* She just claimed me. She *claimed* me in front of everyone in this room. I can't control the smile on my face, nor do I want to.

"You promised me a dance, fish cake," she said, and I fight back a laugh when I see her regret the nickname choice the moment it escaped her sweet lips.

"If you'll excuse me, Tati," I said, pulling away and gathering

Crystal in my arms. Once Tati is preoccupied with another royal, I look at Crystal, her face flush. She is my undoing. My magic pushes me closer to her, a melody forming in the recess of my mind.

"Fish cake? Really?" I joke. She groans, shaking her head.

"I had to be quick!" she said, eyes widening. I chuckle.

"Babe couldn't cut it?" I ask, raising an eyebrow. She rolls her hazel eyes and snorts.

"*Babe* is so basic," she said. I shake my head. Crystal is full of surprises. I twirl her twice before bringing her close. My lips brush her ear, and I grin at the way she shivers beneath my touch. My body ignites at the many thoughts running rampant in my mind.

"You do realize you just claimed me," I said. She moves her hands up my shoulders and around my neck, keeping me close.

"I realize that," she said. I pull back wanting to get a read on her. Her eyes harden with a resolution that leaves me rattled. "I want to be your fake girlfriend, but I have conditions," she whispers. I nod, glancing around to make sure no one is listening. *I wonder what made her change her mind.*

"We can discuss when we're back home," I said. She fights back a smile, and I have a hopeful feeling about why.

"Until then, how about we forget everyone and leave?" I suggest. Her eyes widen.

"Can we?" she asked, her eyes pleading. I know for a fact that Crystal is exhausted from work and has reached her threshold for socializing. Her eyes finds Tati's and there is a flicker of hurt. I grip her chin.

"What's wrong?" I ask. She shrugs her shoulders. I shake my head. "Tell me what's happening in that beautiful brain of yours," I demand. She swallows, her eyes tormented. "You know I'll just keep bothering you." She rolls her lips.

"I came here with you," she started. We glide across the dance floor in unison. "Some of the people here know we are…together," she said. The tips of her ears are slowly turning pink. *That's interesting.* I never noticed that before. She bites her bottom lip, unknowingly teasing me.

"They think we're together, but your first dance was with *her*," she said, her voice borderline jealous. I take a breath.

Was Crystal jealous?

She has to be with the way her lips turned down into a frown, her thick eyebrows furrowed in annoyance. "*Why* are you smiling like that?" she asked, definitely annoyed. I press my forehead against hers, knowing that being this close to her is weakening my resolve and pushing her boundaries.

"She did have my first dance but you, M'Lady, will always have my last."

CHAPTER 9
FAKE GIRLFRIEND DUTIES

Crystal

Ronan sweeps me around the room, introducing me to the different royals. Even though I'm not in the mood for small talk I understand why. So far, I have met with royals from the towns up and down the eastern coast. Out of the corner of my eye I could see the family from the Pacific Coast. The way that Kai cast glances at Mira every few moments has me smiling into my drink.

I spend most of my evening avoiding them but avoiding them meant also avoiding Sailor. One of the ladies follows behind him wherever he goes, ready to sink her claws into him. It bothers me that she watches him as if he is her prey.

"Careful there Crystal. You're sending daggers to Princess Tati," Ronan said, low enough that no one could hear. I let out a strangled giggle.

"I don't know what you mean," I said, hoping to appear nonchalant to this sea of strangers. Mira appears in a short black dress, looping her arm around her cousin's.

"We all see you glaring at the spoiled princess," she said with a smirk. I blush. *Was I really being that obvious?* From the corner of my eye, I see her practically drag Sailor onto the dance floor. My nose twitches watching her press her body against his.

"I would go and get your merman before she tries to shove her tits any further up his chest," Mira commented. My hand clenches around my glass.

"Must you put it that way? You are a *princess*," Ronan pointed out. I raise an eyebrow. I knew they were cousins, but I'm not well versed on how royalty functions.

"Technically I am," she said with a shrug of her shoulders. "But don't treat me differently just because I wear a tiara," she said dramatically. Ronan snorts.

"It's a crooked tiara," he muttered, and she slaps his chest. I smile at their back and forth. They seem comfortable with each other the way that Lily and Lola are with Eleanor.

I wonder if my sister and I could be that way again. Were we ever? My childhood is a blur at this point.

"Is she trying to kiss him?" Mira's question has my head snapping up. I glance at Sailor and see him tilt his body away from her once again as she licks her lips. I hand Ronan my glass.

"Will you excuse me? It seems like my boyfriend has gotten caught in a leech's net."

AFTER SAILOR SPOKE to his brother we walked home. Sailor's cottage isn't my home, but it feels like it. It is warm, inviting, and peaceful with its quaint charm. I look at him, his eyes focus on the stroll ahead.

I thought back to that princess' arms around him on the dance floor. I could tell he was uncomfortable with her. His jaw was set, and he was so robotic when she flirted with him. I hadn't intended for the night to turn out the way it had.

I understood why Sailor asked me to be his fake girlfriend. The women here were swimming around him like piranhas, completely forgetting he was more than just a shiny crown. They ignored how he obviously felt. It hurt to see and...deep down I couldn't stomach watching Princess Tati press her body against his.

When she licked her lips, something possessed me. For once I let my instinct take over. My temper had the reins and *fuck*, did it feel powerful. I marched over and claimed Sailor in front of everyone.

I cringe inwardly. I also called him fish cake. How do couples come up with adorable nicknames? My hands fidget with my clothes. How does a *fake* couple come up with *fake* nicknames?

"How tired are you?" Sailor asked, pulling me away from my thoughts.

"Depends on what the situation is going to be," I answer honestly. Sailor's nice lips that look kissable stretch into a smile.

"I promise no one will be around and you'll be able to dip your feet in some water," he said. I nod and he offers me a hand, leading me to the woods behind his cottage.

As we make our way down the trail, I can't stop myself from giggling. He turns around and raises an eyebrow. His hand is warm and slightly calloused against mine. It feels...nice.

"You're taking me into the woods...at night...and you said no one will be around," I point out. Sailor shook his head with a smile.

"You're always safe with me," he promised. My heart rattles at his words. They feel true.

AFTER A FEW MINUTES I can hear rushing water. I gasp at the sight of a waterfall. It is a small hot spring, judging by the way the steam was rolling off of it. The moon hangs high in the air, enchanting me into my next step.

"It's beautiful," I whisper. Sailor stands beside me, taking it in.

"That's what your sister said," he said. I freeze. I swallow as a rush of hurt crashes over me. He brought Eleanor here. *Of course* he brought her here. *This is where they got the pearl they needed for their potion.*

At least that's what I'm telling myself. I can't deny I feel jealous. He brought my sister here first. And that hurt.

I shake my head. Sailor and I were just friends and there is plenty of time for inside jokes and things of our own. I mean, we had *things of our own* like shows and books. I guess my inner child was selfish.

As the younger sister I'd always received hand-me-downs and for some reason this felt like that. Sailor must have noticed my mood because he tugged at our intertwined hands.

"There is something I haven't shown your sister," he said. *Did he read the hurt on my face?* I stare into his eyes that were dark as the night sky. "But we have to go swimming."

W<small>E WALKED</small> to the house to change into swimsuits before heading back to the spring. I'm a bundle of nerves. I have no idea what Sailor is going to show me and it's late as fuck.

I'm using this summer to live for myself, and today that means late night swimming in a spring with my best friend.

My cheeks heat as I glance at Sailor. I spent so many years focused on work and only hanging out with coworkers at work. And though I loved the ladies of Lavender Falls, with Sailor I felt like I could truly be myself. I'm different around him.

Sailor slides off his shirt revealing a body that makes me clench my thighs. I may be inexperienced in relationships and romance but I'm not blind to my own needs and *fuck* is he beautiful.

He has a tattoo of a trident on the right side of his chest, a mix of waves and seaweed. His body is slightly defined, probably from the hours of carpentry and swimming. He, like most sirens, has a long lean body.

When I finally glance up at his face he is wearing a gorgeous smirk. I look away, undoing my robe. He instantly turns away to give me privacy.

I roll my eyes. He's going to see me in my swimsuit anyway, but I find the gesture endearing anyway. When he turns around, his eyes bounce around my body, drinking me in. My body heats in response to his perusal. *Fuck.* I've never had someone look at me with such hunger. But just as quickly as I see his desire, it vanishes.

"Follow me," he said, leading me into the water. I moan at the temperature. There is a delicious heat that soothes my muscles. We swim closer to the waterfall when Sailor holds a hand up for me to stop. He quickly dives down and there is a flash of light before Sailor pops up again. I gasp.

How can I describe him? His beauty is otherworldly. Dreamy, iridescent scales scatter across his cheekbones, collarbones, and arms. I can faintly make out a beautiful blue ombre tail that I know matches his eyes.

"You're enchanting," I whisper. Sailor blushes against the moonlight and I relish the reaction. Under this serene night sky, I understand why men follow sirens to their deaths.

"Thank you," he said. Swimming closer he hands me a piece of seaweed. "It'll be salty, but I enchanted it, so you'll be able to hold your breath long enough," he said. I cocked my head.

Long enough for what?" I ask. Sailor only grins.

"Trust me."

"I do," I said, taking the seaweed. My nose wrinkles at the salty taste and within a minute my body trembles as a surge of magic rushes through me. Sailor motions for me to follow. We dive underwater and he holds onto my hand, guiding me through the relative darkness. I may be a pixie, but I don't have night vision, and the moon only provides so much light.

I follow him through an opening, and when we finally come up for air I gasp. We are in an underwater cave, the moon hanging directly above us. I swim around the tiny pool, marveling at the cozy hideaway.

"I take it from that smile that you're happy," he said, smugly. I gently splash him with water.

"This place is beautiful," I said, leaning against the pool's edge, wanting to stay in the water. Sailor swims over and floats across from me.

"It was my secret place with my dad," he said, eyes far away. My eyes widen. I didn't know much about Sailor's past. He never really spoke about his dad the way I never really speak about my mom. All I know was that he passed away years ago. "This place is where I would hide to get away from everyone. To...," he trailed off. I nod in understanding.

"My safe place was my room," I said. I swallow, taking a breath. "When my mom died, Eleanor and my dad fought a lot. I started spending more time in my room. It's where I felt like I could get away from the noise," I confide in him.

In my room, I had less of a chance of being accidentally used as a punching bag. I had a less chance of doing something, *anything,* that might start a fight. I swallow, my eyes closing. Water gently laps against my skin and when I open my eyes Sailor is in front of me.

"It must have not been easy...with Eleanor and your dad," he said. I shrug my shoulders.

"I did everything I could to keep the peace, not rustle any...scales," I said, hoping my pun can break the tension. His eyebrows furrow. "Sometimes people get upset at you but it's not actually you that they're mad at. You just happen to be in the crossfire," I continued. "My room was relatively safe from stray rhetorical bullets."

Sailor cups my face, and I lean into it. He hums a few notes that relax my body. I don't know why I'm confessing my secret thoughts, but I can't stop myself. I feel safe with him. And because I feel safe with him, I'm hoping he'll agree with what I'm going to ask. I pull his hand away from my face. He floats backwards.

"I-I have conditions about our fake dating arrangement," I begin. He motions for me to continue. "As you know I'll be acting as your fake girlfriend, but I have no idea how to be one. So, I propose that while I'm faking as your girlfriend you teach me how to be a good one," I said, my face burning. I'm not sure how I managed to get all of that out. His lips twitch.

"Continue," he said. Of course, he knew I had more to say.

"I have a list of things that I would like to experience. Things people do in relationships, and I want you to be the one to show me because I trust you. I feel comfortable to explore...things with you," I said. Sailor inhales sharply.

"You mean sexual things," he clarified, his eyes burning into mine. I nod, silently.

"Yes. My conditions are you help me with my list, and you don't belittle or make fun of my inexperience. I know what I want and just because I'm introverted doesn't mean you should treat me like I'm fragile," I said, my voice growing strong with every word. His lips tilt into a smirk that made my thighs tighten. I saw another flash of desire that made my body come alive. That look, and the way my body reacted to it, is why I know I'm making the right choice.

"Get me the list. I also have some conditions," he said, swimming closer. "Just two," he added, softening his voice.

"Of course. Tell me," I respond. He tilts his head, watching me like a predator. The moonlight was bright, revealing just how blue his eyes were. His blonde locks were pushed back, a slight wave to them.

"First, we have a safe word," he said.

"Fish cake," I said, a smile breaking across my face. We share a laugh, and I feel the tension give away.

"Fine, but that means I need a new nickname," he said, splashing me. I giggle, splashing him back, his eyes bright and playful again. Sailor reaches his hand out and I take it in mine, my heart rattling.

"Deal. What's the second one?" I ask. He takes a deep breath, and I feel his tail towards the bottom of my feet, taking some of my weight. I smile gratefully.

"Call me by my real name from now on."

CHAPTER 10
WE ALL NEED A SUPPORTIVE SEAL FRIEND

Caspian

It isn't until the following week that I finally get to cook breakfast for Crystal. The first week of her being here was filled with a lot of meetings and early mornings on her end. And after our midnight swim I wanted to give her the space she needed, even though my head was swimming with the possibilities of what her list could entail. We felt like ships that only ever saw each other in passing despite living in the same house.

Typically, when I woke up at seven Crystal was already out the door, but last night she walked through groaning about some late shipments. Her eyes were heavy, and she kept yawning. I asked her if she was having another early morning and she shook her head. Apparently, they were behind schedule with two cottages that needed repairs, so her next few days were a bit easier. Her father had graciously given her other work to some coworkers so she could focus on Coralia Coast.

This means that I can make her breakfast and take care of her for the next few days. I smile as I continued cooking our breakfast sandwiches. I faintly hear thumping from her bedroom and move to grab two empty mugs.

There is light shuffling behind me before I feel a certain pixie head press into my back. She groans, rubbing her head back and forth. I glance at the clock on the oven.

"Couldn't you have slept in a bit longer?" I ask, noting that it was 6:30am. She grunts in response.

"This is me sleeping in," she mumbled. I sigh and turn to wrap my arms around her. "Morning," she said, pressing her face against my chest.

"Morning M'Lady," I said. I can't stop grinning. She is being extra affectionate this morning and I'm not going to point it out. I am going to relish this quietness with her.

"Smells yummy," she said. I hum. She finally pulls away and walks over to the coffee pot.

"I'm making us breakfast sandwiches," I said, watching her as she makes both of our coffees. She makes sure to add extra sugar to mine. She hands me the cup taking a sip of her own, eyes closing with happiness.

"How are you feeling?" I question. She glances at her coffee, going over her next words.

"I'm stressed and tired. But I get to have lunch with Mira later which makes me happy," she said with a soft smile. I add a splash of water and place a top on the pan, letting the steam melt the cheese for a moment. I'm grateful to my cousin. It's clear that Crystal felt comfortable with Mira.

"That sounds like a lovely day," I said, plating our food. Crystal moves to grab my cup, and I lead us to my backyard. I have a small garden that is mainly kept up by Aunt Meryl who always needs more space for the herbs in her shop. I have a small patio with an outdoor BBQ station on one side and a seating area on the other.

"Silence or show?" I ask Crystal. She curls up in her seat, tucking her legs under her. She takes another sip, deep in thought.

"Show," she said, quietly. I decide on an old, animated cartoon. We eat in silence as my brain drifts between Crystal's potential list and the trident. I still have no idea where to start to even look for it. I've looked into three books that have said the same thing– that the trident will reveal itself when it is needed again.

"This sandwich is amazing," Crystal said, leaning back into her chair. I shrug my shoulders, nonchalantly.

"I'm a prince of many talents," I said smugly. Crystal giggles, her messy bun moving side to side. I swell with pride knowing that Crystal is content with what I've provided her. She holds her cup with both her hands. Her eyes dart between me and the TV.

"How have you been by the way? We haven't had a chance to talk about you being back here," she asked. I take a deep breath. Talking with Crystal has always been easy, almost second nature like swimming. Around her the words I usually keep to myself tumble out easily.

"Well in the days we've been here I've discovered the coral in our ocean has been dying while I've been gone," I said. Crystal leans forward. "Ronan thinks if I can find this magical item that was a part of our family, I can heal it."

"And *you* have to find it?" she asked. My lips twitch. *Always perceptive.*

I take a sip of coffee. "The magical item is a trident that was wielded by the Second Prince, the first general of The Atlantic Ocean," I said. Crystal's bottom lip pokes out as her brows furrow in thought.

"So, it must be you. Do you need help?" she offered. I smile at her kindness and shake my head.

"You have enough on your plate. Plus, I have a meeting with Kai. He has brought me some books that may have more information," I said. Her cheeks slightly flush, which gives me pause. "Why are you blushing?" I ask. A hint of jealousy snaking its way through me.

"I'm not blushing," she said, defensibly. I narrow my eyes. Did Crystal find Kai attractive? She shook her head.

"As your fake boyfriend, I'm going to ignore you blushing at Kai," I said, crossing my arms. I was *not* going to get annoyed over this. "Anyway, each ruling family has their own trident and maybe his family's information will help me find ours."

"But if you need help, I'm here. I may be your fake girlfriend but I'm also your friend," she said, looking at me in a way that makes my heart leap. Fuck she is so beautiful, even with a bit of dry drool on the corner of her mouth.

"Thank you, M' Lady."

I'M SITTING in Ronan's office waiting for him and Kai to come back when my mom walks in. She looks a bit happier today and a part of me knows it is because I'm back. Guilt courses through me. I stand up, placing a kiss on her cheek.

"Good morning mom," I said. She smiles warmly, pulling me into an embrace.

"My precious boy," she said. I chuckle. No matter how old I am I will always be her little boy. She pushes me to sit down and takes the seat across from me.

"Ronan tells me you're hunting for the trident," she hesitated to say, eyes filled with worry. I nod.

"Yes, and I'm hoping Prince Kai can help," I said, my royal manners kicking in gear. She sits back in her chair, her gaze somewhere faraway. I bite the inside of my cheek.

"You know your Uncle Seward used to say he could sense it," she said quietly. My heart hammers in my chest. My family rarely spoke about my dad, let alone Uncle Seward.

Both had passed away in an accident in the North Atlantic. They were on their way back from rescuing a pod of humpback whales and got caught in a nasty tsunami. It didn't matter that they were the strongest sirens I knew, anyone can fall at the hands of the ocean. She is strong, swift, and wild.

"He could sense it?" I ask. My mom nods, looking at me again.

"He would say how it felt close, but it wasn't the time yet," she recalled, as a door opens in the lighthouse. "Maybe now is the time," she deduced, standing up. Ronan and Kai walk in, bowing to my mom.

"I'll leave you men to it. If there's anything I can do, please let me know. Prince Kai it is always lovely having you around our shores," she said, giving him a warm hug. He smiled politely. "Oh, and Cas," my mom said, turning her attention back to me. I smile. "I would love to have lunch with you and Crystal." She grins before walking away. I keep a smile on my face, reminding myself that Crystal and I are in a fake relationship. Naturally my mom would want to have lunch with both of us.

"Crystal is very beautiful," Kai said, grinning as he slaps a hand on my shoulder. I glare at my old friend. *No shrimp shit I know she's beautiful.* My stomach twists, remembering Crystal's blushing face from this morning.

"She's mine," I snap, feeling possessive. Our relationship is fake for all intents and purposes, but to everyone and *especially* to Kai, Crystal is mine. He throws his head back in laughter while Ronan settles in his seat.

"Relax my friend. I would never steal your woman," he teases. I know he wouldn't, and yet I can't shake this feeling. I grew up with Kai. He's one of my closest siren friends. "How long have you guys been together?" he asked, eyes assessing me.

Fuck, Crystal and I haven't gone over this part. We don't have a cover story. Ronan looks at me expectantly. I have a feeling he suspects my lies.

"We started dating recently, but we've been friends for a while," I rush out. There is some truth to my statement. Kai nods. Ronan clears his throat.

"Alright. We have some things to address," my brother directed, pulling our attention to him. We turn our focus to him. "The coral in our ocean is slowly decaying. Aunt Meryl has been doing her best to keep this sickness at bay. I think the only thing that will save the coral is the Trident of Atlas," he finished. I sit further down in my seat, squirming under his gaze.

My brother knows the story of Atlas, so he knows how much of a responsibility I have in finding and wielding the trident. Kai scratched his ear.

"We know each oceanic royal family has their own trident but the thing about these tridents is that they're only discoverable once they're needed," Kai pointed out. I sigh. This was what I was aware of. I glance at my brother.

"How do we even know they really exist if no other family has seen their own trident?" I ask. Ronan sends me a glare as Kai turns in his seat.

"Do you not trust the story of our kind?" he asked. I lick my lips, feeling the weight of their stares. I'm the only one that keeps questioning the trident. Everyone else is on board and believes this was the solution, but I hesitated.

"I think you've been away from the ocean for too long, Caspian," my brother said. Kai looked between us. I stare down at my hands. When I had run to away to Lavender Falls, I had run from my magic, from my tail. Carrie always made sure she escaped to Boogeyman's Swamp or drove to the nearest beach. But I always had excuses. Not transforming was my self-punishment for leaving home.

"I'm going to look into our books. Maybe you should take a swim, reconnect with your ocean," Kai suggested. My hands twitch against my knees knowing in my gut he is right. I needed to reconnect with the part of me I'd kept hidden for too long.

But will the ocean welcome me back?

I WENT to the extreme northern part of Coralia's beach. It was more secluded because of the rocks, and I knew I would be safe from any possible visitors seeing me transform. After quickly discarding my clothes, I dove in. The transformation is easier this time and I groan with relief.

Fuck, they were right. I miss this. I miss swimming with my tail. The waves are light today, gently swaying like a mother rocking their babe. I hide behind a rock and enjoy floating in the open air. I forgot how freeing this was. Tears prick my eyes. I'd locked this part of myself away out of fear.

I close my eyes and listen to the melody of the ocean, enjoying her soothing song. For a few minutes everything is quiet, and then I hear something. I tuck my tail down, only letting my human half show. I look around. It seems like I'm alone and yet there is some sort of pull. Confused, I dived under and swim further out.

After a few feet the tug grew faint. *Weird.* I thought what I was feeling was coming from this direction. Was this what my Uncle Seward was feeling? Was the tri–

"You're back!" A sweet voice calls from behind. I turn around to see a familiar harbor seal. I smile.

"Hey there," I said with a wave. The seal swims closer, bumping its nose against my hand. I chuckle at the adorable creature. The seal swam circles around me.

"Did you find a way to heal the coral?" it asked. My shoulders dropped.

"Not yet, but we have a few leads," I said earnestly. Its eyes drop.

"You're going to help right?" it asked, swimming up close to my face. I push back slightly. This seal was adorable but lacks understanding of personal space.

"I promise we're doing everything we can to find a solution," I said. While the weight of the promise is heavy, as I stare at this animal (whose home is this ocean), I know what I'm doing is right. Was I afraid of fucking up? Yes. But this seal and so many others need me. It nods.

"By the way, why did you bring that lady to our spot?" it asked. I chuckle again.

"Oh, is it our spot?" I ask, swimming backwards. The seal followed.

"Yeah, it's ours. Yours and mine, Prince Caspian," it said. I try not to cringe at hearing my title. I've gone so long without hearing it that I've forgotten its weight. I'm a prince. Someone whose family is bound by blood and duty to look after their kingdom.

"Fine. The spot is ours but...Crystal is my...girlfriend, and I'm hoping we could share it with her as well," I said, swimming down to inspect the coral again. I fight back a smile.

"Girlfriend?" it asked, slightly confused. "Like mate? Sorry, I don't know all your lingo," it said, zooming ahead of me. My heart races. Mate?

"Sort of," I said, catching a new wave of dying coral. This is horrible to see. So much loss of color and life surrounded me. Maybe if I never left this wouldn't have gotten so bad. But if I never left would Crystal and I have had the same kind of relationship? Would she have trusted me the way she does now?

"You got this," the seal said, bumping my side. I offer a smile, petting its head gently.

"Hey Prince Caspian?" the seal asked, its big dark eyes filled with wonder. "Would you like to race?" it asked. My face breaks out into a giant grin. It's been forever since I've raced in my true form.

"I would love to, but could you tell me your name first?" I ask my new friend. The seal swam around me again as if gearing up to shoot across the ocean. I shiver as my magic soars through my body. I should have never gone so long without this part of myself. Being a siren is who I am, tail, abilities, and all.

"The name is Waldo."

CHAPTER 11
HOW DOES ONE FAKE BEING A GIRLFRIEND?

Crystal

"A plate of chili cheese fries for M'Lady," Sailor said, pulling my gaze away from my laptop. I looked up to his steady blue eyes. His blonde hair was beginning to lighten, and his skin was starting to get some color from being outside.

I was spending a lot of time at Siren Saloon. I found the early afternoon calm, the light sea shanties playing in the background, and the sounds of water from the fish tank soothing.

Sometimes I found myself staring at the multicolored fish wondering if they ever felt trapped or lonely. Did they long for the freedom of the ocean? Or were they comfortable in their tank?

I closed my laptop, sliding it into my bag. Sailor was always serious about me not working while eating. While I agreed with his sentiment it was hard to deny that with every bite of food my fingers itched to type, mentally replying to emails.

Like clockwork, he slid into the seat across from me. "Sitting with me again?" I asked, arching an eyebrow. He gave me his infamous easy-going smile which made my stomach flutter with prancing sprites.

"Of course. We both need lunch," he said casually. The corners of my mouth twitched. He said it like he had been working all morning, but I knew the pub didn't open until 11 which meant he had only been working for an hour. We were also the only other beings here besides Carrie, the cook, and two other patrons.

I bit back a response and decided to go along with him. Sailor handed me a fork then took the first bite.

We ate in silence, which I was grateful for. Sailor didn't pressure me to talk. We sat quietly until one of us broke. Most of the time it was him. But today it was me.

"What are your plans this weekend? I asked curiously. Sailor took a bite of my fries.

"I have a workshop in the morning tomorrow. Most of us were thinking about heading to the tavern tomorrow night," he said. The tavern meant The Drunken Fairy Tale Tavern. Eleanor's boyfriend was one of the owners and it was one of the top pubs to be at.

Which meant a lot of people. And it especially meant my sister and her friends. I swallowed. She hadn't asked me to come hang out. Granted, she was busy with her new event planning job. I'd hung out with her and the ladies a few times when I wasn't swamped with work.

"That sounds fun," I said, munching on more fries. I felt his gaze on me, and it made me squirm. He was probably looking for a reaction.

"Is it your kind of fun?" he asked. My chewing paused. No one had ever asked me that. No one ever considered what I would like to do.

I swallowed before answering. "Um. Sometimes," I said. He waited for me to elaborate. My nose twitched. "Sometimes I like being around people and noise. Watching everyone. Sometimes I join, sometimes I don't. It depends on my mood."

"And do you know what your mood will be tomorrow?" he asked. The corner of my mouth quirked up, threatening to spread into a grin like usual around Sailor. He was always trying to figure me out and I quite enjoyed it for some reason.

"Ask me tomorrow."

I woke up in a relationship with my friend Caspian. I have to get used to calling him that since he asked me to. As his girlfriend I should be calling him by his name...or sweet bun? I wrinkle my nose. My seahorse? I chew the inside of my cheek. This was going to be a process.

My friends in Lavender Falls all had nicknames for their significant other and from the copious number of books I've read everyone gives their partner nicknames. So, I should have a nickname for Caspian. My phone pings, signaling another dreaded email.

We are slightly behind schedule because both cottages turned out to have wood rot which took a significant amount of magic to rectify, pushing us back a few days. I sit at the dining room table, opening my laptop. I squeeze the back of my neck.

Another day, another email. I went through my spreadsheet, ignoring the fact I couldn't add little checkmarks that signified accomplishing my list. Both cottages and b&bs need their flooring replaced. I mentally cursed. With a dash of my fingers across my keyboard I update our schedule and send it out to my dad, Ronan, and Mr. Whitman. Pushing back the schedule allows me some free time. I glance out the window, taking in Cas' serene backyard.

Maybe I could explore Coralia Coast, read more books, and discover new hobbies. I take a sip of my coffee. It will also give me more time to work on the list. I pull up a blank document but before I can write anything my phone rings. I swallow.

It's Eleanor. We haven't really talked since the last time she texted me. As much as I want to ignore her, we are healing our relationship which means answering each other's calls.

"Hey Ellie," I said, using her childhood nickname. She lets out a sound of frustration. My stomach tightens. *Something is wrong. But I can't be to blame because I haven't done anything. Is it because I haven't been responding in the group chat?*

"How dare you," she said. My heart races and my throat closes.

I fucked up.

What did I do?

What did I do?

What did I do?

"You're dating Sailor?!" she screeched. I wince at her tone. I rubbed my forehead. How in the world could she have found out? I was in a different town, two hours away.

"Where did you hear that?" I ask, tapping my pen against the table. Caspian is out with Ronan, getting reacquainted with the town and whatever royal responsibilities he has.

"So, you're not going to deny it?" Her voice went up again. I bite back a sigh. I know she's only being a caring sister. She's probably hurt that she didn't know her little sister is dating her friend. *But can I tell her that what we're doing is fake?*

If Lavender Falls knows we're dating, then there's a chance of our agreement becoming public. I couldn't risk that.

"We are dating," I said, keeping my tone even. Eleanor is quiet and I close my eyes. My hand nervously taps on the table. I knew my sister in and out– until she left. Will she be upset? Happy? I didn't know anymore.

"One, I am so happy for you. You guys are literally adorable," she said. My shoulders drop. I guess we *are* adorable. Caspian for sure is with his golden hair, bright blue eyes, and very pouty mouth. I blush. Now is not the time to think about kissing him.

"Two?" I ask.

"Why did I find out from Meryl?" she asked, sounding hurt. A light bulb flickers in my head. Of course it was Meryl. They had met in the winter and Eleanor promised to keep in touch as a way to form a partnership between the towns.

I was hoping that no one from Lavender Falls would find out. In my head, once all my work was done and Caspian's ceremony was over, we would amicably break up and I would return to Lavender Falls.

A jolt of pain shoots through me. I didn't like the last part. Did I want to move back to Lavender Falls? Back to feeling like I was just Eleanor's little sister.

"Meryl told you?" I ask, buying myself time. "Well, it's very...very new," I said, honestly. This is somewhat true. "I'm still getting used to the whole...you know, dating thing," I said, feeling like my face was getting licked by dragon fire.

"How did he ask you?" she wondered, her voice brimming with happiness. My eyes twitch and I sniff. My body is vibrating with pins and needles. We didn't think this through. I don't even know what our dating timeline is.

"Why do you think he asked me?" I ask, defensively.

"You're telling me *you* asked him?" she said in disbelief. Ouch, okay. I know I'm an introvert but that doesn't mean I'm incapable of making a move. I sit up straighter.

"I actually *did* ask him out and it's barely been a week," I begin. "And I didn't say anything because I've been very busy with work," I rush out. I fidget with my pen. Well, I guess Cas doesn't have to worry about what our story is now.

"I'm not insinuating that you couldn't be the one to start a relationship, it's just that Sailor is a bit more outgoing than you," she noted. *Tap. Tap. Tap.*

"Understandable," I said, forcing the word out. *She is just being my sister.* "I was going to tell you, Lola, and Lily but then we ran into a few issues with our project," I said. By switching to work mode, it gives me the chance to turn off my emotions for a bit and steer towards a more truthful conversation.

"Oh no Crystal! I'm so sorry," she apologized. I relax a bit in my chair. "Is there anything I can do?" she asked. I stare at the blank document on my computer, her question repeating itself in my head. *She wants to help.*

Now she wants to help. Where was she when dad wouldn't come out of his office for days the first week that she was gone? Where was she when I wanted to go to prom but had to cancel because dad got the flu and I had to take care of him? Where was she for the moments when I tried to stand up to dad but then he would guilt me because *she* wasn't around?

I take another breath, my mask of composure feeling snug on my face. "I know Ellie, but I'm fine. I get to relax a bit with this new schedule," I said, hoping to cover up the yucky feelings that are bubbling up in me.

"Crys that's great! You deserve a break," she cooed before I heard someone call her in the background. "I've got to go. We're working on the summer festival and we're trying to convince the Unicorn to let kids pet her," she said. I snort. I feel bad for the unicorn. "But the ladies would love a virtual hang out whenever you're free!"

"Sure. That sounds nice," I said.

"Great. Well, I love you tons Crys. Do everything, I would do!" she sang. I slam the phone down staring at my damn laptop, my face red.

Got to love my sister.

BEFORE I CAN START WORKING on my list my phone rings...again. This time it's dad. I take a breath, my anxiety bubbling to the surface. The door chimes, and I twitch. I take another sip of coffee even though I know I need to stop having caffeine today. I'm still trying to come down from the emotional rollercoaster I went through with Eleanor's call, and now I must deal with my dad.

I close my eyes briefly before answering. "Hey dad," I said.

"I just saw your email and wanted to check in," he said, sounding concerned. This is new. I've sent emails about projects getting pushed back before and he would always call, but his tone would be rough with annoyance. For some reason this softness sends me closer to the edge of breaking down.

"Are you okay?" he asked. Wow, he isn't even demanding details about why the schedule had to be shifted. I go back to tapping the table with my pen. *It's because he's in therapy*, I remind myself. Things are changing and I need to change along with them.

"I am. I figured out a plan which I attached in the email I sent you. We can still finish all key projects by the end of summer with a few adjustments," I said, confidently. I open the schedule, running through it quickly. Yes, with the adjustments I should be fine.

"I saw that. Your updates are always precise and detailed but...how are *you*?" he asked again. I swallow. Fuck, first Eleanor and now him? Both were breaking the patterns I have gotten used to and I don't feel prepared to handle this.

"I'm fine," I said. The phrase rolls off my tongue easily. It isn't a complete lie. I *am* fine, aside from the headache forming and the fact that my hands are trembling with anxiety.

"Are you sure?" he pressed. My nostrils flare. *He's just being a dad who cares,* I chastise myself. When people care–*start* caring, this is what they do.

"I am. It feels a bit weird to have some time to myself," I said, deciding to answer honestly. I want to see how he reacts to that.

"You deserve some time to yourself. You work hard," he said. I ground my teeth and tug at my shirt, sweat beginning to form. *Oh really? Now I deserve time for myself. What about the times I wanted to go to homecoming? Prom? Or the number of parties I missed in college? Team lunches?* I grip the pen tightly. I want to tell him all of this. I want him to feel bad, to realize his mistakes.

I rub my forehead in frustration. But it is too late, isn't it? Nothing I can say can rewrite the past. I just need to move forward. This is my dad's attempt at remedying the past, and I have to accept it.

"I do. Thank you," I said.

"Good," he said. I can almost feel a smile in his voice and that seems to pacify the anger that has been building up. "You know your mom always loved the ocean," he said. My throat tightens. My dad rarely talks about my mom. She was his everything, his one true love. When she passed away my dad broke down, and he has never been the same.

"I didn't know that," my voice cracks slightly. My mom passed when I was 10 and my memories are all hazy. Sometimes I'll get a whiff of perfume, or a certain citrus that will remind me of her. Sometimes I can remember looking in the mirror and watching her yank my hair back into a bun. But those memories were fleeting, arriving when they wanted to and disappearing just as quickly.

My dad sighs and I sink into my chair. "We didn't visit the beach much with you kids because of work but your mom loved the water. She would say how much peace it brought her," he said, his voice catching at the end. I want to ask him more. Her favorite color, how she liked her coffee, anything.

"What–" I began to ask but then he clears his throat, and I know that signals the end of us talking about her. I bite the inside of my cheek. I should be grateful he said anything about her at all.

"I'm sorry. Ask," he said. I hear him shuffling on the other side. "Mr. Fletcher says I need to be able to talk about her even if I'm uncomfortable and that you probably...," he trailed off. Tears prick my eyes and for once I decide to say the honest thing.

"I don't remember her much," I began. "I want to ask you about her, but I know it hurts you," I said. I swallow the lump in my throat and wait with bated breath.

"Crystal...I'm...I had no idea," he said. Another silent moment passes between us, and it allows my anxiety to grow. "From now on please ask. I've been selfish. She was my mate, but she was also your mom," he said. I pause. *Mate?* I knew that werewolves and vampires had mates. Did we have our own...thing? A zing of some sort? Caspian's face flashes in my mind and my cheeks heat.

"Your mom loved the beach. When...we were younger all of us– the Lunas and the Rosarios– would take weekend beach trips," he began. I sit up straighter. I rarely heard about my parents' past. I knew once upon a time in Lavender Falls, they were a gang of supernaturals who were thick as thieves. "Coralia Coast...yes it was in Coralia Coast," he said. I glance around, tears in my eyes.

Did my mom spend time in this cafe? Am I sitting at the same table as her? Hope, sadness, longing, and happiness wash over me. My mom has been *here*.

"I can't believe I forgot. Yes, she was pregnant with you the last time we went to Coralia Coast. She wanted a vacation before you came to us," he said, a nostalgic tone in his voice. "We were at the beach, and she said there was something special there. She hoped to take you when you were older," he said. My hands tremble.

There was something special about Coralia Coast.

I felt it the second we'd crossed into town. I felt at home here, peaceful. There is something about Coralia Coast that just feels right. Lavender Falls is my home, where I spent my childhood, and yet Coralia Coast suited me better.

I look out the window, catching sight of the ocean. My mom had felt what I felt, and something about that connection told me that maybe I was meant to be here.

"Dad?" I ask. He hums. I wipe a tear from my eye. "What mom felt…I feel it too."

I WALK over to one of the cottages to check on the crew's progress and see if they need any help. In our crew we have different kinds of supernaturals. Werewolves did the heavy lifting while a few fairies and pixies pitched in with elemental magic to help with restoration needs.

Like my dad and my sister, I specialized in Earth magic. I could feel the Earth's warm buzz following me everywhere. I wonder if there is a way for me to help Caspian heal the coral.

I sigh. I want to help Caspian. He hides his stress well enough. Whenever he told me I had too much on my plate it made me wonder how much he had and now knowing his truth I'm worried. He had a town and a kingdom on his shoulder, the entire ocean. That isn't easy.

"Ms. Hale!" Connor called out with a grin. I nod at him, returning his smile.

"Hi. I just wanted to check in and see if you need anything," I said. He shakes his head.

"I don't think so, Ms. Hale. We're currently working on the second floor, trying to salvage as much wood as possible so we have enough to work on the second cottage," he said. I smile.

If all goes according to plan, we'll save some wood and have enough left over to pitch Ronan another project. I want–no, *I need* to help Coralia Coast. This is my first solo project as lead. I need to prove to myself that I can handle this kind of responsibility.

"Can you check this wood's rot?" he asked.

"Of course," I said. I use my magic to analyze how deep the rot was and decide which purification ritual will work best for it. We walk over to the giant pile of wood, and I stand wide-eyed. This was a dragon's nest worth of rotten lumber.

I place both my hands on the wood and close my eyes. There is a familiar swirl of my magic low in my belly. It's warm and vibrant, like an old friend. I focus on pushing my magic out through my fingers.

A sting runs up my arms and I bite down on my cheek. This wood is damp and dark. Some pieces are more damaged than others, the darkness nearly swallowing them up whole. I inhale sharply, ignoring the pain and sit on my heels.

"I need some of the fairies to cast a freeze spell ASAP. Even though this lumber isn't attached to the house anymore its rot is still spreading very slowly throughout the cottage," I said, looking up at Connor. "I would cleanse the cottage in case." His eyebrows scrunch together. Connor, like me, is an Earth pixie and we can both feel the wood's pain. His jaw ticks.

I knew from experience this was the hard part of the job. We can feel the pain of the Earth and sometimes it's hard to ignore, hard to let go. I place a hand on his shoulder. His magic was pulsing.

"Deep breaths. We can do this," I assure him. He shakes his head, his shoulders relaxing and I feel his magic settle.

"You got it boss," he said with a warm smile. He holds his hand out and I grab it, letting him pull me up. My sneaker gets caught on a piece of wood and I fall forward. "Got you, boss," Connor said, catching me. I huff out a laugh.

"Thank y–"

"Hello there," a familiar voice said from behind. When I turn around to see Caspian, his arms crossed and slightly glaring at Connor. I pull away quickly.

"What are you doing here?" I ask. Connor steps away, his hands up in the air innocently. Cas steps forward, wrapping an arm around my waist. My face flushes as I look back at my crew member.

"I wanted to check in on my *girlfriend*," he said, looking at Connor. One second, I felt like a gooey mess in Cas' arms and then next I'm annoyed. By his tone he is insinuating something between Connor and me.

"Well, your *girlfriend* is fine thanks to her coworker, Connor, catching her," I said, staring. He finally looks at me and his eyes soften.

"Thank you, Connor, for catching my *girlfriend*," Cas said, eyes still trained on me. I pull away from him, my heart racing. We said girlfriend too many times and now his eyes were making my stomach bounce up and down.

"Oh-kay, well, Ms. Hale I'm going to go brief the fairies like you suggested," Connor stuttered awkwardly walking away. I turn to face Cas, my face red.

"He was just helping me," I hiss. He closes his eyes briefly before scratching the back of his head.

"I know...I...I don't know what happened," he said. I bite my cheek. I wonder if what happened to him was the same thing that happened to me when I saw him dancing with Princess Tati. I tap the ground with my sneaker, unsure of how to exit this awkward conversation.

"Cool. On that note is there something you need?" I ask. He nods and holds up two fingers.

"One, don't forget to get me that list," he said with a wicked grin. My body tingles at the reminder but the feeling quickly vanishes as I watched his smile fall. Whatever he is going to say next is making him nervous, which makes me nervous. "Two, my mom would like to have lunch with us sometime soon."

Fury fuck.

Dragon's piss.

Hellhound's lair.

"L-lunch?" I ask, stuttering. Lunch meant talking. Talking meant having to discuss our fake relationship in a convincing way. We needed to get our story straight especially considering what I told Eleanor. My anxiety is back. I adjust the strap of my bag, needing to keep my hands occupied.

"Lunch sounds great," I said, doing my best to muster up some excitement. Something flickers in his eyes. I hope he can't see how badly I want to crawl into a ball and hide. I promised I would be his fake girlfriend, but all the unknowns were eating me up.

Cas takes my bag and places it over his shoulder. Before I can take it back, he snatches my hand.

"Ready to go home?" he asked. His hand is warm, and all my anxiety melts away with his touch.

"There better be food at home," I said, and Cas throws his head back with a carefree laugh.

CHAPTER 12
PRINCELY DUTIES

Caspian

"Hurry up!" Ronan grumbled. I groaned, leaving Mira and Kai behind. My brother stood, arms crossed. I rolled my eyes.

"What?" I said, glaring at him. This time Ronan rolled his eyes at me. We began walking down the street towards Coralia's Meadery. Ronan's feet pounded against the cobblestone road.

"We're supposed to be at the meeting with dad and Uncle Seward. The meeting with Kai's dad and uncle," he spat. I scoffed.

"I was hanging out with Kai. You know he's a Second Prince too. Shouldn't we get along or some shit?" I said. My brother let out a bitter laugh as the meadery came into view.

"You guys have been friends for years. It's important that you sit in on these meetings," he said. The older I got the more meetings I had to attend, and I was getting sick of it. I wasn't going to be crowned second in command any time soon so why take time away from my youth? I should be swimming with my friends or crashing parties.

"Well shouldn't Kai be going too?" I said, throwing my friend under the bus. I winced. Ronan looked down at me with a smirk.

"Unlike you, little brother, Kai attends all of his father's meetings *and lessons so he gets to enjoy his vacation,"* he said. I glowered. Of course. Kai may know how to hang loose but he's still a do gooder.

"Whatever," I said, my mind already thinking about escaping through the back door in the meadery. I opened the door for my brother.

"Cas? Grow up," Ronan said, walking in.

"Look who decided to show up," Uncle Seward said.

Ronan walked me around town, showing me the different shops that were barely managing to stay open. We are currently in June. The warmer weather should bring a boom of tourists, but looking around now it still feels like winter.

I can't wrap my head around what I'm seeing. Growing up this was the town that beings flocked too for the summer. We always had people covering the beaches and lining up in and out of shops at this time of year. We had so many festivals. We walk by what used to be a meadery and I can't help but smile at the old memories.

We used to have an annual renaissance festival and our meadery was one of the sponsors. There were constant parties and events during the festival. But then the family that owned it moved back to Scotland. It's been closed for a few years now.

"I miss this place," I said. Ronan stares at the shop, taking a deep breath. He patted his journal that was under his arm.

"It's on my list of things to hopefully bring back," he said, sitting on the bench in front of the storefront. I sit with him, anxiety crawling up my back.

We never really worked together. After he took on his role as king I began pulling away. I didn't want any part in taking Uncle Seward's place. And for a while no one pressured me about it. But the closer I got to 30 the more insistent my brother and mom became. Maybe it was time for a change but how can I measure up to my uncle? I swallow the urge to change the subject.

"Can I know what's on the list?" I ask. My brother gives me a hard look. I know why. I never bothered to know these kinds of things before. I avoided talking about them because I felt like I was replacing my uncle, and I'm still not ready to do that if I'm honest.

"I'm working with Crystal to fix up some stuff around town. I would like to bring back the meadery," he said, glancing at the building behind us.

"That means we need someone to open it," I point out. He frowned, nodding. "I...might know someone," I said, my mind returning to Lavender Falls.

"After the summer I'm going to put it up for sale, so I'll keep you in the loop. I want to bring back the bookstore as well, and a bar is needed in this town. The diner doesn't serve alcohol unless it's beer or mimosas on Sundays," he said with a huff. I nod along.

"That all sounds great," I said honestly. Our town needs a makeover. It needs things, establishments, to get the excitement going again. My brother looked at me.

"I'm very grateful for Crystal," he said nonchalantly. The hairs on my arms rose.

"Yes. Me too," I said, watching him. My brother hummed. "How did you two meet by the way?" I ask. The corners of his lips tilt up.

"She reached out to me. I was on the lookout for a company to help with these builds," he paused for a moment. "Her presentation and her conviction about Hale's Lumber's work compelled me to hire her. She's very smart," he said. My hands twitch in my lap.

"I'm aware," I said, trying to keep the surge of jealousy at bay.

"Beautiful," he continues. I glare at him, and he chuckles. "Relax Caspian. I never had an interest in her in that way," he said.

"Then why–"

"Because I enjoy riling you up, and because it's nice to see you act differently," he said. I raise an eyebrow.

"Differently how?" I ask. I fidget under his steady gaze.

"You're happy with her, relaxed," he said. His eyes turn back towards the ocean and a weight settles between us. "I will need your help restoring this town," he said firmly. I swallow, my chest tightening.

"It's not—"

"It will be your duty to help. It's what you've worked for," he said, cutting me off. A flash of anger shoots through me.

"It's what I was forced to work towards," I said, my tone dropping. My brother stood up, looking down at me.

"And what about me? Forced to become king. Growing up knowing one day I would have to wear the crown and rule this entire kingdom," he snapped. His mouth twists into a frown and for the first time I didn't see my cold, grumpy brother. I saw a man that lost a chance at living his life. I had a year to escape; Ronan has never been given that chance.

"Ronan—" I start to say. He waves me off.

"Forget it. I've been fine on my own and I'll continue to be fine. Just work on finding the trident," he said, leaving me alone to head back to the lighthouse. I sigh, staring out at the street. I thought I was coming home, but Coralia Coast didn't feel like that anymore. I clench my fists. I need to see Crystal. I need her warmth.

MY STOMACH IS in knots as I swim back and forth around the coral. First, I had an argument with my brother and then there was my tense interaction with Crystal. I run my tongue over my teeth, grateful that my fangs had retracted. Unbeknownst to most beings, sirens have fangs too, they just weren't as prominent as vampires. We use our fangs to bite into fish when hunting. My heart thumps.

They had popped out because of Connor. I'd seen him smiling down at Crystal while he held her in his arms and I'd hated it. It was ridiculous. I knew I was being ridiculous, but Crystal was mine…for the time being. I groan inwardly. I'd acted like a protective boyfriend, but she wasn't really mine.

A group of sardines swam by, pausing to look at me. I offered them a smile.

"Prince Caspian here to check on the coral," I said. The fish's eyes lit up. I've been coming to the ocean to check on the coral every day, and every day I felt myself reconnecting with my magic. It's beginning to become easier talking to the creatures of the deep sea. Many had exclaimed with excitement at having me back and being able to share their worries with me.

It hurt to see their excitement because it felt undeserved. I'd left them alone with no one and yet they welcomed me back with opened fins. So did the beings of Coralia Coast. My hand glides through my hair in frustration.

The sharks are migrating differently this year because of climate change which has affected some of the fish habitats. A grey whale has reemerged and will be migrating soon as well. While one part of the ocean was thriving, another was suffering.

My stomach sinks. I had missed so much in the year that I was gone. That year should have been dedicated to preparing me to be second in command and officially take on Uncle Seward's duties. I should have been focused on connecting with the sea creatures and learning about their different territories and migration patterns. My eyes burn as feelings of regret began well up. I rub my eyes.

A siren's tears were pointless underwater.

I reach into my sack and pluck out a bottle of a salve that Aunt Meryl has been working on. Thanks to Priscilla's help, Aunt Meryl has replenished a few of her missing ingredients. I decide to work the lotion into a section of coral in the hopes of healing it. The coral is in a fragile state, and I need to be careful. Siren skin is thicker than humans, so I don't need to worry about getting stung.

I call on my magic as I gingerly apply it. I don't know what I'm singing but the notes pour out of me. I've learned that some siren songs just come from the heart.

All sirens can sing and use their voice to manipulate other beings, but very few can use it to heal. I'm not one of those rare sirens, but I still feel compelled to try.

The first notes are hesitant but the more the warmth of my magic grows and infuses with my words the more secure I become.

> Darkness rolls in with coming tide
> Taking us on a painful ride
> Gentle as an ocean breeze
> This decay must be seized
> By my soul, by my will
> Help me nurture what is ill
> Darkness rolls with the coming tide
> And many creatures swim to hide
> All surrounded by pain
> Wash it away with rain
> By my soul, by my will
> Help me nurture what is ill
> With pure intentions
> Relieve this tension
> Bathed in light
> Heal this blight
> And the darkness will roll away with the rolling tide

I hope this works. I adjust my bag and begin swimming away, casting one last glance at the coral. There is nothing I could do now. I just need to wait and hope the salve and my song does something.

· · · 🐚 🐚 🐚 · · ·

WHEN I MAKE it back home, Crystal is curled on the couch, typing away on her laptop. A smile tugs at my lips. She is in a sweatshirt and leggings, her signature look. On the coffee table is an empty mug and from the smell of it, it used to be filled with coffee. She glances at me, her eyes widening as a delicious blush crawls up her face.

"Oh, hi," she squeaked. I chuckle. Her eyes flickered towards her laptop before closing it. I raise an eyebrow.

"What are you hiding?" I ask, resting my arms on the top of the couch. She bit her bottom lip. Honestly, my fake girlfriend has the best lips. They are deep pink, the top lip slightly fuller. Very kissable lips. I swallow as my own face flushes. I need to rein in my thoughts.

"You said you wanted the list," she said, her voice sounding small. I nod, my heart rate picking up. I have no idea what was going to be on that list. I know Crystal reads romance books and she's told me not to treat her like she's fragile. That could mean she was into trying stuff. *But what kind of stuff?*

"May I see?" I ask, my dick twitching. She nodded and motioned for me to sit on the couch next to her. I place a pillow on my lap and reached for her computer. She wraps herself in a blanket hugging her knees, watchful. Taking a deep breath I begin reading.

"Not out loud!" she squealed, reaching to close the laptop. I chuckle.

"If you want to do these things, you should be able to hear them said out loud," I point out. She rolled her eyes and sat back. "Don't be embarrassed," I said. Huffing, she crosses her arms.

"I'm not...sort of. Whatever. Read it," she said, waving a hand in the air. *This pixie.*

"Go on a date, French kiss, give and receive oral sex," I start.

"I have kissed. It just wasn't enjoyable," she added quickly. I nod, remembering our conversation.

"You're okay with doing this with me, right?" I ask. I want to check in again and make sure she is certain about this.

"Yes," she affirmed. I nod, my eyes turning back to her list.

My heart is beating faster than the wings of a sprite. *Maybe I will have trouble reading out loud.* I glance up and Crystal's face and ears are pink. I take a breath before continuing. "Figure out if I like degradation or praise." I raise an eyebrow. She shrugged her shoulders. *This will be interesting.*

"I'm interested in figuring out what I like," she said.

"Blindfold, sexting, role play, dirty talk," I finish. "What about sex on the beach?" I tease lightly. She wrinkled her nose.

"Sand," she pointed out. I chuckle.

"Not if you're careful," I said, wiggling my eyebrows. She gave a dramatic sigh.

"Fine. Add it please," she said with another wave of her hand. The list seems normal enough.

"Receive flowers, romantic moonlit walk, cuddle," I said, my eyes softening. More standard parts of a relationship. Things Crystal never experienced, at least not in a romantic sense.

"Do you have a favorite flower?" I ask. She tilted her head back and forth.

"Hydrangeas, carnations, baby's breath," she rattled off. I smile. Despite this conversation Crystal is at ease discussing this with me.

"This is a doable list," I said, handing her back her laptop.

"Really?" she asked wide-eyed. I nod with a smile, and ideas start forming in my head.

"Yes. We can cross the first one off the list now," I said, grinning. She sat up, clutching her laptop against her chest.

"K-kissing with tongue?" she asked nervously. Even though she stuttered her eyes were hungry. *I am so fucking screwed.*

"The first thing on the list is a date. Already want to makeout with your fake boyfriend?" I tease. I ignore the way that saying fake boyfriend makes my stomach twist. Crystal is helping me, and I am helping her. She rolled her pretty eyes.

"Okay, a date," she said, getting up. I reach for her hand, electricity jumping up my arm.

"I haven't asked you yet," I said. Her brows furrowed. I stand up. I reach for her face with my other hand, my fingers grazing her soft cheek. "Let me show you how you should be asked out," I murmur. "Stay here."

I pull away, walking back out the front door. I glance around my front yard and pull a few flowers from the flower beds hanging on the window. I grab an assortment of daisies, bluebells, and irises. This is simple but I hope the sweet gesture pleases her.

My heart is racing as I knock on the door to my own cottage, anxiously shifting from one foot to the other.

When Crystal opens the door, her hair is down and cascading down her shoulders in soft waves. I notice that her skin has a bit more color from being out in the sun and her freckles are blooming across her sun kissed face. And her eyes? Her eyes are like sunflowers, with a gold iris featuring tiny green flecks framing a black pupil. She is a celestial being and I'm enchanted by her, caught in a spell I never want to break.

"Hi Crystal," I said, grinning. Her eyes widened slightly at the sight of my makeshift bouquet. She crossed her arms and leaned against the door frame, her face recovering quickly. She is going to have fun with this. I can tell by the mischief dancing between her eyes.

"Caspian," she said. I want to melt. Her saying my name feels like a siren's song.

"I brought you some flowers," I said, handing her the makeshift bouquet. Her eyes softened.

"Cas, I love them," she said, staring in amazement. My stomach twists. From her reaction anyone would've thought that I gave her a pot of gold.

"I wanted to know if you would go on a date with me?" I ask. She bit her bottom lip again.

"That depends on the kind of date," she said, her shoulders tensing slightly. Something tells me she doesn't want to be around people.

"How about I buy us some dinner, and we have a movie night in? I can pick you up outside your bedroom at, say, 6PM?" I ask. It is currently four, which means I have time to get food, grab some wine, and shower. Her shoulders relax and her eyes brighten with excitement.

"I would love that Cas."

CHAPTER 13
FIRST FAKE DATE

Caspian

I stare at my outdoor patio. After picking up the food I'd showered quickly and gotten to work. The table has chili cheese fries for Crystal, a burger for me, waters, and a bottle of wine. I'd even added some candles and twinkling lights.

My body is jumpy. I have a ball of energy bouncing inside of me. Tonight, is my first date with Crystal and my first date in a few years. I wish it was under better circumstances. What if I screw this night up? This was important for Crystal. I want her to see how she should be treated.

While our relationship is fake, I want this to feel real for Crystal and for me. I rub my eyes. Even though I have real feelings for her, this is about me fulfilling her list. That's important to me, and I'm willing to take my feelings out of the equation and focus on her.

I'm going to show her what being in a relationship is all about. I'm going to show her how a good boyfriend should act. What matters is making sure she holds the upper hand in spite of her lack of experience.

Crystal had asked for a dress code, and I'd told her sweats would be acceptable. I want her to feel comfortable with me, not stressed. From what I've heard, the scheduling changes at work have given her some anxiety.

In all honesty I'm stressed too. I don't know what is happening to the coral and I haven't found any useful information on the trident. There is also the fight I'd had with my brother. I shake my head. Now was not the time to think about that. All I want right now is to enjoy my night with Crystal.

I knock on Crystal's door, my stomach doing somersaults. She opened the door, and my heart melted. Her hair is pulled back in a ponytail, and she wore baby blue sweats that made her skin glow. I grin and she offers me a shy smile.

"You're two minutes early," she teased. I place my hands inside my pockets to hide a slight tremor.

"You say early, and I say on time," I said. She hummed, stepping out. She glanced at the living room, and I shook my head before guiding her to the backyard. She gasped.

"Cas," she said breathlessly, and my body tingles.

Stars, I can imagine her saying my name like that under...*different* circumstances. I clear my throat as she turns to face me. "You did all of this for me?" she asked in disbelief. My throat tightens at her reaction. Once again, I'm reminded of just how much Crystal has missed out on.

"I did it for *us*," I said, walking her towards our table. "M'Lady," I said, as she slid into her seat. She clapped excitedly.

"Chili cheese fries," she said, grinning. I open the wine and pour us each a glass before sliding in next to her.

"Do you remember the day I found out it was your favorite?" I ask, trying not to laugh. She groaned, shaking her head.

"Please, that was so embarrassing," she said.

On one of the rare occasions that Crystal came out with our friend group, she had gotten drunk. Looking back, we were celebrating her deal with my brother but at the time all I knew was she'd closed an important deal and was proud. She had too many shots and went on a five-minute rant about how much she loves chili cheese fries.

I already knew she liked them because she always ordered them.

But that night she went on a deep rant about the sauce to cheese to fries ratio, which I learned is *very* important. Crystal isn't a fan of having too much cheese explaining that it could overpower the chili.

"I mean I thought it was adorable that you called fries the most perfect carb in the entire world," I said. She took a bite and moaned, making me shift in my seat.

"And I *still* think it's the most perfect carb in the entire world," she said leaning towards me. I sit still, catching her scent. My eyes flicker to her lips and she catches the movement. She is so achingly beautiful and I'm desperate to taste her.

I offer her a glass of wine, wanting to cut the tension. Making out is on her list and I'm fully on board, but first we need to get through this date.

AFTER EMPTYING our plates and pouring a second glass, I pull Crystal towards my side as we watch a superhero movie. She tucked her head onto my shoulder and fuck, it feels so right. Despite her long limbs she curls into me perfectly. My hand finds her foot and I begin gently kneading her heel. She groaned softly.

"You don't have to do that," she said into my hoodie. I kiss the top of her head, and she pulled away.

"Shush. Enjoy my hands," I said with a smirk.

"You're smirking, aren't you?" she asked, eyes trained on the TV. I chuckle.

"You know me so well, don't you?" I tease. She placed a hand on my thigh. My body tightens at her touch. She turned to look up at me, her face inches from mine.

"You and Eleanor have the same humor," she pointed out. I close my eyes briefly. The last thing I need is Eleanor being a cockblock.

"I don't want to talk about your sister right now," I said. When I open my eyes she tilted her to the side, batting her eyelashes.

"Oh? Is there something else we should be talking about?" she asked, sounding breathless. Her hand tightens on my thigh and my blood is flowing south fast. "Or maybe there's something we should be doing?"

There is a hint of uncertainty in her question but fuck, she is pulling me in. Despite her lack of experience Crystal knows what she is doing when she looks at me like that and in her inflections. My hand cups the back of her head.

This is happening. I am going to kiss Crystal. With tongue. Wait, do I have fish breath?

I tilt her head a bit back, leaning down. Her eyes fluttered close. Her hand moved up to my hoodie, clutching it, pulling me towards her.

"Please?" she whispered. One word and I was undone. I would do anything for this pixie. I would get on my knees and kiss her feet. She is sweet, and I had a huge, sweet tooth.

"Yes, M'Lady," I reassure. Our lips brush once, delicately. My heart hammers in my chest. I was ready to sink into her when a phone pinged.

We jump back, staring at each other, chests heaving up and down. That sound snapped us back to reality. She scrambled to grab her phone on the table and flipped it over.

She frowned, tongue running over her teeth, eyes hardening. My stomach sinks. *Something is wrong.*

"Crystal?" I said, worried. She looks up, her eyes refocusing. This isn't good.

"It's an email. They delivered the wood to our restoration plant, but it turns out the process is going to take a lot longer than we anticipated so the timeline on the second cottage is getting pushed back again," she said.

She looks back at her phone, teeth digging into her bottom lip. I can see she'd gone from date mode to fix it mode. I glance at what remainder of our meal. I guess our date was good while it lasted. I quickly roll my lips, the feel of hers just barely still there. She taps my shoulder.

"I'm sorry," she said, frowning. I look at her confused.

"We-we were about to kiss and then I got this email which I should have not looked at, but I did and now I'm going to move things around in the schedule which—"

"It's okay," I said, grabbing her hand. She looked at me hesitantly, which hurt worse than our kiss being interrupted. "It's okay. I understand," I said, pulling her into my arms. She placed the phone down and sagged into me.

"What about the kiss?" she mumbled. Her phone pings again and she groans. But she didn't reach for it. I could tell she wanted to, though. Her fingers are clutching my hoodie. I tilt her face up and give a soft kiss against her warm cheek. She looked at me in surprise.

"Why don't we clean up and get ready for bed?" I ask. Crystal needs to sort out work. Her job involves my town, and I want to help my brother which means not distracting her right now. I can tell from her twitching eyebrows that if she didn't settle this matter now, she would be distracted all night. And I should at least try to flip through a few books tonight.

"I thought we would be…making out," she said, sounding upset. I bite back a grin at her expression. Oh, she wanted to kiss me and that was enough for now. We don't need to rush this.

"Dates usually end in a kiss, but no one ever specifies what kind of a kiss," I smirk. Her eyes widen and go from surprise to annoyance.

"So, we should have another date," she said, matter-of-factly. I chuckle.

"Are you wanting a second date just to kiss me?" I tease. She blushed, rocking on her feet.

"I just like hanging out with you," she muttered. I lean over, my mouth brushing her ear.

"I would love if you would go on another date with me," I said.

Her lips twitched at the side and her eyes narrowed. "I would love to go on a second date with you if you promise to feed me again," she responded. I nod, a swell of excitement coursing through me.

She reached for her empty plate. I grab mine and our two glasses. We make our way to the kitchen, and I quickly push her away from the sink. "Go, it's okay," I said. Her eyes searched my face.

"I said it's okay, Crystal," I assure her. My stomach churns. *Why is she so worried?*

"You promise?" she asked softly. I nod.

As I start to turn towards the sink, there is the softest brush against my cheek. My eyes widen as I stare back at the pixie that was slowly claiming my heart.

"Only fair that you get a kiss back."

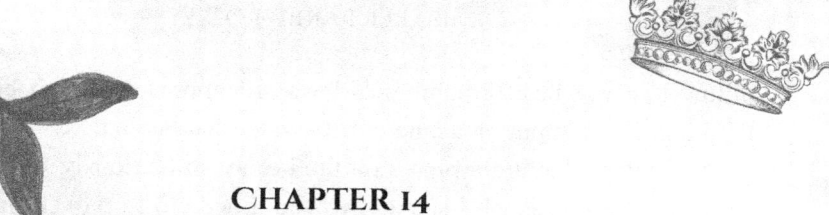

CHAPTER 14
THE OCEAN KNOWS

Crystal

L ips. Mouths. Kissing. Tongue.
　　It's all I can think about. It has been two days since our date. It was wonderful, simple, and perfect. It was so us, though I was afraid to admit that. I was surprised at how relaxed I was during the whole thing, but that's why I wanted to do this with Cas. I felt safe with him.

　　I touch my cheek where his lips were. Stars, I wanted to kiss him so badly. I'd never had these urges before, but then again, I was never around someone who brought them out of me.

　　Even though Cas was sweet, he pushed me. He welcomed my stubbornness, almost seemed to crave more of it, and he made me feel empowered. He made me feel safe to speak up.

　　I'm still holed up in my room. Cas had left to do more research but today I would meet him for lunch with his mom. Sprites flew around my stomach. We had promised to meet early and discuss the details of our fake relationship.

　　I glance at my closet. What did one wear to meet the queen? Should I wear a dress? A skirt? My options are limited since I didn't exactly plan to hang out with royalty when I was packing. I shove a pillow into my face, groaning. If I was Eleanor, I wouldn't be overthinking. I would put on a cute outfit and let that be that.

We will be having a picnic on the beach, so obviously I should do something more casual. I shake my head. I need to stop overthinking. I get up and go to find my favorite jeans. After a few minutes of bouncing between the closet and my luggage I feel satisfied with my look. My phone beeps and I jump, slightly wincing at the sound.

CAS
At the diner!

Kraken's crap.

WE SIT in the back corner of Calder's Diner. As it turns out we will be picking up the food for our lunch. Mira is busy taking orders. In the past few days there have been an uptick of new beings arriving.

"You look beautiful," Cas said, his eyes bouncing up and down. I blush and fidget with my fingers. "What's up?" he asked. I glance out the window towards the ocean.

"I'm nervous," I whisper, leaning in close so no one can hear. He shook his head.

"We'll be fine," he assured me. I narrow my eyes.

"How do you know? We still have to come up with some fabricated story of how we...became a we," I said, my gaze jumping between him and the diner. Cas folded his arms together.

He wore a white button shirt and olive-green khaki shorts. Even in this simple look you can see how handsome he is. Between his perfectly tousled blonde locks, his pouty pink lips and his long, toned body I'm cooked. I bite the inside of my cheek.

"That's easy," he said. I raise an eyebrow, and the prince gives me a heart hammering smirk. "We met when I came over to say hi to your friends at The Drunken Fairy Tale Tavern. I kissed your hand during our introduction and called you a jewel because of your name...and your personality," he began. I stare at him, my mouth hanging open. He remembered the first moment we met. I remembered it too. My hand had tingled the entire night, the feel of his lips imprinted on my skin.

"I'm a jewel?" I ask. His smile softens. His hand grazed my cheek, tucking a piece of hair.

"Diamonds are born in harsh environments. Despite the life you had to deal with you have come out on top. You're beautiful, successful, funny and kind. You shine like a jewel," he said. My bottom lip wobbles at his words. How can he say those things and just be my friend? His finger wipes a stray tear, and he brushes it against his lip. My stomach tightens and there is a glow in his eyes.

"We started hanging out. You needed someone to keep you company while you worked and I needed to bounce around ideas for the carpentry shop with someone," he said. He reached across the table offering me his hand. I take it. His skin is calloused, and I shivered as his fingers played across my palm.

"The more time we spent together the closer we became. It was inevitable for us to fall for each other," he said, looking at me again. There is a softness in his ocean blue eyes that have me falling for every word.

Fake. Fake. Fake.

I keep reminding myself. But I still find myself drowning in his ocean blue eyes.

"W-who asked who out?" I ask. His lips twitch again, and his eyes become playful.

"You tell me," he said. I fight back a smile. He is giving me the choice in our story. Eleanor had assumed it was *him* asking *me* out and I quickly shut that thought down. Cas knew that just because I preferred to keep to myself didn't mean that I wouldn't go after what I wanted.

"I did tell Eleanor it was me," I said quietly. He nodded and a slow grin spread across my face. "I asked you out and you said yes." He squeezed my hand before letting go. I wish he hadn't. I already miss the warmth it provides, the way it anchors me. I swallow.

"Here is your food!" Mira said, sounding different. Her smile is a little forced and her eyes are slightly twitching. Cas looked behind her and smirked.

"For someone who hates royals you sure do attract a certain prince," he teased. Mira rolled her eyes.

"The guppy has been following me around since we were kids," she said, flicking one of her purple braids behind her shoulders. She glanced at Kai quickly. "Poor princey poo," she teased. I shake my head, giggling. I like Mira a lot. She is strong willed, funny, and didn't care what anyone else thought.

"I'll see you tonight?" she asked me. I nod.

"I can't wait!" I said. Mira and I decided to start a book club. Even though it's just the two of us we considered it a club. *We just need a name.* Cas looked between us.

"Wait. What are you guys doing? Can I join?" he asked. Mira gasped before sliding into the booth and wrapping an arm around my shoulder.

"Cas, I finally have a new friend who isn't a snotty royal. A normal and nice friend and she is mine. We must do some things without you," she said. I slap a hand over my mouth to keep the giggles at bay. When I looked at Cas, I expected him to look hurt but instead he was beaming, and I couldn't help but match his energy.

"Well fine. I hope you two enjoy your evening later. Now if you don't mind, my girlfriend and I have a lunch date with mom," Cas said, standing and picking up the bag of food. My heart races and my anxiety makes its way through my body again. Mira squeezed my shoulder and gave me a reassuring nod.

My stomach drops. I made a new friend, but she doesn't know that I'm not really dating her cousin. Isn't it wrong to lie to your friends? But I'm helping Cas, protecting him from the fins of bratty princesses.

WE LAY out the sandwiches and fruits across the picnic table that sits a few feet away from the shoreline. The sun is shining down and there isn't a cloud in the sky. Thank the stars I added an extra layer of sunscreen. The ocean is calmer today and its melody eases my beating heart.

"This looks lovely!" A warm voice said behind me. I turn around to see Cas' mom. She wore jeans and a light sweater. I bite back a sigh. I was so worried that I was underdressed. Cas hugged his mom as my hands trembled.

They looked at each other with such love that it sent a pang through my heart. The memories of my own mom are always fleeting. Some days I have trouble remembering her face, her laugh, her smell, while other days it all comes back to me with a warm swiftness. I blink the tears away quickly.

She turned to me, opening her arms. "I hope you don't mind but I'm a hugger," she said. I step into her embrace and close my eyes. She squeezed me tightly and I feel a sob threaten to burst out of me. This is a mother's embrace, warm and loving.

"Thank you for bringing him home," she whispered. My heart stops. *But I didn't bring him home. I didn't do anything. I'm just a pixie, a friend, a fake girlfriend.* My bottom lip wobbles. Hugging Cas' mom feels like hugging my own mom, and I didn't know how much I've needed this until right now.

"I didn't do anything," I said, pulling away, face flushing. She tsked.

"The fates, my dear," she said, looking up to the sky. An arm snakes around my waist, and I sink into Cas' side. Mrs. Calder clapped her hands. "Let's eat."

AFTER FINISHING OUR FOOD, Cas gathers the trash to toss. We all decide to take a walk across the beach. The waves gently lap at my ankles, easing the tension in my body. Stars, I've missed the ocean. Maybe it is the connection my mom had to it, but the ocean always calls to me. I feel more at peace when I'm near water. My soul is like the ocean, sometimes calm, other times ready to drown me in a storm of emotions.

"The ocean likes you," Mrs. Calder said. I look at Cas and her.

"The ocean?" I ask. She pointed to my feet, and we watch how the waters were gentle as they move up toward the shore. Mrs. Calder smiled, her blues eyes bright like Cas'.

"When you step toward it, the ocean follows you splashing very gently against your feet," she explained. "It calls to you despite the fact that you're an Earth pixie," she pointed out. My mouth hangs open.

"How did you know I was an Earth pixie?" I ask. She wrapped her arms around herself as we walked.

"Ronan told me while we were discussing our options to help the town. Your company–"

"My dad's," I correct. Her lips twitched.

"We looked into *your dad's* company intently. We couldn't trust just any company to help our town," she said. She paused for a moment. "After your first meeting with him he said he had…a feeling. A good feeling. That's when he told me you were an Earth pixie," she said. I nod.

"I mainly use my magic for work," I said. I pause to look out into the ocean. Something about being around water always feels right. I take a step further in and the water remains at my ankles. I smile.

My mom stood at this beach, feeling this water and breathing the salty air. I bend down to dip my hand into the water. At some point she ran her fingers through this sand, this ocean. Waves continued to push and pull at me gently. The water rises, encompassing my hand as if shaking it.

Thank you, I think to myself. The sound of the water eases the tension in my body and when I stand up Cas slips his hand in mine, and I relax into his warmth. I look up at his beaming smile. He squeezes twice and I squeeze back once.

"I guess I'm lucky then," he said. My body tingles.

Fake. Fake. Fake.

His mom snorted, catching our attention. "If only you had a green thumb. This one over here kills succulents," she said. I gasp and slap his shoulder. He held his free hand up defensively.

"I'm sorry! Listen, you need someone to deal with sharks? I'm your siren. But I will forget to water the plants," he confessed. We all laugh, and I relax into step with them on our walk.

My eyes catch the strip of shops that lay at the edge of the beach. There is a hair salon, a grocery store and a few boutiques. The town is quaint and sweet.

Mrs. Calder let out a startled gasp bringing our walk to an abrupt halt. Cas moved to her side, stepping in front of her, eyes surveying the scene.

"What's wrong?" he asked, looking her up and down. Her eyes were transfixed to the wet sand. My heart stops as Cas bent down. I huddled around them as he held up a piece of broken coral. I look at Cas to see that his eyes were glowing. My breath catches in my throat and my eyes widen. I don't watch him use his magic too often.

"It's dead," he said, voice hoarse. His fingers wrapped around the piece of coral as he closed his eyes. His mom placed a hand on his shoulder.

"You have to find the trident," she pleaded. I can see a storm raging in his eyes. He was always the siren that wore easy smiles but today he looked like someone who was desperate and broken. This time I wrap my arms around him, hoping to be an anchor for him through my own anxiety. I was everyone's anchor, what was one more? Especially for Cas I can be.

I STILL HAD some time before my meeting with Mira, so Cas took me to one of his favorite spots on the beach. I watched him the entire walk after we'd said goodbye to his mom, trying to gauge his emotions. The dead coral shook him up. He couldn't stop fidgeting with his hands and his eyes kept darting back toward the ocean.

I want to fix this. I want to change his mood, but I didn't know how. With my dad, I knew I had to give him space and food or change the subject to work. With Eleanor, I could take her dancing. But I still don't know how to make Caspian happy.

We climb over a few rocks to reveal a small strip of sand. This little shoreline is enclosed by rocks, and I smile at the privacy. Cas sat on the sand and patted the space next to him. I accept the invitation, digging my toes into the sand once sitting.

"Don't hide," he said, bumping my shoulder with his. I rolled my eyes. I wasn't hiding from him, just trying to figure out what he needs. "You like it?" he asked, gesturing to our hideaway.

"If you keep showing me all of these secret spots I may never leave," I said jokingly. He grinned and my stomach flipped.

"Mhmm. In that case I might know a few more," he said. My heart pounds. That feels like a promise. We share a laugh and stare into the ocean, letting nature take over our conversation. I lean my hand on his shoulder.

"This is nice...right?" I ask, nerves tickling the back of my head. He laid his cheek against the top of my head, humming. I close my eyes, enjoying the song he is singing. It is soft, sweet, and enchanting and fills me with warmth despite the sea breeze. "That's a pretty song," I whisper.

When I glance up Cas is blushing. His lips are slightly parted, and I have the urge to kiss him again. I want to know if his lips are as soft as they look. His eyes drifted down to my mouth. I lean forward, compelled by him.

"Thanks," he said, his hand tilting my chin slightly up. "We still need to cross item number two off your list," he whispered.

"Yes," I said, breathlessly. He is so close. His breath brushes my cheek. My hands sneak their way to his chest, clutching at his shirt. His nose brushes mine and a desperate noise escapes me.

"I mean I guess their beaches are okay. I just wish they had better everything else," a voice said from beyond the rocks. Cas stares at me. Our moment shatters with the person's voice, a voice that isn't Tati's.

"I mean according to the internet this is a super cute town, but they don't even have a bar," another voice said. Cas' fists clenched.

Ronan stated that his main goal for the town was to make it a place where everyone felt welcomed and could enjoy themselves away from the restlessness of the city. He wants Coralia Coast to be the seaside town version of Lavender Falls. That's why I want to help.

While I'd spent more than half my life away from it, I'd loved my childhood in Lavender Falls. The beings there are welcoming, helpful, and have the best events.

Coralia Coast was once like Lavender Falls and could be that way again. But to do so Cas and his brother needed to work together. They needed to see each other as beings with the same goal and not just squabbling siblings. Sometimes we forget that our own family is just trying to survive in this world like we are.

I bite my cheek, thinking of my sister. But even *with* understanding there can be pain. I can see that there is a rift between Cas and his brother.

"Cas?" I said, trying to pull him away from wherever his thoughts were.

"I missed a lot," he said, harshly. I roll my lips, unsure of what to say next. I wrap my arm around him, holding him close.

"There's still time to fix this," I said, hoping my words and warmth can be enough.

CHAPTER 15
THE PAIN OF THE PAST

Caspian

I knew my mom would like Crystal. Of course she would. Crystal is kind, beautiful, and so understanding that being around her soothes the soul. She is slowly showing me the beauty in the quiet parts of life.

But what we found on the beach left a heavy stain on my heart. The dead coral. It isn't uncommon to find pieces of coral that have passed or been broken off from storms, but I know that wasn't the case here.

After dropping Crystal off at the diner, I made my way back to our new secret place. Shedding my clothes, I dive into the water, my transformation coming with ease now. The water glides around me as I cut through the water. It's a warm day in the ocean with the sun shining above. While the land is my home, so is the ocean.

Fish swim by, eager to gossip with me about the other creatures. Fun fact: jellyfish are the gossip queens. Because many are translucent other creatures don't realize they are even there half the time. They hear everything. A seahorse drifts in front of my face, stopping me. I wave hello.

"Your highness," the seahorse said. I offer it my finger, and the creature taps it with its tail (the seahorse equivalent of a handshake). "Everyone is happy to have you back."

"I'm happy to be here," I said. Half of that is true. The other half of me is worried. What if I fuck up? I didn't know what I was doing. I hadn't paid enough attention when my dad and uncle were alive.

These creatures probably all secretly hate me for running away. And now I spend my time chasing a mystical object that may or may not exist.

"I wanted to let you know that some whales will be visiting soon," it said. I nod. It is common for us to have some whale sightings during the summer.

"I'll let my brother, and the other beings know so we can watch our boats. We'll make sure they have a safe passage," I said. The seahorse swam back and forth excitedly. I couldn't help but grin. Even though I'm apprehensive about becoming second in command, right now it felt...good. That's a good thing, right? It's a sign that I'm on the path I am meant to be on.

Swimming to the coral makes my stomach sink and all my happy feelings go out the blowhole. The salve didn't do too much to slow the coral's decay. Something swam behind me, and I did my best to muster up a smile.

"Hey there, Waldo," I said, turning around. The seal glanced around, his nose twitching.

"Prince Caspian," he greeted. I look back at the coral, and he moved closer, floating next to me. "I'm sorry," he said, his voice sounding small. We'd both hoped the salve would do *something*. I take a breath before placing another smile on my face.

"It's okay because we aren't giving up. There are still remedies we can try," I said encouragingly. Waldo relaxed and his eyes softened.

"Secret spot?" he suggested. This time my smile is genuine.

"Secret spot," I said.

Once we enter the cave my muscles relax. My secret cave. My sanctuary that I share with my dad (and now with Waldo and Crystal) brings me a familiar peace. Glancing around the jagged rock enclosed paradise, it reminds me of the peace I feel when I'm with Crystal. My heart thumps in my chest.

We'd almost kissed again. Every time we share tender touches it is becoming harder to tell if she is faking it or not. I don't think I was faking it. She wanted to kiss me. *But is it because of the list, or because she wants it?*

"This place is magical don't you think?" Waldo asked, pulling himself up onto the rocky shore and diving back in again.

I chuckle, looking up at the fading sun. "I think so. I always felt... called to come here after the first time I came with my dad," I confess. My magic hums louder here, like this is our own version of the Hollow Tree.

My eyebrows scrunch together as I begin humming the melody I'd sang to Crystal. It's her siren song, a song that called her to me and me *only*. And singing it in this cave, its sound bouncing against all the rocks, feels powerful. The words haven't fully formed in my mind yet and I wonder what they will be.

"Hey, I'm going to head back and see if I can find anything that can help the coral," I said to Waldo.

"Anything I can do?" he asked. I stare at the seal fondly. It seems like everyone in my life is willing to help me, which makes me feel guilty. I don't deserve Waldo's help after running away for an entire year.

He slapped a fin across my arm, and I yelped. His beady dark eyes narrowed. "Let me help, my prince," he demanded. I bite my tongue at the *'my prince'* part. I don't want him to help me just because my family rules his home.

"Waldo, you don't need to," I said calmly. He slapped me again and I glared at him. He is really strong for a young seal.

"You're helping *our* home. Let me," he said. I sigh knowing he won't let this go.

"I'm looking for a trident that once belonged to my family. It's hundreds of years old," I said. The seal let out a sound.

"You got it, Prince Caspian. I'll ask around." And with that, Waldo left on his new mission.

A SIREN'S SUMMER FOR LOVE

I'M HOLED up in my brother's study with a few books scatter around me. Once again, I'm left with no clues as to the whereabouts of the trident. What I did learn was the power it wielded. The trident had the ability to amplify the power of any siren wielding it. Most second in commands shared similar abilities: talking to sea creatures, healing with song, and reading energies.

I have two out of three, though I don't use my siren song for much. I don't like the idea of enchanting others to do my bidding.

Instead of harnessing that magic I've learned to fight against it, and I've gotten really fucking good at it.

I flip through another page. Reading energies comes easily to me. I'm able to tell what someone needs based on their emotions. I didn't realize how handy it could be until my father and uncle died. When they passed my family, minus my brother, had been inconsolable. Their hearts were shattered. I still remember the scream my mom let out when we found out the news.

MY MOTHER WAS WAILING in the next room while my brother and I were in the kitchen having breakfast. We had just finished our spring break.

I was a sophomore and Ronan was a senior. We stared at each other wide-eyed. Something wasn't right. My brother's energy bled with concern, and I felt it washing over me. I wasn't awake enough to block out his emotions from latching onto me.

Ronan was the first to stand up. I felt frozen in my seat. I had never heard my mom cry that way. It was high pitched and broken. She was gasping for air.

"What?" Ronan's voice boomed from the other room. Tears

pricked my eyes. I had a sinking feeling that if I stepped into that room my worst nightmare would become a reality. "Cas," *my brother's voice croaked out and I shut my eyes, willing my magic to protect me from the truth.*

But it didn't matter. When I stepped into the room, my mom and Aunt Meryl were on the floor, sobbing into their hands. Mira had her arms wrapped around her mom. Ronan stood with his head bowing in front of one of our guards. The guard's face was streaked with tears and his eyes were bloodshot. He had nasty bruises and cuts all over him.

"N-no," *I said in a strangled voice. Ronan looked at me, his eyes almost devoid of emotion now.*

"Dad and Uncle Seward," *he began but was cut off by the collective cries from our family. I winced. My heart sank and I trembled as everyone's emotions began washing over me like a giant tsunami. I was being swallowed by their anger, heartbreak, and despair. I couldn't tell where my emotions ended and theirs began.*

I fell to my knees, fingers digging into the carpet, willing my magic to come forward and help me come back to center. Dad and Uncle Seward were dead.

Gone.

Forever.

I looked up at my older brother and I already saw the shift within him. His shoulders were straight back as he knelt, placing a hand on our mom's back. He looked at me and nodded. I shook my head, realizing what he was asking me.

"Caspian," *he said, his voice hard. My bottom lip trembled. This wasn't my grumpy brother anymore. This was the new king of The Atlantic Ocean, and he wanted me to diffuse the tidal wave of grief that was trying to drown us. He glanced at our mom, who was shaking her head and clutching at her heart.*

And then a switch flipped within me, and I felt myself shut down. I was a bystander now just watching from the outside. I opened my mouth as a song poured out of me, overpowering the sound of everyone's cries with its melody. My magic wrapped around everyone like a warm blanket, and I watched their shoulders sag and their breathing slow down.

I had never used my siren song to manipulate emotions before. It felt wrong. But in the midst of their grief, it was the only thing to do to keep everyone from drowning.

"I-it's okay. We'll be okay," I whispered. Nothing was going to be the same after today. I would never be the same.

SINCE THAT DAY instead of manipulating others with my songs I vowed to be the one that changed myself in order to help them. I became the happy one, the fun one, the one that made everyone smile and laugh. I traded my royal crown and became a royal jester. And I was okay with that.

Until last year when fate caught up with me and my brother reminded me that I could no longer be that person. I had a crown, a shield, and now a trident waiting for me to take my place. I rub my eyes and try to shove down all of the feelings that are bubbling up.

Atlas used his gifts to bring unity, but I can't. How can I? If I become more like him, there is a chance that this new version of me I enjoy can't ever come back.

"You're here," my brother said, sounding surprised. I bite back a snarky remark. Lately there is a lot of push and pull coming from my older brother. Some moments it feels like the time before my dad's death and other times it feels like we have a wall between us.

"No shrimp shit," I said. He grunted and I ignored him. He sits across from me and when I look up, I raise an eyebrow. *Is he not going to give me shit for sitting in his chair? The king's chair?*

"I don't have to sit there," he said, reading my mind. I snort already seeing his fingers twitch. My brother functioned on routine and that included sitting in his chair. I stand and motion for us to switch. He resisted for a second before giving in.

"Found anything?" he asked. I plop onto the other chair with a heavy sigh.

"Let's see. Aunt Meryl's latest salve didn't do much. She's working on something else from some random book Mira was able to find in the old bookstore's attic.

Apparently, it's creepy and she wants to be compensated for any haunting that may occur from touching it. So far nothing in these books gives any indication on how to find the location of the trident," I said. I chew the inside of my cheek.

"But?" Ronan asked, crossing his arms. There *is* no but. Everything I've read says the trident will reveal itself when it's needed. *But isn't now the perfect time to help?*

My brother is still staring at me, waiting for an answer that I don't have. He looked older now, his hair has grown much longer, and he is even growing a beard. I suppress a chuckle. "What?" he asked, glowering.

"Nothing. Back to your *but*. I did notice a connection between Atlas and I," I said, my nerves bouncing around. My fingers twitch and I clasp my hands.

"Can you please spit it out? You know I don't like the anticipation," he said. I roll my eyes.

"One day you're going to meet someone who is going to make you pull your hair out," I said, glaring at him. For the first time since I've been back and probably longer my brother barked out a laugh.

"You and Mira already do that," he said. I join him, the laughter breaking the tension that we've had for a while. It feels…good. My brother and I were never incredibly close and since our dad's death it felt as though there is sea between us.

Despite not having a big age gap, growing up he always felt distant. He was always serious, whereas I wanted to enjoy our childhood.

"Atlas and I have the same abilities…well, almost," I said. Ronan leaned forward, intrigued. "We both read energies and can speak to sea creatures," I continue. "He could also heal with his siren songs."

My brother nodded. "You can too. You've never tried but your voice is far superior to mine," he pointed out. I swallow, the suppressed memory resurfacing again.

"That was a total accident," I said, wincing.

"You'll never know if you don't try," he urged. "You said the trident would reveal itself to the second born when the time is right?" he asked.

"I assume the second born according to my similarities with Atlas and what Kai has in his book," I said. Ronan nodded, deep in thought. He scratched his beard before meeting my gaze. "What if you need to reconnect with your magic first?"

I swallow. I've locked that part of my magic away since I used it on my family. After that day I felt sick to use it. To manipulate someone against their will, whether for good or not, is wrong.

Is that what I need to do? Connect with the abilities that are currently shrouded in grief and pain? I clench my hands, attempting to hide my tremors.

Am I ready to open that box?

CHAPTER 16
PRACTICE TIME

Crystal

I had spent last night hanging out with Mira, listening to her rant about Kai and how he's been at the diner every day these past few weeks. Afterwards we decided to pick a new romance book for next month's book club.

It felt great to talk to someone new, someone who didn't feel like she was hanging out with me out of obligation. Cas never made a point to make sure that Mira and I were conversing unlike Eleanor with her friends.

She was constantly trying to include me in their conversations, and I did my best. The ladies were always sweet and took care of me but what I have with Mira feels like something of my own.

I sigh. I was only supposed to be in Coralia Coast for the summer, but Ronan has agreed to stretch the timeline. The wood for cottage #1 is being transferred to our lumber yard and would most likely take a week to purify. In the meantime, we will be fixing up cottage #1 while cottage #2 is inspected.

It technically isn't a bad thing, but I can't seem to shake the headache that I have had this past week. I rub my eyes, feeling the pain in the back of my head resurface.

Lunch with Cas' mom was wonderful. *She* was wonderful. She made me miss my own mom. My body had been enveloped in her warmth and my heart felt safe. It took everything in me to not hold on tighter, chasing the ghost of my mom in her embrace.

My heart thumps thinking about my dad telling me that my mom loved Coralia Coast. *Did the fates bring me to this place? Was this seaside town where I belonged?* I loved my childhood in Lavender Falls, but when I'd come back, I'd felt out of place and restless. And so far in Coralia Coast I feel…at ease.

Cas flashes through my mind. Twice we almost kissed and both times we were interrupted. I roll in bed, knowing I need to get ready for lunch with his family. Lately I've been desperate to cross another thing off my list. If our first date was so amazing, I can't imagine what kissing him will feel like.

"WHATEVER YOU DO, do *not* leave my side," Mira said, looping her arm through mine. I let out a giggle as we walked through her mom's home. I can hear noises coming from the backyard.

"Why?" I ask. She scowled. She wore leggings and an oversized t-shirt. I'd stuck with jeans and a blouse. Mira assured me that they only dressed up on royal occasions.

We step past glass double doors to an idyllic garden. There are garden beds everywhere, and even a gondola in the corner. Lemon and orange trees are scattered along the yard. There is an outdoor patio and kitchen. I catch a whiff of barbecue. This is a wonderfully cozy backyard.

"I have friends who love to garden," I said, thinking of Lola and Flynn. "Can I take some pictures to send them?" I ask. Mira shoved me forward which I take as a yes. After snapping a few photos, a familiar weight cradles me.

"Snuggle monster," I said, biting back a giggle. Mira makes a gagging noise.

"A monster? Only in bed," Cas said, teasing my ear. I turn in his embrace, acutely aware that Mira is near us.

"I wouldn't know, would I?" I whisper. His blue eyes brighten, and his hands squeezed my hips. I shiver beneath his touch. We are flirting and I like it. It's natural with Cas. Falling into step with this fake relationship with him is like breathing.

"Hmm. Someone is eager to get–" His sentence is quickly cut off by Mira's loud cough.

"Can you not say that when I'm right here. You're making me gag," Mira grimaced.

"Gag, you say?" Kai teased, appearing next to Mira, who jumped. She recovered quickly and glared at him. Suddenly I was aware of the fact that everyone here knew me as Cas' girlfriend, so every touch right now isn't real in spite of how it makes me feel.

"Don't even Kai. That's my cousin," Cas scowled, pointing his finger. Kai held his hands up with a chuckle.

"Who sneaks up on a siren? Do I need to put a bell on you?" Mira said. Kai's grin only widened. I bite my bottom lip to keep myself from laughing. Cas shook his head, muttering to himself as I look between them. Since being in town I've enjoyed watching their banter. They remind me a lot of Eleanor and Caleb.

"If that's your thing," he smirked, wickedly. I slap a hand over my mouth while it was Cas' turn to gag. I catch Mira's eye.

"Is this why you wanted me here?" I ask teasingly. She rolled her eyes and pulled me away from Cas. I immediately missed his warmth. She tossed her hair over her shoulder again.

"I'll be stealing my new best friend. The mermen can play with each other," she said, dragging me towards the table. I look back at Cas with a grin.

Lunch is wonderful. It's nice to watch everyone banter and listen to Cas share some stories from Lavender Falls, like the mystery of who owned The Drunken Fairy Tale Tavern and the race to save the Hollow Tree. This is just...pleasant. I pull my legs up, wrapping my arms around my knees.

"Should I pack some leftovers for Ronan?" Meryl asked. Mrs. Calder sighed.

"Yes. I thought he would make it, but he got caught up with confirming the arrivals of the next royal family," Mrs. Calder said. Cas rolled his eyes, and my stomach coiled.

"Guess some things haven't changed," he grumbled. I bite my tongue. Cas has issues with his brother the same way I secretly have issues with my own sister. I understood Ronan. He has a responsibility that he needs to be upheld. Unfortunately, Mrs. Calder heard Cas' grumbling.

"You know he has a lot of responsibilities," his mom pointed out. Cas crossed his arms.

"He couldn't spare an hour to spend time with his family?" he asked. I glance between them. From the way they were speaking now I get the sense that this isn't the first time that Ronan has missed a family get-together.

Ronan has things to handle, just like my dad. He missed out on a lot of things in Eleanor's and my life because he was fighting so hard to make sure we had everything we needed.

But being consumed with his job cost him his relationship with his eldest daughter and me my voice and freedom. I shift in my seat, placing my feet firmly on the floor and clasping my hands.

"Sometimes those who have a lot on their plate need to know that they have others they can rely on," I said tentatively, hoping I didn't overstep. The table turned to look at me and goosebumps trickled up my arms. I wasn't typically outspoken, but Cas' attitude made me want to stand up for Ronan.

"Does he have an assistant? Someone he can share the work with?" I asked Mrs. Calder. She glanced at Cas quickly, who had a stoic look about him.

I see.

Cas and Ronan were supposed to be working together and yet here

Cas was while Ronan was managing everything on his own. I place a hand on his arm, wanting him to look at me. I hope he isn't upset with me.

"He's doing what he can for the town and his subjects. He's handling it all, probably trying not to burden you," I said, quietly. This is probably a bad idea. I'm speaking about his family dynamic when I didn't know them all that well. I was a stranger, a fake girlfriend.

A flush creeps up my face as Cas stares back at me. *Is he upset?* His normally warm blue eyes are guarded now, and that guts me.

"She's right," Mrs. Calder agreed. "But…," she trailed off. We look at her and she sighed, staring up into the sky. "I can help and yet… when Edmar died," she said, tears in her eyes. "I was so sad and scared that Ronan just took over and I let him."

We sit in silence for a bit and Cas stares at his hands. The loss of a parent is always hard. You view life differently after it. You remember that even in a world full of magic not everyone lives forever.

Sometimes after grief you get locked in a routine that becomes hard to shake. You mold yourself to survive. Everyone at this table did what they could after their loss and then became like a scratched record, stuck. They became used to Cas making them happy and Ronan running the ship. They've been trapped in a fog, until Cas left and disrupted things.

I reach for his hand, interlacing out fingers and biting back a sigh when he accepted my touch. He squeezed once and I squeezed twice. A ghost of a smile graced his beautiful face. *Maybe I didn't ruin our friendship after all.*

"I'm so sorry for bringing the mood down. How about we have some dessert?" Cas offered.

IT WAS GETTING LATE by the time we decided to leave. Kai kissed Mira's hand farewell which practically made steam come out of her ears. It is truly funny watching them.

Cas and I make our way back to the cottage in silence. Silence for me is typically a comfort but after what transpired at the table, it was making me tremble with anxiety

Today was a long day for him. Between trying to find the trident and a way to slow the decay of the coral on top of just being back home I couldn't imagine the emotional toll it was taking on him.

I'm racked with guilt over defending Ronan tonight. It wasn't my place. I was an outsider in Cas' family and in this town.

Cas unlocks the door, and I tug on his arm, needing to know if we are okay. "M'Lady?" he asked, his eyes brimming with confusion. He's frowning, which is unusual. His shoulders are tense. I don't know what to do. Once again, I don't know how to make him feel better and it's eating me up inside.

"Can we watch something together?" I ask.

Smooth, Crystal. Really smooth.

I'm pathetic. If I was Eleanor, we wouldn't have gotten as far as the cottage without talking things out. *But what if I ask him what's wrong, and he gets angry and ends our friendship?* His eyes search my face. I just need to ask him, but all my courage is swallowed up by fear. He finally gives me a small smile and nods.

Once we are inside, we both switch into sweats and meet at the couch. I sit on one end, and he sits on the other. I'm hyper-aware of how close he is. I curl up, hugging my knees, needing to feel safe. He has an arm around the back of the couch, his fingertips barely brushing my shoulders.

How am I supposed to concentrate on the show when I can feel his warmth, and hear the soft rise and fall of his chest? I bite the inside of my cheek, willing my mind to focus on the anime show we are binging together.

"Hey," Cas said, softly. My head snaps towards him. His blue eyes look melancholy. "What you said back at lunch–"

"I'm sorry," I blurt, cutting him off. My body breaks out in a cold sweat. I hide my hands in my hoodie to hide my trembling. My heart is hammering in my chest. I cannot panic right now. I'd crossed the line and commented on his family's life, judging what I saw as an outsider. I take a quick breath, my fingernails digging into my palm.

His eyebrows furrowed and he adjusted in his seat to face me. His hand cupped my shoulder, and I flinch slightly.

"Why are you sorry?" he asked, pulling his hand away. My eyes water. I flinched. I wasn't supposed to flinch. I don't want him to pull away from me. I glance between him and the TV, feeling my stomach twist. *I fucked up.* I meddled and I was *not* a meddler. I was a peacekeeper.

And I'd flinched. I'd fucking flinched. "Crystal, talk to me," he said gently. I close my eyes, taking a deep breath, hoping to ease the attack that is brewing in me.

Cas is speaking softly, compelling me to open. His face is filled with confusion and concern which hurts me. *I'm not in trouble.* I am okay because he always allows me to speak my mind, but my fear of conflict still has me on edge.

"I overstepped with your family. I said things I shouldn't have said," I whisper. Cas shook his head, offering me his hand. I scoot closer to him, grabbing his hand and placing it on my cheek. His thumb brushes back and forth and the tension eases from my body.

"You did nothing wrong. You were trying to help, and you were very sweet when doing so," he said. My bottom lip wobbles. "Hey, you didn't need to be so worried," he said, pulling me in for a hug. I sigh. He smells like the ocean and pine; a scent I find comforting. I bury my face in his chest as his hand rubs my back.

Fury fuck, why did he have to feel so good?

"I was going to say thank you," he whispered. I pull back just enough to look him in the eye. I blink quickly. He shifted slightly in his seat, gently wiping a stray tear away from my face.

"Why?" I ask. Cas gives me a lazy grin, one that I'm starting to like since it makes his eyes sparkle.

"Because...growing up my brother was always...he was always just prepared, and he could handle everything. I never took the time to see that he had his own shit going on," he said. "I guess we all grew comfortable in our roles." I nod.

"Sometimes it's important to see what the other person is going through, to take a walk in their shoes...or fins?" I hesitate towards the end. Cas let out a chuckle at my pun, shaking his head.

"True and sometimes some of *us* have to be *shellfish*," he said, giving me a knowing look. "It's okay to do what you want, to want something." I roll my eyes at his pun, but a small grin still stretches across my face.

"We're okay right?" I ask, still feeling guilty. Cas leaned in and brushed his lips against my cheek.

"We're good. I promise," he said. He squeezed my hand twice and I squeezed it once. "You don't have to be afraid to speak up if you're upset or worried." I lay my head against his chest, letting his steady heartbeat soothe me.

"Okay," I agree.

We stay like that for a bit, wrapped in each other's arms as our show plays in the background. Cas shifts under me and a whimper escapes my lips. His hands wander from the middle of my back down to my hips and my eyes flutter close.

"I know what you're doing," I said, meeting his gaze. His smile had turned wicked, making my thighs squeeze together. *Wow, he looks gorgeous under me.*

"What's that?" he asked, blinking innocently. I press against him, enjoying the way it makes his cheeks flush. Grabbing the drawstrings of my hoodie he pulls me down until our noses touch. My eyes close as his lips trail towards my ear.

"Tomorrow, we have another welcome dinner," he said. I hum, getting excited. "There will be dancing, and who knows, maybe a kiss," he smirked.

"To show that we're dating," I said, reminding us of our agreement.

"Yep," he said, popping the *p* against my ear. I shiver, pressing my hips against his own. He breathes in sharply.

"We should kiss now," I said, pulling my head up. Cas grinned. I run my fingers through his soft blonde hair.

"What kind of kiss?" he teased. I glare at him, knowing he knows what I mean.

"You know what kind," I said, feeling slightly embarrassed.

"I want to hear you say it," he demanded. I bite the inside of my cheek. "You said not to treat you like you're fragile," he continued. His hands pull my face close until my lips hung just above his, our breaths mingling. My heart is threatening to leap out of my chest now that our bodies are pressing against each other. He feels amazing, so warm and hard.

"Tell me what you want to do to me, Crystal," he whispered. A smile stretches across my face at Cas' words. I'm used to being told what to do and denying my own desires. I'd become comfortable with that. But Cas lets me take the reins.

"I want to make out," I said, excitement coursing through me. Cas grinned, tilting his chin up.

"Alright then. The first step is to kiss me," he whispered. I lean forward, pressing our mouths together. Cas smiled against my mouth. His lips are soft and firm. When I pull back to look at him, his eyes are shining brightly.

"Not bad," he teased. I roll my eyes.

"It was fine for a first kiss," I said, trying to sound unaffected. But I wish I'd never moved away from his mouth. He raised an eyebrow and gripped my chin. He teases me with soft, quick kisses followed by firm ones where he nipped my bottom lip. I find myself pushing for more every time he pulls away.

"Now are you ready for the next step?" he asked, slightly out of breath. I nod; my gaze focused on his mouth. "I want you to do what feels right," he said, right before covering my mouth with his. His soft moan spurs me on. I copy him, teasing his bottom lip with my teeth as his hands move back to my waist, squeezing me, pulling me closer.

Cas opens his mouth, and I gently slipped my tongue in, tangling it with his. It's weird at first, feeling ourselves connect this way. Feeling his tongue against mine, his lips, teeth, hands all creating a symphony within me.

But the longer we go the more I crave. Cas groans when my hands find themselves in his silky blonde locks, pulling tightly. His hands squeeze my hips, and I need more. My core is clenching, my hips grinding into his, seeking more sweet, delicious friction.

I pull away, gasping for air. Cas' chest pants against mine. *This* was kissing? This is what I have been missing? I like kissing. I really like kissing. And I especially like kissing Cas.

By the stars.

I sit back, needing space. I squeeze my thighs together, my core aching for more. Cas sat up and maneuvered a pillow over his lap and I turn away flushing. I made him want me and I wanted him back.

How is this supposed to be fake when our connection feels so real?

CHAPTER 17
GUILTY

Caspian

"Do I have to go?" I complained. Tonight, we will be welcoming another royal family. My family was in the living room waiting for me. I'd had plans to go to a party with some friends from school until my dad had informed me of his plans.

"We have to go," my dutiful brother said. I rolled my eyes. Ronan was no fun. He just cared about following the rules. My dad placed a hand on my shoulder.

"It is our duty as the royal family to welcome the other family," my dad said, his tone serious. I groaned. All I did was go to school, attend lessons, and follow my uncle everywhere. I deserved to have a night off and let loose with my friends.

"But you don't need **me** there. All I do is stand around and smile. You have Ronan! He's great at acting like he shits gold," I said. I could feel my brother's glare on me.

"Caspian!" my mom snapped. My dad sighed and my shoulders dropped.

"I'm sorry Ronan," I mumbled. My brother grunted.

"Caspian. Everyone must be in attendance. We are the Calder

family, rulers of the Atlantic Ocean. We must show a united front and make sure our alliances are strong," my dad explained. I bit the inside of my cheek. I'd heard all this before. The families of the seven seas served the ocean and all its creatures.

But I just wanted a night where I wasn't bound by duty and family. I wanted a break. But royalty wasn't allowed a damn break.

"Kai will be there, you know," my mom pointed out. I sniffed. Kai was from one of the other royal families and was a friend of mine. If he was there, then maybe we could find a way to sneak out and have some fun.

"I'll be waiting outside," Ronan said, over his shoulder. My mom followed suit. I felt the weight of my father's stare on me.

"I know you'd rather be at the party," he said. I opened my mouth to speak, and he waved his hand. "I was young once too, you know. I was not always king," he said, giving me a knowing look. I bit the inside of my cheek. "After dinner, mingle for an hour and then take Kai with you," my dad said with a wink. I stared, mouth agape.

"But–" I began.

"Remember Caspian. Whether you're a prince, a king or anything else, you need to balance your responsibilities with living your life."

I DIDN'T ANTICIPATE that kissing Crystal would set off a tsunami of emotions in me. She was tentative at first, trying to figure out what felt good. Even though we stumbled into our first kiss we quickly fell into rhythm, her mouth leading mine in a dance.

It was magical. Her body is divine. She feels like she was made for me, her long legs tangled in mine, her hips perfectly aligned with my own. But I'm just her fake boyfriend. How am I supposed to make it through her list if she turns me into a damn puddle with just a kiss?

I finish buttoning my shirt, staring at myself in the mirror. Tonight, we have another royal dinner. This time we are welcoming the O'Briens from the Irish shore. I sigh.

I didn't want to go to this dinner and engage in fake pleasantries, wine, and dancing. I hated them when I was younger and that hasn't changed as I've grown up. I want to stay home with Crystal. I'm beginning to enjoy our quiet moments together. I crave the peace I feel when it's just her and I. But maybe going to an event like this with her will make it tolerable.

There is a swift knock at my door. *Barnacle, it's time for us to head out.*

When I open the door, my heart stops. Crystal's dark hair is down in soft waves, and she has on a deep blue velvet dress that highlights the dips and curves of her body. I swallow. I'm going to have to fight every damn being at this dinner tonight.

Her eyes trail up and down my body, drinking me in and making my cock twitch. Crystal and I are friends, close friends, but it is undeniable that we are attracted to each other. Especially now that her cheeks are turning the prettiest shade of pink as she watches me.

"You look stunning," I said. She tucks a strand of hair behind her ear, her eyes darting away from mine.

"You look very handsome," she said. She offers me her hand. "Shall we?" she asked softly. I lead her towards the front door, looking back to marvel at my pixie. *She's not really yours,* my brain chastised me.

"After you M'Lady."

Locking the door behind me I reach for her hand. I lace our fingers together, the restlessness in my body easing. I open the car door for her, and she slipped in. We could walk, but I wouldn't subject her to walking in heels.

The drive is silent, and I couldn't stop tapping on the steering wheel. I'm not sure what was wrong with me but the closer we get the more anxious I become.

The royal families will all be there along with folks around town. The welcome dinners are always open to the public. We take a strong stance in Coralia Coast that we are all equal and should be treated as such, so every being in town, local or not, was always welcomed to join in on royal festivities.

"Are you okay?" Crystal's voice cuts through my thoughts. I quickly glance at her as the dining hall came into view.

"I'm anxious," I said. "But I don't know why." She hummed sitting back in her seat. Her fingers pry one of my hands off the steering wheel and she threads her fingers in mine. My body relaxes in the seat.

"Maybe because you ran away and now you have to face everyone again. Everyone has been welcoming and that makes you nervous," she said gently. I sigh. Of course it makes me nervous. I'd fucked up... royally, no pun intended. I came home to a mess that I could have stopped months ago or at least slowed down.

"I feel guilty," I admit. "I left and now there's so much shit going wrong. Maybe if I'd never left, we wouldn't need to find some mystical trident to save the town," I said, my tone annoyed. It's *my* fault. If I hadn't been such shrimp shit and just taken my place the coral might never have been at risk.

All I need to do is to solidify my position as second in command and wear my uncle's crown. My stomach twists. But I can never replace my uncle. I can't be half the siren my dad or uncle were.

Crystal stays quiet for a moment as my guilt and pain fester.

"Maybe that is true and maybe it isn't, but don't you think your time away from Coralia shaped you in some way?" she asked. Beings were walking into the dining hall as I pulled into a parking space.

"My time away was just me goofing off," I said with a bitter taste in my mouth. Crystal leaned forward, catching my eye.

"In your time away, you helped put on three major events to foster a stronger community in Lavender Falls– something you can easily do here. You witnessed different beings coexisting and working together, especially during the festivals. Your carpentry skills are out of this world from working with Celestino," she began listing off. My throat tightens; a bubble of emotion caught in my chest.

"Each interaction and connection you made in Lavender Falls, whether big or small, helped you to be who you are today. These traits and skills can easily help Coralia Coast too," she continued. She shifts, reaching for both of my hands this time. I meet her gaze and my heart swells at her trust and belief in me.

"The reason I wanted this job, Cas, was because of the way your brother spoke about your town. I can tell that everyone here matters to him. All he wants is to bring what we have in Lavender Falls, here. I know you want that too, and you *can do it*," she said, her smile warming every inch of me.

"And with your help we will," I said, kissing her cheek.

THE DINNER IS in full swing by the time we make it in. I do my best to stay by Crystal's side. I need to meet with other royals to secure their friendships and all that formal stuff, but I don't need any of them getting their fins, claws or hands on my girlfriend.

My fake girlfriend. I remind myself. I bite back a sigh.

That kiss…I can't stop thinking about it. All I want to do right now is steal Crystal into some closet and glide my hands up her dress. I glance over at her.

She is talking to someone from a supernatural town on the west coast. She is in business mode, with a slight squint in her eyes and a pleasant smile. She is calculating, and it is a *very* hot look on her. I know she wants to expand Hale's Lumber and being here with me is a great networking opportunity.

From the corner of my eye, I can see Tati and the other princesses hanging around, watching us. Tati glances at me and her wink gives me shivers.

My mom is speaking to Kai's mom, and he is somewhere around here. I wanted to talk to him about the coral. I'm hoping we can dive down and look at it together one of these days.

"Are you ready for the ceremony?" someone asked. I turn to see an older siren with salt and pepper hair and steady green eyes. I plaster on my fake smile. I don't recognize who this being is, but I need to be cordial Which meant pretending that I'm excited about the ceremony.

"Of course. I've been training for it my whole life," I said. I see my brother walk across the room from the corner of my eye. I will be his second in command, his shadow. I already feel like it, as his younger brother.

Ronan has always been mature and responsible; he has a presence that commands attention and authority. *Or did my brother just assume that role because he was left with no choice?*

"We are all happy you're back, Prince Caspian," the siren said. I look back at the older being. My heart drops as recognition dawns on me. He is one of the fishermen that patrolled our waters and operated one of Coralia Coast's trawlers.

My stomach tightens and guilt washes over me. He is a part of the town, a being that I'm supposed to protect and serve. One who I should have immediately recognized.

"I'm sorry that I–" He waved his hand, cutting me off.

"We understand Prince Caspian. You didn't have a chance to experience life. You never truly have," he said. My throat tightens. His green eyes sparkle with understanding.

"Neither has my brother," I murmur. The old siren lets out a chuckle.

"True, but your brother is different. He hangs out with us, helps us. He's a king who walks with us beings as just another being," he said, patting my shoulder. I stare at him in surprise.

"Once in a while he likes to join us on the boats. He was horrible at first, getting seasick," the siren said. He lets out a rough chuckle. "A siren seasick on a boat." I share in his laughter. "Life can be difficult and it's easy to get swept away by its undertow. We've all experienced moments of swimming away from responsibility," he commented. "You're here. You're helping now and that's all that matters," he said. I nod, tears pricking my eyes.

"One step at a time," he assured me, patting my arm. I watch him walk towards Ronan. My brother offered the siren a small grin, shaking his hand. I guess there are some things I still need to learn about with my brother.

There is a tug at my hand, and I turn to see Crystal with a hesitant grin. Her glass is empty. I lead us back to our table quietly as the beings around us mingled. When we sit down, I wave one of our servers over for another glass. Crystal smiles, her cheeks turning pink.

"Thank you," she said softly. Her eyes flickered across the room as she sat back in her seat. I smile. It's obvious she prefers being where she is now, watching the others.

Her shoulders have dropped slightly, a sign of how tired she is from talking that much and maintaining her image. I felt that way in the beginning too, and then at some point I got used to wearing my small talk mask. But now I have a hard time understanding where the mask ends and I begin.

"If we didn't have this arrangement, you could be with them," she said as she leaned in, bringing her soft citrus scent with her. She motioned to the princesses who were gossiping. I raise an eyebrow. *Why would I be with them?*

"If we didn't have this arrangement I would still be here, sitting with you," I said, looking at her. Her cheeks flush again, her calm facade faltering for a quick second before she nods. My stomach tightens. Crystal is great at hiding from everyone else, but she can't hide from me. She doesn't believe me when I say I would be here with her. I would. Her mouth keeps twitching, clearly holding something back.

"Say it," I demand lightly. She sighs, not putting up much of a fight. I wonder if it is the wine that makes her drop her guard faster.

"I was going to say how they would be more fun than me, to which you would respond with something sweet and then it might seem like I was fishing for compliments," she said, pausing before covering her mouth to keep her giggles at bay. I chuckle which allowed her to safely join in. Her and those damn fish puns.

I grab her chair, pulling her close enough that our shoulders brush. I tilt her chin up, forcing her to meet my gaze. Her hazel eyes widen in surprise.

"A moment with you is much greater than any conversation I could have with anyone else. Even the king," I said, enjoying the tiny sound that escaped her sweet lips. She rolled her pretty eyes at me which only makes me want to kiss her more.

"Your brother is the king," she pointed out, eyes narrowing.

"He's my brother first and king second," I said. There is a light tap to the back of my head.

"Yeah, don't forget it," Ronan said as he glided past us. Crystal giggled again and my heart soars. She is the sweetest being in the world. She is selfless and funny. Occasionally stubborn and brilliant.

And yet I'm just a selfish liar. I roped Crystal into being my fake girlfriend under the guise of helping her with her list, but I'm interested in her as more than a friend. I don't deserve her trust. She pushed a glass into my chest.

"I see you thinking. Less thinking and more enjoying," she said sheepishly.

"I'm sorry you have to be here with me in this predicament," I said. She shook her head, before taking a sip. Her eyes followed the beings around us.

"I chose this. I understood what it meant when we made-" she leaned in to quietly whisper "-our agreement." She looked at me, her eyes softening.

"This agreement feels-"

"Let's enjoy it," she said, cutting me off. I raise an eyebrow, not expecting that answer. *Was she feeling the same confusing feelings as me?* "Let's enjoy what we're doing and if it gets to be too much, we'll say something."

I nodded wordlessly.

Enjoy. I can do that.

IT'S ALMOST time for Crystal and me to make an escape when she tugs at my hand. She had stepped away for a moment and now that she is back her eyes are filled with annoyance. I pull her closer, wrapping an arm around her waist. I catch my mother's eyes, which soften as she looks at us.

"What's wrong?" I ask, dipping down to brush a kiss across her cheek. Her lips twist into a frown and her nostrils flare. Her cheeks and neck are red and splotchy. My heart races and a song threatens to pour from my lips. A song that deep in my bones I know will have the beings here on their knees. My stomach twists.

Never in my life have I ever used my siren song in *that* way. I rarely ever used it, except for that one time in middle school where I had snapped at someone who made fun of Mira. I made a boy shove his ice cream cone in his face. Ronan wasn't happy that I did that. My hands tighten against her body, wanting to control my power.

"Some of the princesses were in the bathroom and they were talking shit," she whispered. "They said Coralia is just a washed-up town," she continued, eyes glowing. I stare at her.

While I understand that Crystal is expressing her annoyance over gossiping mermaids, her defense of my town fills me with pride. She cares so much about my home.

"They–," she paused for a second. I glance over her shoulder at the group that just entered the room, most likely the royals she was referring to. Some of them were local mermaids I recognized. Every town has a group of gossiping selfish beings. Some of the others were from different royal families, Tati included.

"As your friend and boy–*fake* boyfriend, I need to know who," I said, catching myself at the last moment. She sighed, clearly conflicted over telling me whatever happened. "Crystal, you know you can always talk to me," I assure her. She takes a deep breath, nodding.

"They couldn't believe you were dating me," she said quietly. Her fingers dug into my dress shirt, and I bite my tongue, fuming. "They said that I'm just a plain pixie," she said. Her bottom lip wobbles and anger rushes through me. Plain? Crystal? What the fuck.

Fury fuck.

I crushed Crystal to my chest, cradling the back of her head as my gaze burns holes into the floor. My magic courses rapidly through my body. I dig my teeth into my tongue. Never have I felt such an urge to retaliate. My heart is bouncing out of my chest and my scales are reappearing on my hands. I shut my eyes and will myself to calm down.

Coralia Coast is a peaceful town, and we were peaceful. I can't let my emotions take over me. Crystal wouldn't want revenge. Not like this. She didn't like hurting beings. It doesn't matter that I want them on their knees before Crystal, apologizing. The beast within me, the side of me that was a sea creature, craves it.

"They're wrong," I whisper in her ear. Her arms wrap around my waist. "You are anything *but* plain. Your eyes are like sunflowers. Your hair is like the softest silk," I said, sinking my hand into her hair. She leans her head back into my touch. I lick my lips. "Your beauty's reach is beyond the stars," I said earnestly. Her eyes glisten with tears. "You may be quiet Crystal, but your mere presence causes everyone to turn and stop in awe."

"You have a way with words," she said, her arms coming to wrap around my neck.

"I only speak the truth," I said firmly. Her eyes falter for a second.

"*Are* you speaking the truth? Or just saying all of this because of all the eyes on us?" she asked. Music plays and I sway us in a gentle rhythm.

"I would have said these things in Lavender Falls, but I had a feeling you would have looked at me like I was crazy," I said. A beautiful melody pours out of Crystal. *Laughter.* Fuck, did I enjoy making her laugh.

"So, are you saying I'm too good for you?" she asked, raising an eyebrow. I nod. "Fish brain," she muttered, shaking her head.

"Already using our safe word?" I tease. Her fingers played with the ends of my hair.

"How can you believe that while being my…fake boyfriend?" She whispered the last part. I don't want to tell her the truth. That if she'd said no, I would have dropped the whole thing. She was the only one I wanted to *'fake'* this with.

"Because it's you, and when you mentioned what you wanted, well, I wanted to be the one to fulfill them," I said. She seemed to consider this with the furrow of her brow and slight pout of her bottom lip. She took a step closer, her chest brushing against mine.

"The truth is I only ever consider you for this," she confessed. My heart swells with false hope that there can be something more between us. I hear faint whispers around us.

"Do you want to prove them wrong?" I whisper in her ear. She shivers against me before pulling away slightly to look up at me. Her eyes flicker to my lips and I give her a small nod.

"I want them to see just how badly you own me," I said.

She did her best to hold back a smirk. "I like how that sounds," she said, brushing her lips against mine. Her nails dig into my neck, and I take it as a sign to yank her closer. My hands slide down her back, stopping at her waist.

Crystal makes me crave her smile, makes me yearn to feel her skin against mine. She makes me want to be exactly who she needs. And at this moment, she needs me to wash away the hurt they'd left behind. To show them that she is mine.

I cup the back of her head and pull her close. It is as if every heartache I have endured, every misstep I'd taken has led me to her and this moment. Even if it is fake, I'm pouring everything I have into this kiss. Our lips dance to a melody only our hearts can hear, and I want it to keep playing it until everyone recognizes our song. Until they recognize that what we are is real.

When we pull apart, I can't help but lick my lips. She tastes like the berry wine we'd shared. She took a moment to catch her breath, and I smile. For someone who'd hardly kissed, she is a quick learner.

"*You're* too good for *me*," she whispered. I chuckle, pressing my forehead against hers. Crystal glanced to the side and waved at my mom, who is smiling at us.

"How about we head home?" I suggest. She nodded and slipped her hand in mine, tugging me towards the door. She didn't correct me or suggest that it was 'my' home.

It was *ours*.

CHAPTER 18
SNAP

Crystal

Lately I have been having headaches. I know it's because of the combination of stress, lack of sleep, and changes at work outside of my control. But today my headache is worse.

There is a dull ache in the back of my head that is beginning to pulse. I squeeze my eyes shut. *Maybe it was the sweet wine from last night.* I usually didn't drink sweet wines because occasionally it can cause me a headache or worse. I must be mindful of what I drink.

I rub my face. Today I have to check on both cottages and I have a meeting with my dad. We are about two weeks behind on the cottage renovations. I had hoped to have everything done or close to finished by the end of the summer. Even though I go into every project aware that things will never go exactly as planned, I still have hope.

My hands are absentmindedly brushing my lips, my thoughts drifting back to that very public kiss Cas and I had shared. I swallow. It was a good kiss. A great kiss. I like kissing him. I need to remind myself that this is all for show. Our feelings are fake, and we are just two friends helping each other out. The princesses weren't pestering Cas as much lately and I was getting the experience I craved.

My thoughts drift to our conversation. I had no idea Cas could be poetic, that his words could leave me a mess on the dance floor. His words were like honey, sweet and made my heart melt. *How could he believe that I was too good for him?* I didn't know what I was doing and yet Cas walked through life with his shoulders back and head held high. He thought my presence commanded attention when everyone faced him like he was the sun.

As I continue my walk to work, I think of those mermaids in the bathroom. Truly it was a scene out of a movie. Me, in the stall listening to them bitch. They complained about how we were a–how *Coralia Coast* is a ghost town and that they couldn't believe Cas and his family ruled the Atlantic Ocean. Then they talked about me.

My heart sank during those few minutes. I never cared about what people thought of me, but then again, I spent my life in people's shadows. People who didn't think about me at all. This was the first time that anyone had thought of me as less than. Plain.

I grew up constantly comparing myself to my sister. After she left, I reconciled with the fact that we were different. She was shorter and curvier, with a smirk that brought beings to their knees. I was quiet and more reserved.

Hearing those mermaids say how boring I was and how I didn't belong with a prince, it brought all those insecurities back. I spent years pushing past this, and with one sentence they'd made me feel 13 again.

I'd walked into that dinner feeling beautiful. I wore a dress that made me feel empowered and I was with Cas who smiled at me like I was the only pearl in the ocean. And after those five minutes I felt crushed.

If I was more like Eleanor, I would have stomped out the stall and put them in their place, but I froze instead and waited for them to leave.

Then I told Cas. I hadn't planned on telling him what they'd said about me. It felt selfish to, but then again, I trusted him. I told him because I knew he would help ease my pain. And he did. A tiny part of me hated that I relied on him for that. But he erased their tainted words with every brush against my skin and in the tender touch of his kiss.

That kiss, my stars. That damn kiss made my toes curl. I literally heard some beings gasp around us. It filled me with joy and left me longing.

I PAUSED in front of the cottage we are working on; a patch of wilting flowers catches my eye. Crouching to my feet I notice it was a bunch of daisies. Its petals are wrinkly, and its leaves are slowly turning yellow and brown. I don't always use my magic, but there is something about this tiny little flower in a sea of grass that catches my gaze.

I can see my crew coming in and out of the cottage. My hands prick like I'm being stabbed by pins and needles. It has been a while since I've used my magic. I take a deep breath, centering myself into the warm feeling that flows through my body as I harness extra energy.

I tighten my hand into a fist, holding it above the flower. I concentrate on centering its heat towards the center of my hand. Unlike witches, I typically don't need to do a spell. This is simple magic.

Through my connection to the Earth, I can use my magic to muster up some pixie dust. I pull from within myself and from the energy of the land around me. Pixie dust is a physical concentration of pixie's magic. The wielder can use the concentration on whatever they need.

When I unfurl my fist, gold dust rains down onto it. Slowly the tiny daisy straightens, its petals glow and begin regaining color. I smile. The daisy's leaf wiggles ever so slightly as I nod my head.

Earth is made of living beings, and while most humans refuse to understand, nature is alive. The trees have their own language via the rustling of their leaves and the creaks in their branches. Flowers giggle when the breeze sweeps up their pollen. We live in such a beautiful world, if only others could open their eyes to the magic.

"Ms. Hale...uh, we need you!" Connor shouted. I wave goodbye to the flower.

I'M SITTING outside the second cottage where wood is being taken away from a leak. It is slowly rotting. It turns out the leak had been going on much longer than we had thought. I watch as the pile of wood grows bigger and bigger, my anxiety growing with it.

I stretch my neck, feeling a dull ache around the edges of my skull. This isn't good. *But it'll be fine*, I keep reminding myself. For some reason no matter how many times I try convincing my brain to relax, my body won't listen. I can feel the energy in my body slowly slipping away from me.

My phone rings and I squint at its frequency. I close my eyes briefly, knowing it is my dad.

"Hello dad," I said, trying to mask the exhaustion in my voice. I can hear him tapping away on the computer.

"Just wanted to let you know that Lavender Falls received another shipment of wood, and Celestino says the Saturday workshops are doing well," my dad said. I smile. I usually take over for that side of our company. I'm the one who had suggested hosting workshops across different towns on the East Coast as a way to be a part of the community and build our presence.

Because my dad insisted that I focus solely on Coralia Coast, he decided he needed to spend time reconnecting with the original values of his company. I can't lie I feel a bit jealous. The workshops were *my* project. It was the first thing my dad allowed me to do without much of his oversight.

"I'm happy to hear that," I said, my eyes still on the pile of wood. "I'm going to send you another load of wood," I said. He stopped typing and it made my stomach twist. Even though the pause is probably only for a second it feels like an eternity.

"About your shipment," he began. My stomach sinks. "We need extra time. A lot of wood from the first batch didn't survive the purification process." I wince.

There is always a risk of that happening. Sometimes no matter how much you try, the wood is beyond saving

"Understandable. You just send it when you can. The stage was our number one priority. Please prioritize this order when you get the next batch," I said. It is stupid of me to assume that this project will go according to plan, but one can dream, can't they? The pain in my head pulses again. I rub my eyes.

"Have you've spoken to your sister?" he asked. I sit up straighter, my heart sinking. Did something happen?

"No, why?" I ask.

"Just wondering. How are you?" my dad asked. I bite the inside of my cheek. *Do I tell him I'm exhausted? That his relationship with Eleanor stresses me out?* I can't. He is stressed enough as it is.

"I'm doing fine," I said, the lie rolling off my tongue with ease.

I'm not.

I'M FINALLY BACK in the cottage when my headache starts becoming intense. Ronan had texted me to follow up on our meeting, but I had to cancel. I couldn't. I wouldn't be able to handle the sunlight or all the noise.

I immediately change into sweats. I walk around the house closing all the curtains, the light making me squint. This isn't good. My head is killing me, and my teeth ache too. My phone rings again and I jump, clasping my hands over my ears.

Eleanor

What is up with them calling me on the same day? I want to ignore it. I want to shoot her a text saying I'm busy. But if I did that, she would just bother me later and ask if I'm okay. I want to be left alone which means I need to get this over with.

"Hey," I said, trying my best to sound cheery.

"Hey Crys," she said. Her bright tone is like a laser shooting through my skull. I grit my teeth, placing her on speaker phone and moving my phone slightly further away from me. This isn't a normal headache. Instead, the pain I'd had for a few days was forming a migraine. *Fuck*. I should have paid closer attention and try to stop it earlier.

"What's up?" I ask. What I really want to do was ask what she wanted.

"I just wanted to check in on you...and you know...your boyfriend," she said. I cringe. She doesn't know Cas isn't really my boyfriend. She has no idea the lie we'd agreed to. I swallow, the guilt returning.

"Um...good?" I said, unsure what she is suggesting.

"*Just* good?" she asked, fishing for information. My eye twitches.

"What's wrong with good?" I ask. What does she want me to say? Does she want me to talk about how caring and attentive he wis? How he always makes me feel warm and fuzzy? That I'm not afraid to speak my mind around him and he doesn't make me feel weak?

"You're staying at his place, right?" she asked. I blush.

"Yes," I said, firmly. Her questions annoy me.

"How's that going?" she asked in a suggestive tone. I place a hand on my eyes, using the pressure to ease the pain that is building in my head.

"Fine?" I said. She sighed dramatically. She's really getting on my nerves. "Eleanor, we stay in separate rooms. I'm working and so is he. I don't know what you want me to say," I said, my patience waning.

"Hey, no need to get defensive. I'm just looking out for you," she said, her temper rising. Eleanor always had a short fuse. I was the calm and collected one but right now I was a rubber band threatening to snap.

"I don't get why you're calling or what you're trying to insinuate," I said. She scoffed.

"Can't a girl just call her sister?" she asked. My bottom lip trembles as my eyes snap open. My hand reaches out to clutch my pillow as a pile of words bubble up within of me.

I bite my tongue. I can't. It will hurt her, which will hurt me.

"This project has been stressful, and I just got off the phone with dad a bit ago," I decide to say.

"Oof, what did that man want?" she asked. I grind my teeth. She has a problem with him. He hurt her in the past which makes her response valid. She doesn't know how much he wants to rebuild their relationship. She can't see that he's trying. And he *was* trying, wasn't he?

"He wanted to see how the project was going because he knows we've run into a few problems," I begin. "He also wanted to make sure that I was okay," I add in the hopes that she can see that he cares. I wince, knowing I shouldn't be trying to manipulate a decent relationship between them. She grunted. My eyes water.

I feel like a kid again, caught between my dad and my sister just trying to be their bridge. But the bridge is breaking. I'm breaking in half trying to hold them together.

"Have you've tried talking to him?" I ask, remembering my conversation with my dad. There is a pause.

"Yeah, but I've been busy," she said, quietly. My nostrils flare and I begin rubbing my head. Here she is, too busy to build their relationship and I was breaking my back for both without them knowing.

"You know what? I know you don't see it and I know he's hurt you Eleanor, but he *is* trying," I chastise, my temper flaring.

"Crys please—"

"I know. Okay? *I know*. I was in the other room for all your yelling matches. But what you don't know is that every time you ran out, he wouldn't eat the rest of the day. You never heard the way he would pace back and forth in his bedroom until you walked back in the door."

Fuck it.

"I get that he hurt you and that during those eight years either of you could have reached out to the other. I could have reached out," I said, my hands trembling. I worked tirelessly to keep all these thoughts locked up but I'm breaking, and I can't hold them back anymore. "But I didn't want to, because I was tired of having to be the middleman between you two," I said, breathing heavily. That is the truth. Those eight years I was at peace because I wasn't bouncing between them.

I close my eyes, a wave of pain smacking me. I don't care. I don't care anymore. I just need all this pain to stop.

"I'm sorry if I don't share things with you the way you do with me. It's hard for me to handle you acting like a sister when I didn't *have* one for eight years." I slap a hand over my mouth while Eleanor remains quiet on the other line.

I fucked up. I said it. I've finally told the truth. My heart races in my chest as tears stream down my cheeks. I've said the one thing I swore to never say out loud. I didn't know how to act like her sister. I had gone so long without her that I'd become comfortable with not having one. And now with her back I didn't know what to do.

"Eleanor, I'm sorry. I-I'm just so tired," I said, my voice finally cracking. I need to somehow salvage our relationship. I have to fix this. She's only trying to be my sister and I've been ungrateful. There is a pause before she speaks again.

"I never stopped to consider your side, Crystal. I thought-I *didn't* think, actually. I'm sorry. Rest and reach out when you think it's the right time. I know you have a lot on your plate," she said quietly. My heart breaks, my face wet with tears. I finally have my sister back and I fucked everything up. I'm going to lose her again, and this time it's my fault.

But I'm just so tired of holding everything in.

I shove my phone off the bed and slide my head under my pillow, its coolness somewhat soothing me. I take deep breaths, needing the blinding pain to stop.

Some beings don't understand the pain of migraines. The way a simple footstep can feel like someone is stomping on your head. The way light blinds you and makes you feel dizzy. The nausea that's so debilitating that you wind up passed out on the floor with an empty stomach. Your heart sometimes beats so fast from the pain it feels like you're having a heart attack.

And the next day you're a shell of a being. Your brain is covered in a thick fog, while your stomach is screaming for nourishment even though it still can't keep much down. The people around you open their mouths and say words that you can't seem to piece together.

I spent years figuring out my triggers. Period, food, stress, all the above. And sometimes no matter how well I take care of myself, how careful I am, the migraines will attack. The headaches I've had these past few days were a warning.

And now that it's here I have no choice but to succumb to it.

MY HEAD IS GETTING STRUCK by lightning. The pain ricochets from my left side to my back, to my front. I can barely open my eyes. My stomach churns and I know I need to head into the bathroom. I don't want to puke. Puking is bad. If I start puking, I won't be able to stop.

I force myself from beneath my pillow and stumble into the bathroom. I keep the light off, not wanting the buzzing noise to crack my head open. I grip my head, finally cracking my eyes open to take a look at the state I'm in. My hair is slipping from its bun, my skin is pasty and I'm trembling. Tears well in my eyes again as I make my way to the floor.

Cas.

I feel the urge to call him. I want someone to hold me, to take this pain away. I squeeze my eyes shut. There was usually a magical tea that I'd typically drink but I'd left it in Lavender Falls. It was custom made for me.

My hands itch send a text to Cas. Since getting closer to him over these past few months I'm craving his nearness right now. I don't like that. I don't like that I need to hear his breathing, feel his heartbeat, and smell his familiar scent to be comforted.

I don't like that I rely on him to feel safe. I've spent my whole life taking care of myself and now it feels like I'm somehow cheating. I don't need Cas, or my dad, or Eleanor, to make me feel better.

And yet here I am, sitting on the bathroom floor, overstimulated and reduced to tears. Half of the tears are out of frustration over the past several weeks, and the other half are out of frustration from wanting *him–* and this fucking pain. *Stars*, the pain.

Instead of calling him I take deep breaths and stand up. I splash cold water on my face, ignoring the sight of the bags under my eyes and crawl into bed. I don't need anyone. I just need myself. Even if I feel broken right now.

CHAPTER 19
ROYAL BEST FRIENDS

Caspian

"Shit you weren't kidding," Kai said. I invited Kai to swim with me to check out the coral. Maybe there is something he can suggest after seeing the state it's been. My tail is an ombre of shades of blue, while Kai's is a vibrant ombre green.

When we were younger, we would race everywhere. I hate to admit it but he's a faster swimmer than me. I watch him swim near the coral, careful not to touch it. More of its color is fading and it is beginning to stretch towards the shore. We still have a few miles between "our spot" and the shoreline but it still makes me anxious, especially since I can feel the creatures in the ocean getting restless.

"What are the creatures saying?" Kai asked, looking at me from over my shoulders. I swear sometimes it was as if he could read my mind.

"I can't read your mind if that's what you're thinking. I saw you looking over at those stingrays," he said, pointing in the distance. I roll my eyes.

Speaking to sea creatures is a rare ability amongst sirens. I purposely kept my ability a secret. Kai knew about it because it's how

I'd saved him from getting his head bit off by a baby shark when we were kids. Kai has always had a thing for acting before thinking.

"They said that the coral rot is beginning to affect the ocean's food chain, starting with the plankton," I said, grimacing. Kai nodded, his brows furrowing. *This isn't good.*

"It'll start small. It's how any disease works. Whether it's physical or..." he trailed off. My mind flashed to humans and how easily seeds of doubt and selfishness are planted in them. Over the years that greed has hurt our waters.

"I don't think any one of us caused this," I said, swimming closer to him. *I mean, who would?* No siren wants to destroy the ocean. Kai shook his head.

"No, you're right. This doesn't feel like it was done on purpose. I can ask my auntie if she knows any remedies to slow it down. Maybe some of our ingredients can help," he offered. I sigh.

"Anything Kai," I plead. He patted my back.

"Us sirens have to have each other's back," he said, grinning. I smile, a warmth spreading throughout my chest. I didn't realize how much I'd missed our friendship; how much I'd missed being in the ocean with other sirens. I love my friends from Lavender Falls but there is something different about having friends who were royalty and sirens. I feel understood with Kai and Ricky.

"Put in a good word with Mira for me?" he said, smirking. I smack his arm.

"When are you going to give it a rest?" I ask. Him and my cousin have been going back and forth since we were kids. I'm surprised he still followed her like a lost guppy. She never gave him the time of day no matter how much he persisted. Kai shook his head.

"No can do. She's my song," he said, swimming above me. My heart stops. *His song?* I follow him until we both break through the ocean's surface. There is no one on the water today. The sun is high today, and a few seagulls are flying in the sky.

"Your song?" I ask. Kai's face flushed and he shrugged his shoulders.

"You know that thing that our people are always talking about? A siren's song, the mate one?" he said.

"Is it real?" I ask, my stomach twisting. I felt something like what Kai's describing when I'd first met Crystal, but I've hesitated. I've been out of touch with that part of my magic. And to be honest, it scares me. Mates are a serious thing. It means that your heart, your soul, and every cell in your body is tied to another's. Kai nodded.

"I've felt it since we were kids. There's this melody that plays in my head whenever she's near," he said.

"But I don't think Mira feels that way about you, at least, she's never told me that she does," I said. Mira and I are close. We told each other everything, even the things we didn't want to know about the other. I value that trust in my cousin. Kai swam in a circle around me.

"Oh, she does. I caught her humming our song when we were 16," he said, smirking. I stare in shock. Okay, maybe she didn't tell me everything. *Rude.*

"So, it's real," I said, following him. He cocked his head to the side, a curious gleam in his dark eyes.

"You feel it too? With Crystal?" he asked, eagerly. Is that what the melody I keep hearing in my head is? The melody calling me to her? I look near the shoreline and once again that feeling washes over me, a tug to go somewhere on land. *Is that calling me to her?*

But this feels different. It's deeper and warmer. I felt it once before and it vanished.

"I've had so many feelings since I've been back that it's hard to tell which one belongs to who or what," I said, softly. Kai placed a hand on my shoulder.

"Feelings and thoughts can lead to confusion and missteps. But our siren songs are a gift from the stars and the ocean," he said. "They always lead us to our true path."

"When did you get so wise? I'm the older one," I said.

"By like a month," he pointed out with a grin. "I sounded like my dad, didn't I?" he said, breaking into a laugh. This is the Kai I know. I splash water in his face.

"Dude, I hate you," I said. He shook his head.

"No, you don't. You love me. Everyone *does*," he teased.

"Everyone except Mira," I joke. He shrugged his shoulders.

"She'll come around," he said confidently, his eyes glancing back at the shoreline. The air shifts, heavy with his longing. For the first time I see my friend differently. He is like me. Beneath the charm and sunny smile there is someone seeking his own peace.

ONCE BACK ON shore Kai promised again that he would talk to his aunt before we went our separate ways. I'd planned to stop by Ronan's to grab some books when I saw him coming from the old meadery.

"Ronan!" I shouted, crossing the empty street. He looked me up and down, noticing my wet hair.

"Checking the coral?" he asked. I nod.

"Swam down with Kai. He's going to check with his aunt. Maybe she has some ideas to slow it down until...," I trail off.

"Until you find the trident," he said, finishing my sentence. I swallow. Everyone is so damn certain I can find it and yet it feels like I'm trying to grab onto sea breeze. Sure, I feel *something* when I was out in the water, but it's been confusing.

Am I feeling a call or am I just settling back into my powers? It's been so long since I've used any of them. I've been disconnected from myself for a long time– longer than I want to admit.

Talking to the creatures today has left me exhausted. My brain is working in overdrive to understand their languages. When I was younger this was easier. Our words flowed together so simply it was like breathing but now it feels like having to piece together broken sentences.

"You will," Ronan said, firmly. I shake my head.

"No one has seen the trident for hundreds of years. How can you be so sure?" I ask. Ronan looked to the side, where you could make out the ocean between the buildings.

"The ocean. She tells me," he said. I stare at him in disbelief. *Did I miss something in our lessons growing up?* I mean, I probably had since I was always trying to escape them.

"You talk to the water?" I ask. He rolled his eyes.

"I think you, of all beings, know that the ocean speaks to all of us. Some of us just don't listen," he said. "You get the same feelings, don't you?" he asked. I squirm under his gaze. I did. I just didn't know how to follow or interpret them.

"I'm getting something, I just...I don't know what to do with it," I said, feeling defeat. Ronan took a deep breath.

"Let your magic and the ocean lead you. Don't question it. Just follow it," he said. I glance at the ocean again. *Easier said than done.*

"When do you get so wise?" I said. He shoved my shoulder.

"I'm older," he pointed out.

"Just because you're older doesn't mean you're wiser. You still have a barnacle up your ass," I said, chuckling. He crossed his arms with a frown.

"I do not," he said, glowering.

"You're pouting like a guppy right now, I beg to differ," I joke. My grumpy brother glared at me. "Did you end up meeting with Crystal?" I ask, nodding towards the meadery. Ronan furrowed his brows.

"She cancelled," he said. I raise an eyebrow in surprise. *Crystal cancelled a meeting?*

"How come?" I ask. His lips twitched.

"She's your girlfriend, you tell me," he said, shrugging his shoulders. "Also, can you stop making out in public like that?" he asked. I flush, remembering the dinner. I like kissing Crystal, and I like doing it in public where everyone can see that she is mine. I clear my throat.

"One day dearest, older brother, some lucky lady is going to knock that perfect golden crown off your head," I chuckle. He rolled his eyes, sinking back to his usual silence.

"I don't have time for a love life," he glowered. I snort.

"Love is going to find you whether you want it to or not," I said.

My stomach is in knots as I step inside the cottage. Ronan said she'd canceled because she had a headache. But I know Crystal. A headache wouldn't keep her from working. So, something is up.

"Crystal?" I call out. The house is dead quiet and dark. She had drawn all the curtains closed. I bit the inside of my cheek. I tap on her door and hear a deep groan. My heart stops and the door creaks as I push it open. "Crystal what's wrong?" I ask. I freeze.

She was lying in the middle of her bed, curled up in a fetal position with a pillow over her head. Her whole body is tense.

"Crystal?" I ask, softer. She flinches and it guts me. I gingerly walk towards her, placing a hand on her calf. She flinches again.

Fuck. Fuck. Fuck.

She peeks from beneath her pillow, her face pale, and eyes swollen. This isn't good. This isn't a normal headache, and I have no idea what to do.

"I'm f-fine. Just leave," she croaked. The last thing I want to do is leave her here like this. She is in a lot of pain, and I want to ease it. She wiggled her leg, freeing herself from my grip. I step out quietly and walk towards the opposite side of the house. I pull out my phone.

ME

> Hey, Crystal has a migraine. What should I do?

ELLIE THE PIXIE PARTY QUEEN

> Oh no! Ugh I didn't know she gets them but maybe Lily will know what to do!

> Let me know if there's anything I can do or send!

Oh.

Now that I think about it, Eleanor and Crystal haven't spoken in eight years. *Of course,* there are things they don't know about each other. That's why she's been so understanding with Ronan. I rub a hand over my face. I'd left him the way Eleanor had left her. I close my eyes briefly. I need to focus on Crystal right now. I'll deal with my guilt about Ronan later.

> ME
> hey, Crystal has a migraine and Eleanor told me to text you

Lily-aye-aye

Oh no! Okay so everyone has different triggers. Mine is light and hers could be too. Or sound.

if she hasn't started puking that's a good sign. Once you start it's hard to stop. She'll need rest, fluids, and food–stick to bread. It'll help with her stomach. And ginger!

Let me know if you need anything!

> ME
> Thank you so much

I grimace. She had flinched at the sound of my voice, and the house was dark when I'd gotten here.

I take a breath. Food, fluid, quiet environment. I can do this. I quietly switch into sweats and then make my way to the kitchen, being extra careful when opening and closing cabinets. After a quick internet search, I learned that sometimes an ice pack can be helpful.

I place a cup of ginger tea, a bottle of electrolytes, a piece of bread and an ice pack wrapped in a towel on top of a tray. I carefully make my way to her room. This time I'm mindful when opening the door.

When I step in, she doesn't flinch, and I sigh inwardly with relief. I place the tray on the floor before situating everything on her nightstand. Crystal rolls over, slowly lifting herself up. She flinched this time, gripping her head. I lean towards her, stopping halfway. She looked at the nightstand and her eyes softened. Tears filled her eyes.

"For me?" she said, softly. Her face twisted in pain, and I couldn't stop myself. I wrap my arms around her, and she sunk into me. She pressed her face into the crook of my neck and her arms around my waist. I pull back to get a good look at her face. My fingers wander to her temples, and I trace gentle circles. She sighed.

I place a gentle kiss on her forehead before looking in her eyes. I motion to the table, and she nods. When I get up, she tugs at my hoodie. I look down at her. She has dark circles under her eyes, and her ponytail is skewed. She bit her bottom lip, her face tormented by whatever she is thinking.

"S-stay?" she asked. My chest swells. She needs me. She *wants* me. I grab the ice pack and crawl into bed with her. I pull her close to my side as she lays her head near my neck again. I didn't want her on my chest because the sound of my heartbeat might cause her pain. I held the ice pack to her head and once again felt her melt against me. Her hand clutched at my waist until she relaxed after a few minutes.

The last thing I remember is falling asleep in the arms of my friend, who is slowly becoming more.

CHAPTER 20
BRAIN FOG

Crystal

"Bye," Eleanor said, popping her head into my room. I put my fantasy book down and sat up.

"Where are you going?" I asked. Eleanor rolled her eyes.

"To a party," she said. I fight the urge to roll my eyes at her. She was always going off to parties and getting in trouble while I was bound to this house and watching over dad. Couldn't she stay home for one weekend?

"Dad–"

"Is locked away in his office and won't notice I'm gone," she huffed. She uncrossed her arms, and I could see her outfit now. She was in a short dress, her hair curled, and makeup done up. I gripped the sheet beneath my covers. She was probably going to hang out with some boy, something I never get to do.

"Did you–"

"Bye!" she called out with a wave, cutting me off. In the distance I heard the soft click of the front door. I tiptoed outside of my room. I could faintly hear the tapping of my dad's keyboard. He was clueless to Eleanor's departure. I made my way to the kitchen and grimaced.

"It was your turn to make dinner," I whispered into the empty room. The closer Eleanor was to graduating the more forgetful she was becoming. In the beginning when mom passed, she helped around the house. She'd cook meals and clean.

But college was looming over her, and she was pushing her boundaries more and more. She was closer to her freedom while I felt like a bird trapped in a cage that was slowly closing in on me.

Last night her and dad had a yelling match. She came home at 2AM with a hickey on her neck and dad had thrown a fit. I used my headphones to block out their words. It was up to me to make dinner... again. I sighed, grabbing the chicken I set out to defrost earlier.

I bit the inside of my cheek. I was tired. I didn't sleep well because of their yelling, and then Eleanor overslept so I made her breakfast after packing dad's lunch.

I'd nearly fallen asleep during my potion's exam. I was a ghost in my own house. No one thanked me for what I did. No one acknowledged that I made sure we always had fruit and toilet paper. Everyone in town assumed our home was all good. No one saw the cracks mom's passing left. My stomach growled as I began cooking.

"Where is Eleanor?" my dad asked, finally emerging from his office. I was halfway done with my plate.

"She went to see Lily," I lied. I pointed to the food on top of the oven. "She made dinner," I lied again

"Looks good. She did a good job," he said, fixing his plate. I swallowed a bite, the food losing its flavor. Eleanor would most likely get home late, but her "making dinner" would soften the blow.

And it did. Eleanor came up at 2AM. I knew because I was still awake, anxious that she would get yelled at again. But she didn't. She slipped inside. Dad stayed in bed. She ate some of my chicken. I came out for a glass of water even though I wasn't thirsty. I just wanted to see if she would acknowledge forgetting to cook dinner. She didn't.

"This chicken is good," she said, mid-chew. I nodded, feeling hollow inside.

"Dad made it after you left," I lied. The lies came easier as I grew older. I lied to my dad so he wouldn't be mad at Eleanor, and I lied to

Eleanor so she would hate our dad less. It was wrong of me. I knew it was. I shouldn't be the one trying to maintain their relationship, but I only had a few months until Eleanor goes off to college. I just need to survive until then.

Then the house would be quiet.

THERE IS something warm around me, like a blanket. I curl tighter, needing more warmth. My head is still hurting but it's more of a pulsing ache now. In a few more hours it will feel like a dull headache, and I will be in a foggy state. A strong arm pulls me closer.

My eyes slowly open to a dark room. There is a slow heartbeat at my back, a hand on my belly and a leg draped over my hip. I inhale sharply, my memories slowly resurfacing. I had asked Cas to stay. He'd made me tea and then we'd cuddled.

Oh no. I like this. I like this a lot.

Even though my heart wants me to stay, my bladder willed me to get up. I begrudgingly pulled myself away from his warm body. Cas stirred awake. "Crys," he murmured softly. I turn to face him, shoulders hunched. I looked like a zombie.

"Hi," I croak. He sat up, reaching for my hand.

"What do you need?" he asked, blinking away. My heart contracts and tears well in my eyes again. *What did I need?* I'm not sure how to respond. I'm so used to taking care of everyone that I have no idea how to let him help.

"Um, I need to pee," I said, my words slow. He nodded and let me go.

"Would you like another cup of tea?" he asked tentatively.

"Do you have chamomile or peppermint?"

"I have one of them," he said, tilting his head.

"One of those...please," I said. "If it's–"

He kissed my cheek, gently brushing his lips against me as his hand cupped the back of my head with soothing pressure. It makes me lose my words.

"Go and come back to bed. I'll bring you the tea," he whispered. Before I can protest, his lips brush against mine this time. Instead of freezing, my body relaxed into his touch. When he pulled back, he gave me a soft grin. "I'm your fake boyfriend. I'm allowed to take care of you," he said. I nod, too helpless to respond. He didn't need to kiss me, we were alone. But I didn't point that out.

I just wanted more. More kisses, more cuddles, more of him.

AFTER CRAWLING BACK INTO BED, I slid under the covers. Cas is taking care of me. I want to enjoy it. I keep telling myself that it's okay. It's okay for someone else to take care of me. But I can't help but feel guilty. He said he was just doing what a fake boyfriend would do. But he shouldn't feel like he must out of obligation.

I move the pillows so I can lean against the headboard comfortably. The door creaks softly and Cas walks in with two mugs. I can't hold back my smile.

He handed me my mug, and its heat relaxed me. I nod my thanks. Cas crawls under the covers, his side pressing into mine. My face flushes. I didn't think he would stay with me again. I took a tentative sip, my thoughts muddled in my head.

"Is it okay that I'm here?" he asked softly. I nod. Despite the guilt I feel, I like having him here with me. "Do you normally get migraines?" he asked. I stretch my neck, trying to loosen the tension I'm feeling.

"It's something I'm used to," I begin. "I got my first migraine when I was 19. I was really stressed over my exams and wasn't sleeping well. Then it became normal for me to get them. Migraines affect everyone differently, everyone has different triggers," I explain. He nodded.

"You'll notice I avoid red wine because that's a trigger. Food not so much, but if I'm stressed and I eat too much citrus that could trigger a migraine. I was getting headaches on and off the past week from the stress with work...," I trail off. His hands came up to my temples, rubbing in slow circles. I close my eyes briefly.

"Got it. Is there something you can take?" he asked. I nod.

"There's a tea blend I drink, infused with magic to help ease the pain. But I left it back in Lavender Falls. So, for now, regular tea and medicine will have to be enough," I said, staring at my tea. "I feel lucky. Humans don't have the same resources as we do. Some never find a medication that works for them, or they do and it's way too expensive." Cas smiled at me.

"You're adorable," he teased. "Maybe my aunt can brew you something," he suggested.

"Oh, I can get Priscilla to send her the blend," I said. He nodded, the pressure of his fingers easing me back towards sleep.

"I'll take care of it," he said. I lean against the headboard, frowning. I drink another sip, letting the warmth and methanol in the peppermint soothe me. I'm grateful. "Crystal?" he asked. I turn to him, my eyes trying to focus on his face. "What's wrong?"

"Wrong?" I question, trying to mask the uneasiness. There was more to this question, and it made my anxiety flare.

"I can see the wheels turning in your head. I know you're in pain, but your furrowed brows tell me there's more," he said. I take another sip of tea, nervous to speak. "You can tell me. I'm your friend," he urged. I'm embarrassed. I recognize that much in myself. I feel bad for needing him.

"I feel bad," I confess. His face twisted in confusion. "You don't have to take care of me just because you're my fake boyfriend," I said slowly. He placed his cup on the night table and then he reached for mine to do the same.

"Look at me," he said, gently. Taking a deep breath, I meet his gaze. His blue eyes were calm, serious. He took my hand, rubbing gentle circles over my palms now. "Yes, I'm your fake boyfriend but above all else I am your friend. I care about you. I'm doing these things because I *want* to," he assured me. I chew my lip; emotions lodged in my throat.

"Taking care of you makes me happy," he said, pressing his forehead against mine. Exhaustion is sweeping through me, making me feel sluggish. He pulled the covers up and tucked me into his side. I can't bring myself to fight him. With Caspian I follow easily. Sleep is slowly taking over.

"As long as you allow me to, I will always take care of you," he whispered, before pressing a kiss to my temple.

I blink the tears away as I stared at my ceiling in the dark. I can get used to this and I'm not sure if I was okay with that. I'm torn, part of me doesn't want his help and another part of me feels comforted and protected by it.

Since my mom passed away, I'd taken care of everyone around me. I'd neglected myself, my wants and needs. I'm used to it at this point. I don't know how to ask for help.

Cas' arms tighten around me. Maybe…while we fake dated, I could let go of this guilt and just bask in these moments. Maybe Cas can teach me one more thing, that it's okay to accept help. So that one day when someone comes along, I'll be ready.

The word *'someone'* left a sour taste in my mouth.

CHAPTER 21
SIREN ANATOMY

Crystal

"*Oi, minha Crystalina!*" *my mom's voice echoed through the house. My dad was in his office working and Eleanor was finishing her homework. I made my way to the kitchen, following the melody of my mom's humming.*

She had an apron wrapped around her, the one I've always seen her use. She said she'd gotten it when she lived in Portugal. My stomach growled as I recognized the smell in the kitchen. I came around her, eyeing the oven. The sauce was cooking on the stove, and she was cutting *salsichas*.

She looked down at me with her warm green eyes. Her dark hair that matched mine was braided back. She smiled, offering me a piece of *salsicha*.

"Is that what I think it is?" I asked, eyes wide. She simply winked and continued humming. I jumped excitedly. It was rare for my mom to cook *francesinha* since we were the only ones who liked it, and because it was a lot of work.

"*Queres aprehender?*" she asked, the Portuguese rolling off her tongue. I ran to grab a step stool from the closet and pushed it next to her.

"Yes please!" I said. She clicked her tongue, and I cleared my throat. "Sim vos favor," I said, switching languages. She smiled.

"Ta bém, minha Crystalina," she said.

I WOKE up the next day with no pain, though my brain is shrouded in a fog. Very normal after having a migraine. Ronan had texted me, saying to take the day off and that he would make sure things ran okay. I had told him I could come in.

> **MR. CALDER/KING RONAN**
>
> I told Cas to not let you out of his sight, so enjoy your day
>
> Seriously
>
> No work

I don't normally take days off. With the help of my magic, I'm always up and about, making sure I'm there for my crew. Then I got a text from Mr. Whitman assuring me that he will keep me updated.

I stretch my arms up. I've accepted the fact that I have a day to myself. I need to be okay in order to be the leader they deserve. After taking a quick shower, I make my way to the kitchen where I heard Cas moving around lightly.

The smell of coffee makes my stomach growl, and Cas turns around with a warm smile. He points to his head, afraid to speak.

"No pain just…foggy," I said, going straight to the coffee pot. "Caffeine occasionally helps with my headaches and migraines," I said. He nodded.

"That's good," he said, stirring a pot. "Today I am all yours," he said, his tone filled with excitement. He casts a glance at me, and I raise an eyebrow. "We have the day off. So, it's me and you *all* day," he said, and I fight back a laugh.

"You seem really happy about that," I point out, holding onto the coffee mugs. He nodded, turning the stove off.

"A whole day with Crystal? Sounds like the best day ever," he said. I blush. I've never had someone so excited to spend the day with me. It gives me sprites in my belly. His steps are light as I stare at the mugs in my hand and when I look up, he is over me, his hands caging me against the kitchen counter.

"Shall we cuddle on the couch? Binge some movies? Volume on low, of course," he said grinning. I swallow. He smells like the ocean and that eases me.

"You really like cuddling," I tease. He snorted and leaned closer, his warmth slowly radiating over my body.

"I do, and so do you," he said with a smirk. I roll my eyes. "Don't roll those pretty hazel eyes at me. There were plenty of times you pulled me closer," he said. My eyes widen.

"Well, you did too." We both had. I haven't slept as deeply as I did last night.

"I know," he grinned. "So, what shall the day entail M' Lady?" he asked. I take a sip of my coffee. *By the stars I'm grateful for this caffeinated nectar.*

"Binging stuff sounds nice. Um…do you think we could go to the spring later?" I ask. I have been itching to go back to the spring. It is warm, inviting, and peaceful. It makes me feel at peace, like Cas does. His smile widens and my heart swells. He truly is handsome. His hair is now a lighter shade of blonde from spending so much time out in the ocean, and his skin is golden.

"Want to see my scales, don't you?" he winked. I blush. I do that a lot around Cas. He makes my heart race, my face flush, and body heat. He eases my anxiety and stress. *But he is my friend.* We are just friends who are fake dating. He is helping me with my list, and I am helping his image. That is all.

I take a sip from my cup, averting my gaze and hand him his. Cas hums a melody, and a smile stretches across my face. It's the second time I've heard him humming this song and something about it makes me smile.

"FUCK THIS IS AMAZING," I said, moaning at the warmth of the water. Cas chuckles behind me. There is a quiet splash and then something smooth tickles the bottoms of my feet. I immediately kick, giggling. Cas resurfaces, his scales glitter in the sunlight. His skin has an almost iridescent glow when he is in his siren form. He is stunning. I can see the tattoo on his chest peeking above the surface.

He hands me the same seaweed, and I wrinkle my nose. "Eat up so we can go to our spot," he said.

Our spot. I smile at his words. To think that a place where he feels safe is becoming a place we can share fills me with joy.

I ate the seaweed, trying not to gag at the salty taste. We swim for a while until we rise to the surface of the underwater cave. With the sun still peeking from above, the water is warm. I notice a picnic basket resting and gasp.

"Wait, what is this?" I ask. Cas swims up beside me, reaching for the basket.

"A date," he said confidently.

"We get to have a date?" I ask. Instead of responding he grins at me, eyes sparkling. Opening the basket, he pulled out two sandwiches, two bags of chips, and some fruit. I rest my hand on the ledge, watching him set up. He even brought a towel to set the food on top of.

"How did you even get this here?" I ask. I look around. I didn't see an entrance anywhere besides underwater. Cas holds out a sandwich for me and I quickly pat my hands on the towel.

"Well, my dearest jewel, I have this thing called magic," he said sarcastically. I flick his slightly pointed ear. "Hey!" We share a laugh and for the first time this week I feel like I can breathe.

We ate in silence, occasionally swapping chips. The water gentle rocks, splashing across the rocks, making music. Birds fly overhead and the sun is bright. I glance at Cas, enjoying the way the sun illuminates the scales that curve up his cheekbone. I needed this and him.

"How does it feel?" I ask, motioning towards his tail. "Must feel good now that you've been transforming more often," I said. He flicked his tail.

"I forgot how much I missed this part of me," he confessed. I smile. There is beauty in watching someone fall in love with themselves again. He didn't transform in Lavender Falls. It must have been painful to go without transforming so long and then painful once he started.

After cleaning up, Caspian lifts himself out of the water. His tail is huge and a beautiful blue ombre that matches his eyes. My eyes trail his tail in awe, up his stomach, past the tattoo until I meet those mesmerizing eyes.

"Touch it," he said, softly. My eyes widen.

"Y-your tail?" I squeak. Caspian stretches his lips into a slow sultry grin, leaning down until our faces are inches away from each other. I'm still in the water, holding onto the ledge to stay afloat.

"Unless there's another part you're thinking of," he said, eyes twinkling. I shiver. *Wait. Does he–? Did he–?*

"How do sirens have sex?" I blurt. Cas threw his head back in laughter in a way that reminded me of when I'd asked if he had scales on his penis back in Lavender Falls. I wince at the memory and cover my face. "I-I'm so sorry. Sometimes I have thoughts and it's rude of me–"

Cas gripped my hand and pulled me closer. We are face to face and he is smiling at me. I bite my bottom lip to keep myself from saying other ridiculous things. How could I ask him that? It's rude and invasive. With his other hand he pulls at my bottom lip until it's free from my teeth's grip.

"I always want to know what's going on in your brain," he said, his thumb brushing against my bottom lip.

"I shouldn't have blurted it out like that," I mumble. Cas raises an eyebrow.

"Would whispering it be better?" he asked. I shake my head giggling.

"It's just an awkward thing to ask randomly."

"Do you want to know how we have sex in this form?" he asked. I hesitate for a moment.

"I am curious," I admit. His hand cups the side of my face, his thumb brushing my cheek. I'm relaxed once again. "I don't want to… you know, do it. I'm not opposed to, you know, doing it this way! Just like…today I'm too tired," I explain, nervously. Cas eases most of his tail into the water and scoots closer to the edge. He taps his lap.

"Want to sit on my lap?" he asked. I answered by reaching up. He slid his hands under my arms, lifting me up. My feet dip into the warm water and the width of his tail stretches my thighs further apart. I shiver. He's warm underneath me, his scales smooth. Cas takes a deep breath, the tips of ears flushing.

"Whales and dolphins have their penis hidden beneath a slit," he explained. He offers a slightly trembling hand, and I take it. He guides my hand down his stomach. His skin is smooth as he drags my hand down his body and then I hit scales.

I inhale sharply. Even his scales are smooth as I brush downward. He traced my fingers over where his cock would be in human form. Something pulses beneath the scales, and I gasp. I squeeze my thighs and Cas' eyes flutter close. I study his face, watching his cheeks slowly turn pink, his mouth slightly parted.

"For s-sirens it's the same," he said, through gritted teeth as he allowed me to be bolder with my strokes. He has a bulge now and I can make out the slit he is talking about. My heart races in my chest and my core throbs with need. I let out a whimper and Cas' eyes snap open. Cas feels amazing underneath me. I glance up at him. His eyes are hooded; pupils dilated with desire and his mouth hangs slightly open.

"Does that feel good?" I ask. The corner of his lips tilts up. I watch his face, adding pressure to my stroke and he trembles. Power swims through me. Cas, a gorgeous siren prince, is at my mercy. "I need words, Cas," I said, feeling bold. He cupped my cheek, his thumb brushing the underside of my bottom lip.

"Y-yes," he said as I continued to stroke him. His hand traces down my arm and over my hip, sending shivers down my body. Finally, his hand meets mine and my body ignites at how the feeling of us, together, makes him feel good. "Let's stop," he said. My brow furrow in confusion.

"I don't mind–" he stops me with a kiss. His lips are soft. His hand moves to cup my jaw, anchoring me in place as he sweeps his mouth lightly up to my ear. I lean forward, pressing my chest against his, and he welcomes my weight.

"When you make me come I want to make sure your body is completely up for it," he whispered. If he thinks that will stop my ache for him, he is wrong. "Next time. I promise," he said, kissing the side of my neck. I nod, helplessly.

"I enjoyed it by the way," I admit. I want him to know that what we just did is fine–better than fine. I liked it a lot. I lean my head against his shoulder, letting my body relax and my heart slow down. A familiar fog sweeps over me. He traces lines on my back until my head clears. "This was a nice date," I said, softly.

He hummed in agreement. "How's your head?" he asked. I pull back enough to look at him. His blonde hair has dried and is curling at the ends.

"No pain, just a little slow," I said, with a small smile. "Thank you for taking care of me," I said shyly. His arms squeezed around me, and I sighed.

"You don't have to thank me," he said with a pointed look. I roll my eyes.

"I feel like I have too," I confess.

"Why?" he asked, curiously. I tilt my head back to see where the sky is. A cloud passes over us, shrouding us in its shadow. I shiver as the cave cools. Cas pulls me closer to him, enveloping me in his warmth.

"I guess...because I'm so used to taking care of everyone else," I said. A familiar guilt begins bubbling up in my chest. I swallow. Cas tilted his head down, catching my eyes.

"Why the face?" he asked. I bite the inside of my cheek. Admitting that I'm used to taking care of others and therefore feeling bad for someone else doing the same leaves me feeling icky, like a burden. I know I shouldn't feel this way and yet my body does anyway. "Tell me, M'Lady," he urged.

I close my eyes and lean my head back on his shoulder, where I feel safe. "My mom died when I was ten. It was a car accident. I still remember hearing my dad crying in the hospital. Then Eleanor broke down. I was confused about what was happening. I just saw that my dad and my sister were crying," I said, feeling my throat constrict. His arms tighten around me.

"I don't remember crying that day. I thought since they were crying, they needed someone to be there for them. I think that's when it started," I said, tears welling in my eyes. Emotions I tried desperately to hide are coming up to the surface. Cas is quiet for a moment and I'm thankful for it.

"Will you let me take care of you?" Cas asked softly. I bite my lip, hesitating. *I deserve to be taken care of, don't I?*

"I think so," I answer honestly. Cas has a way of washing the guilt away and with him I think at some point I won't feel guilty anymore. Accepting help is easier with him at my side.

"Then wait here while I get more seaweed," he said, lifting me up. I groan.

"Really? More?" I ask, wrinkling my nose. His chuckle is music to my ears.

"If you want to meet my new friend, then yes."

He can talk to sea creatures. He can freaking talk to sea creatures! I stare, jaw dropping as we sink beneath the surface of the ocean. A gray seal swims circles around us. He is so adorable with his big black eyes.

"He says you're pretty," Cas translated. I blush.

"You're very kind Waldo," I said, grinning. A seal named Waldo! I can't believe I'm swimming in the ocean, breathing underwater, and meeting the marine critters. I look around, marveling at the colors and life around me. It's so peaceful and warm here. Cas' grip tightens in my hand.

"He also says he doesn't mind sharing our spot with you," Cas said with a smirk. My eyes widen and I fake a gasp.

"I thought it was ours," I said to Cas. Waldo shook his head.

"It belongs to each of us," Cas said, looking between us. I grin. It's amazing to watch Cas in this form. He comfortable out here in the ocean, gliding through the waves with his ease, communicating with creatures. He seemed to relax into who he is. Even if he doesn't believe in himself, he is meant to be here. I can see it.

"Let me show you the coral," he said. We swim together, Waldo by our side. I gasp. Half of the coral is vibrant shades of orange, violet, and green while the other side is dull and pale. A pain shoots through me. I swim to the floor, feeling the urge to connect to the coral.

"Crystal?" Cas asked, confused. I take a deep breath, centering myself. I dig one hand into the sand. I most likely won't be able to touch the coral but maybe if I connected with the seafloor I can help.

I close my eyes, pouring my magic into finding a connection. There is a dull ache which is most likely the sickness. I sense it from the seaweed that is growing. It's cold and grimy. My stomach twists. My body and my magic don't like this feeling. I'm at a loss for words. I try pushing my magic towards the coldness, but it doesn't do much, not even for the seaweed.

"I can feel the decay," I said, turning to look at Cas. His shoulders dropped.

"Corals are living creatures. I don't think your magic can do much," he said.

"But even with the seaweed, my magic only does a little," I said, in confusion. "I don't have enough power." He nods.

I knew my magic wouldn't work on the coral, but I figured it would on other things. For some reason I'm not enough. I swim up to him, wrapping him in my arms. Cas placed a kiss on my cheek and then my forehead, squeezing me tight. I sag into him.

I wish there was more I could do for him, something to ease his pain. Waldo wiggles his way between us, and I break into a fit of giggles.

"Waldo wants to race back to shore," he said. I look between them.

"Both of you would beat me easily," I said, pointing at them. Waldo shook his head back and forth and then bumped his nose against Cas' shoulder. Cas turns around, giving me his back. He looked over his shoulder at me with a smile.

"Hang onto me guppy," he teased.

"Won't that be exhausting?" I said. Cas' face drops immediately, and I fight back a laugh.

"My jewel, don't insult my strength in front of Waldo."

I latch onto his back, wrapping my arms around his waist and pressing my cheek onto the middle of his back. Cas reaches down to wrap my legs around his waist. I breathe in sharply, feeling his hands on my thighs.

"Hold on tight, M'Lady," he said, looking at Waldo. I didn't know a harbor seal could look competitive, but I'm learning a lot today.

"1…2…3!" Cas counted down before shooting us across the ocean. I squeal, feeling the rush of water zoom past us and hearing the power of Cas' tail cutting through the water. My heart races against my chest.

I squint my eyes, barely making out all the fish moving out of our way. I smile against Cas' back as his carefree laughter vibrates against me. I join with him.

Ever since we'd come to Coralia Coast Cas has been more anxious and stressed out. Maybe this day was something we'd both needed. I keep my eyes closed, enjoying Cas' warmth and the sound of the ocean. I didn't realize we were near the shore until he squeezed my thighs.

"W-who won," I said, clinging to him for stability. Cas swims us up until to the surface. We are a few feet away from the shore now, near our little spot on the beach that is separated by rocks. There are a few beings on the beach today. We aren't sure if they are humans or not, so we swim closer to the rocks to hide ourselves.

Waldo's head pops up. He pouts, or at least he looks like he was pouting. I stifle a giggle. He really is adorable.

"I won, of course," Cas said, smiling. I couldn't help but smile back. He is the only one I can trust with this part of myself. He has a magical way of filling my quiet space with color, sunshine, and sandy beaches. Waldo snorts in the water.

"You know I did!" Cas whined. Waldo splashed water at Cas, and I continued to laugh. His eyes sparkled with delight. Cas needed this.

"What do we do now?" I ask. He tilted his head up towards the sky before looking at me.

"Well, we have to go back to the spring. I need my clothes," he said. I blushed, remembering how he shoved me towards the spring so he could undress.

"R-right."

AFTER AN AFTERNOON IN THE WATER, I curled up on the couch with a cup of tea and a blanket. Cas sat down next to me, pulling me towards his body. I melt under his touch. He began humming the same tune as before while he flipped through the channels.

"I had fun today," I said, blowing into my cup. Cas squeezed my arm twice and leaned over. His lips tickle my ear, sending a flush through me.

"So did I," he whispered. He settled on a show, and we sat in silence while my brain replayed our time in the cave, when I'd opened up to him about my family. I hadn't spoken about my mom in years, and it felt good to talk to someone about her. My memories of her were fleeting but for some reason I'd felt like reminiscing today. I guess grief is like that sometimes.

Some days you hardly feel its shadow and other days it's wrapped around you so tight you can't breathe. But today? Today the shadow of my grief feels like a warm hug. I want to talk about my mom because talking about her helps me keep her alive.

"Cas?" I said. He turned to me like he always does, giving me his full attention.

"C-can I tell you something about my mom?" I ask, my voice quivering. I don't want to cry. I want to talk about her without crying.

But isn't the reason for my tears because I love her so much? He turned off the tv, shifting his body so we were facing each other. Then he took my cup and placed it on the table before holding my hands.

"Of course," he said, earnestly. My smile wobbles under his attention.

"I don't remember much like I said. Sometimes the memories are hazy and sometimes they are clear. I was thinking about how she would make this dish that I really liked," I said. And just like that a spark in my memory forms. My mom is humming in the kitchen as the smell of garlic, beer and tomatoes wafts throughout the house. *She was always humming something.*

"It's called *francesinha*. It's a Portuguese sandwich. It's messy but so delicious," I said, my mouth watering. The last time I'd had one my mom had made it for me. "It's a sandwich with bacon, *salsicha*, *linguiça,* steak and cheese. Everything is covered in this tomato-garlic-beer sauce, and you put a sunny-side up egg on top of it," I said, grinning.

"That sounds so good," he said. I squeezed Cas' hands once and he did the same twice. Excitement courses through and I jump to sit on my knees.

"Oh, it's so good! I think you would like it. You have it with French fries to soak up all the juices."

"It has to be fries because fries are the most perfect carb," he teased. I nod in agreement.

"Of course. I can never finish one by myself. Usually, my mom would help me eat it because my dad and Eleanor never liked it," I said, still grinning. "My mom taught me how to make it, but the memory is hazy," I said, my nose twitching. "I remember her getting annoyed because I would say the ingredients in English," I said, a giggle pouring out of me. Cas smiled, pulling me to his chest.

"Both the dish and her sound wonderful," he said against my head. I sighed, needing him to hold me as I reminisced.

"She would have loved you," I whisper. Cas' heartbeat picked up underneath the palm of my hand. She would have. My mom was a warm soul who always laughed. In a lot of ways, she was like him. She would be sad about Eleanor and my dad, but I think she would be happy that I found someone like Cas— a *friend* like him.

"Of course she would have. I'm great," he said, and a giggle pours out of me. I shift my head to look into his beautiful blue eyes. I can see flecks of green. He tucked a stray strand of hair behind my ear.

"That's why she would have loved you," I said. He raised an eyebrow.

"Because I'm cocky?" he asked. I shake my head, my hand moving to brush his cheek. He hums in joy.

"Because you make me laugh."

CHAPTER 22
THE SIREN SQUAD

Caspian

It was early Saturday morning. Today Ronan would be with Uncle Seward reviewing the migration patterns that would be passing through town soon. Which meant I was stuck with dad and probably another boring lesson.

There was a swift knock at my door, and I groaned, getting out of bed. When I opened the door, my dad stood before me in old jeans with paint stains and a raggedy college shirt. I raised an eyebrow in surprise. Typically, my dad was always dressed in slacks and a polo shirt.

"Throw on some old clothes and meet me in the garage," he said. I nodded wordlessly, following his order. When we met in the garage, he handed me a cup of coffee and a breakfast burrito. I noticed he'd pulled out a pile of wood and some of his tools.

I shivered as I took a sip. It was getting colder, which meant snowfall was quickly approaching. While I loved summers in Coralia Coast there was something special about cold mornings at the beach during the winter.

"Are we not doing a lesson today?" I asked. My dad pulled out an old notebook and shook his head.

"I want to make a new dresser for your mom. Think you can help me?" he asked. I stared at him in shock. When I was younger, he would make a lot of our furniture and toys. He, of course, made whatever my mom wanted him to.

"There's no books that need reading or treaties to learn about?" I asked. My dad let out a breathy laugh.

"That will always be there. Today's lesson is to remember it's important to take a break to do things that make you happy," he said.

"Building things makes you happy?" I asked, before taking a bite of my burrito. He smiled at me and for the first time in a while I saw my dad and not the king.

"Making something with my bare hands and watching people enjoy my creations makes me happy. It definitely makes your mom happy," he said. "It's also a great stress reliever."

I glanced at the tools and continued eating in silence. I had never thought about carpentry. It was just a cool thing that my dad did. I remember loving the building blocks and toy cars he made me. It did bring me joy.

My dad organized his tools with relaxed shoulders and a pep in his step. He seemed excited to share this with me. Not Ronan and I, just me. Another thing that was just between us. I grinned into my coffee cup.

"I want to learn," I said.

° ° ° 🐚 🐚 🐚 ° ° °

IT'S BEEN a few days since my excursion with Crystal. I wish that day had never ended. So many things happened. I got to show Crystal the ocean, she met Waldo, and we examined the coral together. I showed her parts of me that I was starting to love again.

Sharing that part of me with her was magical. It filled me with a sense of ease. The corners of my mouth twitched, remembering how she'd tried to use her magic to help the coral.

I knew it would be futile but the fact that she'd tried, that she'd cared about my home meant so much to me. Even Waldo liked her.

And her opening up to me about her mom? It had broken me. I understood her pain. I lost my dad at a young age. When you lose a parent it's like losing a piece of yourself. There's an ache within you that never goes away. At some point you learn to live with that ache.

The difference between Crystal and I is that I had my memories. I had memories of swimming with my dad, him telling me to pay attention, him grilling fish for dinner, and taking us on trips. She'd missed out on so much by living for other people. I clench my fists.

Who am I to judge her when I did the same thing? I walk around like I'm the sun, people's happiness reflecting the warmth I give them. But I've been burning up carrying their light for so long.

I scratch my chest, remembering her mention that her mom would have loved me. It filled me with so much pride. I would have loved her mom too. She'd given birth to someone who is gentle and kind.

In that moment I'd wanted to talk to Crystal about my dad, something I never did with anyone, not even Ronan. I'd closed that part of my life off, saving myself from the pain his death had caused me. I sigh, letting the sound of the ocean soothe me.

Does that feel good?

I swallow, my cock twitching. *Kraken's crap.*

My face heats and my body tingles, remembering her hands on me. She felt so good on top of me, and my cock was begging to be let out of its slit. Crystal was a quick learner. Her hand was magic against me, and she'd seemed...into it. She'd seemed into the thought of being intimate with me even in my siren form. In all honesty I was nervous about showing her but...it felt freeing to know she liked *all* sides of me.

My heart was hammering in my chest with each of her strokes and the song that I've been humming ever since I'd met her threatened to pour out of me.

Claim her.

The siren in me, the primal part wanted her, *needed* her to be mine in every way possible. I ran my tongue over my teeth before taking a deep breath, letting the salty air calm my body. I can't. I won't. If I were to take her that way and...bite her...it would seal us to each other.

No.

I'm her fake boyfriend. I'm her friend. I'm teaching her how to be intimate, but we aren't anything more than friends. We can't be, unless she wants to be.

"Caspian!" a voice called out from behind me. I turn to see Kai with Ricardo, the Second Prince of the Southern Ocean. Many of the royal families have been gathering for my ceremony. My throat tightens.

In a few weeks I will be tying myself to my kingdom and my duty. Am I ready for that kind of responsibility even though I feel unworthy?

"Hey Ricky!" I said. I hugged him briefly.

The last time I saw him was after graduation. He has let his dark hair grow long and it was pulled back into a messy bun. I could see a half sleeve tattoo peeking out from beneath his shirt sleeve. Ricky and Kai shared the same deep tan skin. He had high cheekbones and brown eyes, and a small gold hoop hung on one nostril. "When did you get a nose ring?" I ask with an arched eyebrow as we began walking towards the apothecary.

Ricky wrinkled his nose. "Got it to impress a siren," he said, grinning. I chuckled, not surprised in the slightest.

"Did it work?" I ask. He crossed his arms, smirking.

"She liked it, and so did a warlock. Now I just keep it because it looks good on me," he said. I rolled my eyes.

"I'm just now realizing that we are all way too confident," I said, shaking my head. Ricky wrapped an arm around me, pulling me closer.

"Can't help that we are a good-looking group of mermen," he said, wiggling his eyebrows. Kai tossed an arm around my other shoulder.

"By the stars we are," Kai said. I looked between both of them, my heart feeling lighter. I haven't hung out with them in years. Of course I miss my friends from Lavender Falls, but Kai and Ricky know the side of me that I've spent the past year hiding. They understand the weight of my duty.

"You know most beings aren't impressed by that," I said with a pointed look at Kai. He rolled his eyes, shoving me into Ricky.

"She will see me one day," Kai said, shoving me into Ricky. Ricky's eyes widened.

"Dude, you're still hung up on Mira?" he asked.

"He never gave up," I said. Ricky's mouth dropped.

"When you know, you know," Kai said, eyeing me.

Fuck, I do not want to talk about Crystal right now. If we do, my mind will wander back to our moment in the cave. To every moment we've shared here and the confusing feelings I have. Is she the one? Is my siren song for her, or someone else?

"Oh yeah, I heard our little Sassy Cassie got a girlfriend. When do I meet her?" he asked, his tone mischievous.

"So, you can tell embarrassing stories about me? Yeah, no," I said as we continued walking.

"I promise I won't," he said before breaking into a smirk. "I'll only tell the *semi-* embarrassing stories." I roll my eyes.

"That doesn't make me feel better," I point out. He shrugged his shoulders.

"I would like to meet the woman who has stolen my best friend's heart. Gotta make sure she doesn't hurt you," he said. My stomach sinks. I think I have a better chance of breaking her heart than her breaking mine.

"She could never hurt me," I said. *But I can hurt her*. I'm a prince with responsibilities that can take me away. My feelings for her are growing, feelings she might not reciprocate.

We stop in front of my aunt's store where books and potions wait for us.

I look at my old friends. If I'd learned anything from my time in Lavender Falls it is that it's good to ask for help. It didn't make you weak, just made things easier. Even though asking is never easy.

We stood in front of the shop, nerves dancing up and down my body. Ricky opened the door and Kai motioned for me to head inside.

"So…ready to help me save my ocean?"

I DON'T KNOW how many more books I can read about the trident. Apparently, every ocean kingdom has its own legend. But each one stated *"when the time was a right the song of the trident would play for its true heir."* Is now not the right time? The coral is dying, and its sickness is spreading. How can this not be the time to make an appearance?

I groan, closing another book. Ricky stretched his arms over his head. I look over at Kai who is helping my aunt make potions. I wince. They are all helping me, and I feel useless. I'm the one that is supposed to find the trident and I'm doing a shitty job at it. I can't hear any damn songs anywhere besides Crystal's. Why is finding a giant fork so damn hard? I rub a hand over my face. *Stars, that is a shitty thing to think.*

"It'll be okay," Ricky said. I shake my head.

"Have you *seen* the coral?" I ask. His smile faded.

"I haven't, but Kai described it to me. I'm so sorry this is happening but I'm sure you will fix it," he said, earnestly. I bite my cheek, my eyes glued to the pile of books. How can Ricky believe in me when we've haven't even seen each other in five years?

Everyone is so fucking sure I can do this and I'm not. Can't they see that I don't know what I'm doing? That those years of training as my brother's second were utterly useless? *I* am useless. I can't save the coral or this town. I'm only good for a laugh, and what good is that?

I freeze.

I'd run away from home to get away from those kinds of thoughts. Everyone in town loved me because I could make them laugh on their worst days not realizing how exhausting it was for me. They couldn't see that it was all an act. Everyone wanted me to *be* something. The jokester. The dutiful prince. The happy son. The wild brother. They expected me to be something more than what I see myself as.

There wis a sharp slap to the back of my head. I yelp and turn around to find Aunt Meryl glaring at me. I narrow my eyes.

"What the kraken was that for?" I ask, rubbing my head. She rolled her eyes.

"I see what's swimming around in that head of yours," she said with a knowing gleam in her eyes. I shift my gaze away from her.

"I don't know what you're talking about," I said, crossing my arms. Aunt Meryl began putting the different colored potions carefully into a sack. Ricky watched her intently and she took notice.

"These potions are more like salves. I don't need the jars breaking inside of the bag with the way you all zip through the water," she said. I give a fake gasp. I knew the meaning behind her statement.

"The only reason I broke your cup that one time was because Kai over here bumped into me!" I said. Kai gasped.

"That was because Ricky bumped into *me*," Kai exclaimed.

"Because *you* kept checking Mira out and weren't paying attention," Ricky said, narrowing his dark eyes. Aunt Meryl sighed.

"All the more reason for this particular bag. Your friend Lilianna enchanted it for me," she said. I offered her a small smile and get up to make some tea in the corner. I can't lie I miss Lavender Falls. I miss my friends even though I'm happy to be around my old ones.

"Oh, tell us about Lilianna and Lavender Falls!" Ricky said from across the room. My lips twitch.

"First: Lilianna is happily in love with my friend. Second: I think you all would love it there. It's like...how Coralia Coast used to be," I said, handing Aunt Meryl the tea. She smiled in thanks.

Things changed when my dad and uncle died. They were a bright light in our community. My dad was fair and stern. My uncle made everyone laugh, and he'd looked out for every being. When they'd died it was like they took our sun with them. We have been struggling ever since. Many beings moved away and closed their shops.

"They have a friendly zombie who helps take care of the cemetery. My friend Caleb owns the pub called The Drunken Fairy Tale Tavern and it's awesome. But don't tell Carrie that," I said, laughing.

"How is she?" Aunt Meryl asked, eyes softening. I smile.

"She's doing great. She fits right in with everyone," I said honestly.

While Carrie grew up here, she always felt like she belonged somewhere else, and that place ended up being Lavender Falls. I've always felt like I belong in Coralia Coast, but that I'm not good enough to be what the town needs me to be.

"Are they coming for the ceremony?" Kai asked. My stomach tightens at the mention of the ceremony.

"They are. They're very excited...I think," I said, brows furrowing. Aunt Meryl clicked her tongue. My stomach twists again as guilt washes over me again.

"Uh oh. What did you do?" Kai asked. I grimace. Ricky placed his chin in his hands and Kai copied him. I rolled my eyes at their dramatics.

"You clearly did *something*," Ricky said, smirking.

"I...um...sort of hid my identity," I grumble. The mermen gasped. "I needed a break okay! A break from–" I glance at Aunt Meryl, who gives me an understanding smile. "I just needed time." They looked at me then at each other before nodding in understanding. Ricky stretched back in his chair.

"I get it. I'm always running from responsibility," he said. I snort.

"You're the third in line," I point out. He raised an eyebrow.

"You think they want *my sister* to be second in command?" he asked.

"She *is* smarter than you," Kai pointed out. Ricky threw his hands in the air.

"That's what I keep telling them!" he exclaimed. "I don't see what's wrong with her taking her rightful place." I wince. Poor Ricky. I forgot his family tends to run things in a very old school way. "She's not giving up and I will never take her place," he said with conviction. Kai's eyes turn to look at me. His gaze unsettles me.

"Did you hide who you are for a whole yeah?" Kai asked. I swallow, nodding. It was exhausting ping ponging between all these emotions. "What was your new name?" he asked. My cheeks heat remembering my brother's reaction. I scratch the back of my head, feeling nervous.

"Sailor," I mumble. Ricky bit his bottom lip for two seconds as his body shook. I grimace as both sirens burst into laughter. "Hey, I know!"

"You-you...Sailor...dude!" Kai sputtered. I roll my eyes and Aunt Meryl shook her head with a smile.

"Clearly Mira has the creativity in this family," she said. At the mention of Mira, Kai lit up. I smirk.

"You're right. *Mira* did get the creative gene. *Mira* is so creative," I tease. Kai glared at me, trying to maintain his smile.

"I can't wait until she gets it together and settles down," Aunt Meryl sighed, handing me the bag. Kai sat up straight, sobering up.

"But we'll see," she said nonchalantly, turning away–but not before I could see another smirk on her lips. When she went to the backroom Kai relaxed.

"Dude," I said to Kai, shaking my head

"Dude *me*?! Dude *you*! You made it obvious" Kai said. I scoff.

"Kai, everybody knows," I said.

"Okay, but that's her *mom*," he said. Kai's feelings for my cousin have always been obvious. He would follow her around and do anything she asked.

Actually...I do the same around Crystal. It never bothered me that he had a crush on Mira because Kai respected everyone. I trusted him around her and now that I know that she's his siren song I would never dare get in their way. But clearly Mira is getting in the way of her own happily ever after.

"Sailor? You couldn't have gone for, I don't know, Max?" Ricky suggested, changing the subject. I shrug my shoulders.

"It just came out when I was with Carrie, okay?"

∘ ∘ ∘ 🐚 🐚 🐚 ∘ ∘ ∘

WE DECIDED to dive into the ocean in the afternoon. Ricky took a quick swim around, assessing the damage. He said he would talk to his mom and then get back to me. Afterwards headed towards the diner.

Across the road I can see Crystal talking to Ronan. I slowed my steps watching her share a laugh with my brother.

I couldn't lie, there was a stab of jealousy. Sure, I make her laugh and smile but so could he. Maybe I should be happy that she's getting along with him because that means she's comfortable with my family and hometown. *Maybe that means*...I shake my head.

"Hey little brother!" Ronan shouted. I roll my eyes.

"We're almost the same height!" I said back. Crystal's eyes widened before softening. I grinned as they made their way over to us. My heart races watching her walk towards me. I immediately open my arms to hug her. I wrap my arms around her tightly, feeling my body sag with relief now that she's in my arms.

"Hey there sweet muffin," she said, her cheeks flushed. Her nose twitches and I chuckle at the awkward nickname.

Clearly, she wasn't a fan of it. I kiss the top of her head. I wasn't touching her because we have an audience. I want to. I need to. Someone cleared their throat behind me.

"Ah, Crystal, I want you to meet a friend of mine," I said. She pulled away slightly, keeping one hand wrapped around my waist. I bite the inside of my cheek to keep from smiling like a lovesick fool. She smiled at Kai, nodding her head before looking over at Ricky.

"I'm Crystal Silva Hale," she said, using her full name. For some reason that made me smile. She stuck out her hand and Ricky reached out.

"I'm Ricardo Alexandre Gomez, Second Prince of the Southern Ocean," he said, speaking his full title as he took her hand. Crystal's cheeks turned pink, and she glanced at me quickly.

"Wow, you have rich friends," she said. My friends laugh and I faintly hear my brother chuckle.

"Are you suggesting you care about money?" I ask. She rolled her pretty hazel eyes.

"No, I do well on my own," she said. Ricky and Kai snap their fingers while I grin.

"So, you don't care that you're dating a prince?" I teased. She raises an eyebrow, crossing her arms.

"Please, when we met, I'd thought you were a happy go lucky bartender who was good at building stuff," she said. I have to fight back a grin. I love this side of Crystal.

"You still build?" my brother asked in shock. I shift on my feet while my friends look at each other. Crystal watches us all, confused. She doesn't know why I even know how to do carpentry.

"Um hey, do you think you could bring dinner tonight?" Crystal asked, trying to break the weird tension. She squeezes my hip, and I look down at her. She is perceptive. My hand cups her cheek and I feel compelled to kiss her. Her eyes wander to my lips, and my heart rate kicks up. But before I can lean down, Kai pulls me away.

"Can you buy *me* dinner too?" he teased. I roll my eyes, squeezing Crystal's hand once and she squeezes twice back.

"You have money," I said. Kai sighed dramatically.

"But I'm in your kingdom, treat me," he said. Ricky swung an arm over Kai.

"Me too, sweet muffin," Ricky joined in with a wink which made Crystal snort.

"He's *my* sweet muffin," she said teasingly, and it fills my heart with pride.

"Yeah, I'm her sweet muffin," I said. Ricky held his hands up defensively.

"True. I wouldn't dare steal your siren. There are plenty of fish in the sea," Ricky said. I chuckle, shaking my head.

Before I can respond there is a gentle brush of lips against my cheek. I look at Crystal. She stares at me again; her hazel eyes filled with warmth. She shines brighter than any pearl in the ocean or any star in the sky.

"May I have chili cheese fries?" she asked gently. I nod.

"You can always have whatever you want M' Lady," I said, pressing a kiss to her forehead. I watch her follow my brother, probably going to check the meadery out again. I turn to my friends. "But you two can pay for your own food," I said.

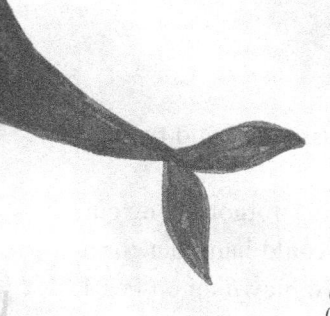

CHAPTER 23
SIP N' SPILL

Crystal

The first cottage is now complete, and the crew is halfway through the second. Soon we will be fixing up the meadery. I got to go on a thorough inspection with Ronan, and it made me excited. I've helped rebuild homes but never a meadery. He said he would be putting it on sale soon, and I knew the perfect being to send the listing to.

I blush, remembering how we'd bumped into Cas and his friends. My lips tingle. I kissed him on the cheek in front of them. Sure, it was an innocent kiss. But when I'd wrapped my arms around him, all my worries melted away and it was just him and I.

When I looked up at him, I wanted to kiss him. I wanted to feel his lips on mine again. I didn't even feel shy showing him affection around his friends, especially showing affection. It feels natural to be with Cas. I shake my head. What we have is fake. The innocent touches are for show and the kisses are just practice.

I quickly change into sweats, remembering our list. I pull at my hoodie strings. Maybe today we can knock something else off. I can't help but smile at the thought. I haven't forgotten our moment in the cave. It consumed my thoughts late at night. I blush, my hand twitching. He felt great beneath me. I wonder how his co–

My phone buzzes and I jump. It's Lily. *Fuck.* I forgot about our FaceTime call. I had promised the ladies that we could hang out for a bit. I swallow. I haven't spoken to Eleanor since I'd blown up on her. I close my eyes. I really fucked up last time. What I'd said hurt her, and hurting her, hurt me.

I click 'answer', seeing the faces of the beings who had welcomed me back to Lavender Falls: Eleanor, Lily and Lola. They were at Lola's apartment.

"Hey," I said, doing my best to sound cheerful. Lily and Lola beamed, their faces taking up most of the frame. Lola had her braids pulled up into two buns while Lily had hers in two French braids. My sister hung back, her auburn hair loose and longer than I remembered was a tad longer.

"Pixie pie I'm going to need you to sip something to spill something," Lola said sweetly. I blush. They ladies like to have Sip n' Spill sessions during their ladies night. I haven't spoken to them about my *new boyfriend*. I go to the kitchen to grab a beer.

"How is everyone?" I ask, trying to buy myself time.

"Well, by the end of the summer Miss Unicorn and baby Rarity will be leaving us to go to the Gasping Greenwood," Lola said, sadly. During the spring she helped deliver a baby unicorn. She's only being known to have ever done that. It was magical. Lola is the smartest and sweetest vampire I know.

"I'm finally confessing my love for Celestino at the end of the summer," Lily said, blushing. I smile. While everyone knew Lily and Celestino were in love, Lily had a hard time verbally saying it out loud. She's been planning to say those three little words in a magically romantic way.

Honestly, I kind of envy her. I want magical romantic moments. Well, I'm having them, but they aren't real because Cas and I aren't in a real relationship.

"Caleb hogs the blanket which has made me kick him out of bed three times," Eleanor said from behind them. I raise an eyebrow.

"And?" I asked, knowing damn well where this was leading. Eleanor rolled her eyes.

"He's very thorough with his apologies," she said, smirking. I shake my head, laughing and cracking open my beer. I take a sip, and the ladies all move closer to the camera.

They stare at me, waiting for the details on my fake relationship. My stomach churns. The guilt of lying to them about their close friend and lying to my own sister has been eating me up alive. They stare at me wide-eyed and happy, eagerly awaiting details.

"We're fake dating," I blurt out. I stare at their blinking faces. There is a pause before they scream in unison. I wince.

"*WHAT?!*" Lola yelled, popping in front of the camera.

"ARE WE IN A BOOK??" Lily exclaimed, pushing forward. My sister hangs back, watchful.

"Are you okay with this?" Eleanor asked, looking at me with concern. I take another sip. My sister has a right to be concerned. It's what a good sister would do in a healthy sibling relationship. But it still bothers me. It's not like I didn't think this through. I even told him no at first. Then I processed what he'd asked for and figured out what I could get out of it. I knew *exactly* what I was getting into.

I move to the couch, wrapping myself in a blanket as I wait for their disappointment at the truth. But surprisingly, it didn't come. They didn't seem to be.

"How do you feel about it?" Lily asked. I bite the inside of my cheek, tilting my head side to side.

"Cas is my friend. I like him a lot and I trust him. I want to help him," I said, honestly. Lily glanced at Lola.

"And everything is okay with you too? He's not taking advantage of you?" Lola asked. Even while Cas is their close friend, I'm grateful that they are checking in on me. I nod.

"He's been very respectful. He doesn't push me, and he always makes me sure I'm okay," I said. I glance at my sister. "I feel safe with him." My sister stared at her hands.

"E-Eleanor?" I asked, hesitating. She has something to say. I can tell by the way she keeps rolling her lips back and forth. "Say something," I urge, my anxiety growing. The knots in my stomach are so tight I can't keep drinking my beer. She sighed.

"I say do everything on your list. Fuck him. Enjoy. Have fun. Let loose!" she blurted out. My eyes widen. The girl's' mouths hung open. "What?" she asked, crossing her arms. "Crystal deserves to have fun! And at least she's doing it in a safer way than how I did it," she said. My bottom lip wobbles. I thought she would get mad at me or be disappointed. Eleanor moved to sit in front of the camera.

"You're both are consenting adults and seem to be having honest communication with each other," Lily said, nodding. "That's important."

"The fact that you were able to open up yourself to even talk about it with him says something," Eleanor pointed out. I nod. I had met other men in college and at work. They'd flirted with me here and there and it had always made me unpleasant. But Cas is different.

"Exactly. Just stay safe and never be afraid to speak your mind," Lola chimed in.

"You deserve to have fun. You *can* have fun," Eleanor said, with a serious look. I nod. She brought her drink in front of her face with a smirk. "And you come first," she said with a wink. My face flames and laughter erupts around me. I relax, sensing that my sister is back to her normal self, and that maybe our relationship isn't as fractured as I'd thought.

The front door clicks, and my eyes widen. Eleanor grinned wickedly.

"Enjoy!" Lily said.

"Be safe!" Lola snickered.

"You come first," Eleanor shouted. I quickly hang up, dropping my phone on the couch. My whole face is on fire, especially when Cas walks up to the couch with our dinner. He smirks, his blue eyes boring into me.

"You *will* come first," he said, and my thighs clench.

A SIREN'S SUMMER FOR LOVE

WE SAT ON THE COUCH, eating our food and, enjoying our anime like we usually did every night. Cas is drinking a beer, and my eyes followed the movement of his throat as he swallowed. I had to put up with his agonizingly soft touches against my arm, my thigh, the way he dabbed a napkin on my chin a few times throughout dinner. His shoulder would brush mine occasionally and it was getting me riled up. He was doing this purpose. The corner of his lips would tilt at my reactions each time. *This damn siren.*

We hadn't talked about knocking another item off my list, but the tension keeps rising between us. I chew my bottom lip. I know which item I want to do; I just need to say it. From the corner of my eyes, I notice Cas' glance. His lips are twitching again. He raised an eyebrow at me, and for some reason that movement annoyed me.

That fish face knows what he is doing to me. Instinctively I reach for his beer, placing it on the table before crawling onto his lap. He raised his eyebrows, his hands going up in defense.

"What's up cupcake?" he said, his eyes glowing. I fight back a laugh, staying silent. I reach for his wrists, placing his hands on my hips before grabbing the sides of his neck and, enjoying the feel of his warm skin. We stare at each other in silence, desire brewing between us. I glance at his lips, and he gives me the slightest nod. That's all I needed.

I brush my lips against his, sagging into him immediately. Cas softly groans, his hands gripping my hips. I squeeze my thighs, enjoying the feel of having him underneath me again. I nip at his bottom lip, and he opens willingly. Our tongues tangle with each other. One of my hands slides into his hair, tugging at his soft locks. Cas groaned again and I couldn't help but smile.

I rock forward, gasping into his mouth. His cock is hardening beneath me, and I scoot up until I'm right where I need to be. Cas' hand comes up to cup the back of my neck as I rock forward.

"Fuck," I whisper against his mouth. He chuckles, deep in his throat. His other hand wanders down, cupping my ass, assisting me with the motion. "C-Cas," I whisper, as he trails kisses down my neck. A whimper escapes me when his teeth dig into my skin. "Yes," I hiss. My hand pulls at his hair, earning me another delicious groan.

My other hand is moving down his chest. I slightly lift my hips, wanting to stroke him. Cas tilted his head back, resting it against the couch. His cheeks are flushed and his lips slightly swollen. He looked gorgeous like this, his blonde locks a mess, his bright blue eyes, hooded with desire for me.

"I don't know what I'm doing but it feels good. Doesn't it?" I ask, my breathing coming in short bursts. Cas lifted his head, pressing his forehead against mine. Our breaths mingle as my hand continues to stroke him through his sweats. One of his hands join me and I sag further onto him. The feeling of both of us working together to make him come undone was pulling me closer to the edge. I rock harder, seeking more friction.

"For someone who's never done this before you have a way of making me fall apart with just one touch," he said, the corners of his mouth tilting into a smile. I blush at his words. "But how about we switch positions. I don't want to come yet," he said, nipping at my bottom lip. I nod, scrambling off his lap.

I look up at him as he stands. He runs a hand through his hair as he tries to regain control of his.

"Do you want to continue?" he asked, checking in. There is an ache between my thighs that we started, and I want relief. I wanted *him* to give me relief.

"I do," I said, squeezing my thighs together. Cas sees the motion and takes in a sharp breath.

"Bedroom?" he asked. My heart races in my chest. I nod, wordlessly. "Yours or mine?"

"Mine," I said. He offered me a hand, and I took it, enjoying the way our skin felt against each other. Cas escorted me to my room, shutting the door behind us. He motioned for me to sit on the bed and stood in front of me.

"Safe word?" he asked. I grin.

"Fish cake," I said. He tucks a stray strand of hair behind my ear, and I lean into his touch.

"What are you comfortable with me doing right now?" he asked. My heart swells. This is why I wanted to do this with Cas. I knew he would be considerate of me. I trusted him to make sure I was okay and taken care of.

"I want you to touch me until I come," I said, my eyes focused on his chest. I can't deny that I still feel slightly embarrassed. Cas shuffled forward and his fingers gripped my chin, forcing me to look at him. My cheeks flame as his hand moved to cup my cheek.

"Never be embarrassed to ask for what you want," he said, his voice gravelly. He leaned forward until our lips brushed. "Now M'Lady, tell me *exactly* what you want," he demanded. I swallow; my eyes focused on his swollen lips for a second.

"I want to feel your fingers on my clit," I whisper, our eyes connecting. Cas gives me the most breathtaking smile, filling me with excitement.

"Just my fingers?" he asked. I smile, tilting my head to the side and batting my lashes.

"I'll let you know," I said. Cas licked his lips and nodded.

"Yes, M'Lady." His hands come up to my hips, tugging at my waistband. I nod, standing up. I watch him lower my sweatpants and underwear, raining kisses down my legs. It's odd.

I always assumed that when this moment would come that I would feel awkward. That the urge to cover up would consume me and I wouldn't be able to relax. Yet here I was with a Cas, half naked, and I'm comfortable.

Cas stroke the back of my legs, reverting my attention back to him. I shiver, keeping my eyes on him. He pointed to my hoodie. I shake my head.

"Cold," I said, giving him a nervous giggle. Cas settled on his knees and my stomach flipped. His hands are on the back of my legs, and he places his cheek against my thigh.

"I'll make sure you stay warm," he promised, placing a kiss on the inside of my thigh. I ran a hand through his hair, and he closed his eyes briefly. I give it a slight tug and his eyes snap open, pupils dilated. A pretty flush stains his cheeks. I feel empowered.

"Eat me," I demand, releasing him from my grip. He lets out a shaky breath and I crawl onto the bed, resting my head against the pillows as he moved on top of me.

"Such a good girl for me," he whispered. My eyes widen and my lips stretched into a smile. He remembered my list and...I like what he said. It made my body buzz with excitement.

"I think you're being good for me too," I tease. He smiled before kissing me once again until my legs opened and he settled himself between them. I moan, rocking my hips. I'm so much closer to him now. We stayed this way for a bit, m. Mouths moving against each other, his hands stroking my sides, my legs around his waist. We this way until I was trembling and begging for more.

I place my hands on his shoulders, pushing him down. He nipped my bottom lip before smiling as he made his way down my body. I rock my hips up, needing relief.

He placed kisses on the inside of my thighs, holding them apart. I watch him from beneath my eyelashes. I'm nervous and excited about the promise to euphoria.

"You smell so good," he said, his nose running up my thigh. I twitch, my core aching. "You know, sirens have heightened senses," he said, his blue eyes catching mine. "And *fuck* is your scent driving me crazy, Crystal." His teeth dig into my thigh, and I hiss, my fingers clutching the sheets.

His fingers finally stroke me, and I moan loudly, my eyes closing. His fingers work me until he finds a pace that has my thighs moving to hang over his shoulders.

"More, Cas," I beg, slipping my fingers between his hair again. I want his mouth on me. I want to feel his tongue. "Mouth," I command.

Cas gives me a wicked grin before taking my clit in his mouth. I arch my back, a new wave of ecstasy coursing through my veins. He takes his time to find the pattern that sets me on edge, shifting from back-and-forth flicks of his tongue to gentle sucks. I squeeze my thighs against his head, rocking against his mouth.

"Only good little sluts get to come," he mumbled.

I blink.

Everything in me stops and I stare at Cas. He lifts his head away from me and raises an eyebrow. "Not into that?" he asked. It's not that I hate it, but it doesn't give me the same thrill. Something about it makes me freeze and anxious.

"It's...okay? But it makes me feel like I'm making a mistake," I said. Cas sits back on his feet, watching me.

"Well, nothing that is happening right now is a mistake," he said. I nod, wordlessly. I give him a soft smile.

"I preferred the praising," I admit. Cas places his hands on the top of my thighs, squeezing one. I reach and squeeze his shoulder twice.

"Do you still want to continue?" he asked. I rose to my elbows.

"Caspian, what just happened is us learning about my body. I'm happy we know what I don't like but you are *not* stopping now," I said. Cas smiled, pressing kisses against my thighs. I smile back. "Keep going." I run a hand through his hair, letting him bring me back to the brink of ecstasy.

"There's my pixie. You're going to be good and come for me, right?" he asked, before swiping his tongue against my clit. My back arches as my eyes closed.

"*Please*, please," I said, needing more. His finger teases my entrance and my core clenches at the emptiness. He slid the tip of his finger in and my hips buck. "Yes," I said, my hand slipping under my hoodie to tug on my nipple. Cas groans against my clit, causing me to clench again. I open my eyes to see him staring at the hand I'm using to touch myself.

I swallow, pulling up my hoodie so he can get a better look. His eyes flash brighter with excitement. He pulls away for a second, eyes drinking me in.

"You're so beautiful Crystal," he said. My heart skips. He looked at me with adoration. I closed my eyes, not wanting to read into it. If I did, my mind would steal me from this moment from me. *He's just being a fake boyfriend* and helping me. "Look at me," he demanded. My eyes open at his command. "Do you want me to..." he trailed off, his finger going in another inch. I tilt my hips up with a smirk.

"My toys have gone deeper than that," I said, teasingly. His eyes widened and he threw his head back within laughter.

"I knew you weren't so innocent," he said, smiling. He inserts two fingers gently and my back arches. This is what I need. Toys are fun, sure, but this was different. My friends assume I'm completely innocent but I'm not. I'm just not as vocal about what I do behind closed doors.

Cas sucked on my clit, his fingers stroking me. I'd made myself feel good before, but this is different. This is *better*.

My fingers tug on my nipples, and I rock against Cas' mouth. He began humming. It was the same melody that I've caught him singing before. It heats my body, driving me higher. *Is this his magic?*

I gasp as his fingers began thrusting faster. His tongue flicked back and forth, and there is a familiar warmth in my stomach, spreading. His humming is getting louder, and I rock harder against him until I'm spasming, my body tightening as he sends me over the edge.

"*Y-yes!*" I cry out. Cas smiled against me, slowing down his strokes until my body sank into the mattress. I struggle to catch my breath. Cas pulled away with a smile. He crawls up the bed until we are face to face. His lips shine with my cum on his face. I tilted my head up, capturing his lips.

A thrill goes down my spine, tasting myself on him. We stayed like that for a bit. Mouths and bodies melting into each other, until he pulled back. He straightened my hoodie before getting up to go to the bathroom.

"What are you doing?" I ask when he returns. He gripped my ankles, tugging me down the bed and then placed my legs over his shoulder.

"Cleaning you up," he said. I moan, feeling the warm cloth against my sensitive clit. "How do you feel?" he asked. I smile.

"Good. Great. Happy," I answer honestly. Cas leaned down for another kiss, and I hiss at the stretch.

"Mhmm. You're going to have to stretch more, M' Lady."

After taking a quick shower, I notice Cas isn't on the couch. I go back to my room and find him on my bed with his laptop. He lifted a cup of tea to me and patted the space next to him. I crawl under the covers, leaning onto him.

"Hope you don't mind, I came back here," he said. I shake my head. Cuddling in bed is much more comfortable than on the couch. *As friends*, my mind chastised me.

"What about…you know…you?" I ask, blushing. Cas grinned.

"Tonight was you," he said. My eyebrows furrowed.

"I distinctly remember on my list it mentioned giving," I point out. Cas chuckled and it warmed my soul. I take a sip of the tea, sighing. He grabbed his.

"I know. Trust me. But tonight, I wanted to enjoy *you*," he said. He leaned over, his lips brushing my ear. "Which I did, by the way."

I chew my bottom lip. As much as I enjoyed the orgasm, he gave me I wanted him to enjoy one as well. I wanted to touch him, to learn what he likes.

"Fine, for now," I said, reaching for the laptop to play on the next episode of our show. "Next time you're mine," I said. He hummed, pulling me to his side and slipping his hand under my hoodie, gently stroking my side. I slipped my own under his and sighed at the contact.

When I looked over at him, he was smiling at me. The tips of his ears were pink, and his eyes darted to the screen quickly.

I wondered if he likes the idea of being mine.

CHAPTER 24
A STOLEN MOMENT

Caspian

N*ext time you're mine.*
I'm screwed. So, fucking screwed. She has no idea that I'm already hers. Ever since the day I met her at The Drunken Fairy Tale Tavern I've been following her around like a guppy. And now that we've spent weeks getting to know each other on a deeper level, *touching* each other, I'm falling deeper and deeper.

My heart rattles in my chest. I lick my lips, missing the taste of her on my tongue. Her body was sensational under mine. I squeeze my eyes shut, trying to remind myself that I was *just* her friend—a friend helping her with a *very* naughty list.

"Caspian!" My mom's voice called out. I pause. I cannot be having dirty thoughts about my fake girlfriend out in public. I shift on my feet, before turning around with a smile.

"Hey mom!" I said, giving her a quick hug. Her eyes darted around.

"No Crystal?" she asked, sounding slightly disappointed. *You and I both.* I shake my head.

"She's finishing up the second cottage this week," I said. She nodded before giving me a secretive smile.

"You know I like her," she said. I blush. *Once again, you and I both.*

"Y-yeah? I do too," I said, knowing that while we were in a fake relationship, my feelings were very real. I was using Crystal as a buffer with my mom. I knew being back would entail completing a long list of duties, including courting princesses.

"I was worried when you first came back," she said.

"What do you mean?" I ask. She sighed and the sound made me crumble slightly. I wasn't a horrible child growing up, but I certainly didn't comply with everything that was expected of me.

"I love you Caspian, I do. But it was hard to watch you fling yourself around and ignore what your father and I said. I know the rules were tough. You didn't ask to be born a prince," she began. I swallow. "When you ran…it hurt, but I knew you needed that time for yourself. I didn't grow up as a royal. I' always had had the freedom you craved. That's why I never went after you even though I knew where you were."

"How did you know I would come back?" I ask, my fingers twitching at my sides. She gave me a smile that made the sides of her eyes wrinkle. She didn't have as many of those when I'd left. My heart constricted. She is aging. *I'm aging. Things are changing.*

"Because I know that deep down you love this town and its beings," she said. I blink back tears. I don't deserve to be a prince. I don't deserve to be second in command. There is no way I can fucking do this.

"I wasn't worried that you would come back. I knew you would. I was worried that you would still be jumpy and struggling to settling into this next phase of your life. I was happy when you told me about Crystal," she said. I give her a tightlipped smile. But I'm not settling down because our relationship is fake, a way to keep her, and any stray princesses, off my back. "I see the effect she has on you," she noted. I blush.

"What do you mean?" I ask. She tilted her head from side to side.

"You seem calmer, especially at those dinners you typically would try to get out of," she said. My eyes shift to the ground. Crystal brings me peace. Around her, I'm at ease.

"You guys would have cute babies," she teased, shifting the tone of our conversation. My face flamed.

"Mom! That's a little soon," I said, feeling uncomfortable (*but weirdly happy*). She shrugged her shoulders.

"Hey, I knew from the moment I met your father that he was the one," she said. That gave me pause. My mom rarely talked about my dad since his death. What I did know was that they met when they were young. My mom was non-royal, which wasn't really a big deal.

"Really?" I ask, curiously. She gave me a pained smile before casting a glance at the ocean.

"Aunt Meryl and I were visiting Coralia. We went for a swim, and I'd ended up getting tangled in some seaweed," she said. She laughed and I joined her. Why did every siren have a story about getting tangled by seaweed? Was it a rite of passage?

"Your father and uncle were out on a swim when they found us," she said. I smile. "When our eyes met…there was something there. As he helped me out of the seaweed he started humming a song. It was a song I'd never heard before and yet it felt as though I knew the melody," she said, looking at me again. Her eyes had gone misty.

"I never knew that," I said. She sighed.

"A great love means every other emotion is heightened. Your father brought me great joy, great love, great annoyance," she said, shaking her head. "And when we lost him, that pain was also great." I nod, remembering her wails and how I used my powers to calm everyone down. "I know we don't talk about him often but maybe we can start to again?" she asked, tentatively.

"Yeah, that sounds cool," I said, clearing my throat. I hadn't expected our conversation to go this way at all. My mom kissed my cheek.

"By the way, there is another dinner tonight. I will see you and Crystal there," she said, patting my back. I groaned inwardly. Another damn dinner.

I sigh, before heading down to the beach to meet up with Ricky and Kai.

WE DECIDED to split up and head to different corals around Coralia Coast and to see which salve would work best. I've come to somewhat accept the fact that I will have to trust that the trident will appear when I need it. It has too. My stomach tightens. I must trust in a magical item that hasn't been seen for hundreds of years. My hands clench. I hate it. I don't like that I don't have tangible proof of its existence.

Something nudges me from behind. When I turn around it's a giant loggerhead sea turtle. I smile, staring into its dark eyes. It has a red-brown shell with a yellow belly.

"Hi there. I'm Prince Caspian Calder," I said, smiling. The turtle dropped its head slightly.

"Your highness," it said, slowly. My heart began sinking. This turtle seems lethargic. "Our food source...," it trailed off. I inwardly frowned.

Coral is vital to the Earth's survival. It offers protection, as well as housing, food, and medicine. When one part of the food chain is affected, it'll slowly trickle towards other parts.

"I know," I said, nodding. "The crustaceans have been a bit sparse this season. Towards the east you'll find more seaweed. I'll be talking to a few more sea creatures and then reporting to the King to see how we can help manage the rising food scarcity," I said. The turtle nodded, bubbles escaping its mouth when it sighed.

"Thank you so much, Prince Caspian," the turtle said before, swimming away. I stare out into the vast ocean. The words had tumbled out of my mouth without thinking. I just knew what to say and, how to move forward. *Maybe I'm not as incompetent as I feel.*

The turtles are heading east. Around me there are some black sea bass and mackerel. I close my eyes, taking a deep breath. I allow myself to float in peace, my ears picking up on the sounds around me. Soon more predators will start to close in and shift closer to shore if I don't fix what is happening with the coral.

The last thing I want is more sharks. I understood the diet of sharks. Carnivores serve as a check and balance for the local food chain. When it comes to the food chain, a balance is needed, especially with carnivores. But the last thing I want is for them to get so hungry that they turn to eating sirens and humans, even if we aren't their first choice.

I shake my head, swimming towards my favorite beach area. I promised Kai and Ricky we would meet there once we were done working. The sun is starting to set. Crystal and I have another dinner we must attend tonight. Another night of me holding her close and wishing she was truly mine.

I stop as I approach some familiar rocks. I turn around, feeling like I was being watched. My heart races and there was an invisible pull somewhere. A few notes begin playing in my mind. The melody seems familiar. It reminds me of the one that I hear when I'm around Crystal. They were sweet notes that fell into a waltz like rhythm.

"That's pretty," Kai said, appearing next to me.

"Sounds familiar," Ricky said. I look back out at the ocean. The water is a brilliant blue color though it is slowly turning dark against the setting sun. Something is out there yet nearby. *But what? The trident?* I don't have time to explore. I need to go.

"Yeah. I just can't figure out where I've heard it."

○○○ 🐚 🐚 🐚 ○○○

I WRAPPED my arm around Crystal's waist, enjoying the feel of her satin dress as she spoke to Ricky's younger brothers.

She looks beautiful as always. She is wearing a satin black dress with a slit that makes me want to take her to a secluded closet and drop to my knees. Her laugh is low pitched, and she is resting a palm against my chest. I watch her laughing at something Ricky said. Stars, I love when she wears heels.

"Wait. What's happening?" I ask, pressing a kiss to Crystal's temple. She blushes and I smile. I'm learning more and more that while Crystal is shy and quiet she has a fiery spirit. She looks at me, eyes narrowing as my hand comes to her exposed lower back. Her chest rises sharply. I smirk. I also love teasing her.

"I was telling Crystal about the time you got drunk and couldn't transform back into your human form, so you slept in a bed of seaweed and woke up with starfish stuck all over you," Ricky said with a grin. My eyes widen.

"We swore to never speak of that," I exclaim. Everyone laughs and when I catch Crystal's eyes I can't help but join in. "Well, I'm going to grab a drink. Please don't tell any more embarrassing stories about me," I add. Ricky shrugs his shoulders. There is a tug on my sleeve.

"Get me one too please," Crystal asked. I kiss her cheek, using her request as an excuse to keep touching her. She seemed to welcome every brush and touch from me, which I'm taking as a good sign.

I head to the bartender and ask for two dry white wines. I want something stronger but figured we can keep it light today. I stretch my neck from side to side. I might have overdone it on my swim today.

Today was the longest day I spent in the water and my muscles are killing me. Tomorrow I will have to check to see if any of the salves Aunt Meryl made have worked. Even if they only slowed down the decay a second, it is all I need to keep pushing forward.

"Hey," a deep voice said from behind and I closed my eyes briefly. I take a deep breath before turning around.

"Ronan," I said. Since my coming back I've felt uneasy around my brother. We had somewhat of a close relationship growing up. But now as we grew older and into our roles our dynamics have changed.

He'd spent a lot more time shadowing dad and, learning the ropes of how to be a king. And then when dad passed, the divide grew deeper. I'd pulled away from him, wanting to escape the duty and he so easily threw himself into it.

"What's up?" I ask, trying to act casual. I also feel immense pressure around him. There is a lot at stake, and he is probably waiting for me to fail or bolt, maybe both. He shrugged his shoulders, his gaze taking in the party before us.

"You know the usual. Talking, listening. *A lot* of listening," he said. I raise an eyebrow in surprise. My brother never complained unless it was about me. Then again, I guess I'd never bothered to check on him. Crystal threw herself into taking care of her family while I ran from mine. Staring at my brother, his eyes were bloodshot. My mind turned back to the turtle that I'd encountered.

"Have you checked on the sea creatures?" I ask. He eyed me.

"You mean have I done *your* duty?" he asked. I clench my jaw. He was right. It is my duty, and I can see what failing to do it has done.

"Between revitalizing the town and preparing for the ceremony I haven't had the time," he confessed, his eyes on the ground. Uneasiness ripples through me. My brother didn't have the time to check out the waters. He is busy on land, working with the other kingdoms and, rebuilding our town. That's why my position is needed, why *I'm* needed. I have the special ability to communicate with marine life.

I wondered what would have happened if I'd never left.

Maybe the coral would be different. Maybe our marine life would be thriving instead of dwindling like our town. My eyes catch Crystal who is now talking to Mira and my mom. But if I had never left, I wouldn't have met Crystal at the time that I did. And then maybe we wouldn't have the close friendship that we do now.

"Well, I spoke to some marine life," I said, shifting on my feet. "Food is running scarce. I'm worried the sharks will begin to swim closer to shore," I said. Ronan's eyebrows furrowed.

"We have an understanding with them," he pointed out. I nod. It's true. Sharks didn't like eating beings. We weren't their right kind of nourishment. They stayed away from boats and the shore and in exchange we made sure they had plenty of food. But food supplies are dwindling due to the coral's health.

"I know, but when one part of the food chain suffers it's only time before the other parts begin to get affected. You can't really blame them when they are forced to go somewhere elsewhere for food," I point out. My brother sighed, tapping the bar. The bartender poured him a glass of whiskey.

"Of course. I'm not upset. I get it," he said. "This is why we have to find the trident and heal the coral as soon as possible." He took a sip. My nostrils flare and my temper rises.

"I know. I'm trying," I said, with gritted teeth. "All I can find is that I have to rely on some *"feeling"* that I know nothing about and hope it calls to me," I said with a roll of my eyes. I'm fucking trying. I'm trying every day. To my surprise, my brother didn't call me out on my snappy attitude.

"Do you know why our symbol is the trident?" he asked. I raise an eyebrow.

"It's always been our symbol," I said, shrugging my shoulders. My brother sighed. The kind of sigh that lets me know he is annoyed with me.

"That mystical trident we're so desperate to find is part oof our history. That's why we have it as our family crest," he said. I stare at him in confusion. I don't remember that. I don't ever remember learning that.

"Did you really not pay attention to *anything* dad said?" he asked. I rock on my heels, feeling embarrassed. I *did* pay attention to dad. I paid attention when he was yelling at me to pay attention. My brother shook his head. "It's our symbol because of Atlas. *Atlas* was a bridge between the ocean and the land. His trident helped bring that unity between the worlds. That's why our family, our *kingdom,* honors him. Sure, he wasn't the king when he'd found the trident, but he was still as *important,*" my brother said, staring at me. I take a sip of wine.

Atlas is twice the merman that I am. I'm someone who runs from tough times, who makes people laugh. I'm more of a court jester than a prince. But staring at Ronan gives me a sliver of hope that I can be something more than a joke.

"You're going to find it. Just trust *who you are,*" he emphasized.

"How can you trust me when I left?" I ask, quietly. The question has been eating me up alive since I've returned. My brother stared at me for a second, assessing and I squirmed under his gaze. He shook his head.

"You ran and I was pissed at you, Caspian," he began. I force myself to keep his gaze. "But you did a lot. You watched over mom when I was working, took care of Mira, helped Aunt Meryl with the shop." He swirled his whiskey. "While you didn't really do your duty to the ocean you were committed to helping the town. You love Coralia. I knew you would return," he said. I stare at my brother in shock. I did avoid the ocean as much as I could growing up. I swallow.

"Being in the ocean reminded me too much of uncle and dad. It reminded me that I had a duty that they died for," I said, trying to keep my emotions in check. My hands tighten around the wine glasses.

"I get it, trust me and trust yourself," he said, tapping his glass against mine. I stared at his retreating figure. What if I fail? What if the coral and the creatures die because of me? My heart rate kicks up and my throat tightened. I need to get out of here. I can't be around all these beings who trust me.

I left the wine glasses on our table and went to pull Crystal away. I need to breathe. I need to be out of this room with all these beings who are looking at *me* for answers, for help.

Crystal doesn't say anything when I grab her hand and walk her out of the ballroom and into the hallway. She doesn't say anything when I open a door into an old meeting room, unlock the balcony doors and step out to stare out onto the ocean. There is a soft click. She'd closed the doors, keeping us outside.

I take a deep breath, letting the salty air try to soothe my racing heart. She placed her warm hand on mine, which is clutching the railing. The moon is high in the sky, and I can faintly hear the music from where we are.

"What's wrong?" she asked softly. My hands tremble slightly. *Where do I begin?* How do I tell her that the confident, always laughing siren is just a mask I wear? It's not who I really am. I don't even *know* who I really am.

My brows furrow as I stare at the sandy beach. Crystal has opened up to me so many times these past few months, and it's only right I do the same, because I trust her. I feel comfortable admitting these things to her.

"I've always enjoyed making others laugh," I start off. "But when my dad died, something changed. Making others happy and smiling turned into a chore, a necessity," I said. She curled into my side, her head on my shoulder. "And now that I'm back...they expect so much more of me. They no longer want the agreeable, sunshine person they made me into, and I don't know how to be anything else."

My heart is beating wildly at this point. Words I never thought I would say pour out and I feel like I can't catch my breath. *What's wrong with me?*

Crystal wedged herself between me and the railing. She cupped my face and tilted my head slightly down, forcing me to look at her.

"You don't have to be anything but yourself, even if you're still figuring it out. You can figure it out and know that your friends, your family, and your kingdom will be there with you while you do," she said. I blink several times, feeling tears in my eyes.

"They're relying on me to fix something that I don't know h-how to," I said, my voice coming out strangled. She tilted her head to the side, wiping a tear from my cheek.

"And that's okay. Everyone understands the situation that we are in. They know the task is difficult, but they *trust* you," she said, keeping her tone soft yet firm.

"How can they trust me when I left them?" How can my family, my kingdom, welcome me back so easily when I easily ran from them? "I left them, Crystal. I left and didn't look back," I pause. "I don't even know if I would have even returned if Ronan wasn't with you that day," I confess. And that was it. The dark thought that has kept me on the edge the entire time I've been back. Everyone has been so sure I would return and yet...I don't know if I would have.

She is quiet for a moment; her hazel eyes are dark in the moonlight. "What you did wasn't easy, Caspian. You made a difficult decision because you needed to find yourself, to *save* yourself. They understand," she said, wiping my tears gently. But did I find myself? I'd found new friends, a new family. And most importantly, I'd found her.

"Everyone here supports you. Everyone is here for you on the days where *you* need a laugh, need help, or need anything else," she said. "They rely on you, and they expect you to rely on them too. It'll work out," she said, her lips tilting up into her shy smile that made me weak.

"H-how do you know that?" I ask. She tipped her head back, wrapping her arms around my neck to looking up at the stars.

"I trust the fates. The stars have what's best for us planned out. If I'd never convinced my dad to start therapy, I would never have reconnected with my sister, which meant I wouldn't have met you when I did. And I'm *very* happy we met," she said, her cheeks turning pink in the moonlight. My hands move to grip her hips, and she looked back at me.

"Trust, faith–"

"And pixie dust!" she said beaming, finishing my sentence. We break out into laughter and my shoulders relax.

"Thank you," I whisper. I press my forehead against hers. While I can still feel the anxiety and pressure swirling around me, the storm within has calmed down. Because Crystal is right. If everyone trusts me, then I need to trust myself and my gifts.

My arms loosened around her, and I begin to pull away when Crystal tightens her grip. I raise an eyebrow. She blushes again. "Don't pull away yet. This is nice," she said, her eyes looking sideways.

I smile. How can I pull away now? We are intertwined in the same thread, connected in a way that goes beyond what I could've imagined.

"Don't want to head back to the party yet?" I ask. She shook her head.

"I'd rather be out here...with you," she said, pressing a kiss against my cheek. My hands on her hips flex and my cock twitches.

"Crystal," I said, my voice sounding out of breath as her lips brush down my throat. "Outside M'Lady?"

She pulled back a bit to look at me from beneath her lashes. She has a coy smile on her lips that I can't wait to kiss. I need this moment with her. Just two beings, outside, following their desires.

"Crystal? Kiss me. I need to forget the world for a bit," I said, my hand cupping the back of her head. She stuck her bottom lip out in a pout. I can't help but chuckle.

"If you forget the world then you'll forget me," she said, teasingly.

"Not if you're my world," I said, grinning. Her face flushes and her eyes widen, before rolling them. While I can tell from her flush and smile is that she'd liked what I said, but she doesn't quite believe me. But I will prove it to her.

Her hands wander down to grip my dress shirt. Fuck, I love when she gets aggressive. She pulls me close, our lips brushing each other. A thrill travels up my spine. She smells like the ocean and citrus. Out here with her, just her and I, I'm at peace. The same peace our little cave provides me with.

"Alright Romeo," she said, right before kissing me. Our lips dance with each other, teeth nipping and tongues teasing. I press my hips against hers, trapping her against the railing. My other hand wanders down. She widens her stance, exposing that glorious leg. I grip her thigh, lifting it to wrap it around my waist, enjoying how the dress falls away from her.

She may have thought I was joking but she is slowly becoming my world. Her smile captivates me. Her eyes lure me toward feelings I didn't know I could feel. Her soul soothes the tormented sea within me.

"Don't you dare ruin this dress," she whispered against my mouth. My grip loosens against her hips, the fabric dropping slightly.

"I want you," I murmur, kissing down her neck. "I need you," I said. Her hands wander up my chest and into my hair. Her nails dig into my scalp, and I groan against her skin.

She pulled my head away for a second before our mouths crashed together once again. We were tongues and teeth, fighting against each other.

"Cas," she gasped into my mouth. She pulled another groan from me. My hips buck against hers. Her heel digs into my lower back, keeping me close.

"Say my name again," I beg. *"Please."*

"Caspian," she whispered against my ear. Her teeth tugged at my earlobe, and I swear I'm going to lose all sense of control and take her right here. *Fuck.* My fangs ache with the need to claim her as they stretch to scratch her neck.

"Did you know we have fangs M'Lady?" I whisper against her skin. Her hips buck against mine, seeking friction.

"Is it like werewolves and vampires?" she asked, her voice soft. I suck on her neck, earning another moan.

"Yes. I have to be careful with them, but you make me crave you so badly," I said, not caring about what the fuck I'm saying. My grip on her hips tightens as her lips brushed my neck. Now I was the one freely giving her my moans. Her hands slid down my waist and my breath hitched.

"I like this," she whispered, her hand cupping my aching cock. I let out a strangled breath. She is going to be my undoing. The corner of her lips tilts up. My hand slipped under her dress, brushing against her panties. *She's so wet.*

"You like this too," I said, gripping the back of her neck. She hummed and my eyes closed briefly as we stroke each other. Her hips move faster and this time she bites my neck stifling another moan.

"Grip me harder," I choke out. She followed my instructions. Too quickly, beneath the moonlight and surrounded by the roar of the ocean, our bodies came together. Our hearts raced against each other as we tried to catch our breaths.

"You wanted to forget, didn't you?" she asked, her tone teasing. I nod, my hips pressing against her hand. Our mouths met again, and I relished her taste. We are a mess of tangled tongues and limbs, holding each other up against the railing.

Laughter rings from inside and we freeze. I force myself to pull away and Crystal stares at me, her face flushed. Then we break out in laughter. She clears her throat, her gaze drifting away. I leaned forward, sneaking in one more kiss.

"We should probably get cleaned up and go back in," I said, pressing my forehead against hers. Crystal licked her lips before sighing.

"I suppose we *should* keep mingling," she said, sounding slightly disappointed. I chuckle.

"Don't worry, soon we'll be home," I said.

"With tea!" she exclaimed. My heart skipped. I'd said home and she didn't correct me. I nodded. A cup of tea with her in my arms is the perfect way to end a night. It's a night I want to happen every day until I'm called back into the ocean one last time.

She straightened her dress and adjusted her hair. She tapped around her face in an attempt to smooth out her makeup. I smile as I watch her. Her lips slightly swollen and I can't help but lick mine. I adjusted my pants. *I needed to head to the bathroom.*

"How do I look?" she asked, cheeks still pink.

"Beautiful," I said, offering her my hand.

CHAPTER 25
SISTER SISTER

Crystal

I walk down the familiar path towards the second cottage. While we've already finished the project, I wanted to double check one more time. What was left on my list is now the bed and breakfast, meadery and bookstore. Ronan said that we can move the last two projects to the fall since the bed and breakfast is expecting more beings with the impending ceremony.

We are nearing the end of the month, which means summer is almost over and the ceremony will be soon. I swallow, remembering Cas' confession from a few nights ago. I hadn't realized that we are so similar. The feelings about himself are very much like mine.

I grew up quiet and observant, and when my mom passed away, I took on the role of caregiver– a role I was never supposed to have. Cas took on the role of providing comedic relief. I understood him. I always question myself around those who expect things of me that I feel like I can handle.

Am I smiling too much? Are my questions and curiosity dumb? They sure are a sign of how little I've experienced. Maybe I'm too serious, too much of everything and at the same time not enough.

I rub my lips, remembering our time on the balcony. It was different. It was heated, aggressive, and needy. Cas had kissed me like it was going to be our last kiss ever. Stars, and I sure I hope it isn't. We gave in to our desires that evening and it went beyond my expectation.

The cottage came into view. It looks like Cas', but this one is light green with a white trim. It's cute and quaint. The front porch has been rebuilt, and I can still feel traces of the magic I imbued it with. In a few days the wood will settle into place and bring warmth and protection. I smile, feeling proud of my projects.

I'm enjoying this. I like being in charge and helping to rebuild something that was once beautiful. I like bringing life back into things. I'm also falling for this town and its quiet nature.

My phone buzzes. and It's a text from Ronan. He's heading to the meadery now. I snap a few photos of the cottage to send to my dad. I bite my lower lip and decide to send it to Eleanor too. We still haven't had a proper conversation about my emotional blow up.

As I headed towards the meadery, my phone beeps.

ELEANOR

Mom would have loved it!

She would have. She walked this town before, and she fell in love with it. Now I am too.

"THE MEADERY NEEDS A LOT OF WORK," Ronan said, his brows furrowed. It's true. The meadery is broken down and we will need to nearly rebuild its entire structure. The walls and ceiling beams all need to be refortified along with the ceiling beams. The bar also needed to be gutted. While Hale's Lumber Industry's main duty is to provide and treat the lumber, I've created a department to handle reconstruction.

Coralia Coast is our first big project for this department. The cottages and the stage were minor projects. But the meadery is and the bookstore are major rebuilds. I can see why Ronan wants to move this to the fall. It will take us some time to make sure everything is up to code, especially if he wants to sell the property.

"You had mentioned that you knew someone who might be interested in acquiring the meadery," Ronan said, his nose wrinkling. I stifle a cough. The inside is littered with dust, broken tables and chairs. I nod. There's a certain blonde back in Lavender Falls who I know prefers mead to her family's whiskey.

"Yes. Mead is her thing," I said. Ronan raised an eyebrow when I said *her*. I raise my eyebrow back. His face relaxed.

"I don't care who it is as long as they are interested and serious," he said. I smirk. If she is interested, it will be fun to see their personalities clash.

"That makes me glad," I said. I stifle a chuckle. "I'm going to hold you to that," I said, walking back out.

Ronan followed me out, his eyes immediately moving toward on the ocean. I can just make it out between the buildings.

"How are you feeling by the way?" I ask. He took a moment.

"Regarding what?" he asked. My lips twitch.

"Well, I know you're confident in what *I'm* doing, so you're not worried about that," I said, trying to ease the tension. Ronan's chuckle is rough. The King didn't crack too many smiles let alone laugh, so I'm happy I can break past his icy demeanor.

Both Ronan and I take care of the people we care about. We hold a lot of responsibility. It's a constant weight that dictates the way we move in the world.

"Cas has been stressed," I said, quietly. Ronan's eyes drop to the ground, and he nods.

"I know he's under a lot of pressure, but so am I," he began. He curled his hands into firsts. "I don't mean to minimize what he must do. There's not much I can do to help him," he said. I kick a rock with my foot, my stomach twisting with anxiety. I don't want to overstep.

"Of course there is," I said. Ronan shook his head.

"The trident has to come to *him* in order to heal the coral," he said. I sigh. While I know where Ronan is coming from, I understand what being a younger sibling is like. It's constantly hoping that the ones who are older will take care of you when you need them. Both Cas and I were left to take care of ourselves, unsure of if we could trust the ones who walked before us.

"While that's true, Cas doesn't trust himself. He's worried about letting you all down again," I said. "He believes that you think he'll run away again. He's struggling to be the prince that you all need because he's spent his whole life being your clown. That's the role he's used to," I said. This is a bad idea. I'm getting into the middle of their family drama when I have drama of my own. Ronan sighed, running a hand over his face.

"He doesn't trust us to be there for him because he's always been there for us," he admitted, quietly. I nod.

When he finally looked at me his eyes mirrored a similar storm I've seen in Cas. A broken and tired look. "But I don't know how to be there for him. We've always had this…trench between us," he said. I nod again. Eleanor and I have a space between us too. A one-sided trench that I made her aware of.

"You need to go to him…swim to him?" I said. I really need to stop with these ocean puns. But Ronan cracked another chuckle so maybe it was a good one.

"He did mention that I need to go down to the ocean," he said, eyes back on the water.

"Maybe you should see what he's been so desperate to fix, what he's afraid he can't fix," I said. "This is something that you should do together." Ronan

"Thank you for Crystal. I'm sorry if my family issues have interfered with your work." I shook my head and offer him a smile. We walked towards the bed and breakfast, where my crew is awaiting instructions.

"You're good for him," he said. I blush. He's saying that because he thinks we are dating. But we aren't. It's all for show. Even though I'm slowly believing in our act.

THE BED and breakfast need some parts of their flooring to be replaced, and I contracted Celestino for some furniture. I smile. I had promised Celestino when we partnered to supply his carpentry shop with our lumber that I would help bring him business and I'm finally able to fulfill that promise.

I decide to pick up dinner for Cas and me on the way home. I smile inwardly. I feel like a real girlfriend. The door of Calder's Diner dinged. Mira turned around, her eyebrows furrowed within annoyance. I looked around and found myself clashing eyes with Kai and Ricky. I smile politely.

"Hi," I said, feeling shy. I'd talked to Ricky a bit at dinner, and I've spoken to Kai a few times, but these were Cas' friends, and I feel out of place around them without him being here. Ricky stood up and pulled me into a hug. My eyes widen.

"Hey there, Crys!" He sounds excited. Ricky is a big ball of energy and a flirt. Kai stood up and followed suit. I glance at Mira who rolled her eyes at the mermen.

"Lovely as always, Crystal," Kai said. He looked at Mira. "But not as lovely as Mira." He gave her a wink. I bite back a laugh, watching Mira's face turn red. She grabbed my arm, pulling me towards her.

"Alright mermen, back to your seats and wait for your order," she commanded. Kai bowed to her.

"Yes ma'am."

Mira dragged me into an empty booth and slid in next to me. I place my chin in my hand, wiggling my eyebrows.

"Don't start," she warned.

"I don't know what you mean," I said. She groaned.

"He comes in here every day," she said with an exasperated tone. I glance back at Kai, who waved at us.

"Why don't we like him again?" I ask. Kai is always sweet despite having rude cousins. Sure, he liked poking at Mira, but I have a feeling that Mira secretly likes his teasing. She sighed, sitting back.

"Nothing," she grumbled. I look between them, and she sighed again. "He's annoying and persistent and I have other things to focus on," she said.

"Like?" I ask. She turned to face me with a fake smile.

"Like your order. What'll it be, bestie?" she asked. I roll my eyes, letting it go for now.

"Chili cheese fries," I said as she made a face. "I like them, okay? And get the lobster roll with mac n' cheese for Cas," I said. While I wasn't a big fan of seafood, I know Cas likes it. Mira's lips pulled into a smirk.

"I'm guessing you guys won't be making out later," she teased. I blush.

"I don't know what you mean," I said, turning to face the window. She hummed.

"Don't think I didn't notice you two sneaking off the other night," she said. My face is on fire.

We did sneak off and I had hoped no one really noticed. Cas had opened up to me about his fears. He'd laid his heart out for me. The more time we spent together, the closer we grew and the more tempted I am to tell him more about my thoughts that lurked in the back of my head and the deepest parts of my heart.

"Don't worry. I don't need the gross details about you and my cousin. I'll get your food," she said, sliding away. I sit back in my seat and watch the waves crash onto the shore.

･ ｡ 🐚 🐚 🐚 ｡ ･

Cas isn't home yet when I get there with dinner. The cottage is quiet and there is faint rustling from the flowers scratching against the windows from the breeze. I quickly shower and switch into sweats.

I sit on the couch, eyeing my phone. I have been meaning to talk to

Eleanor. Even though we'd video chatted the other day, the ladies were there too, and we weren't able to actually talk. I'd said hurtful things, and it is slowly eating me up inside. I'd hurt my sister. I groan, knowing I needed to get this over with.

She picked up on the first ring which surprised me. The line is quiet.

"Hey," I said, weakly. Eleanor sighed.

"Hey there," she said. "How have you've been?" she asked. I lean my head against the couch, staring at the ceiling.

"Not bad, I guess. The project is back on track, and we have a better plan for the upcoming work we're going to be doing," I began. "Ronan is happy with our work. Some of the royals that are here want to have meetings with us too," I said, my lips tilting in a smile. My dad is getting more inquiries about potential contracts to do rebuilds in other supernatural towns.

"Crystal, that's great! Seriously," she said. "I never thought the company would do anything like that," she said. I take a breath. I understand her.

My dad, growing up, only focused on being a lumber supplier. I was the one that had the idea that we could do more. My memories of mom were always surrounded by love and helping others.

"I knew that Hale's had the capability to do more, give back and help," I said. Eleanor sighed and it made my heart freeze. My stomach tightened in anticipation.

"I guess…I never thought about the company that way. For me the company felt like a burden that I was forced to have someday have," she said. I swallow. Instead of her having it, it fell to me.

"Well, how are you?" I asked, hoping to change the subject. I didn't want to go down that path and slip by saying another hurtful thing.

"Fine, I guess. Our summer festival is starting soon. It's the weekend before Sailor's ceremony. We're still invited right?" she asked.

"Yes, you are. He really wants you all there for it," I said. Cas was able to learn about parts of himself with them. I can tell from the amount of laughter they shared back at Lavender Falls and the guilt he harbored from keeping his identity a secret that he needs them. There was a bit of silence.

"How is he?" she asked. Eleanor was friends with Cas longer than I was. They'd hung out all the time, did karaoke together and took shots. They are close friends, and I knew she was hurt that he kept his secret from the group.

"He's struggling a bit honestly. It's a lot of responsibility that he has. He ran from it, and he feels guilty over that choice despite the fact that everyone seems to be okay with it," I said.

"We texted a few days ago when he was getting ready for one of the dinners," she commented. A giggle poured out of her. "He sent me a drink recipe Mira shared with him. I smile, happy that he was still talking to them.

"You know, this town really is beautiful and everyone is nice," I said. Eleanor and Lily had told me that Coralia Coast was cold and that the beings felt standoffish. I guess there was a bit of that in the beginning. But it seemed like with Cas returning, he'd brought the sun's warmth back to this seaside town.

"He's really stressed and anxious about the coral," I said, quietly. He's frustrated and I wished I could help him.

"Oh no, the trident right?" she said. I guess Cas had been updating them on what has been going on.

"Yeah. He still can't find it, but....," I trail off.

"But?" she asked. I sigh.

"In the books it says that the trident will come to him at the right time. That he'll know. I think he just has to trust himself– and his magic– more," I said. He spent so much time away from his tail, from what makes him so special that there's a disconnect.

"Oh absolutely. Crys, he never transformed here. When I went to Coralia it was the first time, I'd ever saw his tail," she said. "I've also never *really* seen him use his abilities that much."

"Exactly," I said. The conversation became quiet. I wasn't sure what else to say. *Is now the time to apologize? Do I talk about something else, like maybe Waldo?*

"How are you?" she asked, filling in the silence. I bite my cheek. That is a small question that came with a loaded answer. How *am* I? I'm exhausted from work, juggling my feelings, faking who I am. Sad, because my life didn't go how I ever thought it would. Happy, because I have chili cheese fries. Lost, because once again: *life*.

"I'm okay," I said, masking the multitude of emotions with two words.

"You can talk to me. I know…I know I haven't been there," she said. Her voice sounded small, hesitant. This is my in, right? The opening to telling her exactly how I feel about her, about our dad and my childhood.

And yet I can't do it. I'd spent years burying my feelings, wearing a masking to hide what I actually feel. My throat constricts.

"Everything is going well." I forced the words out, my eyes burning. *I'm a fucking liar.*

"Well…I had lunch with dad," she said. My heart stops. I lick my lips, a wave of uneasiness washing over me.

"Oh?" I squeak. *Oh?*

"It was fine, I guess. He's still…our father," she said. My stomach sinks. She called him father. She always did that as a dig to showcase their turbulent relationship. I made a noise. "He apologized for our past relationship, but then criticized my career choice, *then* apologized again and said he hated talking about his feelings so I said so maybe we shouldn't talk at all," she said with a groan. "I know, that was a bit harsh," she rushed out. I stared at the blank TV.

Suddenly I'm fourteen again with my sister and my dad fighting. By that point I'd gotten really good at numbing myself to their words and dissociating from the moment in order to protect myself.

"Then he went to meet Lily's mom for who knows what," she said.

"He's friends with her," I pointed out. Mom and dad were close to Lily's mom, and Celestino and Lola's parents. She sighed, and the sound irritated me. My fingers twitched at my side.

"I guess," she said. My nostrils flare. Did she even *try* to reconcile? Sure, according to her eyes he fucked up the conversation, but he *had* apologized. Did she?

"How do you feel about it?" I ask tentatively.

"About Lily's mom and father?" she said, her voice pitching higher. I roll my eyes.

"No, about your lunch with dad," I said, my voice annoyed.

"I mean, it was fine or whatever," she said.

"Or whatever?" I push. Their relationship isn't my problem now, but it *was* my problem for four years and her indifference still stings.

"I don't know Crystal. It's not like our relationship is peachy. Sure, he apologized. But he made my life miserable for years," she said, sounding like her teenage self again. A wave of anger washes over me.

Her life was miserable?

I bite down on my cheek hard. I want to scream at her. I want to yell. What about me? What about me having to listen to the yelling and slamming of doors? I cooked, I cleaned, and I did my fucking best to keep the peace in the damn house.

"Understandable," I said, masking my hurt. I'm over this conversation. I want to crawl into bed and forget the world for a bit. "Oh! Cas just got here, and he brought dinner," I said, lying to end the conversation.

"Wait! How are you guys?" she asked.

"Still in a fake relationship and sleeping in separate beds," I said, despite the fact that we did share a bed twice. *And I've been wanting to again.*

"Well remember that you deserve happiness in whatever way you want it," she said, her voice back to its bright tone. I hold back a snort.

"Thanks, Ellie."

CHAPTER 26
I Like Hiding

Crystal

Cas didn't come home until an hour later. By the time he came in the food had gotten cold and I was curled up in a ball in my room. The conversation with my sister had completely drained me. I was in a fight with my brain and my heart.

My heart wants to mend my dad and Eleanor's relationship now that a shift has finally happened within each of them. I can see how stubborn they both are. I can feel that their individual pain is blocking them from reconciling. But at the same time, their relationship isn't my problem. I can't fix their relationship. I'm the youngest daughter, the little sister. I have my own things I need to be worried about.

There is a soft knock at my door, and I quickly wipe my face. Cas steps in, already changed into a pair of black sweats and a blue shirt. I smile, weakly. He's so handsome and sweet. Too fucking sweet to someone whose brain is always in the clouds.

"Hey, you didn't eat dinner," he said, coming closer. I clutch at my covers. I take a breath, hoping to settle my emotions before he can read into them.

"I was talking to Eleanor and then I was waiting for you," I said, doing my best to sound bright. Cas sat on the bed and my stomach twisted. He is going to see through the façade. He is getting good at it. I blink quickly.

"Crystal," he said. I shiver at his tone, which is demanding yet soft. I jump out of bed and head towards the kitchen, trying to get away from his knowing gaze.

"How about we heat up the food and watch a movie?" I said, shoving my emotions down. I guess old habits die hard. I take a deep breath, forcing my brain to shut off and shoving my heart in a box. Cas says nothing, which I'm grateful for. I don't want to think right now. Thinking leads to feelings which will lead to tears, and I'm don't want to cry.

○ ○ ○ 🐚 🐚 🐚 ○ ○ ○

ONCE ON THE couch we turn on a movie and eat in silence. Occasionally Cas would glance over. He was checking on me, waiting to see me crack. But I won't, because I don't want to. I chew the inside of my cheek, feeling my emotions at the edges of my brain. They are poking at me, begging to be released.

I take a deep breath and stand to clean up our dishes. Cas follows behind me and I inwardly groan. *He's waiting for me to say something.*

"How was your day?" I ask. Cas pulls me away from the sink and lifts me onto the counter.

"Stay," he demanded. I roll my eyes.

"Yes sir," I said, teasingly. He chuckled and it eased a fraction of my heart.

"One of the salves my Aunt Meryl made seems to be helping the coral. It isn't healing it all the way, but it *is* slowing down the rot much faster than the other remedies," he began as he washed the dishes. My legs swing back and forth.

"That's a good thing," I said, watching him. He had a few bags under his eyes, and I noticed his hair was getting longer.

"It is. My brother…is actually going to come down with me at some point. Some of the predators are starting to feel the effects of the dying coral," he said, his voice worried. His eyebrows dipped and his shoulders tensed. I guess Ronan took my advice. It eased me slightly. If only I could do the same for myself with my sister.

Cas and I had many things in common, from food, to music and shows to our relationships with our older siblings. We both had problems with them. They just manifested in opposite ways.

"That's good," I said. He looked at me and I looked away. He's sharing this with me in hopes that I will cave and share my own troubles with him. I have before and I want to now.

"And you?" he asked. I smile. I'm right. He saw through my mask and that's terrifying.

"Fine," I lied. Fine and okay have become permanent words in my lying vocabulary. But Cas is smart. He turned off the water and placed his wet hands on my cheek. I jump, startled by the wet heat.

"Your hands are wet!" I said. He kept his steady gaze on me.

"And you're lying," he said. I frown.

"I'm fine, Cas," I said, my voice trembling. Tears pricked my eyes, and I cursed. I don't want to fucking cry. I'm tired and done with the day. Cas snorted which only angered me more.

"You're lying," he pushed, hands still on my face. I tried to pull away, but he tightens his grip, wedging his hips between my legs until they opened. "Crys," he urged. My throat tightens.

"I'm fine," I said through gritted teeth despite my eyes burning.

"Crystal, I can see your tears," he said, his voice softening. My heart races and my hands tremble. *Fuck it's happening.* A tidal wave of anxiety is forming in me. My body is weakening and I'm struggling to keep it together. His thumb brushes my wet cheeks.

"S-sometimes the lights can be overwhelming," I stumble to say. Cas' blue eyes soften, and his hands move down to my waist, pulling me closer. I wrap my legs around him, resting my head on his shoulder.

"Sometimes beings can be too. Life and work," he said, pulling my hands to wrap around his waist. I inhale sharply.

"B-but I'm fine." The lie is tumbling out of me despite the tears raining down my face. I hiccup, my heart beating faster.

"M'Lady," he said, tenderly. "It's okay to not be okay," he said, pressing his forehead against mine. I shake my head, shutting my eyes.

"I have to be okay. E-everyone needs me to be okay," I said, my breathing shallow. "If I say I'm not okay then…," I trail off. My control is slipping, and it feels like the air around us is being sucked out of the room. I'm dangerously close to spilling all my hidden thoughts.

"Tell me," he begged quietly. I sniffle, my hands digging into the back of his shirt.

"If I say I'm not okay then I have to admit that I never feel okay," I begin. My brain has checked out and my heart is finally pouring everything out. "I'd have to admit that I'm exhausted every day because every day I'm constantly worried about everyone and everything. That I feel stifled all the time because…because I'm just in a constant state of anxiety and sadness and no one sees me," I said. *Fuck. Fuck. Fuck.* **Shut up.**

I press my face into his neck, the tears flowing freely as I try to breathe. But I can't breathe. I'm horrible. How can I be admitting this?

Cas' hand rubbed my back reassuringly. "Keep going," he whispered. I let out a pained noise.

"I'm walking a fine line between being okay and not okay every day. I can't trust myself or, my feelings. I've spent so much of my life being there for others that I don't know how to be there for myself." I paused to take a deep breath. "I-I don't know who I am because I've spent my entire fucking life being what everyone else needed and I'm tired. I'm *so* fucking tired of being needed and I hate myself for even feeling that way."

"Crystal-" I push Cas away, covering my mouth. I'm shaking all over.

"I sound like a shitty being for admitting that. I'm—listen, I'm fine. I just need to cry in my room. This happens every once in a while, but it's fine," I said, trying to keep my head above water. Cas stares at me, his lips twisted in a frown. He is upset with me.

Of course, he is. I admitted that I was tired of being needed and he probably feels guilty about being my fake boyfriend. Imagine having a fake girlfriend as needy and sad as me.

Cas doesn't say anything. Instead, he lifts me off the counter, presses a kiss to my forehead and whispers, in my ear.

"Follow me."

It's close to midnight and we are back at the spring. Cas carried two fluffy robes with him. He hadn't spoken the whole walk down here and it made me nervous. Was he upset? Did he feel guilty? How can I take everything that I said back?

"Strip," he said. My eyes widen. The corner of his lips twitched. "Strip and get in the water please," he said, turning around. Cas had already seen me naked and yet he still gives me my privacy. I strip out of my clothes with nervous fingers.

I groan as I step into the warm water. I wasn't sure how the spring stayed hot even though it connected to the ocean but I'm not going to complain. The water feels amazing against my aching muscles. There is a wave behind me, and Cas' fingers brush my shoulder. I turn to look at him.

His cheeks are flushed, and his eyes glowed brightly against the moonlight. The darkness hid most of our naked bodies from each other. A toe brushed my calf.

"You didn't transform?" I ask. He shook his head.

"I want to be here with you in this form," he said. My hand trembles as I reach for him.

"Hold me?" I ask. Cas wrapped his arms around my waist, pulling me until we were flushed against each other. We sigh in relief. "Thank you," I said, quietly. He presses a kiss to the side of my head.

"You don't always have to be okay, Crystal," he whispered. Tears blur my eyes again. "I know you feel like you do because you've spent so much of your life taking care of others and being there for them. But you can rely on them too. You can rely on your sister," he said. My heart twisted. I swallow.

"I hurt her. I said things that hurt her," I confess. Cas took a breath, and it sets me on edge.

"What you told her, was it what you were feeling?" he asked. I gave a weak nod. Feelings I'd buried deep and carried with me against her and dad had poured out of me in the heat of the moment.

"Her pain does not take precedence over yours. You can't continue to hurt yourself by not telling others the pain they're causing you because you're in fear of hurting them." His arms tighten around me. "You can't live life if you feel broken inside. You're good at acting Crystal, I'll give you that, but I see how much pain you're in and you need to talk about how you feel, or the wound is only going to grow," he said. I squeezed my eyes shut.

"And you?" I ask, my voice sounding small in my ears. "*You* need to be honest with yourself and stop running. Everyone is here for you. You're more than a crown and pretty smile," I said, quietly.

"I guess we're both fakes," he whispered against my head. His breath was warm.

"Is this our first fight?" I ask, my fingers trembling against his back. *Are our words heated enough to break our growing friendship?*

"I think this is us looking out for one another in a calm and rational way," he said, and I chuckled, the tension easing.

"This isn't easy," I said. My trauma and pain created a habit that keeps me silent. But sharing with Cas, *being* with someone who didn't originate that habit made breaking these emotional chains of trauma slightly easier, bearable.

"It's not, but we're here for each other." He placed a kiss on my forehead.

"I know you've heard about my dad because of Eleanor, and I won't lie– he wasn't the best. My mom was his soulmate and losing her destroyed him. Him and Eleanor are similar, and so they just fed each other's fire until one day it got bad enough for her to leave," I said. I pulled enough away to stare into his eyes.

"It didn't matter that I'd spent years trying to keep the peace between them– lying about the amount of times dad made dinner for us, so she could see that he cared. Or how Eleanor always got him the better gifts to show that she noticed him," I said, no longer able to hold back my tears.

"I did everything. I became what they needed, and they never noticed me. They never noticed how much pain I was in. I don't even know who I am, Cas." The hurricane of emotions that I kept locked up were breaking out. "I've worn so many masks and now I'm just a shell of someone I don't even know," I said, breaking down in his arms. Cas allowed me to sob into his chest. His fingers massaged the back of my head, and I felt his lips against my cheek.

"I know who you are," he whispered. I snort, my body worn from crying, from admitting the feelings that I've held back for so long. "You're brave. You're so strong. Kind. Funny. Beautiful. Intelligent," he rattled off. I squeezed my eyes shut. "I'm saying these things because they're true, Crystal. You are so much more than what you give yourself credit for," he said. I press my forehead against his tattoo. His heart is a steady beat and that soothes me.

"Your dad has changed since I first met him. I can see he's trying, and Eleanor does too, it's just hard for her to trust him," he said. There is a twitch in my eye.

"And it's hard for him–"

"But they're *not* your responsibility. Their emotions have *never* been your responsibility, so they need to work it out on their own and together without you," he said. I take a breath. "I know it's hard. You were always in between them before but let them fight their own battles."

I lift my head to look at Cas. His blue eyes seemed troubled. "Focus on you. Do what *you* want. Go for what you want and don't worry about them. They're busy living their own lives and you should be too," he pointed out. I swallow.

"And you?" I asked. Cas had a strained relationship with his brother. And I understood it because I understood Ronan. He took on the responsibility for his family and the kingdom when their dad died, and I related to the burden of responsibility and in a similar way.

"What do you mean?" he asked, his grip around my waist, loosening.

"You and your brother," I said. *Fuck, maybe I shouldn't have brought him up again.* Cas looked away from me and down into the water, his eyes faraway.

"I should share too, huh?" he said. My eyes widened.

"You don't have to! I just thought you were helping me and–"

"I guess...he reminds me so much of dad and I just always feel like a disappointed. Disappointment I can handle but hope and faith? I've fucked up enough," he confessed. "Ronan took on his duty so easily while I fought mine tooth and nail." I shook my head.

"You're not a disappointment. I know you ran, but you ran because you needed space. Sometimes we have to get lost to find ourselves. And you found a great group of friends and everyone here, including your family, is just happy you're back now," I said. I press my face into the crook of his neck. "I'm happy you're here," I said, quietly. Cas squeezed me.

"We're a mess," he said, huffing out a laugh. I smile.

"But we're a mess together."

Cas stares at me, searching for something. His eyes are soft, tender. It eases me. "You have me," he whispered.

"I h-have you?" I asked. My heart is beating in my chest again. I have him. But I didn't. Not the way I wanted to at least. His eyes travel all over my face. He gently brushes my cheek with his lips.

"Yes," he said. "I'm here to be there for you, for when you're too tired to stand, when you need someone to make you laugh or smile, anything," he said. I let him hold me for a few more minutes.

"You don't have to do anything but be here with me," I said softly.

Eventually we pull apart swimming around the spring, hanging out behind the waterfall and enjoying the peace and quiet. I like this spring. I feel at home here and Cas has said the same thing.

"I always felt connected to this place," he said, looking at the moon. He eventually shifted into his tail so he could hold me better and

I could rest my legs. "I would always sneak away to this spring late at night or during study class," he said, his tone light. I look back at him, and he smiles.

"I ditched a lot of things," he said, sheepishly. I giggle. I can picture a younger sunshine blonde siren, running around with an infectious laughter.

"I feel it too. This spring is special," I said. I take a deep breath, feeling my worries melt away with each gentle wave of the water.

CHAPTER 27
CROISSANTS AND GRIEF

Caspian

I wake up to Crystal's warm body pressed against mine. After our late-night swim, we had come back home, and I followed her to her room. I walked her to her bed to tuck her in, but she'd scooted over and patted the bed quietly, inviting me to join her.

I crawled under the covers and pulled her close. My heart ached when I came home yesterday to see her curled in this bed alone. I could hear her sniffles through the door. She held back a lot. It's something that I've always noticed about her.

She is careful with her emotions, always watchful of how much she shares about herself. She spoke a bit about her childhood. She was the one who'd stepped up to take care of her family, like my brother had.

Last night there was something different between us. Somewhere between the hushed words, high-strung emotions and skin to skin contact, something shifted between us. We'd opened up to each other in a way we never had before. Our relationship is evolving, and I have no idea if she senses what I was sensing, if she feels what I'm feeling.

I sigh, breathing in her citrus smell. Crystal is making me see my brother and my community in a new light.

I'm struggling to trust the beings who said they cared about me because I didn't trust myself to not run away again. I did it once before, so didn't that mean I was capable of doing it again? I'd run away in fear of my responsibility, afraid of it and yet Ronan had no choice, he never did. I never saw him complain about it. Instead, he just pushed on with his grumpy attitude.

I glance at Crystal who is still sleeping. She will be waking up soon for work soon. She has been so stressed with being my fake girlfriend, dealing with my town's renovations, and yet she found time to hang out with Mira and me. I want to show her that I'm there for her, for whatever she needs. I brush a strand of hair away from her sleeping face. She takes care of everyone, including me.

I kiss her cheek softly and pull away. Her hand reached for me and I lightly chuckled.

"I have to make our coffee M'Lady," I whisper. She stretched her arms over her head, groaning. I can't stop grinning. She slowly blinked her eyes, trying to focus on my face. *She's adorable.*

"Oh," she squeaked.

"Morning, M'Lady," I said. Her face slowly turned pink, and I had the urge to kiss.

"Morning," she said, her voice scratchy.

"I'll go make our coffee," I said, kissing her forehead. Fuck it. If I'm her fake boyfriend, I'm going to act like it until she tells me to stop. The corner of her lips twitched.

"I can make you breakfast," she said, hand on my arm.

"Will you be making *yourself* breakfast too?" I ask. Her brow twitched.

"I'm actually having breakfast with Mira," she said. I narrow my eyes playfully.

"Did she pressure you into eating with her? She can be very assertive" I ask. Her brows pinched in the middle.

"She just wanted to have breakfast, and I said I would love to," she said. My heart skips. This beautiful being is stitching herself into every thread that made up my life.

"Well, I'm kind of jealous she gets to have you," I said, crawling back under the covers to pull her close. A giggle escapes her. Stars, I would make a fool of myself all the time if it meant I got to hear her laugh.

"She gets me in the morning, and you get me later after work," she said. I pout playfully which makes her laugh more. With every passing day, what is happening between is blurring the line of our friendship. Our "fake" relationship was shifting.

Crystal turned around in my arms, our noses brushing as she stared at me. I swallow. Her eyes were as alluring as a siren's song. She has complete hold of me, and I don't want to let go.

"I can have you?" I whisper. Crystal's bottom lip wobbles slightly and a swell of emotions threaten to overtake me. She nodded quietly. I close my eyes, pulling her to my chest. We stay like this for a few moments. Two beings whose hearts are beating as one, enjoying the early morning peace.

"So, you don't want me to make you breakfast?" she mumbled. I shake my head and kiss the tip of her nose.

"I'll make our coffees, and you can go and get ready," I said. I like taking care of Crystal. I'm used to having to take care of everyone's emotional needs, that providing something physical for her makes me feel important and useful.

"Okay. Dinner together later?" she asked, pulling from my hold.

"Looking forward to it."

I WAS WALKING to the beach to meet Ricky when my phone rang. It was Celestino. I wince. I was actively avoiding talking to him even though I'd left Lavender Falls on good terms. Guilt still consumed me around my deception.

"Hey," I said, casually. Celestino scoffed.

"'Hey'? *That's* how you greet your best friend?" he asked. I gasp.

"Are you finally accepting our friendship?" I tease. I nod in hello to the beings of the town as I walk by them.

"Well clearly you don't with your cryptic one worded replies in the group chat," he said. My smile falters. It's not that I'm actively avoiding them, I'm just…scared. "You know we're not upset with you. We're just checking in," he said, his tone hesitant. I swallow.

"I know…I just feel…," I trail off, trying to find the right words.

"Like a shitty friend? You know that's okay." My eyes widen.

"It's okay that I'm a shitty friend?" I said, my voice getting louder. A few passersby's glance at me. Celestino lets out a chuckle.

"You feel shitty because you regret what you did, right?" he asked.

"Of course," I said, earnestly.

"Which means you wished you had told us sooner and going forward you plan on being a better friend that sends text messages with more than one word in them," he said. I shake my head, my grin returning easily. I don't know what I did to deserve these beings in my life but I'm grateful. I have people who care about me. I needed to let them care.

"So, two words in my texts. Got it," I tease. Celestino snorted and I heard the door open on his side.

"Perfect. Caleb and Flynn just walked in. You can catch us up now especially on how you're dating Crystal."

WALDO IS SWIMMING above us impatiently. Kai looks at me and I shrug my shoulders. The second I hit the water Waldo was waiting for me. Ricky had stayed back to help Ronan with something, so Kai was with me to check on the coral.

"What's up with him?" Kai asked as we swam after Waldo. I concentrate my eyes on Waldo, my magic illuminating his energy. He's anxious. But I'm not sure why.

Waldo takes us to a different patch of coral. Its color is dulling much like the others. We haven't seen this area before, though. My stomach sinks. It's spreading faster. We're about 200 yards from the shore.

Kai's and Waldo's eyes are on me. I'm meant to fix this. I'm the only one. I ball my fists. I'm supposed to be the one that saves the coral, and I can't yet. *Why me? What am I doing wrong? This is why I shouldn't even be–*

My head snaps to the right. There is a tug of magic pulling me, a soft melody playing inside my head. "Do you hear that?" I ask. Waldo shakes his head, and Kai looks around in confusion.

"I don't hear anything, and I have better hearing than you," Kai pointed out.

I swim towards the feeling. Something is out there, calling me. Was it the trident? I stop. No, this isn't right. Whatever is tugging me feels like Crystal. But that can't be right. *Why would I be sensing Crystal this far out?*

I take a breath and go back to Kai, who pats my arm. "Let's do some rounds around the different areas of the corals and I'll check on the marine life," I said. Kai nodded and swam off.

"Come on Waldo," I said. I don't know what I was doing. But everyone tells me I need to reconnect with my magic, and so that's what I'm going to be doing.

If the fates granted me the ability to speak to the sea creatures, then it's for a reason. Maybe the ones who have been living longer have an idea of what can be done.

Or maybe they know where the trident is.

I'M STIRRING a pot of sauce after spending the afternoon in the ocean. Many of the creatures are aware of the dying coral. Some of them have been having to move to other parts of the ocean. Some places are being overrun with fish and crabs seeking shelter.

The ocean and its creatures are shifting their patterns to account for crisis. I made sure to tell them that King Ronan is doing his best to find a solution for the coral and that I, as the Second Prince, am also working tirelessly to find a solution.

They are very appreciative of my honesty and have watched each time I've tried a different salve on the coral. Kai had eventually left to see my Aunt Meryl and report back on the salve that had shown some promise.

That feeling in the ocean.

It feels like when I'm with Crystal. It's the same warmth and peace. *But I shouldn't have been feeling her presence all the way out there.*

After transforming I went straight to the grocery store. Crystal occupied my mind. She'd had a rough summer so far and I decided I wanted to do something for her, something that would remind her of home.

I just hope I'm doing it right. The sauce is red-orange color. It's like tomatoes, garlic, and red peppers. I added the beer and prayed I didn't just fuck everything up. It had taken two different transportation spells to get all the different meats.

This sandwich is a fucking beast, but Crystal was so happy when she was telling me about it. I smiled to myself. The brightness about her when she spoke about her mom made me ache. I didn't talk about my dad often, practically never.

I love my dad, but when he passed it changed our family. My mom was heartbroken and rightfully so. She'd lost her soulmate, her other half. My brother had to step in as king, earlier than we'd all planned, and I was there to witness everything. I made everyone laugh and smile even though I'd just lost my dad and uncle. My dad, who despite getting annoyed with me whenever I wanted to be lazy, provided me with a space to have fun and be silly.

Stars, he showed me a place to run away to so I wouldn't leave home and yet…I had. Instead of running to my secret cave I ran out and I didn't look back. Sometimes I wonder if my brother hadn't been in Lavender Falls would I have ever come back? If I'm honest, I don't think I would have. Carrie would have pressured me to, but I would have stayed put.

And now being back I'm feeling like myself again, like who I was before the death of my dad and uncle. My powers are growing stronger. I'm growing more confident in them and *fuck* I missed swimming with my tail. In spite of not feeling good enough to be the Second Prince, I found that talking to the marine life and helping them with their problems is second nature. But the trident is still missing it, and I need it to heal the coral.

My head snaps up when I hear the soft click of the door. There is a small gasp followed by fast footsteps.

When I turn around Crystal's ponytail is slipping, her jeans have patches of dirt on them, and her bag is falling off her shoulder. She's holding a box of baked goods in her other hand.

"Welcome home," I said, smiling. Why did those two words make my heart race and my mind jump to a future that isn't promised?

"T-that smell," she said, placing her stuff down on the counter to come towards the pot. Her cheeks are flushed and her eyes water. I wince. Maybe I fucked up. What if it tastes bad? What if reliving the memory of her mom causes more pain? She swallowed and I waited with bated breath. Her wide hazel eyes meet mine. "Can I have a taste?" she asked, softly. I nod, too afraid to speak.

She took a spoonful. Her tongue darts out to lick her bottom lip. I watch her eyes close, her eyebrows twitch and her cheeks flush darker. When she opens her eyes, tears run down her face. I reach for her instinctively, crushing her to my chest.

"I'm sorry if it's shit Crystal. You talked about the dish and your mom, and I thought maybe making this could be something nice," I rush out. She buries her face in my chest as her shoulders shake. I hold her tight as her tears begin soaking my shirt.

"Caspian," she whispered. My knees nearly buckled. She used my full name. I pull slightly back to look at her. She has the biggest smile on her face. "A bit more salt and it's pretty close," she said, through her tears. My shoulders drop and I press my forehead against her.

"Are you sure?" I ask. "Did I didn't overstep or something?"

"You're doing too many nice things for me," she whispered. My heart cracks a bit. I hate that she feels undeserving of my kindness. I can simply hold the door open for her, and she will feel guilty about it. I cup her face, forcing her to look at me.

"You, Crystal, are deserving of every ounce of goodness that comes your way," I said and brushed a kiss against her right cheek. "You don't need to feel like you have to earn kindness or feel obligated to return the sentiment when it's given to you freely," I said, placing a kiss on her left cheek. I brush her tears away with my thumb.

"Accepted but sometimes I want to do nice things for you because you do so much for everyone else," she whispered. I chuckle. *She's a sweetheart through and through.*

"Accepted," I said. She kissed both of my cheeks, mimicking me.

"Good boy," she teased.

"Crystal, please we have to eat first," I said. She throws her head back laughing and the air around us eases. I point to the box. "You went to the bakery?" I asked. She shook her head, her ponytail nearly falling out.

"Ms. Serena just keeps giving me things every time she sees me," she said. Ms. Serena owns the bed and breakfast and was one of the best bakers. I open the box and gasp.

"You're telling me she gives you her sea salt caramel croissant for free?" I said in disbelief.

"Yes! I guess she just likes me."

"Crystal, how am I suppose to compete for your love if she is giving you sea salt caramel croissants?" Her eyes twinkle and before I can reach to grab one, she closes the box.

"I do have a list, don't I?"

───✧✧✧───

WE ATE in comfortable silence outside. Every so often Crystal's eyes would soften against the setting sun and her shoulders would shimmy. I was so worried that I'd overstepped somehow. Instead, she looked at me like I'd hung the sun and cleared away her dark days.

"You sure it's not bad?" I ask. I can cook a decent meal, but this dish had so many layers to it. She nodded her head mid-chew.

"Just needed more salt and some hot sauce," she said, after taking a sip of a water. "Cas, this is beyond what anyone has ever done for me." Her fork scraped at the plate as her eyes turned away. "You didn't need to do this," she said. I roll my eyes. Crystal struggles with letting others take care of her. She is always used to always being in control.

"But thank you," she said, making eyes contact. She's learning slowly. I move to sit next to her, pulling her to my side. She sighed immediately and I bite back a grin.

"My dad would have loved this," I said, softly. Her hazel eyes widen as she looks up at me. I don't talk about my dad or uncle much. It hurts to. Their loss is a deep crack in my heart. Since being with Crystal I've learned that the crack they left didn't need to be cold and empty but could be filled with the memories I was given.

"He loved anything with a lot of meat in it," I said. "My uncle loved having barbecues throughout the summer. Actually, we used would have the renaissance festival come to town for a month and he would host these feasts that matched each weekend's theme for the festival." Crystal squeezed my hip, her eyes shining, and I couldn't stop myself from continuing.

"My Uncle manned the grill, but it was actually Aunt Meryl who would tell him when to flip the meat and plate the food. Then my dad would bring out his guitar and sing some songs and we would spend the day eating and drinking," I said, laughing.

As much as I hated being a prince, I had so many happy memories with my family. We ate, danced, sang, and swam together. "When they passed away things changed. Ronan threw himself into being king with my mom's help. Aunt Meryl had to start running the shop solely on her own," I said, softly. "After their deaths, things in our family, around town, shifted. It's felt like our town has been stuck in a fog."

I stare at my hands. I did my best to help everyone on land, but I distanced myself from the duties I had to the ocean. The town suffered during this transition and looking back our tourism dwindled. We've been hanging on to a buoy just to stay afloat.

Crystal intertwined her fingers with mine, pulling my focus back to the present. Against the sun her eyes looked like melted honey. Her freckles were more prominent now and I have the urge to trace them with my fingers.

"Well, it's a good thing you have a lighthouse," she said with a grin. A lighthouse? I shook my head, a chuckle pouring out of me as, my body instinctively moved towards hers. I kiss her cheek once, twice.

"We do. We definitely do," I said. She leaned her head against my shoulder, her other hand running up and down my chest.

"Grief isn't easy. It'll never be. Some days you think you're okay and then a smell, a sound, *anything* will remind you of them and you'll remember they're not there anymore," she said, her voice wobbling. "My mom wasn't there for my prom, to helping me pick a college, and she won't be there when I need a wedding dress." I blink back tears. My dad and uncle have already missed out on so much and will continue to.

"It hurts but sometimes it's okay to hurt. The pain reminds us that we're still here, alive and breathing. I use the memories I do have of my mom to strive for a better life," she said. She looked up at me, her eyes glistening with tears. "I'm working on living for myself because of her. What do their memories push *you* to do?" she asked. My heart cracked open, memories began flooding my mind again. I take a deep breath.

"They would be disappointed in me," I admit. The corner of my lips twitched. "Uncle Seward would smack me upside the head. My dad would shake his head at me and then...," I trailed off. Both of them had pushed me towards accepting who I'm supposed to be. My stomach twists and Crystal's hand cups my cheek.

"And *then* what would they say?" she asked. My hand traces her cheek towards her right ear. Her eyes briefly closed on a sigh.

"They would say that I need to believe in myself more, and trust myself more," I said begrudgingly. She tapped my chest three times.

"See? You know what to do," she said, confidently. I shake my head again, squeezing her. She squeals, the sound making my heart want to spring out of my chest.

"Grief becomes easier to manage once you accept it," she said, quietly. I take a deep breath. While my uncle and dad are gone now, I carry different parts of them with me. From their laugh, to my dad's eyes, my uncle's snarky attitude, and my love of dancing.

I grew up thinking I wasn't like them. That I could never live up to their legacy. But I can. I just have to try.

CHAPTER 28
BENEATH BLANKETS

Crystal

I'm meeting Cas' mom at the diner. She had asked me when she saw me eating with Mira. There was no way I was going to refuse her, even if it did make me nervous. I didn't have time to tell Cas about it. Between getting up early for work each day and crawling into bed with him at night I've been wiped. He's also been so busy, spending hours in the ocean every day.

Mrs. Calder strolled in with a wide smile and I stand immediately. She opened her arms to me and my heart thumped. I freeze for a second before returning her hug, feeling a slight pain in my chest, my heart cracking slightly. All of a sudden, I'm a kid again. She smells like jasmine drifting in the ocean breeze.

"I am so glad we are having breakfast," she said, her blue eyes bright. I smile, sliding into the booth.

"Me as well," I said, politely. Mira took our order quickly. I shift slightly in my seat under her watchful gaze.

"Thank you so much for joining me. I know your schedule has been extraneous," she said. I nod. There was no way I would have said no regardless.

"I'm happy Ronan selected my dad's company and I've been enjoying your town," I said. She nodded.

"We have been bustling with a few more tourists. I can't wait for the meadery and bookstore," she said, sounding excited. I smile.

"I think both of those things will help," I said, earnestly. The meadery will be a big selling point in getting tourists to stay. Mrs. Calder took a sip of her water, glancing at the ocean. There was a faraway look in her eyes.

"You're good for him," she commented, softly. My eyes widen and a flush creeps up my face.

"I am?" I question. She giggled, sitting back in her seat.

"He's different around you. A *good* different," she clarified. I raise an eyebrow. Would she still feel this way if she knew we weren't really together? I squeeze my hands beneath the table. "Cas has always been a ray of sunshine. Even as a child. He loved making others happy," she said with a wistful smile. "But as he grew older, he struggled," she said, her voice dipping. I stay quiet. "He kept pushing his responsibilities off and then when Edmar and Seward died he changed."

She sighed deeply before looking at me. "When his father and uncle passed away, making us happy became his obligation," she said. "He twisted himself into what others needed to the point where it became a reflex. I don't think he realizes he does it," she said. I reached for my cup of coffee. "And I should have done better. I let Ronan take over in my grief and then I was more queen widow than mom." She winced and wiped her nose.

"Grief has a way of stealing our time," I note. She looked at me in surprise. "I can understand that," I said. She nodded.

"But a new tide is on the horizon. I know it. So, thank you for what you're doing for my town and allowing Caspian to be simply Caspian." She reaches for my hand, and I take it. "Thank you for bringing my boy back to life," she said, grinning.

I nod my head, uncomfortable with her praise knowing the truth is that what Cas and I have isn't real. We are just two friends whose line of friendship is being washed away.

GUILT CONSUMES me as I sit on my bed. Mrs. Calder has no idea that our relationship is fake. It's an entire lie and we are way too good at acting. She thinks that Cas is himself around me not realizing he is performing around me, *with* me.

Her son is too good to me. He makes me coffee every morning. He holds me until I fall asleep, eases my anxiety, and takes me on midnight swims. I glance at the vase of flowers on my dresser. Cas took the time to make me a recipe from my childhood. He brought a piece of my mom back to me. So much of his thoughts and consideration went into my own happiness.

An idea forms in my head, and I rush to quickly text Mira.

ME
> Do you have twinkling lights and extra sheets?

MIRA/NEW FRIEND
> whatever naughty thing you're going to do with my cousin I would like to NOT know the details

ME
> MIRA! It is not like that! I want to do something nice for him

MIRA/NEW FRIEND
> And the sheets....

ME
> I'm trying to make a fort for a cozy movie night

MIRA/NEW FRIEND
> OH MY STARS! we loved doing that as kids!

ME
> ...I've never made one...

A SIREN'S SUMMER FOR LOVE

MIRA/NEW FRIEND
Give me thirty minutes

"This is insane," I said, watching Mira place the last corner of the last sheet on top of a lamp. Not only did she bring sheets and twinkling lights, but she also brought extra couch cushions. From where? No idea.

We placed the pillow on the floor to make a makeshift mattress against the couch. Two giant sheets were spread out to cover the couch, all the way to the TV that will cocoon us. Two strings of twinkling lights stretched out from each lamp, holding up the sheet and met at the TV.

I covered the makeshift mattress with cozy pillows and blankets. We moved the coffee table against the TV stand. I placed two boxes of pizza, a pitcher of spiked iced tea, popcorn, and sour candy on that I found stashed away.

"This is very cute," Mira said, hands on her hips. She smiled, admiring her workbook.

"Do you think he'll like it?" I ask. Maybe this is too much. It is, isn't it? I'm only his fake girlfriend, and maybe this is too much for a friend to do.

"He's going to love it. and I'm going to leave before he comes in, sees what you did and then shoves his tongue down your throat," she said. I threw my head back laughing.

"Thank you, Mira," I said. I'm happy I have Mira here. She is a good friend. Stubborn yet, sweet, blunt but hilarious.

"What are friends for?" she said, casually. I bite back a smile.

Friends.

I PACE BACK AND FORTH, waiting for Cas to arrive. The second he opens the door he'll see what I've done. My stomach is in knots waiting for him. My brain is split in half. One side of me trusts that he will like this. But the other half of me is nervous, worried that I'm doing too much.

The door clicks and I spin around, my ponytail smacking me in the face. I grip the bottom of my sweatshirt, sprites flying in my stomach. Cas steps through the door looking gorgeous as ever. He's wearing a white shirt that makes his tan skin glow with shorts. His hair is tousled back and looks dangerously soft. When our eyes meet, a smile stretches across his face and then they widen as he takes in the state of the living room.

"Crystal. What is this?" he asked, walking in. My brows furrow as I notice he has a box of pizza and a bouquet of carnations in hand.

"That's going to be a lot of pizza," I murmur. He glances at the box and then me.

"What do you mean?" he asked. I take the flowers from him, inhaling their subtle scent. Cas winks when he catches me with a smile. I grab his hand as he slips off his shoes. I lead him towards the fort and lift the blanket to reveal inside.

"Is this our fort?" he asked, his eyes lighting up. *Ours.* This is ours. Hearing him say it gives me fuzzy feelings. I blush like I always do around him.

"This is not because of what you did the other day. I just wanted to take care of you, do something for you. Just because," I said, heart racing. His eyes land on the pizzas and he chuckle.

"Guess we'll be eating pizza tomorrow," he said.

"I love pizza for breakfast," I said. Cas sighed happily, a smile stretching across his face.

"Fuck Crystal," he said, shaking his head. He places his box of pizza with the others before wrapping his arms around me.

"What?" I ask, concern bleeding into my voice. He stares at me; eyes filled with joy.

"I'm happy I met you," he whispered. My heart kicks up again and my magic buzzes in excitement. I'm happy too. I am beyond grateful for Cas even if we are just friends. He's brought me warmth, hope, and peace. Things I never thought I could have or even deserved. "I'm going to shower. Get nice and cozy for me," he said. I nodded, sharply.

"Yes, sir," I tease. The tips of his ears turned pink, and I smile. I'm beginning to enjoy making this sunshine siren blush.

After finishing a box of pizza, I curl up against Cas. He's warm and his heart is pounding against my cheek in a relaxing rhythm. Cas holds a cup of spiked iced tea to my lips, and I smile before taking a sip. Mira is great at mixing drinks and this one tastes divine. I hum happily at the taste.

"Mira has always been our bartender. She actually taught me how to make drinks actually," Cas said. I sit up as much as I can.

"Really?" I ask, enjoying a peek into his childhood. Cas took a sip from the same cup, and I watched his throat work.

"Oh, I was horrible at mixing drinks. I used to make everyone gag. But Mira has a creative brain and she's good at blending flavors," he said. I hummed, taking another sip.

"You and Mira probably have had a lot of adventures," I said. Cas eyed me.

"I mean we hung out, swam, and studied. The real adventures happened when Kai was in town," he said, chuckling. My ears perked.

"The seaweed incident?" I ask. Cas groaned, shaking his head.

"And ever since then I have never let myself get that drunk again," he said. I laughed. Laughing is easy around Cas. Everything is easier with him. He opened his arms.

"To my arms M'Lady," he said, with a smile.

"I might want to kiss though," I said, placing the cup on the table and crawling into his arms. Cas presses a kiss against my temple, a little thing that I enjoy every time he does.

"Kiss me," he said. I shake my head, nerves settling in.

"Friends don't kiss," I said, fidgeting with his shirt.

"Yes, they do," he said, his body shifting. I glance at him.

"Not the way we do." An unreadable look passes over his face. Did I ruin the moment? Cas reaches for my face, pulling me close until our lips brush.

"You, Crystal, can always kiss me, however you want," he whispered, his lips teasing mine.

"And if I want more?" I ask, feeling brave. Cas' lips brush over mine.

"You can have whatever you want, my jewel," he whispered. My stomach tightens and there is an ache in my core. I stared into his eyes.

"I know what I want," I said, feeling bold. Cas provides me with the space and trust to speak my mind. There's something I've had been wanting to do ever since the last time we were intimate.

Cas turned his body, and I straddled his lap. "Tell me," he said. I place a hand on his chest, my fingers trailing down. His breathing hitches and I smile. By the time my hand reaches his cock it's already hard. His breathing has gone shallow.

"It's my turn to give," I said quietly, gauging his reaction. He swallowed.

"Are you sure?" he asked. The corners of my lips twitched. *This siren.*

"I know what I want, remember that," I said, reminding him of our agreement. He chuckled.

"Then," he began as he pulled my ponytail free. My dark hair cascaded down my shoulders. My mouth hangs open slightly as he pulls my hair back, retying it. "We have to fix this. Don't want your beautiful hair getting in the way of me watching you," he said. My face grows hot as he tightens my ponytail and then kisses me.

I relax into his touch. His hands wander down my shoulders until they land on my thighs. Our mouths move against each other. I cup the back of his head, pulling him closer. I nip at his bottom lip, begging him to open. He groans, and it gives me all the encouragement I need.

My hand lands back on his hard cock. His fingers dig into my thighs, and I smile as our tongues tangle. Cas rocks his hips against my hand, and I rub him up and down.

"Pants. Off," I demand. He grinned, his face red and his lips swollen. His eyes are dark with desire, and it excites me. I shift off his lap.

"Yes M'Lady," he said, voice already hoarse. He lifted his hips, pulling down his sweatpants and boxers low enough that his cock sprang free. I lick my lips and Cas groans deeply as he pumps his cock.

"My turn," I said, moving his hand away. I give a firm pump, and he hisses. I raise an eyebrow. His hands dig into the couch, and I watch his face.

"Keep going," he said, his chest rising and falling fast. After a few pumps I lean forward, giving his head a tentative lick. His breathing picks up and I lick again. He bites down on his bottom lip, and I grin wickedly.

"Fuuuuuck," he moans as I take him further into my mouth. His hand grips my ponytail, and I rock forward, trying to ease the ache between my thighs. "I won't last long," he said.

I smile inwardly, bobbing up and down. Cas' breathing grows faster. His hand keeps my head pressed down and I follow his rhythm. He's thick and hard in my mouth. I open my mouth, my jaw slightly stretched to take him further.

I gag as he hits the back of my throat, and he tries to push me.

"You don't have to go deep to make me come," Cas said, his breathing erratic. My eyebrow twitches. I take him back in my mouth and his hand stays away, letting me have control. "Crystal this feels s-so good," he said, his hips lifting.

Cas is getting closer and closer to the edge and it's all because of me. With each pump, his groans filled me with confidence. I'm going to make this siren come by my hand and mouth. I'm going to own him in this moment.

"You're taking me so well." His voice is hoarse, and his body tenses. "I'm going to come," he said, pushing me away. I shove his hands away, keeping my mouth latched on his cock. My tongue swirls his head as I suck. My hand twisting as I pump again. I glance up at him and the second our eyes connect Cas' body goes rigid.

"C-Crystal," he moans deeply, his cum shooting into my mouth. I choke slightly and wait until he is done to pull away, nostrils flaring.

Oh no.

Cas' eyes widened and he reached for the empty cup on the table.

"You don't need to swallow!" I shake my head and my throat

closes. *Why is this hard?* Cas rolled his eyes playfully. "You don't have to," he pressed. I close my eyes, willing my body to relax but it doesn't work. I reach for the cup, spitting out his release. He places the cup back on the table and pulls me forward. I cover my mouth quickly.

"No! I need to wash-"

"Let me taste myself," he whispered, pulling my hand away. He kisses me sweetly, coaxing me to open and this time I moan. After having taste, he pulls back, smiling at me. "My pretty pixie," he whispered. I blushed, staring at him. Cas' eyes flickered back and forth.

"You want to brush your teeth, don't you?" he asked, a laugh threatening to pour out of him.

"Desperately," I said, laughing.

CHAPTER 29
THE WEIGHT OF A CROWN

Caspian

"You see Caspian, everywhere the light touches the oce-" I splashed Uncle Seward, cutting him off.

"You were not about to rip off a classic movie quote," I said, glaring at him. My uncle let out a boisterous laugh that eased the tension in my shoulders.

We were swimming around the coral. I was shadowing him again. The older I've gotten the more my brother and I began following our roles. Ronan shadowed dad and I was with my uncle. I liked being with him. He was fun and carefree.

He tossed me a grin and a quick wink before speeding ahead. I watched his blue tail disappear and I followed suit. The ocean was quiet in the early morning. I passed by a few fish, waving.

"Stars, have you gotten slower?" he joked. I pulled up on his left.

"You made me get up at sunrise!" I said. He snorted. He'd banged on my bedroom door at 5:30AM telling me to get ready. I was at a party last night and felt dead to the world.

"It's important to come out to the ocean during the first rays of light," he said, giving me a pointed look. So much for having fun. I guess this was going to turn this into a lesson. "Look around," he said.

The ocean was a deep blue. The sun was slowly rising, and the temperature was still cool. A few turtles were swimming to my left, near the coral. I smiled. The coral was an orchestra of radiant colors, and small crabs were beginning to wake from their slumber and slip out. It was quiet, peaceful.

My shoulders dropped and I let my body fall backwards, slowly floating to the surface. I took a deep breath, inhaling the salty, crisp air. The water seemed to hold me in place, rocking me gently.

"I come out here when most of the world is resting to enjoy some quiet time with the ocean, to connect with her," Uncle Seward's voice was soft. I blinked my eyes, watching a lone bird cut across the sky.

"This is nice," I said. Water gently brushed my chest, covering my heart. My body seemed to melt in the water. The ocean was a beautiful yet ominous presence. We did our best as sirens to protect her and all of her beauty and in turn she watched over us. But the ocean was as merciful as it was relentless.

"It's important to connect yourself with the part of you that makes you, you," he said. I straightened myself up to look at my uncle.

"And what makes you, you?" I asked. His lips stretched into a smirk.

"Besides my amazing smile and great head of hair?" he teased. I rolled my eyes with a snort. "Well besides my good hot physical appearance—don't make that face at me—. I would say my ability to turn a situation around," he began. I listened quietly.

"Life will never go exactly how you plan it, and you won't always be prepared for what it gives you. But if you believe that you can handle anything and surround yourself with people who support you, then you can deal with the cards that you are dealt with. I like what I do for our kingdom. I think my compassion and empathy lends itself to the job," he said.

"But don't you feel like you have those traits because of your position? That you had no choice but to be that way?" I asked, nervously. Being second in command was about communicating with the shore, ocean and its creatures. It meant being a bridge between two worlds.

"A job can shape who you are. I won't lie to you on that. But how I was raised and how I walked through the world also has had a hand in making me Seward Coralia Calder. Experiences provide lessons that can either make you or break you. It's up to you whether you want to sink or swim," he said.

I DON'T WANT to be here. I'm sitting in my brother's office with my mom going over plans for the ceremony. It's making me anxious. I keep fidgeting in my seat. At the moment they are discussing food, table settings, and outfits.

The ceremony would be happening on the beach. The whole town is invited and therefore there's a lot to prepare for. But the closer we get to the ceremony the more the invisible deadline I have to save the coral grows near. I'm still not sure about the trident, even though lately I've been having weird feelings in the ocean.

Maybe it's the same thing my uncle felt. It could be the trident calling me. But every time I swam out the feeling disappeared and if I was too close to shore it would evade me. It's frustrating.

"What do you think about this, Caspian?" my mom said, pulling me from my thoughts. I blink.

"He wasn't listening," my brother said, glaring at me. I roll my eyes. "You can't daydream like when you were in high school. The ceremony is next weekend," he snapped out.

"I'm well aware," I said. My mom sighed, which twisted my stomach. She has nervous energy about her today. Glancing at Ronan I can see he was worried. I force my mouth to twist into a smile. The last thing I want is for them to worry about me. I stressed them out enough while growing up. They believed I could do this, and I need to show them I can.

"The ceremony will be beautiful, and it will happen," I assure them. "Just please add chili cheese fries to the menu. I swear Crystal can eat every day if she let herself." My mom giggles and writes it down. The ceremony is going to happen no matter how inadequate I feel. It needs to.

"And you'll heal the coral," Ronan insisted. I cross my arms. So far all we've managed to do is slow down the sickness, but if I said that out loud, they would say something that I'm not in the mood to hear.

"You know dear *older* brother. I don't remember you having this much confidence in me when I was younger," I said. My mom shook her head. He gave me a blank smile that gave me the shivers. "If you smile like that, you'll never get a date," I point out. His face drops immediately.

"You were more annoying back then," he said. I raise an eyebrow.

"Aren't I still annoying?" I ask. He nodded, signing a paper.

"Of course, because you're my *little* brother," he emphasized. He places the pen down before looking at me again. "And my smile is fine," he grumbled.

"You boys give me gray hair," mom said, shaking her head. I let out a chuckle. She tapped my shoulder. "Your friends will be here, right? Would one of the newly renovated cottages work for their lodging?" she asked. I smile. It warmed my heart to hear my mom wanting to make sure my friends are okay, friends I made away from Coralia when I was someone else.

"That would be perfect mom. They're all excited," I said, remembering being on the phone with them. Apparently, Lily finally said 'I love you' to Celestino. Flynn and Lola are collaborating on a whiskey recipe, and Eleanor and Caleb are still...banging it out.

"I'm excited to meet your friends," she said, smiling at me. "Oh, does Crystal have a dress?" she asked, concerned. Automatically my magic opened up to her. Since the death of my dad and uncle it was instinct to keep my mind open to my family so I could be there to ease whatever clouds they have.

"I don't think so," I hesitated. My mom pursed her lips and then waved her hand back and forth as if sensing my magic. I gave her a sheepish grin.

"I can send her a few dresses," she said. *An idea formed in my head.* Crystal is already dealing with enough and if there's something I can take off of her plate that will give her a break I will.

"Send them to me," I said. My mom smiled at me, arching an eyebrow. I flush under her gaze.

"My son, the romantic," she teased. "You guys are going to be the cutest couple there," she said, dreamily. *I bet she's already planning our wedding.* Ronan snorted and I glared at him.

"Can we focus for a second?" he asked. My brother's mouth twisted into a frown when he looked at me. I didn't like that look. "We're going have to pull Uncle Seward's crown out from the vault," he said. I breathe in sharply.

"Ronan—"

"You will wear his crown," he demanded. I stare at him wide-eyed at him. I can't. There is no way I can wear his crown.

"I can't. It's his," I said through gritted teeth. Ronan pauses for a moment.

"It was his crown, along with every other second born Calder in our family. It's a part of our legacy and as the next generation it is rightfully yours. If he was here, you know he would give it to you," he said. I closed my eyes, a wave of emotions swimming deep in my chest.

He is right. I know it and yet I don't like it. My dad and uncle have been dead for years, but wearing Uncle Seward's crown feels like it would solidify their passing.

"I know what you're feeling Cas," Ronan said, his tone soft. When I look at Ronan I see our dad. He's a near spitting image of him.

Fuck, I've been so selfish of my own grief. *Of course* he knows. He's had to wear our dad's crown since 18, a week after the funeral. To deny wearing our uncle's crown would be ignoring Ronan's pain.

I take a deep breath. I can't run away, not anymore. Even if the pain feels like it might drown me, it's my turn to step up for my kingdom.

"Wear the crown. Find the trident. Heal the coral," I said. I rub the back of my neck, feeling my nerves prick beneath my skin.

"That's my boy," my mom said, beaming.

My brother's tail is silver. My tail took after dad's while his took after mom's. I couldn't remember the last time my brother and I had gone for a swim together. Ronan is finally checking out the coral with me. Waldo appeared, swimming by my side.

"Hey Waldo," I grin.

"You didn't tell me the King would be visiting us!" His dark eyes widened. My brother bowed his head.

"He's just my brother," I joke. There is a sharp slap on both my arms.

"He's the king!" Waldo said.

"I'm also the king," Ronan said at the same time. I chuckle.

"You're my brother before you're my king," I said, giving him a pointed look. Ronan offers a sliver of a smile.

"Remember that," he said. The seal bumps my arm.

"Are you guys going to check the coral?" Waldo asked. I nod.

"Anything new to report?" I ask. Waldo has somewhat become my ears for when I'm not in the ocean. We slow down once we reach the coral that has been suffering the longest. My heart sinks staring at it. Ronan rubs a hand over his face.

"Sharks are doing their best to not switch their hunting grounds, but their food source is becoming scarce," Waldo said. His nose twitched. "Let's say some of us are looking a bit tasty to them." I grimaced.

"I'm sorry," I said. Fuck, we needed to hurry. My brother swam up next to me.

"What's wrong?" he asked, noticing my face. We can only pause the food chain for so long before mother nature takes over.

"Sharks are getting antsy," I said. Ronan kept a cool expression. His tongue ran over his teeth and that was his tell. He's worried. I watch my brother carefully. He straightened his shoulders, his eyes hardening with resolution. I'm not looking at Ronan my brother but Ronan the king.

"Understandable. Some of the animals may need to move closer to shore," he said. I shook my head.

"That's going to push the predators closer too," I point out.

"It'll be tentative-" my brother began but something snapped up my attention.

The feeling again.

I twist my head to the right. Is the feeling coming from that direction? With the rolling of the waves, it's hard to tell.

Crystal?

I shift to the left. Is this the trident or is something calling me to check on Crystal? Was this a mate thing? I flush. I have been trying to avoid the whole mate thing, but my siren side comes to life at the thought of mate. But I can't place where this song is coming from and from who or what.

"Well, I don't like the idea of giving the sharks a temporary territory," he said, trying to get my attention. I don't like that idea either. But the sharks need to eat.

"We might have to wait until I find the trident," I said. I look between Waldo, Ronan and the vast ocean. "I will find it," I said. And for the first time I believe it.

I was back at the cottage waiting for Crystal to get home. Today I don't feel heavily burdened. Yes, the coral is dying, and the ceremony is next weekend. But swimming with my brother and communicating between him and the marine life filled me with a sense of purpose. I haven't had that feeling in a long time.

I saw the importance of my role. I felt it. I wonder if this is what Uncle Seward meant in our conversations. I'm going to find the trident. Whatever I'm feeling in the ocean has to be it. I just needed to follow it, follow my heart.

"I'm home!" Crystal called out. My stomach swoops. Fuck, I want that to be real. I want her to be coming here, to our home and into my arms because she is mine. Her arms wrap around my neck, and she kisses my cheek. I chuckle.

"Someone's happy," I said as she came to sit next to me.

"I woke up feeling...okay. The bed and breakfast will be done next weekend, and we won't be starting the meadery until the fall which gives me some breathing room," she said. "Today is slightly above a decent day," she said.

"A decent day?" I ask, curiously. She nodded.

"Every day I try to shoot for a decent day. Not every day can be great, but it can be okay," she explained. I admire her outlook. It's something I need to adopt.

"I think I had one of those too," I said, placing my arm on the back of the couch. Crystal scooted closer. Her eyes shifted.

"How are you feeling about that?" she asked. I take a breath.

"I think I'm okay with it. I dived into the ocean with Ronan today," I said. Her eyes widened and she placed her legs in my lap. I moved to squeeze her calves, and she sighed quietly.

"How was that?"

"Good actually. Growing up I thought I would hate this. I felt like I couldn't do it. But out there in the water with him, navigating what needs to be done, could be done and translating made me feel...important. Smart. Needed." I smile. "I liked it," I said, honestly. Crystal beamed and it made my heart leap.

"Looks like we both had slightly above decent days," she said. She reached for a hug and when my arms wrapped around her, I pulled her fully onto my lap. She made a sound of surprise. My arms tighten around her. She is meant to be in my arms. Her body folded around mine perfectly. Her citrus scent fills my senses. Her heart kicked up and I smirked. She twitched in my lap.

"I *just* sat in your lap," she said. I chuckled.

"Well Crystal, when a siren finds another being attractive hormones will surge causing rapid blood flow to their–"

"I know how that works!" She erupted in giggles, cheeks ablaze.

"Oh really? Want to show me?" I ask, waggling my eyebrows. She snorted.

"You couldn't have come up with something better?" she asked. I nodded quickly, sticking my bottom lip out.

"You're right," I pouted, before clearing my throat. I adjusted her on my lap, and she gasped again, eyes fluttering close. I grip her chin. "Look at me," I said and her pretty hazel eyes met my gaze. They flared with playful desire.

"Tonight, I want you to be greedy. Take whatever you want, however you want. You want to ride me? Do it. You want me to bury my face between your thighs until I'm gasping for air? So be it. So, tell me M'Lady, how do you want me?" I said. She let out a tiny gasp, a quick inhale filled with need. Her hands came to my chest, fingers digging into my shirt. Her chest rose and fell rapidly.

"I want you, all of you," she whispered. My hands cup the back of her head, and I kiss her hard. Crystal immediately responded. I slip my hands down until I reach her ass. I stand, taking her with me and she wraps her legs around my waist. I hiss, feeling the heat between her thighs.

"Are you sure?" I ask, pressing my forehead against hers. Her hands tremble against my face.

"Yes," she said. My heart is pounding out of my chest. It's finally happening.

"Your room or mine?" I ask, kissing her neck. My tongue trails up until I latch onto her earlobe. Crystal shivers against me with a low moan.

"Yours," she whispered.

I PRESSED her against my door, my cock grinding against her core. She is divine. Her legs tighten against my waist, and she moans as I rock against her. Her hands roughly pulled at my hair as we kissed. My other hand stumbled to find the doorknob. I need her on my bed before I come holding her against the door.

Once inside the bedroom I lay her on my bed. I press kisses down her neck, taking my time to nip and suck until she is frantic.

"Hot. Too hot," she said, her hands pushing up my shirt. I nod, pulling it off. She rakes her nails down my chest. I hiss. Fuck, did I love this side of her. I pull up her blouse, kissing her stomach, making my way up until I need to pull the blouse off. She whimpered for my lips.

Kissing Crystal is like a shot of adrenaline, and I'm addicted to her taste. Our tongues fight for dominance. I reach behind her, unclasping her bra. I groan, feeling the weight of her breasts in my hands. My cock is hard, aching.

"I've been wanting to taste them," I said, sucking the top of her chest. She moans loudly. I push her back until her head lands on the pillows. With one hand I tease her nipple, and I use my mouth to give the other attention. My tongue swirls around the hardened peak and Crystal bucks as I press my cock against her core. Her body is hot. Her hands get tangle in my hair, pressing me impossibly closer to her.

"Caspian," she whispered, and I grind against her core faster. "Caspian," she said again and again. I let go of her nipple with a pop and bite down on her shoulder as a wave of passion washes over me until I explode.

"F-fuck no," I stutter. She freezes beneath me, and I pull back to see worry. "Baby I didn't mean no as in what we're doing," I said to clarify. Her face shifted from worry to confusion.

"Oh?" she said but it felt more like a question.

"I sort of busted quickly," I said, blushing. Her eyes widened comically, and I couldn't help but laugh. "The way you said my name... fuck Crystal. I couldn't help it." This time she blushes. It wasn't often that she said my full name. My name on her lips would gladly bring me to my knees.

"Really?" she asked, a mischievous glint in her eyes. My boxers are sticky, but I ignore it for a second to steal another kiss.

"It was hot," I said. She smiled against my lips as her hands wandered down my back. I know watching me become undone does it for her. She likes having control. "I'm going to get rid of these and clean up and I'll be back," I said.

"It's fine," she said quickly. I shake my head, my hand slipping under her sweats. My fingers graze her soaked panties. Crystal's eyes fluttered close.

"I'm a siren. I have the stamina. So, when I get back, I want you naked."

CHAPTER 30
IT'S FINALLY HAPPENING

Crystal

I'm trembling beneath Cas' bed cover. It's finally happening. I thought when I would be in this moment, I would feel some form of trepidation but instead I feel excitement. I trust him completely with myself.

When the door opens Cas is naked and he's right. Sirens have stamina because he's ready to go. His body is lean and dips slightly in places, teasing the muscles I know he has. I can see his tattoo clearly, a symbol of his family from what he has told me. I lick my lips.

"Fuck baby if you look at me like that I'm going to come again," he said, wrapping his hand around his cock. He kneels onto the bed, crawling towards me. I let him peel back the covers and he settle between my legs.

He's warm and when his chest presses against mine, we sigh in unison. His skin feels amazing against mine. When my eyes meet his steady blue gaze my heart pounds.

"This is happening," I whisper. He offers me a small grin.

"Only if you still want to," he assured me. I place a hand on his chest, feeling his heart race.

"Are you nervous?" I ask. He lets out a chuckle, slightly shaking his head.

"Of course I am," he said. I cock my head, arms wrapping around his neck, to pull him flush. He places a kiss on my forehead and each cheek. "It's you." I inhaled sharply.

"I'm nervous too," I admit. "But I want to." He squeezed my hip once before moving his hand down. I moaned, bucking my hips up at the feel of his fingers. Dipping between my folds he teases my entrance. Cas' eyes briefly closed as he pushed his finger inside. A string of curse words left his lips.

"Please," I beg, quietly. He pressed his forehead against mine before giving me a slow sensual kiss. It tastes like promise, reassurance, trust and so much more that my heart is ready to burst.

"Fish cake?" he asked, checking in once more and I giggle.

"I'm ready," I said, pressing a kiss against his cheek.

"Touch yourself while I get a condom," he said. I nod frantically, replacing his fingers with my own. He pulls away. I faintly hear the sound of ripping as my fingers pumped in and out of me. I close my eyes, concentrating on the feeling I'm orchestrating. Cas tugged on my hand, taking my fingers into his mouth. He groaned deeply, enjoying my taste and I shivered.

I hook my legs around his waist, pulling him close. He held one of my hands above my head, locking our hands.

"You ready M'Lady?" he asked, the head of his cock pressing against my entrance. This was finally happening. Cas' eyes shifted from desire to concern. If I told him to stop, he would but I don't want to.

"Yes." His cock slide between my folds and I arch.

"Crystal," he said, his voice low and needy. I stare into his blue eyes as he notches the head of his cock at my entrance. "You can back out," he said, cheeks flushed. I shake my head despite the slight discomfort.

"All of you," I whisper, lifting my hips. My body tightens and we groan at the same time. This feels good despite the pain. Cas shudders above me, slowly rocking.

"If it hurts too much I can stop," he said. My free hand snakes down his back until I cup his ass and push him deeper. I scrunch my nose at the sting.

"You will make me feel good, Caspian," I hiss. He pushes in and after a few moments of slow rocking the pain eventually gives away to pleasure.

I gasped.

This is better than anything I have felt before. He thrusts slow and deep. "Cas," I beg as his pace picks up slightly.

I wrap both my legs around him and he slightly lifts up his chest, the angle changing subtly but enough that I'm clenching, my body giving away to him.

"Crystal, fuck," he grunted. He drags his cock out and slams back inside me. I whimper; the roughness makes my body shake. His eyes are watchful. "Yes?" he asked, checking in. I nod frantically.

"Harder," I plead. Cas shifted to sit up and I whine. He grips my hips and pumps into me mercilessly. I press my cheek against the pillow, a new sensation ripping me at the seams. I didn't know it could feel this good.

"You feel so good," Cas grunted out. "Mine," he whispered. My heart skips at his declaration.

Mine. Mine. Mine.

It repeats in my head, sending me closer. Too soon I'm panting his name, begging for more. I grab my breasts and tug at my own nipples which pulls a groan out of Cas. When I look up, his eyes are brighter than I've ever seen them.

My ears perk as his groans and moans take on a musical quality. He's on pitch and the notes pouring out of him have me soaring higher. My body is burning up and my magic is buzzing.

"Sing to me," I beg. Cas' eyes widened but he obeyed.

His voice carries across the room as the headboard slaps against the wall to the rhythm of his thrusts. The sound of our bodies becoming one echoes with his voice and I'm so close that a cry breaks out of me. His magic presses against my skin, caressing me until I peak at the highest level of euphoria.

My scream blends with his song, my back bows and my nails dig into his arms as I finally give in. Cas' thrusts slow and with a low grunt he collapses on top of me. We both struggle to catch our breath.

My eyes close, overwhelmed with every sensation. I stroke his back until his body relaxes against mine.

"Crystal," he said quietly with a tenderness that makes my eyes prick with tears. His voice is filled with so much gentleness I want to run away. This is too much. We are too much and not enough.

"Caspian," I said, my voice filled with longing. His hand cups my cheek and the look in his eyes gives me pause. His face fills me with hope that he might feel the same.

"How do you feel?" he asked. I fight back a smile. My body is tired, spent and deliciously warm.

"Good," I said. "And you?" I ask, hesitantly.

Mine.

He said I'm his. His magic was released. But did it mean anything or was he lost in the heat of the moment? The tips of his ears turned pink.

"Exquisite," he said, grinning and I relax, matching his wide smile. "I'm going to clean you up," he said, pulling away, taking his warmth away. I shiver and he places the covers on top of me. "Sleep with me tonight?" he asked, his gaze on the bed. I raised an eyebrow.

"Didn't I already?" I tease. He rolled his eyes.

"Ha ha. Stay in my bed tonight?" he clarified. "I want to hold you." I nod and Cas presses a quick kiss against my lips. With my heart in his hands, I watch him walk away. I'm screwed. This agreement we have is being torn up by waves of emotions I've never felt.

I WANTED MORE WITH HIM. More kisses, touches, words, everything. Something happened that night between us, something broke and healed. I had no idea my body, my heart could feel that way, like I was going to explode into dust and be put back together again. That's how Cas made me feel.

We haven't had time to have another night like that. It was the day before the ceremony. Cas is an anxious mess. Every day he would come home from the ocean, pacing back and forth, his lips turned down in a frown.

We would shower and then go to our separate bedrooms for the night. But Cas always ended up knocking on my door and pulling me to his side to sleep. I'm not sure what we are doing. Are we still just friends? Maybe something more? I want to clarify but he's been so stressed the past few days.

Thankfully I'm on break because we won't be touching the meadery until the fall. Our friends arrive today and I'm a mix of anxiety and excitement. I miss them. I truly do. I'm nervous about the possible questions and looks at the situation I'm in with Cas.

There is a knock at the door, and I rush to open it. I smile, seeing our friends.

"Crystal!" Lola said, barreling into me with a hug. I choke, her vampire strength taking my air.

"Sunflower, she can't breathe," Flynn said, pulling her away. I giggle, stepping out of their way. The entire group waltzed in. The house immediately felt smaller, and I wished Cas was here.

"Hey guys! Hope the drive was okay," I said. My sister stayed in the back by Caleb. My stomach sank. We technically haven't had a conversation about my blow up. I figure we will pretend as if that call never happened and go back to normal. It's what we always did.

"It was fine," Caleb said, squeezing Eleanor's waist. I swallow. He probably doesn't like me at the moment. I upset Eleanor which most likely upsets him. I plaster on a smile.

"Where is Sailor?" Lily asked. My stomach twists. Unease ripples through the group.

"He's out by the coral," I said. Everyone gave each other looks.

"He must be under a lot of pressure," Celestino said. I nod silently. This whole week he's been a mess. I did my best to encourage him when needed and distract him when called for. But I understood anxiety. We are best friends. You could only be distracted for so long. Soon enough in the quiet pauses of day to day, anxiety will whisper softly in your ear.

"But I know he's going to be so happy you're all here," I said. Once again, I glance at Eleanor who is glued to Caleb's side. She gave me a reassuring smile. I can't get a read on her and it's bothering me.

"How is everything going?" Lola asked as we made our way to the kitchen. I opened the fridge, handing everyone a beer like I owned the place. I feel comfortable hosting them here as if Cas' cottage is my home. It feels like home because of Cas. Stars, I wish he was here.

"Really well. In the fall I'll be working on the meadery and later on rebuilding the bookstore," I said. Eleanor's eyes brightened.

"That's what we need! A bookstore," she said.

"Oh, my stars we don't have one!" Lily said, walking towards Eleanor who nodded furiously.

"Well, we know I can build a bookcase," Celestino said, wrapping an arm around Lily's waist, pulling her back to him. She blushed.

"A meadery?" Caleb said, glancing at Flynn. I pointed to the brothers.

"What you're thinking is what I'm thinking," I said. Flynn shook his head with a chuckle.

"She doesn't like whiskey as she likes to remind me," he said. Flynn and Caleb Kiernan have a whiskey distillery run by their father. Caleb isn't really a part of it, but Flynn is one of the lead developers. They have another older brother, Greg who is a baker and a younger sister, Bridget, who is figuring out her life.

"I have a feeling it'll be a good idea," I said with a grin.

"The town seems different," Eleanor noted. I take a breath. Caleb, Eleanor, Lily, and Celestino have been to Coralia Coast. They said there was a somber, melancholy vibe about the town, a sadness of sorts. They were right because I felt it too when I first arrived.

But since Cas' return and watching him slowly open up to his community, who were excited to welcome him back, there's been a shift.

Everywhere I walked they smiled, asked about my day and gave me thanks for rebuilding their town. That's why I liked these projects. Not only could you *see* the improvement when assisting a town rebuild but you could *feel* it.

"I think it was Cas," I said, a small smile on my lips. Lola's eyes sparkle.

"Ah, so you call him Cas," she teased. I roll my eyes. I forgot that they still called him Sailor.

"He asked me too," I stated, trying not to blush. I don't want to divulge the specific reason as to why even though the ladies knew. They looked at me and I took a sip of my beer. Caleb crossed his arms.

"So, what's it like dating a prince?" Flynn asked. I glanced at the girls and Lola winked. I'm not sure if the guys know about my arrangement with Cas or not.

"Well, he buys me all the chili cheese fries that I want," I said. Eleanor finally broke away from Caleb and wrapped an arm around me.

"And make sure he always does," she said, waggling her finger. I look around the people I spent my childhood with and for once I don't feel out of place.

THE SUN IS high and shining. I took everyone to the secluded rocky part of the beach that Cas and I enjoy. We packed a bunch of food and drinks. The men are kicking around a soccer ball while us ladies are standing in the water, enjoying the gentle waves.

"This is amazing," Lily said smiling. I nod. Fabian has actually come with them and was chilling under an umbrella. He is Lily's familiar, an adorable fennec fox. I smile seeing Trixie, another magical fox, and Fabian's crush a foot away from him.

"How are those two by the way," I ask, motioning towards them. The ladies giggled.

"Oh, Trixie is playing hard to get but Fabian is winning her over,"

Lola said, just as Trixie scooted slightly closer. I shake my head laughing.

"You seem happy," Eleanor noted. I look at my sister, feeling flushed.

"I am," I said honestly, my hands dipping in the water. I've been enjoying the work I was doing in Coralia Coast and while what we have is fake on the outside, every day it was feeling more real. I inhale the salty warm air.

In Lavender Falls I was constantly anxious. I felt like my sister's and dad's shadow. But here I'm at peace. For once I have both my feet firmly planted on the ground. Sometimes we are meant to move away from everything we've ever known to discover the place where we truly belong.

"Are you guys…still fake dating?" she asked, her voice dropping. My heart skips. We are still fake dating. To everyone in town we are in love but behind closed doors we are just friends. But Cas doesn't look at me like he used to. Now he looks at me like I'm the only thing that matters and I'm believing it. I sit down, the water coming up to my chest.

"Yeah," I said, sounding disappointed. The ladies sit down with me. The water turns still and my shoulders ease.

"Crys?" Lola said. I take a deep breath. What I feel for Cas goes beyond what I ever felt for anyone.

"I like him a lot," I admit easily. "But I don't know…I think I know how he feels, and I've been wanting to talk to him about it, but he's been so stressed," I said. "I've never felt like this for someone so I'm afraid to trust it."

That is the real truth. Is this what deeply caring for someone feels like? What about love? I've never been in love. How do I distinguish between emotions I've never felt? Eleanor reached for my hand.

"How do you feel around him?" Lola asked. I take a deep breath, my fingers gliding through the sand below.

"Warm. Relaxed. It's like all the thoughts that occupy my brain just fade away when I'm with him," I said.

"What else do you feel?" Lily asked, glancing at Celestino. I huffed out a laugh.

"With him I don't feel afraid to speak my mind or say what I want. I feel brave," I admit, a smile tugging on my lips.

"If it makes you feel at ease, I don't think Sailor is faking it with you," Eleanor said. My eyes widen. She grinned, her smile reminding me of our dad's. "Since the day he's met you at the bar you've had him wrapped around your finger. We could all see it."

"Trust us, Crys. We've been watching him trail behind you like a puppy," Lily said. Cas wouldn't be making my coffee every morning or surprising me with flowers if he didn't feel deeply about me. He sees me and I see him.

There's a splash and I freeze. Turning to my right, out in the ocean is a large dorsal fin. Eleanor's hand tightened.

"I-is that a shark?" Lily stammered. My heart is pounding in my ears.

"Why is it so close?" Lola hissed. Sharks aren't normally this close to shore but with the coral dying, patterns in marine life have had predators shifting their routines. Cas has been worried about this and now a shark is here. Sure, we have magic but that doesn't ease the tension of this situation.

"The coral has been affecting everything," I said, quietly as the shark swims closer. Lola scooted closer.

"I can talk to it," she said. Lola has a special gift like most vampires. Her gift is the ability to communicate with animals. I cock my head to the side. Something is different though. My magic buzzes beneath my skin. I don't feel afraid for some reason.

I dipped my head underwater, watching the shark. It seemed to be glancing around as if looking for something or someone. When our eyes connected it made a straight line towards me.

Eleanor yanked me back. "Crystal, what are you doing?" she asked, trying to drag me out of the water. Something in my stomach tightened. My magic willed me to stay. One thing every magic user has been taught was to trust your magic. It would never steer you wrong.

A SIREN'S SUMMER FOR LOVE

"Wait," I said, pulling my arm free. More splashes sounded behind us as the men arrived.

"Let's go," Caleb said, grabbing Eleanor.

"*Querida*," Celestino said to Lily. Flynn left Lola alone, knowing she would be okay with her gift and vampire strength.

"Crystal," my sister hissed. But I ignored her.

"I need to stay," I said. I don't know why but I can't move, I shouldn't. Everything in me is telling me I need to stay. I swallow, sticking my hand out. The shark stops in front of me. I duck my head back down and it turns sideways to stare at me. My brows furrowed. The shark looked at me like it recognized me.

Lola's head appeared in the corner of my eye. Sounds passed between them. The shark glanced between us looking…sad. She cocked her head to the side before tugging me up.

"He knows you," she said, gasping for air. The shark slapped my hand with its fin before swimming away.

"What the kraken was that," Eleanor said, back at my side. She wrapped a protective arm around me as I stared at Lola. For once I'm not bothered by my sister acting like an older sister. I found comfort in it. She didn't pull me away from the shark, instead she honored what I said, trusted me.

"What do you mean the shark knew Crystal?" Celestino asked. Lola's eyes softened for a second. Then Waldo appeared. He swam towards me, dipping so my hand rested on his head.

"Hey there," I said softly. His eyes look sad. My stomach tightens. Something is wrong.

"What the fuck is happening?" Caleb asked as fish gathered around us. Wait no, the sea creatures aren't gathering around us, they are gathering around *me*.

"What the stars?" Eleanor whispered.

"Waldo?" I said. His eyes closed briefly.

"Did you just call him Waldo?" Lily asked. I chuckle as he moves his head side to side against my hand.

"Crystal, you're literally surrounded by crabs and fishes," Eleanor said, pointing down. My eyes widen as the marine life circles around me. They all stare at me with concern. I look at my friends who are worried.

"I don't know what's happening," I whisper. "I'm not doing anything." Waldo made a noise and Lola raised her eyebrows.

"The shark said their princess is needed," Lola began. My brows furrow. "He is saying you are needed, that something happened. They're all saying it," Lola said in disbelief. Waldo makes more noises, getting my attention.

"Princess?" I question. Lola grins, her eyes bright when she looks at me. My heart begins beating rapidly.

"They say Prince Caspian needs you," she said. Her voice softened at the end and my eyes widened. I'm not their princess but Cas needs me. I need to get to him. I turn to Waldo.

"Where is he?" I ask. Waldo lets out a noise.

"He says our special spot," Lola said, slightly confused. I nod. I have never gone to the cave without Cas' help. The swim is too long without magic or proper gear for me. Every time I went, I needed the seaweed laced with his magic to dive down. I look at Eleanor who stares at me with a smile.

"Go to your prince. You know where we will be if you need us," she said. My eyes water. I hug her tightly. I run out of the water, throwing on my clothes, not caring if I'm soaked.

"Lily!" I call out. She wrapped a towel around herself.

"Do you need me?" she asked. I nod.

"I need to be able to breathe underwater for a bit," I said. No one questioned me and to that I'm grateful. Now isn't the time for questions. Cas needs me.

CHAPTER 31
A SIREN'S TEARS

Crystal

With the help of a spell and following Waldo I'm able to enter our secret cave from the ocean's side. When I emerge from the water, Cas is sitting on the rocky edge, his head in hands. He's in his siren form. He looks beautifully sad.

I swim closer and place my hand on his tail. He gasps, eyes widening. He wipes at his face before dragging his hair back. Above shore you can see a merman's heartbreak. So, ow many of them have hid their tears in the rolling of the ocean's waves?

"H-how are you here?" he asked, voice breaking. He bent over, reaching to pull me out. I settle against his tail; his arms wrapped around me.

"Lily helped," I said, running my fingers through his golden hair. He closed his eyes, his lips tilting up. "Our friends are here and they're happy. They've noticed the difference in Coralia," I said. His shoulders relaxed. He loves his town, and I knew it would ease him to know his friends see the difference.

"Really?" he asked. I hummed.

"You've brought something back to the town," I whisper.

"We both have," he said. He pressed his forehead against mine, his arms tightening. "You're doing good, Caspian," I said. His bottom lip wobbles slightly and the sight makes my heart crack. I tilt my head up, capturing his lips. His grip around me tightens. He pulls away gently.

"Am I?" he asked. His voice is broken and small.

"Look at me," I command. His blue eyes glistened with tears.

"I know you're worried and scared. But you have beings standing beside you," I remind him. Tears fall down his face and I quietly wipe them away.

"Remember how you said you were tired? I'm tired. I'm so fucking tired and overwhelmed," he said, his voice breaking. His hands tightened on my hips. "Every time I go to the coral, there's barely any improvement. And everyone is counting on me to fix it, and I don't know if I can." I stay quiet, knowing he needs to pour out the words he keeps close to his chest. He hasn't had the chance to truly break down. "Life is dying, and I have to fix it," he croaks. "I should have stayed. I should have paid better attention when I was younger. I should-"

"We can't take back the past. There are so many things I should have done or said but it happened, and I can't take it back," I remind him. I should have spoken to my dad sooner, to Eleanor. I bring his head to my shoulder, tracing lines up and down his back.

"I think I feel the trident but every time I do the feeling disappears and it's so fucking hard to trust something that I've never dealt with," he confessed.

"You feel the trident?" I ask. He takes a shaky breath.

"I feel something but...," he trailed off.

"Something I've learned since reconnecting with everyone, since meeting you is to trust myself more. The only way we will get through this crazy life is by going after what we want and trusting ourselves to get there," I begin. "Not making a move, not doing something opens the opportunity for failure," I said.

"But sometimes when you try you fail," he said, quietly. My lips twitch.

"But at least you tried and now you can move onto a new step," I reply. My lips twitched. "You know a shark came to me," I said. Cas' head snapped back quickly. His nostrils flared and his eyes roamed my body. I giggle. "I'm fine, Cas. A shark swam up to me, so did Waldo, a few crabs and fishes," I recall. He shook his head.

"What?" he asked, in disbelief. I nod.

"Lola was with me to translate but they said…they said," I trailed off, feeling embarrassed. His hands wandered down my thighs, lifting me so I could straddle him. His scales feel smooth beneath my skin, and I shiver.

"Tell me," he urged.

"They said their prince needed his princess," I said, my voice dropping. Cas takes a deep breath.

"My princess," he whispered, his eyes softening with a look that I'm becoming attached to. A look that tells me we are something more. Cas' eyes are slightly swollen from the tears he hid in this cave, his cheeks flushed. My heart joined in his pain.

"I'm here for you," I assure. "Honeysuckle," I add. Cas blushed, a chuckle pouring out of him.

"Honeysuckle?" he questioned. I shrug my shoulders.

"I knew it would get you to smile," I said with a grin.

"You always do," he said. One of his hands cups my cheek and a tear rolls down his eye. This time I don't think the tear is for something sad.

"What do you need?" I ask, my hands stroking his hair again.

"You. Just you," he pleaded, gently. My heart swells.

"You have me," I said, repeating his own words from before. I press my lips against his and my body softens. Cas feels incredible against me.

He presses me against his cock, and I moan. He nipped my bottom lip, and I opened, our tongues fighting for dominance. With Cas I burn hot. It's a delicious, sweet heat that keeps me craving for more.

"Can I have you? Like this?" he asked, against my mouth.

"Yes," I cave. I reach to undo the knot of my bikini top. I toss it behind him and my nipples pebbled against the breeze.

Cas' cock emerges from the hidden slit, and I shiver at the sight of his cock. It's a deep blue color that matches some of the color of his scales. My core clenches at the sight. I look at him and his chest rises and falls heavily. I grip his cock in my hand, pumping a few times. His moans are on pitch and a melody floated out of him. The same melody he sang the last time.

The sound ricochets against the cave walls and I gasp as his magic presses against me. His fingers slip under my bikini bottoms, and I moan as he strokes my clit. I press my face against his neck, my lips trailing wet kisses. And then all too quickly his name is pouring out of me, and I tremble as an orgasm takes over.

"I need to be inside you now," he whispered against my head. I nod, helplessly, still craving more. Cas pulls away from me and we shift until we were on the edge. I gasped at his strength as he readjusted me on his lap. He gives me a delicious smirk.

I shimmied my hips slightly up. He pushes my bottoms to the side and checks in with me, like he always does. I nodded desperately. He lines his cock at my entrance, and I roll my hips slightly.

My body tightens, my core tenses at the delicious stretch. I rock slowly, trying to ease him inside and sigh once our hips are flushed against each other. His hand cupped the back of my neck, pulling me in for a kiss.

"By the ocean and stars, Crystal," he murmured against my mouth. I drag my hands through his hair, tugging as I rocked in tempo with the waves that were splashing with the movement of his tail.

"Caspian," I whisper, my voice filled with need.

This is different from the first time. In his siren form Cas stretches me, filling me up and it's the best thing ever. We're ravenous, consumed by the fire burning between us.

"This feels too good," I said as his hips bucked. I grab his hand, placing it over my eyes. I faintly heard him curse when he realized what I was doing.

In this moment I want to only feel and hear Caspian. In this moment we are just two beings becoming one. The water crashes against the cave and Cas hums his siren song.

I latch my arms around him, pulling close so my nipples rub against his chest. I let him take over. With one hand on my waist, he rocks me. I enjoyed him getting lost in the rhythm as his hand remains over my eyes. I moan, loudly when I feel his fingers against my clit. This is beyond anything I have ever felt, and I don't want it to end, not with him.

"Caspian, yes," I whimper as his fingers and cock sent me closer and closer over the edge. "We need this," I beg.

Cas continued to sing, his magic filling the cave and I screamed as waves of ecstasy crashed over me again. Cas pulls out quickly, rubbing his cock against my stomach until he finishes. He kisses me as the echoes of his song resounds around us. My eyes blink quickly, adjusting to the light. Cas' face is flushed, his eyes bright and he pulls me in for an all-consuming kiss.

We kiss until our hearts ease and bodies relax. Looking into his eyes I smile which he returns easily.

But then there is a loud crack, and Cas wraps his arms around me, taking me underwater as rocks fell from above. My heart kick back up in fear as I cling onto him. He swims further down, covering my head. After a few moments the rumbling stops.

We come up for air, quickly. Thankfully now is when Lily's spell has ended. We look around the cave and Cas gasps. My mouth drops. A bright, golden object is floating in the middle of the air above us. I can make out a crack in the wall of the cave off to the side.

"Is that...," I trail off.

"By the stars," Cas whispered. He reached up, hesitating until I placed a hand on his arm, urging him forward. The trident has to be five feet long, a beautiful gold, etched with swirls of waves and seaweed. It reminds me of Cas' tattoo.

When his fingers wrap around the staff the air around us grows hot, the water bubbles and I cling to him. The magic from the trident courses through Cas and me. My eyes widen. Cas' skin glows, his blue eyes brightening, reminding me of glaciers.

"C-Cas?" I ask, trembling. He turned to look at me, a smile stretching across his face. "Why are you looking at me like that?" I ask. He gives me a bruising kiss, and I relax.

"I've been having this feeling out in the ocean. This tug of peace and home. But every time I felt it, I thought of you because it's how I feel when I'm with you," he began. I blushed. "The reason I've always come back to this place wasn't just because of my dad but something else drew me here and it was the trident," he said. My heart swelled. I pulled him into a hug. His tail came up to hold up some of my weight.

"I knew you could do it," I said. I pulled away, wiping my tears.

"Thank you," he whispered, his voice slightly cracking. I cock my head, giggling.

"What did I do?" I ask in confusion. Cas looked at the trident and then at me.

"You reminded me of what home felt like. Without you I wouldn't have found the trident and I sure as the stars above wouldn't have felt like I could wield it," he said. "You reminded me to believe in myself, trust myself."

My heart is in my throat. I chew my bottom lip. I wasn't to tell him that I did nothing. If I made him see who he truly was then he did the same for me. I remind him of a home and to me he is my home.

"I just wanted you to remember that you are capable of doing things, not just for others but for yourself," I said, quietly. Cas kissed my cheek, then the other and lastly my lips.

"Thank you, Crystal, for giving me the strength to follow my heart and magic," he said.

"Would it ruin the moment if I said we should stash some condoms here for the future?" I ask, sheepishly. Cas threw his head back in carefree laughter and I grinned. He pressed a firm kiss against my mouth.

"Anything for my jewel," he whispered, holding me close.

MAGIC IS cool especially because Cas is able to turn the five-foot trident into a mini charm to wear around his neck with some loose rope we found. We make our way to the cottage where our friends are waiting.

His hand is in mine, and I glance at him as we stand outside the door. He leans forward to place a kiss on my temple. I'm falling for Cas and his actions. His words tell me he feels the same way. I'm going to talk to him, eventually, after everything.

Entering the cottage our friends cheered. Cas' body relaxed and his smile brightened.

"Friends!" he shouted, opening his arms. The ladies tackled him in a hug.

"Your majesty!" they joked. Cas' ears turned pink, and he rolled his eyes. I can't help but laugh.

"Please no," he said, shaking his head. Caleb handed him a beer as Celestino hugged him.

"There's my annoying best friend," Celestino teased. I smiled watching the scene before me.

"You know you love me," he said, playfully glaring at him. I take a deep breath. This is much needed. A reunion with friends, drinks, and food. Cas needs this, I need this. Sometimes you don't realize how much you've missed something until you're reminded of it. Cas meets my eyes and gives me a wink. He stretches out his hand I take it.

○ ○ ○ 🐚 🐚 🐚 ○ ○ ○

WE MADE our way outside and Flynn used his magic to ignite the fire pit. We all sat around, and I glanced at everyone. I never had this. A group of friends to share stories with, laughter, worries. My throat tightened. I truly missed out on so much in life.

A warm hand intertwines with my own. I glance to see Cas' sparkling eyes. He raised my hand, kissing my knuckles softly. I melted easily for him. This is real. What I feel for him is real. And with the fire dancing in his blue eyes I can see he feels the same way.

"So can someone explain to me how a seal gets a name like Waldo?" Eleanor asked, breaking our bubble. I shook my head laughing.

"How does one get the name Eleanor?" Cas retorted. Eleanor tossed a napkin at him which he deflected into the fire.

"But I figured his name would be like Squirt or something," she said, teasingly. Caleb whispered something in her ear that made her blush. Flynn groans and throws a napkin at his brother's face.

"Dude, I didn't hear you, but we can all guess what you whispered," Flynn said. Lola hits his chest playfully, smirking at her elf boyfriend. He quietly blushed, staring into the fire.

"So, Sailor, ready for the ceremony tomorrow?" Celestino asked, watching. Cas froze for a second next to me. If I didn't have his arms wrapped around me, I might not have noticed. He takes a sip of his beer. He's hesitating. Is he still unsure even after what he said?

"I think so," he said, staring into the fire with a small smile. I grip his hand, and he glances at me. He squeezes twice and I squeeze once.

"Now that you guys are here, I have the trident," he said pointing to his necklace. Lily's eyes widened and Celestino stood up abruptly.

"No way!" Celestino said. Cas chuckled, squeezing me once before getting up. He slid the trident from its rope. His eyes concentrated on the charm before he said three notes that caused it to enlarge to its full height.

Fuck, he's hot.

"That is so cool!" Flynn said, getting up to walk over. Cas nodded. The look in his eyes is slightly bittersweet.

"It's beautiful," Lily said. It is and in Cas' grip it looked right. Like he was always meant to wield it.

"You did it," Caleb said, firmly.

"I just hope I can wield it," he said, quietly. Celestino shook his head. He placed a hand on his shoulder.

"You can. You just need faith," Celestino began.

"Trust," Caleb called out. Cas met my gaze with a twinkle.

"Don't even finish that," Eleanor warned. Everyone laughed and my worries melted away with the crackling of the fire. "But you can do it. You've made it this far," she said.

"I'm happy you guys are all here," Cas said. He comes back to sit next to me, pulling me close. I catch Eleanor's eye, and she grins.

"The cottage is gorgeous!" Lola said. Lily smiled, nodding along.

"You're doing an amazing job," Eleanor said, and my heart soared. "Both of you are doing amazing things for Coralia Coast," she continued. My nose twitches and I blink back tears.

Cas' hand squeezed my hips twice and I leaned against his shoulder. Tonight is a break for us, a break from everything that has been going on. For the rest of the night, we are going to enjoy spending time with our friends and each other.

CHAPTER 32
A SIREN'S CALL

Crystal

It's finally the ceremony that Cas has been anxious about. He's been gone since the morning. I assume to do any last minute preparations. Now that he has the trident, he can finally heal the coral. I'm still worried because according to him he isn't sure how.

I decide to take Eleanor to the spring for us to have a much-needed talk. The last thing I want to talk about is the rift that has always been between us. But the only way I can be happy is if I air out my feelings. Sometimes I need to put my pain first. Cas taught me that. My stomach is in knots the entire way there but luckily, she fills the silence.

"It looks so different in the summer!" she said, buzzing with excitement. When she had visited there was snow covering the ground. The sun is almost at its highest peak, but the trees provide enough shade.

"It's honestly changed quite a bit since I've gotten here," I said. "I can tell the town missed Cas," I said. Eleanor smiled.

"I've never seen him so relaxed. Like, sure in Lavender Falls you could tell he was happy, but I don't know he seems different here, more himself," she said. She turned to look at me. She winked. "He's different with you too," she said. I blush.

Once at the spring we shrug off our shoes, dipping our feet into the water. We both sigh. My body relaxed. For an earth pixie the water sure feels like home. We both lay back against the grass, staring at the clouds. For a second I forget why I brought her here. For a second it feels like how we were before mom died and dad's heart was broken.

"I talked to father," she said, breaking the silence. My stomach twists and I lick my lips.

"How was it?" I ask. I dig my fingers into the ground, needing to keep the trembles at bay and feel grounded.

"We actually talked...about the past," she said. She turned her head to look at me. There are tears in her eyes. Feelings are swirling inside. Hurt. Anger. Exhaustion. Envy. "I'm sorry I never noticed all the things you've done for us," she began. My bottom lip wobbles. Fuck, I didn't want to cry.

"Crystal, I am so sorry for not being the older sister you needed. I am so sorry that we put you in a position to take care of us when we needed to be there for you," she said.

"Eleanor. It's fi–"

"It is not fine!" she said, sitting up. "You did everything to keep us from fighting, to take care of us and I abandoned you," she said, her voice cracking. My eyes flicker to the sky. "I left you behind," she said. I bite down my cheek as tears cascaded down my face. My sister is hurt, and I want to tell her that it's okay but it's not. My pain is also valid. I sit up, wrapping my arms around my knees protectively.

"You needed to be free, on your own for a bit," I said. "At first, I was hurt. But I knew at some point you would leave. You and dad are too similar. He shouldn't have pressured you into taking over. He needed to see that you had your own dreams," I said. Eleanor shakes her head.

"That may be true but Crystal, you needed to be a kid and not think about those things. We should have done a better job," she said. "It's okay to admit that you were hurt. That you hated us," she said, quietly. A noise escapes me.

"I didn't hate you. I just hated the situation we were in and I just...I wanted to be seen," I said, voice cracking. I sit up and Eleanor wraps her arms around me tightly. "You guys were in so much pain, and I could see it. I wanted to help." Eleanor stayed quiet.

"I see you Crys. Both father and I do," she said. There was a rustle behind us and my dad appeared. I watched as he sheepishly walked up to us. He's dressed in a button down and jeans. This is the most casual I've ever seen him.

"D-dad?" I ask. He kneels in front of us. He places a hand on mine, squeezing gently. I sit a bit straighter, and my body stiffens. He must have noticed because his shoulders drop, and his eyes soften.

Instinctively my body is prepared to hear their argumentative words. I'm preparing for a fight between them. Fuck, I hate this. I look between them, unsure what is going to happen.

"I don't know if you remember this Eleanor, but your mom and I visited Coralia when she was pregnant with Crystal," he said, his eyes softening. Eleanor looked at both of us.

"I think I remember. It makes sense why Crystal feels connected to here," she said, smiling through her tears.

"What? How?" I ask. She rolled her eyes, sighing.

"The way you showed us around town yesterday. The way everyone got excited to see you, talk to you? What I have in Lavender Falls, you have here in Coralia Coast," she said. I sniffed, wiping my nose. I glance at dad, expecting to see pain. I don't want him to think I'm abandoning our hometown that we finally reconnected to. Instead, his lips tilted up into a rare smile.

"I-I have found a home here," I said, quietly. My dad wraps his arms around me and kissed the top of my head. My eyes widen in surprise.

"You belong here, Crystal. And I don't want you as COO," he said. I stared at him in confusion. He smiled down at me, a smile I hadn't seen in years. "I want you to head the rehabilitation division. Helping towns like Coralia Coast, expanding your community projects. It's where you thrive," he said. Tears continued to roll down my cheeks, my heart racing. "You are so much like your mom. A pixie with a wonderful and giving heart." I nod, taking a breath.

I'm finally going to do what I love. I'm going to be in charge. I let out a cry. I'm finally doing it, accomplishing my goal. I wipe my face, sniffling. Looking at the two of them it's finally time for me to speak my mind.

"I don't want to be the messenger between you too," I admit. "I'm tired. I'm tired of trying to be there for both of you emotionally. I'm tired of trying to be what you need and not knowing what I need," I said. "I missed out on so much. Hanging out with friends, experiencing life because I was worried if I wasn't around, you both would fail in some way," I continue. Eleanor swallows and my dad's face falls. "I love you both so much, but I can't be in the middle anymore. I'm tired all of the time because you both taught me to walk on eggshells." I take a deep breath, once again anticipating some sort of backlash. They stayed quiet for a few minutes.

"Your mother would be disappointed in me," he said, quietly, eyes on the water. "When she passed, I was lost, and I've been lost. I hurt you both in ways that you'll always carry the scars with you. I have many things to make up for. I hurt you both badly and I know my words can only mend so much. But I will prove it to you." He sighed slightly. "I'll mess up. Old habits die hard," he said, his lips twitching in a way that reminded me of Eleanor.

"But you can always learn," Eleanor said, giving a wobbly smile. I stare at both of them. The old me was slipping away and I can now see a brighter future where I don't have to mitigate between the beings I care about. Instead, we can finally stand together.

"Mom would be so proud of you, of both of you. I have a lot to make up for. I caused you both so much pain, but I hope you can be patient as I try to correct the wrongs I've made," he said. My dad's broken heart is slowly being mended. I never thought I would see the day. I gave up hope a long time ago that we would be in this position. I glance at dad and Eleanor. She smiled and placed a hand on his shoulder.

"Like I said. *Dad* and I had a long talk," she said. He cradled her elbow, his eyes softening. My mouth drops. Eleanor always called him father, a way to keep her emotional distance from him.

"So, what does this mean for us?" I asked. I fidget with my hands, unsure what happens next.

"We should have a family video chat once a week, whether it's dinner or breakfast," Eleanor offered. Dad nodded.

"And I'm going to start taking more time off to be with you both and…my future sons-in-law," he teased. My eyes widen and Eleanor laughs.

"Did dad just try to be funny?" I said, mocking a gasp.

"Do you think he was possessed by a ghost?" Eleanor asked, running with the bit. He rolled his eyes and once again I'm reminded of Eleanor. I smile at both of them. Here we all are, sharing laughs and smiles. My eyes water again. For the first time in a long time, I can breathe.

"Thank you," I said, softly. They looked at each other and then at me.

"Thank you for being more than what was needed but you don't have to anymore," he began. My bottom lip trembled as he pulled me in for a hug. My body collapsed against his. His heart is steady. "You just have to be my daughter now," my dad said.

AFTER CRYING SOME MORE, we all left to go get ready for the ceremony. I'm still in shock that he and Eleanor are getting along. There is a shift between us, a weight is finally off my shoulders. Now I can just be a little sister and younger daughter.

It will take time though. It's going to be hard to relinquish the need to fix their problems. It will take a while for the resentment and jealousy to fade but now I'm willing to say those feelings out loud. I'm afraid to tell my dad and Eleanor how I feel. I need to if I want to continue to mend our relationship. I need to talk about my feelings if I want to truly live and not let life pass me by.

My thoughts drift to Cas as I step inside the cottage. He hasn't answered his phone all day and it's making me anxious. I'm not sure what he is doing. After finding the trident he seemed more comfortable with himself and his role.

We also still need to talk about our feelings. Throughout the summer our friendship changed. It's blossom into something greater than I thought it could. My feelings for him deepened. I reached for him when I was happy, sad or tired.

Walking into my room I paused. Lying on the bed was a gorgeous, silver dress with a slit and a scooped neckline. Lifting it up, the back was open and in the lighting the silver reflected hues of blues. I blushed. The shades reminded me of Cas' tail. There is a note on the bed.

My siren song,

I wanted you to have something special to wear for the ceremony. I never thought this day would happen. But since meeting you I've learned to trust myself more. You make me want to be a better siren, a better friend, a better brother, son and lover. Not for others but for myself.

I hope when you wear this dress you feel beautiful. Because to me you are more beautiful than any pearl in the ocean and any star in the sky. I hope after the ceremony we can have a little chat about a certain arrangement, M'Lady.

Always yours,
Caspian
aka fish cake
aka sweet muffin
aka honeysuckle

A bubble of laughter escapes me. Cas picked out this dress for me. A dress that showed every siren and marine creature that I'm his. I smile, taking a deep breath. I went to place the note on my nightstand and noticed a vase filled with blue hydrangeas. I smile.

I'm getting my siren, and my siren is becoming who he was always meant to be. Now we just need to get through the ceremony.

ONCE DRESSED I meet everyone by the stage on the beach. The whole town plus the royal families are there looking their best. I smile and politely speak to everyone. From the corner of my eye, I can see Kai glaring at the person talking to Mira.

"You look beautiful," a voice said from behind. My dad wore a button shirt with slacks. I smiled, reaching for a hug.

"You look very handsome," I said, patting his shirt. He chuckled. He has slowly been smiling a lot easier the past few months and it warms my heart to think his spark is returning. "You've been doing amazing work. Your mom would be so proud of you," he said, his eyes going misty. I blink rapidly. The tears are always easy when it comes to my mom.

"She is," I said, quietly. "I feel her presence all the time, like a warm hug," I said. My dad pulls me into a hug, kissing the top of my head. There is a soft cough.

"If it isn't Mr. Hale," Cas' mom said. She's in a beautiful green dress that shifts the color of her eyes from blue to almost green.

"Dad this is—"

"Marina," my dad said, cutting me off. I look between them.

"Wait, you two know each other?" I said. Mrs. Calder laughed.

"Your father and mother visited once," she recalled. My eyes widen.

"But I didn't know you met during that time," I said. My dad grabbed the back of his neck, nervously.

"He also probably didn't mention the fact that a group of seahorses tried to attack him," she said, raising an eyebrow. I smile at my dad's lore and stifle a giggle.

"No, he did not," I said, crossing my arms and giving him a pointed look. My dad rolled his eyes and just that motion caused me to laugh.

"I had a life where things happened," he stated. I snort despite knowing it's true. He isn't just my dad. He was someone's son, is someone's friend, and was someone's love. He had a whole life where I didn't exist. There's a bit of pain, in knowing that he probably experienced things and that I couldn't be there for him. But I guess that's life.

"Please promise me if there are any other stories you know to tell me," I told her. She nods, before glancing at the ocean.

"Have you seen Caspian?" she asked. I shake my head. She nods, pursing her lips. "I know he'll be here. Well, why don't you go hang with your friends and I will introduce your father to the potential clients you've been winning over?" she said with a wink. I blush under her praise and watch them walk away.

I move to pull Mira away from some princes that she was clearly not into. She sighed in relief as we walked over to my friends.

"Everyone, this is Mira, Cas' cousin," I said. Eleanor threw her arms around her.

"Your hair is different!" Eleanor noted. Mira giggled.

"Yours too. I remember some of you guys! How are you?" Mira asked.

"It's so good to see you! The town...looks very happy," Lily said with a smile. Mira chuckled.

"The summer is a magical time for new adventures," she said, eyeing me. I blushed.

"Crys was telling us about the meadery and bookstore. Honestly, we could use a bookstore," Lola said, looking at Eleanor who nodded. Mira's smile widened.

"Yes!" she said, cutting her eyes to me and I nodded. "A family used to own it before they moved away. The meadery was basically our local pub and the renaissance festival used to pass by here mainly because of the mead," she said.

"I've always wanted to go to a renaissance festival," Lola said. Flynn wraps an arm around her, watching his girlfriend smile with excitement.

"Maybe with the meadery back who knows," I said, ideas forming in my head. My dad is right about my need to give back. I love helping expand communities and I have ideas for not just the company but for Coralia Coast.

"Stranger things have happened," Lily said with a knowing smile. I winked at Caleb and Flynn.

"I'm so happy you guys are here and especially to see the town at its best," Mira said.

"Oh, it's beautiful," Lola commented. It's Lola and Flynn's first time in Coralia Coast. The crew decided to use Cas' ceremony as a mini vacation after surviving another festival in Lavender Falls. Apparently, a baby unicorn went on the loose. Mira glanced quickly at the water, her eyes assessing something I couldn't see.

"Wait you two make drinks right?" she asked Caleb and Flynn. They nodded.

"Come with me. We all need a drink and I'm the honorary bartender around here," she said. I took a step to follow her, and she pointed to the ocean. I raise an eyebrow in confusion, but she motions for me to go to the water.

When I glance at the sea, its waves are crashing against the shore and for some reason it worries me. I place my heels by the stage, letting my feet dig into the sand. I feel anchored here. I make my way to the ocean, lifting my dress to feel the water. It's cool, inviting. The waves relax, lapping at my feet softly, and so I wade further in. I see why Mira wanted me here.

This time when the ocean called me it wasn't in a somber melody but a peaceful one. The ocean is as merciful as it is merciless. My emotions, my heart is like the ocean and right now I feel its song deep within.

My magic buzzes beneath my skin. Cas said that I provide the same feeling as the trident. Well, the ocean did the same for me. How I feel about Cas is how the water makes me feel. It understood my hopes, my fears and sadness. It and Cas didn't push me away. Instead, they allowed me to feel the emotions, ride its waves.

Taking a deep breath, I think of Cas, of where he might be and might be feeling. I begin humming the same melody he's been singing to me. I recognize it now. It's our song, a melody that draws us together. I'm not a siren but I hope our song can reach him, wherever he was.

CHAPTER 33
HOME

Caspian

"One day you'll wear my crown, Cas," Uncle Seward said. We were out floating in the middle of the ocean, watching the whales migrate. They were massive creatures. I enjoyed watching something so big be so graceful. It was beautiful. Scary but beautiful.

"That won't be for a while," I said, rolling my eyes. My uncle and dad always talked about the future as if it was about to happen. He chuckled.

"You never know," he said with a shrug of his shoulders.

"Why do you and dad always have to be so morbid?" I asked, making a face. Uncle Seward splashed me.

"We are preparing you," he said. He turned back to watch one of the whales rise from the sea. The waves pushed us back. "You and your brother will lead the Atlantic Ocean, protect it, nurture it. I know you're tired of hearing it but it's true," he said, his tone shifting. He sounded like dad, and it made my heart thump and stomach twist.

"What if I don't want this?" I asked quietly. All I ever wanted was a normal life without a crown looming over my head. He took a deep breath.

"One day Caspian you'll see the importance of yourself in this big wide ocean," he said. I snorted.

"I'm just a merman who can talk to fish," I said. He dunked my head into the water.

"Yeah, and it's fucking cool," he said. I shook my head, spitting out water.

"One day you'll wear my crown. You'll be ready," he said. I frowned. No, I wouldn't be. I would never be ready because I didn't want this.

"How do you know?" I asked. He looked at me, his blue eyes shining.

"Because I felt the same way you do," he said. My eyes widened in surprise. Uncle Seward swam around the ocean and the sea creatures followed him. He listened to their problems and always lent a helping hand. With my dad they worked side by side, cleaning up the beaches on the east coast, taking care of everything and everyone. He was meant to do this.

"What changed?" I asked. He stared back at the whales, seemingly lost in thought.

"One day I met someone who made me realize my potential."

CRYSTAL. My siren song. My best friend. The being I'm in love with. Her quiet curiosity makes me smile. Her warmth and giving heart make me want to be better. She's never pressured me to be anything more than what I am. She believed in me even when I didn't believe in myself and she allowed me to feel broken.

Sitting around the coral I hold the trident in my hand. Its magic is buzzing within. Its strength is a welcome weight. It's real. I have it, the item no one has seen for hundreds of years. It's been calling me this whole entire time, urging me to find it. And I did. Because of Crystal.

Today is the ceremony. Everyone is probably at the beach waiting for me. I swallow, feeling nervous. I look around at the dying coral. I finally have the trident, but I have no idea how to use it. Which of my magic will even work? Talking to the coral?

"There you are," Ronan said. I twist to the side. His eyes land on the trident and his mouth drops. "I knew you would find it," he said. I swallow.

"Did you? Really?" I ask, my voice sounding small. He said he believed in me but wasn't he just waiting for me to drop everything and run? It's all I've ever done. His brows furrow as he swims to sit next to me on the sandy ocean floor. His tail is much longer than mine given the fact in our human form he is taller.

"I did Cas. I always knew you would," he said. I shake my head.

"How? I never gave a shit about this growing up. All I did was complain, ditch lessons, and go to parties. I fucking ran away," I said, my voice breaking. My eyes burn but it doesn't matter since I'm underwater. Ronan places a hand on my shoulder.

"You needed to leave to find yourself," he said. I bit my cheek, feeling my emotions break again slowly. "You've always given yourself to everyone. You always did your best to make everyone happy, but you needed to leave to find your own happiness," he said. I stare up at him in surprise. He sounded older, wiser, like dad. His eyes are trained on the coral, and I'm struck with the realization again that I never considered the pressures he's always felt. Fuck, I've been so selfish.

"I'm sorry," I said.

"For what?" he asked, looking back at me. I take a second to gather my thoughts.

"You've always known you were going to be king. You've carried that weight with you without a break for yourself," I said. "Weren't there times you wanted to run?" I ask. He doesn't answer right away, and I sit quietly waiting. I've been too blinded by my own pain to see his.

"Yes. All the time Cas. But I couldn't. When you left, I was jealous, but I also knew you needed it," he confessed.

My brother grew up with the mantle of king on his shoulders and not once did I ever see him falter and yet he always understood me before I understood myself. I take a deep breath before pushing myself off the sandy floor. Gripping the trident in one hand I offer my other.

"Don't you want a break?" I ask. He huffed out a rough laugh.

"All the fucking time," he said. He glanced at the coral again. "I think bringing the town back to life will help," he said. I nod.

"You'll have a different kind of stress. A fun stress," I said. He eyed me.

"Since when is stress fun?" he asked, grumpily.

"Depends on what or who is causing it," I said with a smirk. We share a slight chuckle and the trench I always felt between us is slowly closing. I lift the trident, enjoying the weight "As your Second, as your brother, you can count on me for when you need a break," I said. His eyes shift. He isn't staring at me like I'm his annoying younger brother but as his equal, with pride. He gripped my hand, and I pulled him up.

"We will do great things," he assured me. We will because we care for the ocean, this town and our family.

"I wish they were here to see it," I said, quietly. My brother placed a hand on my shoulder.

"The ocean sings their song. They know," he assured me. I smile before turning to the coral.

"Any ideas on what to do with the trident?" I ask. Ronan frowned.

"All I know is that it's supposed to heighten your powers," he said. I sigh.

"I talk to fishes, Ronan," I said. He rolled his eyes at my dramatics.

Lala la lalala la.

My ears pick up a familiar melody. I spin around but I don't see Crystal. Yet the ocean carries her voice to me.

"What is it?" my brother asked, looking around for danger. I stare at him.

"You don't hear that?" I ask. He tilted his head for a moment and then shook it. I stare at the direction of the shore. Crystal is in the water, singing my siren song, *her* siren song. The song that fills my head whenever we're together. My eyes widened in realization.

"I think I know what to do," I said. I grin at my brother. "A siren song. It can cause damage, bring happiness, take away pain and-"

"Heal," my brother said, finishing my sentence. "But not everyone can heal," he hesitated.

"I can. I know it," I said with conviction. My magic surges through me. I'm right.

"You can use the trident kind of like a tuning fork, sending your song across the ocean," he said. I rolled my lips. I hadn't used that side of my magic in a long time. I used a bit of it with Crystal because it heightened our desires. And then prior I used it on my family to ease their pain when my uncle and dad passed away. It's a part of me that makes me anxious.

"Ronan...," I trailed off.

"What's wrong?" he asked.

"I haven't used that power in a long time," I admit. He took a deep breath, swimming up to me. He lifted my hand holding the trident and reached for my other. Once my hands were wrapped around the trident he placed his hands on my shoulders.

"You are the Second Prince of the Atlantic Ocean. You have been blessed with many gifts that you always use for good, with a pure heart," he began. My stomach tightens. "You heard a song with Crystal, right?" he asked. I flush under his gaze. Crystal is my soul mate and from the moment we met I've heard the sweet and slow melody of our hearts connecting.

"Then close your eyes, listen to the ocean, feel the creatures that occupy her home and listen to the song that forms in your heart. Your heart, your magic will never leave you astray," he said.

"Where were these pep talks when I was younger?" I tease. Ronan flicked my forehead. I took a deep breath.

"You didn't listen, now focus," he ordered. But I can see his lips twitching to smile.

I take a deep breath, and magic vibrates from the trident, up my arms. The ocean needs me, and I need her. I promise that I will protect the ocean and all its living creatures. My heart hammers as music fills my brain. A melody begins forming and my larynx drops as I take in a deep breath.

Notes carry and the trident is glowing brightly. Ronan swims behind me quickly, holding me in place as the power of the trident pushes me back. I watch the waves created by my voice moves across the coral, out into the ocean.

> When the darkness rises
> Let my song be heard
> When shadows leave you paralyze
> Heed my words
> When the rough waves of life leave you adrift
> When the thunder cracks the ground below your feet
> When you feel sick and broken
> This melody of love will be your guiding light
> Heal what is hurt
> Repair what is broken
> Find what is lost
> Let your beauty be awoken

The song continues to pour out of me, and my body ignites. I watch everything around me faintly glow. I wait with bated breath as the color in the coral slowly begins returning. My eyes once again burn. By the stars, I did it. I'm doing it. The coral is healing.

"Kraken's crap," I said. My brother slaps my shoulder.

"I fucking told you; you could do it," he said. I rub my eyes, knowing my tears will just float out into the ocean. My uncle is right. My dad is right. I'm meant for this role. I'm meant to take care of the ocean, be the bridge for my brother. I'm more than just a pretty smile and a good time. I know my place in this bright big ocean and for any moment when I might lose my place, I know my friends and family have my back.

"Now are you ready to wear the crown and be by my side?" my brother asked.

ISABEL BARREIRO

THE BEACH IS FILLED with beings that I grew up with, beings that saw me rise and fall. And now I'm back and ready to take my place. I undo the first button on my dress shirt, needing relief from the heat. I was tired from all the magic I had used up. From behind the curtain, I can see my new and old friends sitting together, getting along.

I smile. I always had a feeling that one day they would get alone. My eyes snag on Crystal in the dress I picked out. I grin. It's taking everything in me to not walk over and kiss her. She is achingly beautiful. She is magnificent. Ethereal. And soon she will be mine.

My mom sits in front row with Aunt Meryl. She is gracious and I owe her so much for allowing me to leave and find myself. I really owed the whole town. My brother walks to center stage and everyone stands.

"Thank you to everyone for being here. Today is a special day as most of you know," Ronan began. I take deep breaths, my heart racing. "Today my brother, Caspian will take his rightful place as my second," he said, turning to face where I'm waiting. My heart races but not with nerves, with excitement.

I walk out and people gasp. I have the trident in my hand. It's real and it's also mine. I glance at my friends and wink. Crystal beams joyfully and it fills me with pride. I'm becoming the being that she deserves, and I will spend every day making sure.

I stand before my brother. This is the moment we've waited for since we were kids. If only dad and uncle Seward were here. Ronan must have noticed what I'm thinking because his eyes soften. Mira appears next to him with her father's crown, and I bite the inside of my cheek. My mom left her seat to stand next to her with the royal book, the one where my name will be written below my uncle's.

Staring at his golden crown my lips twitch. It matches the trident. Swirls of golden waves, twisted into points. Once again, my eyes prick with tears. My name will not erase his. Instead, it will be enshrined *with* his. I wouldn't be who I am without my dad or my uncle. I feel honored knowing that I can proudly have my name with theirs.

"Kneel," my brother commanded. I bend down on one knee, keeping my trident upright. I glance at Mira who has tears in her eyes.

"They're here, with us," she whispered. I take a deep breath, my body feeling warm. Glancing out at the ocean I can't stop myself from grinning. Everyone turned to see a bunch of sea creatures poking their heads from the water. I'm the bridge and it's only right that they should be here to witness this moment.

"Caspian Coralia Calder, Second Prince of the Atlantic Ocean, do you accept your position as your king's right hand? To serve and protect the ocean and all of its living things. To be as merciless and merciful as the ocean?" he asked. I take a deep breath, closing my eyes briefly.

One day I met someone who made me realize my potential.

Sometimes we need a place, a person that helps to ease the weight off our shoulders.

Sometimes we need to be reminded of why we do what we do but also that we can't do everything,

You cannot take care of others if you don't take care of yourself. Remember that.

I look over at my friends and family, my town. When I didn't believe in myself, they believed in me. They've always known what was in my heart. They trusted me, loved me. I look back up at my brother, smiling.

"I do," I said, my voice strong, carrying in the ocean breeze. He cracks a small smile, placing the crown on my head. It's a welcome weight that makes me straighten my back. I slowly stand and turn to face the crowd and the ocean. Mira stepped up, handing me a pen.

Without hesitation I sign my name below my uncle's with thunderous applause surrounding me. We will forever be together in these pages. I close my eyes briefly, another song playing in my head. One from my childhood, a song by my dad. I smile. I was going to carry his song, his teachings and legacy with me for the rest of my life.

I bang the trident against the stage signaling my turn to speak. Everyone quieted quickly. There was something I needed to say.

"Thank you everyone," I start off. "Most of you here watched me grow up and you know how much I didn't want to be standing here today. It's why I ran away which once again most of you are aware about. Honestly, I wasn't sure if I was coming back," I said. "But I made new friends who believed in me the same way you all believed in me, and it made me realize something." I look around, making sure to catch everyone's eye like my uncle taught me.

"You all saw my heart, my potential not because of the family that I belonged to but because you saw *me*. So, thank you. Thank you for always being there, trusting me when I didn't trust myself. I promise to serve you all righteously until I am called back to the ocean," I said. Everyone cheered and my eyes caught Crystal's. There was one thing left for me to do.

It was time for me to confess to my mate.

CHAPTER 34
REUNITED AND IT FEELS GOOD

Caspian

I spent most of the ceremony party saying hi to beings and giving my thanks. Kai is hanging with Ricky and talking to Mira who keeps rolling her eyes. Kai's cousins are talking to other royal members, thankfully occupied.

"I'm so proud of you," my mom said, holding her arms out. I step into her hug. I take a deep breath.

"Sorry it took me so long," I said, feeling guilty. She shakes her head.

"I've always known your heart, my sweet boy. I'm just sorry you felt like you had to take care of everyone else's but your own," she said, tears in her eyes. I swallow.

"Mom–" She holds up her hand, cutting me off.

"I'm thankful for all the laughter and smiles you have provided us. But I should have done better. I should have been there for you," she said, voice slightly breaking.

"You did more than you could," I said, pulling her back for a hug.

"I am so proud of the being you have become, and I know dad and uncle Seward are smiling from beyond the ocean," she whispered in my ear. My chest tightened. "Now go hang out with your friends. They've missed you," she said, pushing me away. I chuckle, walking away.

"Look who decided to grace us with his royal presence," Celestino teased. I rolled my eyes. Celestino threw his arm around my shoulder, flicking the hair that was poking out of the crown. I shoved him away.

"You're always going to crack royal jokes aren't you," I said. He glanced at Caleb and Flynn.

"Yes," they all said. I smiled. I loved having them here in my own town and I loved that for the first time I didn't have to hide myself from them.

"Thank you, guys, for coming and once again I am sorry for keeping this a secret," I said. I still carried some guilt from lying to them for a year. Lily shook her head, placing a hand on my arm. The warmth of her magic eased my heart.

"We all have secrets to protect ourselves. But you know now that you can trust us to be there for you," she said, smiling. I nodded.

"Yeah, and trust us to kick your butt on the dance floor," Eleanor said, holding her hand out. I laughed, taking it and leading her to the makeshift dance floor in the middle of the beach. I glanced around trying to find Crystal. Eleanor noticed and leaned over to me.

"Her and dad are talking to potential clients," she said. I nodded. I will get my time with her when it's right. Everyone followed my suit, and it felt like I was back in Lavender Falls with all of them. We shared the dance floor, mingling with the beings around us. I am filled with happiness, the weight of all of my worries melting away.

"How come you never told us how hot your friends were?" Ricky said. I chuckled.

"They are all taken," I point out. Ricky sighed dramatically and I bumped his hip.

"By the way I had no idea you used to make shit drinks," Caleb said, leaning over. My eyes widened and snapped to Kai and Ricky who wore giant grins.

"Who the fuck—"

"We needed to bond with your friends?" Kai said, throwing an arm around Celestino's shoulder. I take back liking my groups of friends interacting.

"Yeah, and I had no idea you went skinny dipping in a swamp," Ricky teased. I groan as the music continues to make us sway.

"You know I have stories about all of you," I retort. Everyone threw their heads back in laughter. Sure, I feel embarrassed, but I'm so fucking happy to be having a moment like this, with all of them.

I enjoyed myself with my friends. I introduced them to Kai and Ricky properly. We swapped embarrassing stories. The ocean crashed excitedly against the shore, calling me.

Lily, Lola and Eleanor were gossiping with Mira while the guys decided to play soccer on the outskirts of the stage. Things are finally winding down. I roll up slacks, letting the water wash over my feet.

"Thank you for showing me what I needed," I whisper to the ocean. I needed to thank her for everything she's done for me this summer.

The sun is beginning to set, and in the distance, I can make out some whales. The same whales I watched with my uncle all those years ago. His crown is now on my head, and it served as a reminder of my memories with him. It symbolizes that my uncle will always be there with me.

Someone cleared their throat behind me. I turn around and my heart stops. She is a vision, too beautiful to stare at but I can't tear my eyes away from her.

"I've been looking for you," she said, fidgeting with her hands. She had pulled her hair into a loose ponytail. Her hips swayed as she walked towards me, the dress sparkling in the setting sun.

"Your dress," I said, taking a step. She waves her hand, not caring. I smile and open my arms.

"I just need you," she said, dragging her dress through the water. I pull her in for a hug. Her familiar scent washes over for me and I feel like I can finally breathe.

"How do you feel?" she asked. I hold her tighter. I tilt back to look into her eyes. They were browner today and still beautiful.

"I feel good," I said, honestly. She grins and my heart eases. "I healed the coral," I said with a small smile. Her eyes widen and she squeals. I laugh. I love getting her to react. Her emotions when she let down her guard, shone from her face and vibrated throughout her body.

"How?" she asked. I begin humming our song, swaying our bodies. She lets out a startled gasp. "Did you hear me?" she asked. I nodded. "But how?"

"You didn't use some magic?" I ask, confused. I heard Crystal's voice when I was down below. It's how I figured out what I needed to do. A wave crashed against the back of my legs, and I smile. I see what happened.

"No, Cas. I just felt compelled to walk to the water and then something about the waves made me want to sing the song you always sing," she said. I glance back at the ocean. The ocean takes care. She is loving and kind but also protective and fierce.

"The ocean must have called you," I said. "The ocean knew I needed you and carried your voice to me," I said, smiling down at her. "She connects us all and we are connected," I said. Crystal blushed, her eyes softening.

"Cas?"

"M'Lady?"

"Can we dance in the water?" she asked, softly. I step away and offer her a hand. She placed her soft hand in mine, and I led her further into the water. The waves relaxed as we wrapped our arms around each other and swayed to the song that was drifting from the stage.

I pulled her close and her face nestles into the crook of my shoulder. I take a deep breath. Once again, her scent relaxes me, easing the burden of the day away. In the back of my head, I hear a whisper of forever. I want this forever, her forever.

In her embrace I'm strong. In her eyes I'm capable of anything and everything. Her arms tighten around me, and I smile. I wouldn't have found the trident without her. I wouldn't have found myself without her.

"Thank you," I whisper.

AFTER SAYING goodbye Crystal and I headed home. We showered and switched into comfy clothes. She brought out two mugs of tea and we grew comfortable on the couch. She nestled against my chest, and I sighed happily.

I can see this being our life together. Our days filled with work but coming home every night to tea and cuddles. It's a simple life that I welcome openly. My hand stroked her cheek. I needed her to be mine, truly mine.

Now is the time for us to discuss our little arrangement. I don't want to go around faking our relationship when it feels so incredibly real. My feelings for her are real and strong. She is my mate, my one and only.

I run my fingers through her hair and her lips tilt up. She is the sweetest being I have ever encountered. She is everything.

"Crystal?" I said, getting her attention. She looks up at me, blinking. "I'm going to say something cheesy, but I mean it."

She blushes. "Okay," she said, her voice squeaking.

"Every siren has a soulmate, and we hear this song in our head that only they understand," I said. "You're the only melody I can hear, the only one I want to hear, my siren song." My heart is racing against my chest. Her eyes well with tears.

"Oh," she said, quietly. "Is that the song you're always humming?" she asked. I nod. Someone else would have been hurt from her reaction but I've long learned that sometimes she needed time to process.

"You said that in the note," she pointed out. I nod again. "Could you sing it for me?" she asked, her lips stretching into a small smile. I stroke her cheek.

My heart sings a song

Its notes spell out your name
When I'm with you my pain seems to fade away
You erase my darkest clouds
Your voice is the melody that keeps the nightmares
    at bay

Can't you see you are my one and only
Roses paint my cheeks whenever you are near
Stay with me until the stars call me home
The taste of your lips is sweeter than any wine
All I need is your hand in mine
Love you, I always will, my north star, my siren song

With a red string, our souls intertwine
Forever yours, forever mine

    Tears run down her cheeks as she quietly listens to the song that has filled my heart since I first met her. She reaches for my hand, and I stare at our intertwined fingers. She places tender kisses across my knuckles. My sweet Crystal. I lean forward, catching her watery gaze.
    "Can I kiss you…for real this time?" I ask, taking a chance. I want this kiss to be about two beings who share feelings for each other, feelings that run deeper than the ocean. This isn't a show and tell for the world; this is for us. Her cheeks are stained pink, and her hands tremble when she cups my face.
    She brushed her lips against mine, giving me the promise of something more. I hold the back of her head, keeping her in place. Her body sags into mine, and I catch her. I pour everything I feel for her into this kiss. I want her to feel just how badly I ache for her.
    The kiss is slow, sensual, a promise to one another. Her hand rakes through my hair and I shiver. She grows bolder which only makes me want more of her. She takes a bite of my bottom lip, pulling back slightly. I chuckle at her playfulness. She pushes herself closer, sitting in my lap.
    "That was a nice real kiss," she said. I stole another, sweeter this

time. My hands wander down her shoulders, to her hips, massaging away any tension she has in her body. She melts easy for me, like always.

"I like being real with you," I admit. Her hands fiddle with my shirt and when she looks up at me, I see my whole world.

"Can this...be real?" she asked. I grin, pressing my forehead against hers. She wants this as badly as I do. Crystal isn't just my best friend. She is the being I plan on walking through life with.

"Yes," I whisper against her lips, pulling her for another slow kiss. I want to savor every inch of her. I scoot down, laying on the couch, keeping her on top of me. Our hips are aligned, and our mouths move against each other perfectly.

Stars, I love kissing her. Her hands tighten against my chest, and she is breathing faster. Her hips slightly rock against mine before slowing down. Her body relaxes and I can't stop myself from smiling against her lips. It's amazing how during these two months of living with her, being with her, I've been able to read more into her, understand her better.

"Tired?" I ask, pulling away. She blinks a few times before nodding. I chuckle and kiss her forehead. "Then let's just stay like this and watch a few episodes before bed," I said. She nodded, kissing my cheek...and then my other...and then my nose. I raise an eyebrow.

This is a new side to Crystal. She was playful at times and loved to tease me, but this was...cute. This is adorable and cozy. Her shy smile with her blushing cheeks makes me want to squeeze her.

"Someone is being affectionate, and I do find it adorable," I said, rubbing my nose against her cheek. Her soft laugh is music to my ears.

"I just feel...happy," she said. My chest fills with pride. Her happiness doesn't have to be chained down by reasons or stipulations.

"And I'm happy," I said, staring at her. I brush some loose hair back, enjoying the way her eyes flutter close, and she leans into my touch. "I love that this is real," I said, softly. Crystal blinked a few times, her nose twitching before looking at me.

"I've never been in love," she whispered. My heart skips. I'm in love with Crystal. I've always been. She came into my life quietly and has buried herself in my heart. Every cell in my body lights up around her, craves her, and cares for her.

"Me either," I said, offering a hopeful smile. A tear slips down her cheek and I swipe it with my thumb. She is there for my tears, and I'll always be there for hers.

"But can we figure it out together?" she asked, sounding hopeful. I trail kisses across her face, slowly making my way back to her mouth.

"You and me, always. Crys and Cas," I said. "Our wedding hashtag will be cute," I tease, and Crystal slaps me in the chest. I mock an offended gasp which quickly turns into laughter. "I'm not joking, I'm being very serious right now. It'll be a very cute wedding. Small of course. Don't worry we won't invite all the kingdoms. If we do, I'll just steal you away before the party starts to help you relax," I said, waggling my eyebrows at her. She clicked her tongue and nodded.

"You seem to have this planned," she said, narrowing her eyes. I do because she's mine and I'll do what I need to, so she always knows.

"I knew the moment I saw you, M'Lady. You are my north star, my shining pearl in the sea, my siren song. I wouldn't be who I am right now without your steady faith in me," I said, hoping she can feel the sincerity in my words. I want her to see herself the way I see her.

She stayed quiet for a moment, and my heart raced, hoping I didn't fuck this up despite the fact that we decided to try this for real. Was what I said too much for her?

"You know I have a tendency to hide and get overwhelmed," she said, drawing circles against my heart. She tilts her head, her eyes softening. "But I feel safe with you. I feel seen with you. I've never felt that in my life," she said, her voice cracking. "You bring me peace and adventure. You feel like how home used to feel like," she said, softly. I cup her cheek, pulling her in for another kiss.

"We're so cute," I said with our noses squished together. "Fuck I could make out all night with you."

"Just that? What if I want more? I still have a list," she said, eyeing me. "I also strangely don't feel that tired anymore," she said, sitting up to straddle me.

"Anything for M' Lady."

CHAPTER 35
HAPPILY EVER AFTER

Crystal

"Can I spend a weekend in September at Coralia?" my dad asks on video chat. Eleanor's head snaps into frame.

"If you go in September, Crys do you think you and Cas could come up for the winter festival?" she asked. I smile at them both. While our dynamic has a long way to go, we have been making progress. I nod.

"That's fine with me. Eleanor, do you happen to have Bridget's number? I have to talk to her," I said with a grin. Eleanor took a sip of her coffee.

"Oh yes!" she said. My dad cleared his throat.

"I sent Celestino some wood to start working on the bookcases," my dad said to me. Eleanor groaned. She's still convincing Mayor Kiana that they need a bookstore, which they do.

"That's great. I think we'll be tackling the bookstore in the spring, but I have to find someone to run it," I said. My dad raised an eyebrow. "It's going to be owned by the town by the way. Apparently, the old building, is a landmark," I said. My dad's phone beeped.

"Maria is calling. I promised I would have brunch," he said. Eleanor smirked.

"Dad does brunch?" she said in disbelief. He rolled his eyes, and I giggled.

"I had a life, okay?" he said, running a hand through his salt and pepper hair.

"And it's time for you to live it," I reminded him.

We are getting close to the end of summer and I'm looking forward to fall. My workload with Hale's Lumber Industry is easing as I'm transitioning into my new role. Dad, Eleanor, and I have almost weekly video chats.

I have a siren by my side that makes breathing easier. He pushes me to come out of my shell and experience the world. Being with him is natural. It always has been since the beginning. I'm enjoying falling for someone who feels like home, and I enjoy finding my new home here in this town.

Coralia Coast is bustling with tourists. A band is set to perform, and it's been drawing a crowd. The townspeople seem happier, like a weight has also lifted off their shoulders.

"Ms. Crystal, lovely day," Ms. Serena said. I smile. Ms. Serena is the owner of the bed and breakfast that I had finished fixing. She is a sweet gentle witch with crazy gray curls and warm brown eyes. She enjoys leaving me baskets of croissants which Cas is insanely jealous of.

"It is. How's everything at the b&b?" I asked. She placed a warm hand on my arm.

"Lovely. The town as well. Thank you for everything," she said. "There are brighter things ahead for Coralia Coast now that you are finally here." I stare at her confused.

"Now that I'm—"

"Well, I must be off dear. Have to prep the bed and breakfast!" she said cheerfully, waving me off. I stare at her retreating figure. According to the townsfolk there is something slightly odd about Ms. Serena, but I don't find her odd, just uniquely charming.

I glance at the outside of the broken down meadery. My phone beeps and I smile. A friend from Lavender Falls will soon be arriving to check out the place. I have a feeling she is going to want it. I usually have good insight when it comes to beings. Now there is only one thing left to do and that is enjoy the day with my boyfriend.

Boyfriend.

I still blush whenever I think of Cas as my boyfriend. He's my first boyfriend and probably my last. His heart speaks to me in ways I only dare to imagine. He is mine and I am his. I'm on a new path that is wonderful, nerve-wrecking, exciting, and terrifying.

But that's life. It has the probability of being unexpected. There is always a chance of getting hurt however when you are knocked on the ground the only other direction is up.

The roar of the ocean calls to me and I follow her song. In the distance I can see fins popping out of the ocean. One is a startling ombre blue that warms my heart.

I make my way to our secret spot on the beach and begin undressing. The water is getting colder as fall looms over.

"M'Lady!" A bright cheery voice calls. I swim out until a pair of arms wrap around my waist. Strong arms lift me up and I gasp for air.

"I didn't know you were joining us," Cas said, his blue eyes shining. I shrug my shoulders.

"I finished the day early and figured I deserve to relax," I said. "By the way Bridget is going to be visiting soon."

"Oh, I can't wait," he said, pulling me closer. He kissed me all over my face and I giggled. Cas is definitely the more affectionate one in the relationship but that's what I love about him.

Love.

Boyfriend.

Stars, this summer is turning out to be something. I never thought that I would fall in love and yet Cas came into my life quietly and steadfast. He pushes me to go out into the world, and I do, knowing that I can be safe in his arms when I return. He doesn't expect me to be any more or less than what I am. I don't have to try to be anyone but myself with him. For once I can simply be whatever I want.

I wrap my arms around him, pulling him close. He grunts, feeling my legs wrap around his waist.

"Crystal," he said with a warning tone that makes my stomach twist. I raise an eyebrow.

"No one is here," I said, lowly. He fought back a smile. I enjoyed teasing Cas. His blue eyes are bright, and his hair is much lighter from his hours in the sun.

"Yes, but we have a group of whales migrating and you know fish, crabs, jelly–"

"Then take me to our little cave and have your way with me," I said, sounding giddy. Cas shook his head.

"My, my, has my little pixie come out of her shell," he teased. I lean over, giving him a gentle kiss. A kiss of promise, patience, and love. He blinks in a daze when I pull away.

"What can I say you're rubbing off on me," I said. Cas smirked like I knew he would.

"I see what you did there," he said, giving me a playful glare. I cocked my head innocently. "Rubbing off on you. Is that what you want, M'Lady?" he asked. I shrug my shoulders.

"That, your heart, peace, the meadery to work out," I said, listing my wants off the top of my head. Cas pressed a kiss against my chest, where my heart was and then my neck, teasing me with his fangs. I placed my hand over his tattoo, gently tracing over it. His hand came to cup my cheek.

"You have my heart, my body, and my soul," he said, softening his voice. His words are a promise stitched on my heart.

"You have my heart, my body, and my soul," I said, repeating his words. They are like vows, vows we will eventually make to each other in front of others, someday. "This has been the best summer," I said.

"It was a siren's summer for love," he said with a wink. I roll my eyes.

"It was our summer for love," I said blushing. I gasp as Cas adjusted his hold on me.

"Well fuck Crystal you said love. Now I have to have my way with you in our cave," he said, pressing a kiss against my neck once more and this time I felt his fangs. I threw my head back in laughter.

In the distance I can hear the whales singing their song and in front of me is the most beautiful, sweetest siren.

Life isn't easy and it never will be, but I can finally see a brighter future where I'm smiling.

THE CLOSING OF A CHAPTER

Lilianna and Celestino, childhood friends who found love in each other under the moonlight continued to love and grow as the years went by. Lilianna found the courage to speak her love out loud while Celestino stayed by her side through all the trials of life.

Caleb and Eleanor loved fiercely and stayed true to their promise of always communicating their worries and hardships. Eleanor's ideas helped foster the community of Lavender Falls. With a heart as big as hers, she made sure all were welcome. And quiet grumpy Caleb stayed by her side to make sure she always shone bright.

Lola and Flynn learned that working together was their biggest strength. Flynn was always with Lola to help her out in times of need and Lola washed away his dark clouds. Together the garden grew enough to sustain Lavender Falls and its neighboring towns. Every once in a while, a certain unicorn and her family visits the ones who saved their lives.

Lastly, Crystal and Caspian. Sometimes love comes quietly, sometimes it is always there. They lived happily in Coralia Coast. Prince Caspian grew in his duty as second in command, healing the ocean. Crystal helped to revitalize the town and many others. Together they lived a quiet, fun-filled life that they have always wanted.

Each of them had their ups and downs, their struggles and achievements because it's life. Life is never easy, but they surround themselves with people who push them to go after their dreams and hold them when they break.

They eventually went on more adventures together and with the beings they met along the way. It's a beautiful thing when you make a family of your own. Sometimes friends turn into family, sometimes families break and sometimes they heal.

Lavender Falls, a small town tucked into the Northeast where everyone can let out their inner beast. A quiet witch who accomplished every task, a warlock who returned home, broke her mask. A stoic elf, his secret revealed, a flirty pixie's broken family finally healed. A sunny vampire and grumpy elf have been rivals from the start whose hearts now will never part. A siren bound by fate finally found his song, his mate.

The End for Lavender Falls

Acknowledgments

For a while I thought this book was cursed. From Google Docs crashing for 2 weeks, to Microsoft Word crashing, documents not downloading, accidentally deleted chapters it's been a JOURNEY trying to get this book done.

And here we are.

The last book in my first ever series. Like Crystal I never dreamed that I could do something like this. I didn't think it was possible or that I deserved it.

Becoming an author, what little me always wanted has finally given me hope and light that the future I've been scared to dream can finally happen.

I'm so grateful for Lavender Falls and all the characters that have pieces of me. This story itself was the hardest. It was the most emotional out of all my books. Of course the one that has given me the most problem would be the hardest to write.

This book deals a lot with being the parentified daughter, the good one, the person who gives so much to everyone. And if that's you, if you see yourself in Crystal and Caspian just know it's okay to be selfish, it's okay to say no and give yourself a break.

Thank you for reading my series. I'm still learning and growing and I hope you can see that through this series. And thank you for taking a chance on me.

Thank you to my mom who continues to give me more than I deserve. I can't for the day I can give everything back to you.

Thank you to Bear, the Caspian to my Crystal, the Celestino to my

Lilianna, the Lola to my Flynn and the Caleb to my Eleanor. Thank you for loving me even when I feel like I don't deserve it.

Thank you J for all of these covers. It's been amazing watching you grow as a cover artist. I can't wait for the day we get traditionally publish.

Thank you to Ruby, Alise, Kaylea, Ime and everyone who has been the subject of my rants while trying to finish this book. Sorry for the endless texts and voice notes.

Thank you to Michelle, my editor, my friend for dealing with my tenses and commas. I'm also excited for your journey! Can't wait to work on more stories with you.

The story is over for Lavender Falls but who knows when will visit Coralia Coast again. I have a lot more stories in store and so I hope you can join me!

About the Author

Isabel Barreiro is an anxious bookworm who loves being a dork and knowing random facts. Did you know a bumblebee bat is the world's smallest mammal?

During the day she's a freelance social media manager and at night she's binging anime shows or kdramas. Her brain has five hamsters running around on fire which makes the day to day interesting.

Despite being born and raised in Miami she prefers mountains and the fall/winter season. Maybe one day she'll have her small town life that she loves writing about. (Please it's my dream). She loves cooking and crafting and being an extroverted introvert.

You can follow her on Instagram/TikTok:
@authorisabelbarreiro
You can receive my newsletter on substack:
A Bookworm's Diary by Isabel Barreiro

You can also check out the first book in the Lavender Falls series, Falling For Fairy Tales on Amazon! A workplace romance between two childhood best friends who reunite to put on a magical pub crawl.

Want something a bit darker? Isabel also has a mafia book under a penance! Check out: The Mafia's Seamstress by Isabel Catrina on Amazon!

Made in the USA
Monee, IL
03 September 2025